HUMANITY UNLIMITED PUBLISHER'S PACK TWO

TERRY MIXON

YOWLING CAT PRESS

Published by Yowling Cat Press ®

Digital edition date: 6/21/2023

Print ISBN: 978-1947376557

Individual Works

Tree of Liberty Copyright © 2017 by Terry Mixon

Print ISBN: 978-1947376069

Blood of Patriots Copyright © 2019 by Terry Mixon

Print ISBN: 978-1947376212

Cover art - image copyrights as follows:

Dreamstime/MarcioMauro

DepositPhotos/zittto (Rui Miguel Morais Vale Sousa Pereira)

BigStockPhoto/Creativemarc

Donna Mixon

Cover design and composition by Donna Mixon

Print design and layout by Terry Mixon

Audio edition performed and produced by Veronica Giguere

Reach her at: v@voicesbyveronica.com

ALSO BY TERRY MIXON

You can always find the most up to date listing of Terry's titles on his Amazon Author Page.

Note: the links below (ebook only, obviously) redirect you to my website where you can click a button to go to Amazon. This allows me to participate in Amazon's associates program and earn a little more. Sorry for any inconvenience.

The Last Hunter

The Last Hunter

Bonds of Blood

Alpha Strike

The Enemy Revealed

Command Authority

The Grand Conspiracy

Shield of Humanity

Fog of War

Ships of the Line

Operation Liberty

The Empire of Bones Saga

Empire of Bones

Veil of Shadows

Command Decisions

Ghosts of Empire

Paying the Price

Recon in Force

Behind Enemy Lines

The Terra Gambit

Hidden Enemies

Race to Terra

Ruined Terra

Victory on Terra

When Luck Runs Out

Gunboat Diplomacy

The Imperial Marines Saga

Spoils of War

Imperial Recruit

Enemy Action

The Humanity Unlimited Saga

Liberty Station

Freedom Express

Tree of Liberty

Blood of Patriots

Single Novels

Scorched Earth

Storm Divers

The Vigilante Series with Glynn Stewart

Heart of Vengeance

Oath of Vengeance

Bound By Law

Bound By Honor

Bound By Blood

Box Sets

The Empire of Bones Saga Volume 1

The Empire of Bones Saga Volume 2

The Empire of Bones Saga Volume 3

The Empire of Bones Saga Volume 4

Humanity Unlimited Publisher's Pack 1

Humanity Unlimited Publisher's Pack 2

Want to get updates from Terry about new books and other general nonsense going on in his life? He promises there will be cats. Go to TerryMixon.com/Mailing-List and sign up.

DEDICATION

This book would not be possible without the love and support of my beautiful wife. Donna, I love you more than life itself.

ACKNOWLEDGMENTS

I want to thank the folks that support me on Patreon. You got to read this book as I was writing it and that kept me working. You have my deepest thanks.

In particular, I want to thank those who beta read these books and the patrons that supported me at the $10 level and above:

Bryan Barnes
  Tracy Bodine
  Michael Falkner
  Michael Goad
  Cain Hopwood
  Kristopher Neidecker
  John Naiser
  Bob Noble
  Andrew Olivier
  Jon Paul Olivier
  Bill Smith, Tom Stoecklein
  Dale Thompson
  Jason Young

Finally, I want to thank my readers for putting up with me. You guys are great.

TREE OF LIBERTY

BOOK THREE

Harry Rogers and his friends found alien tech scattered across the solar system and the government of the United States wants it. Them and everyone else.

His diabolical family also managed to steal an alien spaceship and flee the system. How long until they bring trouble back?

As the revelations set the world on fire, Harry must stop shadowy enemies from enslaving humanity. If he can.

1

Harry Rogers examined the rolling landscape below his hilltop perch. The only sign of movement was the occasional four-legged scavenger darting between the parked cars. The lack of a police presence told him that—against all odds—the pitched battle fought below hadn't drawn anyone to the hidden base in the wilds of France.

Getting into the area without using the decrepit road had taken a few hours, but he hadn't wanted his team to stumble across any of Nathan's men or the people they'd been fighting. Or the police.

To all indications, the place was deserted.

Frankly, finding it at all had taken a lot of hard work and more than Harry's fair share of luck. His father, Clayton Rogers, had an extensive network of informants keeping an eye on the goings of his ex-wife Kathleen Bennett and his other son, Nathan.

Those people had pieced together where Nathan had been and where his mother had fled after the United States seized her holdings and tried to arrest her. That had gotten Harry to Paris.

The computers on *Freedom Express*, the mobile ship the human resistance to the alien Asharim had build a thousand years ago, had shown the general location of a nearby base and that had allowed Harry to find this remote area once he'd convinced Brenda Cabot to bring him and his people back to Earth through their portable gate.

In all, it had taken almost half a day to locate the base and get here, which was pretty damned fast, considering they'd been out beyond the orbit of Pluto.

"It looks clear," Harry said softly. "Take your people around to the left. I'll go right. Those birds circling up near the big hill probably lead to the base and the heaviest fighting."

Rex Jamison, the lead scout in Harry's old private military company, lowered his binoculars. "Roger that. IR says none of the vehicles have been running in the recent past. As isolated as this area is, people might not have been able to pinpoint where the shooting came from. If they even heard it."

Sandra Dean looked up from the scope of a .338 Lapua Magnum. It was her preferred weapon as a trained and experienced sniper. "The flechette weapons are silent. We know your brother picked some up. If he were ready for the attack, the only noise would've come from the attackers. That could've been muted inside the base."

"We'll rendezvous there once we've secured the area," Harry said. "Keep an eye out for trouble, Sandra."

"On it."

He'd brought a dozen of his best men and women with him for this job. Here on Earth, it was their highest-priority task. His mother and brother, Kathleen and Nathan Bennett, had used a quantum tunnel in this base to get to the Asharim ship in the outer system.

They were still untangling the story of who the powerful aliens were, why they'd come to the solar system a thousand years ago, and what had happened to them. All he could say with any certainty was that they were the biggest threat humanity had ever faced.

That worried him, but there was nothing he could do about it right now. Best to focus on the problems he could actually deal with.

Nathan obviously knew how to use the gates. He probably had codes for the ones in this base. Harry meant to see them locked down tight to prevent anyone from sending waves of troops back through to Earth. He had to prevent that at all costs.

As he led his group around the area on his side, he considered how others might have thought he needed to be in New Zealand. The US had tried to kidnap his father in a wilderness area that, according to one of his people on the scene, was even more remote than this place.

Clayton Rogers and two local associates had disappeared before anyone had managed to call for help. The New Zealanders had gotten searchers into the area but found no sign of them or their attackers.

They'd sent ships to confront the US Navy destroyer that had launched the raid, but it had made it back into international waters. Even as badly as the US military had fallen, they were still far more advanced than pastoral New Zealand, so the destroyer had gotten away.

Either the US had his father, or his father had escaped into the base he'd been searching for. One way or the other, nothing Harry could do would change that situation right now. Besides, his father was a douche and deserved some trouble for being an asshat.

He'd head for New Zealand as soon as the France situation was under control. If nothing else, the people who'd vanished with his father deserved rescue.

Working slowly, they cleared the surrounding area over the next hour. No people or signs of conflict, though he smelled death and decay coming from the hill. This was going to be ugly.

He and his people had dealt with stuff like this far too many times in the Middle East. Mainly Iraq and Afghanistan. They knew what to do.

Harry slipped his nose plugs in. In the old days, people had put ointment on their upper lips. This was much better. It completely blocked the odor. That wouldn't do anything for his eyes, but he'd seen death before.

That's what they found in a cave up on the hill, too. Both outside and inside the well-concealed doorway. The attackers had left it open when they'd rushed inside. Parts of bodies littered the ground and corridor inside. Blood and other less savory bits painted the walls in a ghastly mural.

"It looks as if your brother made some new friends," Rex said as he moved inside, shooing the carrion birds away. "Looks like they headed for the elevator."

"Search every floor," Harry said. "Start at the top. I'll hit the bottom."

He stepped back out to get radio reception. "Sandra, we're going in. I'll leave someone out here to relay any warnings. We're going to move as much of the gore inside as possible. The birds will eventually draw official attention."

"Copy that. I've sent the drone out toward the main road. If anyone seems interested, I'll let you know."

Harry pointed to three of his men. "You guys drew the short straw. Get these bodies inside. Collect all the weapons and any other intelligence you find. Set aside any car keys. We'll be relocating the vehicles tonight, if no one finds us first."

Once he'd let Rex out on the next level down, Harry rode the elevator to the lowest floor. The people that had built these places liked to bury their power centers and the gates to the quantum tunnels deep.

There were a number of bodies and even more blood inside the elevator car. Nathan had fought for every inch of this place.

Harry didn't find the power room, but he did find a hangar even larger than the one on *Freedom Express*. Dozens of military-looking vessels sat there, waiting for someone to come along and use them. Black Jack McCarthy would be pleased.

The fighting down here had been brutal. Bodies littered the area around the elevator and stairs, and extended most of the way to the quantum tunnels. A particularly unlucky man lay in one of the arches, cut neatly in half from head to crotch.

That had to be the man Harry had watched die on the Asharim warship when Nathan had blown up the first gate.

"We're in the right place," he said, examining the arch. It didn't seem damaged on this side, but they would take no chances.

They'd probably used one of these vehicles to activate the quantum tunnel. The one with a raised canopy seemed like the best candidate.

Harry looked inside while his men searched the hangar and watched the elevator closely. If there were any hostiles left alive in this base, they wouldn't be springing any ambushes on his people.

The screen came alive with a swipe of his hand. There was the gate controller. He tapped the button and brought up the code. That particular sequence wouldn't work with the gate destroyed, so he wouldn't try it. And if by some chance it could work, he had no intention of letting Nathan know they were coming before they were ready to pour through in force.

He started to pull back, but something on the floor caught his eye. An envelope.

Harry picked it up and looked inside. Then he smiled. His French was lousy, but this looked like a deed and a bill of sale. Probably to the very property they were standing under.

Nathan's name wasn't on anything, so he'd bought it under an alias. The bill of sale had his signature on it, though. Harry had seen the bastard's handwriting far too many times to be fooled.

Of course Nathan and their mother would want clear title to the find. Luckily, Harry knew people who could forge someone's handwriting so well that even the wronged party couldn't be sure they hadn't written the fake.

He'd accumulated a lot of his brother's papers over the years, so there were samples aplenty for the forger to use. By close of business tomorrow, he'd have a fresh bill of sale transferring the property to Humanity Unlimited. Or at least the name of someone untraceable that linked with the corporation.

In a way, they'd already paid Nathan and his mother for it. The two had stolen the spaceship Harry had found near the Mayan pyramid. He'd make sure the bill of sale indicated the base changed hands for the "Guatemalan ship." The irony was exquisite.

First, though, he needed to clear the place of bad guys. No time for gloating until the base was safe from discovery. He only hoped that his brother and mother didn't bring the wrath of God down on their heads while he secured all the pieces they'd left scattered around the globe.

The elevator doors slid open, and one of his men hurried over to him. "We have a problem. Sandra just spotted a couple of cars heading up the road. We're about to have company."

* * *

"YOU'RE ASKING us to take a lot on faith," General Jim Wayland, the senior Army commander advising the president, said. "This all sounds like some kind of drug induced fantasy. You haven't been smoking the wacky weed, have you, Mister Secretary?"

Secretary of State Josh Queen glared at the man in Army green. "No, but I came prepared to demonstrate this in a way that even you can understand, General."

He rose from the table where he'd just finished briefing the president, vice president, national security advisor, director of homeland security, and the senior military officers present.

"The scientists tore the wrecked ship apart and found a stash. It had this inside, among other things." The pistol he pulled from his case was sleek and dangerous looking. The Secret Service had thrown a kicking, screaming hissy fit when he'd forced them to allow it into the meeting. Only the president's stern insistence had allowed that to happen.

Queen laid it in front of the general. "I suppose I could blow a hole in something to demonstrate it, but that seems likely to get me shot. I'm sending it off with you to test for yourself. I have no idea how many shots it has left, so be sparing."

He cued the video of the weapon blowing a nice chunk out of a concrete wall. Everyone looked suitably impressed.

President George Blankenship shook his head. "Based on everything you've shown me, I'm inclined to believe this is as bad as you think it is. Until I say differently, we treat this as the most serious issue on the table. Everything we've seen is now classified top secret/SCI under the code word 'Prometheus.'

"It seems fitting, since we're stealing the knowledge of fire from the gods. Icarus was a close second, for obvious reasons. I want every effort expended to find the people who are spying on us and locate their little hidey-hole. Every bit of tech we can find and examine gets sent to Area 51 for secure testing."

General Weyland cleared his throat. "Sir, you do realize we don't actually have aliens there, right?"

The president smiled. "I'm not that far around the bend, Jim. It's a secure area with the brightest minds we have. That has to be where we keep this secret."

He looked at each of them for a moment. "Gentlemen, I want every angle examined. We have to get ahead of this, or you'd best start learning Chinese. Call Homeland with any breaks. Secretary of State Queen is in overall command. Dismissed."

Once everyone was gone, the president gestured for Queen to join him on the couch off to the side. He poured them both a stiff drink.

"Is it really as bad as all that?" the president finally asked.

"It's potentially much worse," Queen said grimly. "Former FBI Agent Cabot said this could be an extinction-level event. I'm inclined to think she was understating things. Rogers and the rest could very well bring an alien invasion down on our heads. One that we'd be powerless to stop."

"*War of the Worlds* bad? That's frightening. I want to know what you think of the main players. What kind of people are they? Who's in the driver's seat?"

Queen didn't need to look at his notes. "For the moment, that would be Jessica Cook. I looked her up before the meeting. An engineer with specialties in space construction. From what she said, she's also the number two in their company. She has a bigger stake than Harry Rogers does, in any case. I'm not sure why."

"What do you think of her?"

"She's bright and resourceful. She seemed like a straight arrow, but I'm disinclined to trust loose cannons not to roll over me. The same with Harry Rogers. He's not a twisty bastard like his father."

Blankenship sipped his drink. "What about Clayton Rogers?"

"I thought he was in it for the money. Now? Who knows? He's a bad one, though not as bad as his ex-wife and other son. They're lunatics."

"I thought you were going to pick him up. Where are we on that?"

Queen grimaced. "Nowhere. We weren't able to find him or the team we sent after him. It's as if they vanished off the face of the Earth. And with this technology, that's a very real possibility.

"Someone called in the local government to do a search and rescue mission, so we had to break off our examination of the area. Maybe, once the New Zealanders give up, we can find the gate they used."

The president sipped his drink without speaking.

Queen took that as a hint to keep speaking. "Frankly, those three don't worry me nearly as much as Cabot and her group. They could be anywhere and want anything. We know nothing about them."

Blankenship sighed. "A secret society of humans with ties to aliens. It's like something out of a science fiction novel. I can hardly imagine a group that has been active since the Middle Ages."

The president frowned. "This is more like a Dan Brown novel."

Queen would have laughed if the situation hadn't been so ridiculously dire. "That's the rub. Their organization has been active since around the time the Vikings found North America. They could have people anywhere in the country or be insinuated into anything.

"They could have someone in the Secret Service right out in the hall. They could have put taps into the NSA when it formed. They could literally have people anywhere, and we have no way of knowing."

"Trust only the people you have to," the president said as he set his half-finished drink down on the side table. "Put them through every bit of testing you can. We can only let paranoia make us so crazy.

"You're the man on point, Josh. I need you to get us a ship of our own before the Chinese find out about this. Or one of those gate things. Find someone in the secret society and make them talk. We can't be in the game unless we get a seat at the table. Make it happen."

Queen tossed his drink back and set his glass beside the president's. "You can count on me, sir."

2

J ess Cook craned her neck to stare out from the lifter's window as it passed over the immense buildings below them. Monumental snowdrifts covered everything, except that wasn't snow. It was the planet's frozen atmosphere. Not just the humidity in the air, but the gas itself, chilled into powder.

This far out beyond Pluto's orbit, the sun wasn't more than a bright star in the sky. It didn't provide any warmth worth mentioning. Or any illumination. Only the lifter's spotlights allowed them to see what they were passing over.

The view using *Freedom Express*'s telescopes was a lot brighter, but it had technology to enhance the ambient light. Her Mark One eyeballs thought of this world's normal light level as Stygian blackness.

"I'm going to pick one of the buildings for a closer pass," Black Jack McCarthy said from the pilot's seat. The ex-marine lieutenant colonel had really taken to the small craft.

No surprise there. He'd been a very talented pilot in atmosphere, and he'd been studying hard to learn how to use all their spacecraft. The copilot was the regular pilot, and she was watching his actions closely.

Jess knew that he wanted to get all the proficiency he could and then learn to fly the abandoned small craft they'd found scatted around the solar system. Particularly the fighters in the French base.

"Is there a place to land on one?" she asked.

"Maybe. Some of the roofs seem flat enough, but we won't know what's under the snow until I melt it off."

"How are you going to do that?"

He grinned. "I'm going to hover over one and dial the thrusters up. The heat and blast will clear us a spot."

She shook her head. "It'll also make for a really icy place to put our feet. Do you want me to slip and fall off one of those things?"

"No, but I'm a pilot. I just deliver the packages. Still, if you slip, the snow looks deep enough to save you."

"I'd rather not find out," she grumbled. "Make the blast long enough and the ice will convert to gas. It won't be completely safe, but that's better than risking a cracked helmet."

"Yes, ma'am," he said. "That one ahead looks good. It's taller than the ones around it, so we won't have to worry about dodging any unforeseen obstructions in the flight path."

"Make it happen, Colonel."

He smiled a little. "I'm just one of the boys, now. Call me John."

"Maybe I should've called you Black Jack. How did you get that call sign, anyway?"

"I'm really good at cards. Hang on. I'm going to hold us steady over the widest area on the roof."

The lifter came in slowly and stopped a dozen meters up from the snow. The exhaust blasted snow everywhere, blinding her.

"I have the radar altimeter keeping us at a good height above the deck," McCarthy said.

The white fog around them slowly thinned, and Jess found that she could see the actual roof. Part of it looked like some kind of landing area.

"Over there to the right," she said. "Is that a landing pad?"

"Might be. Let's clear it off and see."

The large slab of thicker material had a bright white circle that would hold the lifter easily. The small cross in the center made it look like a target.

"Well, unless they were asking for an orbital strike, this is indeed a landing pad," McCarthy said. "We need to be careful putting weight on it, though. We have no idea what its limits are or how much it might've weakened over time and under these conditions."

He moved the lifter over the probable landing pad and slowly settled down, never letting off the thrust completely until it demonstrated that it was up to the task of supporting them. Only then did he shut the thrusters down.

"Okay, we're down," he said. "Now what?"

"We see if we can find a way in and determine who used to live here," Jess said as she unstrapped.

"Good luck. This planet is too damned big to search in a meaningful way. Christ, it's about the same size as Earth and looks like it's covered by a single damned megacity. We won't even be able to examine the orbital in the near future because it's so massive."

That was true enough. The cylinder in orbit around the frozen world had an interior the size of Manhattan. Even with the quantum tunnel to bring people in from Earth, there just weren't enough bodies in the company to search it closely.

They had teams looking for the life support and power controls, but it might take months to find them. Or years.

The orbital had power, thankfully. The lights were on minimal settings, and the incredible quantum gate for spaceships worked. Unfortunately, the departed tenants had turned off the life-support systems. It was like an Arctic freeze inside the damned place.

The teams working inside it were in heavy cold-weather gear, much to Doctor Michael Crockett's annoyance. The archaeologist wasn't used to working under such trying conditions, and he wasn't shy about telling anyone who'd listen.

"We can only do what we can," Jess said. "You'll keep an ear on us?"

The ex-marine nodded. "The suit radios are good for quite a ways, but if you don't hear from me every few minutes, I want you to turn around and come back, no matter what interesting baubles you've found."

She smiled. "Yes, Mother. We're going to be careful. Don't come after us if we drop off for a little while. Give us an hour, and head back to orbit for more help if you can't get ahold of us for longer than that."

"They covered this kind of thing in the marines. We don't leave people behind. They also taught me to never give an order I knew wouldn't be obeyed, so I'll pass that lesson on to you now."

She stood and put her hands on her hips. "If we're not responding, one more person isn't going to make a difference. We'll need a full team for extraction. If you two don't go get them, they won't know where to find us."

He scowled. "You're annoying when you're right."

"So I hear. Don't worry. We'll be very careful."

Jess marshaled the team, and they exited through the airlock and onto the roof. The surface was still coated with a crust of ice, and the footing was treacherous. They all took care moving because a smashed helmet meant death.

Once she'd assured her footing, she stared up. The number of stars she could see above them was incredible. Vacuum did that.

There was an entrance off to the left. Wide doors of what looked like glass reflected the light streaming from the lifter.

No, they wouldn't be glass in this environment. Glass would never survive the intense cold. It had to be something else.

"This wasn't designed for vacuum," Ray Proudfoot said. The chief engineer of *Liberty Station*—their original ship—pointed at the handles. "These are for use in a shirtsleeves environment. There aren't even two sets of doors."

"That makes sense," she said. "No one would build a world-spanning city on a planet this far out of a system."

"How the hell did it get out here?" Everett Anderson asked. He was in charge of the tactical team Harry had insisted she bring along. As if there were anything more hostile than the environment on this ice ball.

"There's no telling," she said. "If the orbital station is any indication, the Asharim had something to do with it. I'm at a loss as to how or why."

The doors looked as if they were meant to slide open, but a tug failed to move them. They were frozen in their tracks. Doors like this could usually be swung open in an emergency, so she tried that and they rocked the slightest bit. Ray lent her a hand, and they popped open.

The interior of the building was pitch black, but their helmet lights lit the way in. More frozen atmosphere covered the floor a few centimeters deep.

"Uh-oh," Ray said. "That doesn't bode well."

His light had picked out a huddled form covered in frost and snow. A distinctly humanoid form.

"This isn't the first dead human we've found," Jess said sadly.

"Not the body," the engineer said softly. "The wall beside it."

She raised her eyes and stared at the sign. It welcomed them to Youngstown Emergency Trauma Center and pointed the way to the emergency room. In perfect English.

* * *

CLAYTON ROGERS WOKE with a stiff back. The stone floor inside the cave was the most uncomfortable surface he'd ever slept on. At least they'd let him and his companions sleep without restraints.

That had really pissed the CIA operative off. Agent Ulysses wanted them tied up hand and foot. Clayton had no idea where the man thought he and his people would get off to. They were all trapped on an alien world with an army of some kind camped only a few kilometers away.

Without a way to control the quantum gate deep inside the cave, they wouldn't be going anywhere soon. Since they'd brought the powerless controller from the other side along with them, odds were very good that no one would be able to come after them, either. They'd have to save themselves.

The special operations troops had made an early morning approach to the encampment they'd spotted yesterday. The people looked human enough, based on the descriptions that they'd brought back, but primitive. Maybe Revolutionary War tech levels.

As to whom they were fighting, no one could guess. Heavy-worlders were his personal wager. That seemed as if it would be a very short fight, though.

They were human enough to pass in society, but the Asharim had genetically modified them to be able to live in a three-gravity environment. The poor bastards had been military slaves to the powerful aliens.

A sailor came back with Penny Cash in tow. She'd just gone out to use the concealed latrine the men had dug.

She thanked the man and sat down across from Clayton. The third member of their abortive escape attempt, Mick Bird, was consulting with the Navy commander. His extensive outdoor skills might be critical in this situation.

"The army hasn't moved," Penny said. "That's what they tell me, anyway. It seems as though they might have been there for a while."

"That seems odd," Clayton said. "I know armies used to stay in one place over long winters, but why now? It seems warm enough to me."

She shrugged. "Damned if I know. Maybe they're waiting for their opponents to do something spectacularly stupid. Or maybe they're in hiding."

"Not with all that smoke from the fires. Speaking of which, how will we cook the food that they're hoping Mick can quietly kill? How do they even know that it's edible? With our luck, we'll poison ourselves."

"There are some animals being cleaned at the army camp. The scouts said they look like deer. Maybe they got through here at some point in the past and became part of the biosphere."

Penny looked back toward the entrance to their chamber. "While we're alone, we should discuss escape plans. First, are we even going to try?"

"No," Clayton said with a shake of his head. "All we know about this world is in the cave system here. Such as it is. We saw the dead alien city and the army. We haven't left this hill and have no clue what awaits us. Let's not jump out of the frying pan just yet."

"Then we need to make contact. We're not going to stay hidden for very long."

"That's not our call," he said dryly. "The men with the guns are in control now."

That answer didn't seem to satisfy her. "No disrespect to Commander Krueger, but I don't like leaving my fate in the hands of others."

"Believe it or not, I agree with you," a voice said from the dark tunnel leading toward the entrance. Commander Krueger stepped out of the passage and gave them a nod. "Voices carry in places like this."

The situation amused Clayton. Of course their plans had been overheard. That's the way things had been going for them.

"How are your people holding up?" he asked the officer. "This has to be a strain on them."

Krueger sighed. "It's sinking in, but we're special operations. We'll hold together. I know I wasn't the only one to lose sleep over the impossibility of our situation last night. I'm worried about Ulysses, too. Worried enough to detail someone to keep an eye on him."

Clayton nodded. "I hope we can find another way home. Hell, just a way to power the tablet would probably work for us."

"You said you agreed about not leaving our fate in your hands," Penny said. "What did you mean?"

"That the mission has changed," the officer said as he sat on a handy rock. "We can't get you back to Earth easily, so the new mission is to survive and learn about our new neighbors. If we reach an agreement, will you abide by it?"

Clayton smiled. "I'm a straight dealer, Commander—no matter what Ulysses might have told you. If I make a deal, I stick to it. You just need to be sure the details really mean what you think they do. Technicalities matter."

"Well, this is pretty straightforward," Krueger said. "I want you and your people to give me your parole. We all act as a team until we get back to Earth. If we can do that, then I don't have to guard you like prisoners, and Mister Ulysses can go piss up a rope."

"Colorful and vivid. I agree, but with one caveat. If we can get back safely, you have to let us go."

The officer shook his head. "I caught you fair and square."

"After we escaped to another world," Clayton riposted. "That seems to negate your point."

Krueger seemed amused rather than offended. "I have control now. That gives me the edge."

"Then release Penny and Mick. They have nothing to do with the charges against me."

The other man considered that. "Agreed. They weren't in my orders anyway. That just leaves you."

"Excellent. As for myself, if I can manage to do so without endangering any of your people, I reserve the right to depart once we return to Earth. Isn't that part of your creed as well? Escape and evade?"

Krueger smiled a little. "Once we get back to Earth, you're welcome to try. We have a deal."

"What happens now?"

"Breakfast. I'm afraid there are only MREs."

The sound of rapid footsteps in the tunnel interrupted them. It was Gunnery Sergeant Danvers. He stepped over to Krueger. "We have a problem, sir. A party from the army camp is headed our way. Maybe thirty people."

"Bring everyone back inside," the officer ordered. "We'll just have to hope they don't find us in here."

3

Kathleen Bennett didn't recall falling asleep, but she woke when the lid to the sarcophagus-like machine slid open above her. She sat up, trying to remember how she'd ended up inside the thing.

Nothing.

She remembered seeing it in the room her son Nathan had stuffed her into aboard the alien ship but not climbing inside. How odd.

After another moment trying to remember, she shrugged and stretched her back. She felt good. Really good. She must have really needed that nap.

Then the full memory of the day's events caught up with her. The fighting, the terrorists, and the way they'd tortured her. She looked down at her foot and saw that the bandages had fallen off. To her astonishment, her missing toe was there.

Feeling as if she were dreaming, she wiggled it. It moved just like all the rest. It was as if the bastards hadn't cut it off. How was that even possible?

Well, there'd be time to figure that out soon enough. First, she needed to find her son and see what was happening. They needed to secure control of this ship. It was the golden goose, and she meant to have its eggs.

She slid out of the device and noticed something else was different. Her clothes didn't fit properly. Her pants wanted to slide off, and her bra was like a clamp around her torso.

With a quick look around the strange room, she located a wall screen that would serve as a crappy mirror. She walked over to it, holding her pants up. What she saw stopped her dead in her tracks.

That wasn't possible.

Gazing back was a view of herself that she hadn't seen in far too many decades. She looked like she had in her mid twenties. The parts of her that life had filled out had slimmed back down, and the parts that age had deflated had ballooned back up.

Yes, this had to be a dream. A nice one, but she needed to wake the hell up.

The sound of the door opening made her turn.

Nathan Bennett came in and stopped dead in his tracks, his jaw dropping as his gun came up. "Who the hell are you? How did you get in here?"

"Try not to be more of an idiot than you have to, boy." Her voice was different, too. Less gravelly. Fuller. Younger.

Her son slowly lowered his gun, but he didn't put it away.

"Well, this is a surprise, Mother. You've found the fountain of youth. I can see you in there, now. You look younger than I do."

"How did I get into that machine?"

He leaned against the console. "You don't remember? The men I had guarding you said that you got into it under your own power."

"I remember coming into the room alone, so I won't rule it out," she granted. "What's happening out there?"

"Nothing as interesting as what's going on in here. You've been out almost twelve hours. The terrorists are still alive and kicking, though we have thinned the herd. I think there are two or three dozen left."

She'd have to do something about her clothes, but she had no idea what. They would have to wait.

"What about our forces? Do we still have guns?"

"Yes, but we're short on ammo. The new weapons are almost dry, but I might be able to find some more ammo somewhere on the ship. We have regular guns and ammo from the dead ragheads. Enough to finish the job, I think.

"But that will have to wait for a little while. We need to have someone look you over. One of my men is a medic."

She shook her head. "What would he see? You don't have any instruments that could look inside me. Forget it. I need something to modify my clothes. They fit like crap."

He grinned. "That's because frumpy clothes don't work on hot chicks."

"I'm your *mother*. Don't be more of a pervert than you must."

The deck under their feet shifted a little. Hardly enough to notice but more than it had before.

Nathan stood straight abruptly. "I think we better go find out what that was. Nothing good, I'll warrant."

No, probably not.

* * *

BRENDA CABOT WALKED down the streets of Washington, DC, as if she hadn't a care in the world. No one would guess she was one of the most wanted fugitives in the country. The former FBI agent had no doubt she was number one on the most wanted list.

Her stylish hat and overly large sunglasses were more than enough to botch facial recognition programs on the numerous cameras watching over the nation's capital, but she made certain to walk in a different manner than she normally used. More of a sexy saunter.

Since that was completely out of character for her, it would screw with any of the more esoteric movement recognition programs running on the surveillance systems. Yes, that was actually a thing.

Piazza's, the trendy bar she breezed into, had a reputation as one of the hottest nightspots in the city, but it was early for the pretty people. The Families used the place as a means to keep an eye on what happened in the halls of power just over a dozen blocks away.

The Families had been part of an underground movement in the alien society after they'd taken primitive humans as slaves. They were as deeply buried in modern society now. They'd had a thousand years to become part of every organization that mattered, operating out of sight and with extreme subtlety.

The bartender was always one of them, so he didn't blink when she made her way into the back with a wave. A rack designed to hold wine bottles sat empty in the corner. It was old, and they'd upgraded one of the rooms to control the environment better for the expensive vino they stocked for the rich and powerful. It never drew the slightest interest during health inspections. That made it the perfect place to hide a secret entrance.

She bent low and found the hidden catch. It clicked softly, and the entire rack swung out, along with the wall behind it.

A newly revealed set of stairs led down into an abandoned portion of the old subway system, though not directly. There was a little walking through a dank tunnel to get to the station. That always set her into the right frame of mind for their secret lair: the Vault.

The Families had sprayed the crumbling walls with sealant to keep most of the seeping groundwater out, so the place was actually quite comfortable. The dehumidifiers and air conditioning routed in from buildings above the station helped a lot with that, too.

A massive door set in the wall of the abandoned station kept the lair secure. They'd bought it when a local bank had closed. Getting it down into the abandoned subway had been a chore, or so the older members of their group claimed.

In any case, it would keep any intruders at bay long enough for the people inside the Vault to escape by other routes if anyone ever discovered the place.

Two men wearing body armor and holding automatic weapons nodded to her as she walked past. They'd hold the door if trouble came knocking. Someone inside always monitored the bar to be sure no one raided the place.

Past the vault door, a wide room that looked like a CIA monitoring center awaited her. A dozen people stared at state-of-the-art monitors and listened to hidden bugs planted throughout the city—or in some cases, around the world.

A tall black man in a subdued suit gestured for her to come over to the raised platform above the rest of the stations. Cyrus Patterson had once worked for the CIA in a room very similar to this one, so he'd been the perfect choice for their intelligence chief.

"Brenda, I'm glad to see you made it here safely." He gripped her hand for a moment. "I'm so sorry you had to come out into the open like this."

"It's okay, Cyrus," she said as she set her purse, hat, and sunglasses onto his desk. "This is way more important than what I was doing before."

His smile widened. "Actually, I said that because the FBI is sweeping all their buildings and we've lost a number of bugs. It won't be long before they turn their attention to other critical areas. That's what I'm sorry about, not your loss of a social life."

She swatted his arm. "Ass. You never change. Now that we have the portable gate set up in the house over by the river, what is our situation like?"

"The government has gone all paranoid, which makes sense since we still have them penetrated six ways to Sunday. They're kicking off the king of all witch hunts. Everyone is a suspect, so everyone is keeping their heads down. It'll take them weeks to vet the critical people. We're safe enough for the moment."

Cabot pulled up a chair and sat. "What about our assets? Are they likely to find anyone? Do we need to start pulling people out?"

"I think not. Just like you, we made sure they had no links back to the Families. Some of them have been in place for decades. They're often the people doing the vetting. This has to be a nightmare for the alphabet agencies."

"We can't be complacent," she said firmly. "They have smart people working hard to find us now that they know we exist. They won't stop looking."

"Exactly, so we've picked out a number of bad apples to throw their way. People we've been aware of for a while that have dark little secrets they'd rather keep to themselves. We've left careful and subtle clues linking them together.

"The counterintelligence teams will unravel quite the conspiracy when they find them. One that doesn't lead back to us. Best of all, none of our people have to 'discover' them. A couple will pop up in a day or so without endangering any of our folks."

Brenda looked around the room while she considered that. A massive witch hunt was to their advantage. It wouldn't last forever, but it would put the opposition into disarray. Right now, time was a critical factor.

"Okay, that sounds good," she finally said. "What are our top issues right now?"

"We've had someone keeping an eye on Harry Rogers since you brought him through our gate. He found a hidden base in France, just like you said he would. Dammit, but I wish we'd known about it. Think of all the equipment that has to be there."

She shrugged. "The Families have been looking for just that kind of thing for centuries. We missed this one, but there are other bases scattered around the world, I'm sure. Rogers knew about the one in France. He'll know about others. We can trade our assistance for one."

He grinned. "I like the sound of that. In any case, we used our man in the French national police to be sure no word leaked about the site. No one has uttered a peep about it, so he hasn't had to smother any awkward information. It's still clean."

"It makes me mad, too," she admitted. "Centuries of hard work and some guy just waltzes into what should be our hidden fortress. Still, you're right. We'll manage to get on his good side. We just have to gain his trust so he doesn't poke the Asharim."

"I might be able to help with that. There was a big national security meeting at the White House. We don't have the full details, but one of our people picked up some of the fallout. They're going to use the military to solidify the US claim to the Yucatán Spaceport in Mexico and fortify it."

"That's not a big surprise," she said. "The US doesn't have a space program anymore. Idiots."

"True, but that's going to change. They leaned hard on the Indians and 'bought' their Mars ship. It's almost ready to go, so Roger's people there can expect company in about three months."

That wasn't unexpected, but she'd hoped it would take longer. "What about the Chinese?"

The Indians and Chinese had been engaged in a race to Mars. The US co-opting the Indian ship would definitely gain the attention of the most powerful nation on the planet. With their powerful military, they could potentially act out in unexpected ways.

"They're monitoring the situation. The fact that *Liberty Station* made it to Mars in a matter of days and that the US is now heading after them isn't lost to their senior people. They still don't know about the Asharim, but that won't last forever. One of their spies will pick up something eventually."

The Chinese would have no problem using force to take any advanced technology. They'd rightly see it as a direct threat. That could get very ugly in record time.

"We'll need to let Rogers know," Brenda said. "He'll want to get weapons to Mars so they can defend themselves. Thank God there are only those two ships. Any chance we could sabotage them both?"

"It's possible we could do something to the Indian ship but not the Chinese. It's too well guarded."

She sighed. "I want options on my desk as soon as possible. Too many people know about the technology for it to stay quiet much longer. If we have spies that are hearing about it, the Chinese will, too.

"Rogers and Cook will need someone to hack the big gate soon. They'll want to track down where that ship went. Do we have anyone that might be able to help?"

He considered that for a moment. "I think I know just the man. Kevin McHugh. He's one of my guys. A real hacker."

Brenda raised an eyebrow. "One with skills in Asharim tech?"

"He told me there had to be similar ways into those kinds of systems. He's built up a number of tools and techniques over the last few years. He's your guy, but he's based out of Virginia."

"Call him to Washington. If I'm right, he'd best pack for a long trip."

4

Chen made his way into the depths of the Chinese Embassy in Washington, DC. A room there was proof against any external monitoring, and he wanted no one to be aware of what he was about to pass on to his superiors.

Even though the guards knew him well, they were thorough in checking him for listening devices. It was always possible that someone would manage to plant a device on him, so he approved of their caution and diligence.

He left his cell phone and other electronics in a lockbox on their desk. That kept them safe from either of the guards getting their hands on them. Paranoia ran both ways.

Inside, the secure room was much as depicted in various entertainment programs: high-tech gear off to one side and a large screen dominating one wall. A technician awaited his pleasure in front of the controls.

"Leave me."

The man rose, bowed, and retreated without a word.

Chen secured the door behind him, activated the jamming technology built into the walls, and disabled all the recording devices. He manipulated the controls and opened a channel to Beijing.

The man who appeared on the screen was of lower social rank than Chen, but that didn't stop him from virtually sneering. "Imperial Palace. How may I assist you, Ambassador?"

"I must speak with the president's secretary. The matter is urgent."

The other man made a show of checking his watch. "She has most likely been asleep only a few hours. It would be best to call her back at a more reasonable hour."

"It is not your place to question my judgment. Wake her."

The man's expression subtly indicated he thought Chen was making a mistake, but the screen blanked.

Fifteen minutes later, the screen once more cleared, and Chen saw the president's secretary. She'd obviously risen hastily and looked somewhat peeved.

"Ambassador Chen," she said coolly. "The hour is early."

"Are you alone in the secure room?"

She glanced to the side. "No. The technicians are here."

"Send them away."

Her eyebrows rose. "They have the highest clearance."

He said nothing.

She searched his face for a moment before nodding. "Everyone, leave me."

The man Chen had spoken with earlier shot a disgruntled look at him as he crossed behind the president's secretary. A second man kept his face blank as he followed him.

The woman watched them until they were gone and then turned to face Chen. "I am alone."

"Be certain that no recording device is activated."

"I have already done so. Proceed."

"This is a matter for the Dragon, not the president."

Her eyes narrowed. "You are not supposed to contact us through official government channels. This is dangerous."

He nodded. "The information is too critical to use my normal courier. Only this heavily encrypted line will do. The United States government has come into the possession of Asharim technology."

The woman's eyes widened. "Are you sure?"

"I am. One of our sleeper agents has seen it with his own eyes. An independent source intercepted a message about the acquisition, as well. There is no doubt."

"Forgive my misgivings, but this could be a trick of some kind."

He shook his head. "The technology was a flechette pistol of the standard design. Our man saw a video of it blowing a chunk of concrete the size of my head out of a wall.

"The Americans confiscated it from Kathleen Bennett, and it is merely the smallest of a sizable cache of similar equipment. The largest appears to be an Asharim cargo lifter in questionable condition but also recognizable. There is no mistake."

The woman considered him for a moment before nodding. "I will see that the Dragon is made aware of these developments in the morning. It would be too conspicuous for me to contact them any sooner. Watch for a special courier in the next day."

She wasn't genetically one of the Dragon's members—it only took one look at her petite frame to realize that—but she was still one of their leaders. The Dragon needed people of non-heavy-worlder extraction in many areas of their work, so some families had been with them for many hundreds of years.

"I will have as detailed a report as possible ready at that time," he said.

"My people are still gathering data. One complication is that it will not be long before spies outside our control become aware of these developments."

Her expression darkened. "That is unfortunate. Can we seize the trove?"

Chen shrugged. "Possibly, but I would not count on it. The Americans are moving it to a secure facility under extremely heavy military guard. While they are not as strong as they once were, they can defend themselves here in their home quite well."

"Pity. I will need a story to tell the president when she wakes. Someone will report your call."

"That will be no challenge. The Americans have sent military forces to secure the Yucatán Spaceport and cajoled the Indians into selling them their Mars craft for a significant—perhaps even ruinous—premium. The US seems suddenly desperate to get to the Red Planet. That tells me there must be more technology on Mars."

"That is troubling but not really a surprise. The rebels were scattered all across this system when we suppressed them. I do not recall specific mention of anything on Mars, but it would shock me if there were not."

"The Chinese vessel incorporates more powerful engines than the Indian ship, but it is less powerful than the fusion drive Rogers employed. It will still take us months to get to Mars, and the forces we can send will be small. His mobile station is far larger than our ship, so he will outnumber us."

"True, but we can send crack military forces with heavy weapons. Roger's ship is unarmed. He could not smuggle anything serious through the Yucatán Spaceport."

"Such as a stolen fusion reactor?"

Rogers had powered his Mars ship with a prototype fusion reactor stolen from his ex-wife. That briefly made Chen wonder if Kathleen Bennett had used Asharim technology to build it. No matter. They'd find out soon enough.

He inclined his head to grant her the point. "We can stop the Indian ship. Rather, the American ship, I suppose. We have weapons in orbit capable of destroying the thing. That will generate unfortunate consequences here on Earth, however. In the end, that decision is not mine to make."

The corner of her mouth quirked up. "No, I suppose it isn't. You have done well, Ambassador. The courier will have further instructions for you. Good night."

The screen went blank, and he took in a deep breath to settle himself. The great game was entering a very dangerous phase. If it came to war, China could crush the Americans but only at a terrible cost.

Well, so long as the Dragon triumphed in the end, it was worth the blood and fire. Let the world burn. They would soon be leaving it behind anyway.

* * *

JESS WANTED to rub her face, but her helmet prevented that. This situation was not only impossible, it was ludicrously so.

Time travel? Where someone brought another Earth with them? Yeah, preposterously impossible.

They'd need to get a good reading of the continents to confirm everything under the global ice sheet matched Earth, but it was hard to dismiss a frozen planet filled with huge buildings and the bodies of people that sure looked as though they'd come from the future.

They'd examined dozens of bodies so far, and the majority of them had IDs from Virginia or the surrounding states. All with dates corresponding to more than two centuries in the future.

"We're going to have to wrap this up," she finally said. "I want everything documented in a way that won't make Doctor Crockett lose his mind. We'll take a few bodies back with us for the medical team to examine. Let's finish searching this floor, and we'll put a beacon on the roof to lead some follow-up teams back. Stay in pairs."

She gestured to Ray Proudfoot and led the way deeper into the offices just off the landing platform. They'd made a single pass through, so their footprints marred the perfect sheet of frozen gases that covered everything.

This level had probably housed senior executives, if these people followed anything like the practices on her Earth. Those in power seemed to think they needed to be higher up than anyone else and have a better view.

The central area was an open space filled with desks. Probably people that supported the movers and shakers in some way. The latter were probably in the offices along the perimeter of the building, with the most powerful having corner offices.

There were some bodies here, but not as many as one might expect on a workday. Whatever had happened to them, it had come at night, or it had taken time. Not too long, though. Otherwise, there'd have been no one here at all.

"What do you think happened?" she asked Ray as she headed for the largest of the corner offices.

"I've been running possibilities through my mind. It's hard to speculate on something this crazy."

She opened the door and looked into a spacious and luxurious office. One that Clayton Rogers would've been proud to occupy. "Well, we're going to have to speculate on what happened here, impossible or not," she said. "After all, we just found out we can travel across the universe via quantum tunnels."

"Point."

The office contained three bodies bunched together on a couch, two larger forms with a smaller one between them. This was the first child they'd found, and it made Jess's heart ache.

Ray moved to the spacious desk while she stepped closer to the dead. "Since we're talking the impossible, I suppose that a planet that suddenly lost its sun might die this quickly. I'd have to run some numbers, but just look at how quickly temperatures at home fall overnight.

"Without any solar radiation, that trend would keep on going as heat radiated into space. Faster, really, since the heat on the other side of the planet wouldn't be there to help smooth things out. The US would be like the Arctic in a matter of days at most. Perhaps even quicker."

She nodded, knowing that he couldn't see her. "That would jibe with the cold-weather clothing. Whatever it was didn't happen all at once. These people were inside a building that presumably had power, yet they're dressed in as many layers as possible."

Like the rest of the bodies they'd found, these three were dressed for extreme cold but not with dedicated gear. Just whatever they could put on in layers.

The two larger forms turned out to be a man and a woman. The child was a girl based on her braided hair and bright hair clips, perhaps ten. Definitely prepubescent. She had something in her lap.

Jess brushed the snow off the girl's lap and found a small black cat curled up there. That made her choke a little more. She loved cats.

She couldn't cry now. She had no way to wipe her eyes.

A search revealed an ID on the man, and there was a purse beside the woman. They had the same last name and address in Youngstown. This was a family.

"There's a fairly advanced-looking computer over here," Ray said. "It might only be a terminal, but there's a possibility I can get something from it."

"Take it with us, then. I've got a family over here. I think we should take them with us as a unit. They died together, so we should keep them that way."

A search of the short table beside the bodies revealed a pill bottle. They'd probably taken a lethal dose of something before the intense cold froze them. She also found a pet carrier on the floor.

"We're going to need to be very careful moving them," she said as she turned to face Ray. "They're completely frozen, and I don't want to break parts off them."

"That's gruesome. I've got the computer and monitor—or what I suspect is the monitor. It's a strip that sat on the desk at about the right place. Maybe a projector of some kind."

"Let's get it out to the lifter, then. I'll send someone back to get the bodies."

She was able to lift the cat free. The poor thing was just as stiff as one would expect but small enough that Jess could carry it easily. It took a little work to angle the small body so that it went into the carrier, but she managed it.

The two of them retreated to the roof. She tagged some of the other team members to secure the bodies. They'd put the family in the cargo area in back of the lifter. That way the family could stay in vacuum until the medical team collected them.

Half an hour later, Jess's team was ready to go. They'd barely made a dent in the exploration, and definitely had more questions than answers. Doctor Michael Crockett was going to go nuts.

She filled McCarthy in as he took them up.

He looked at her and shook his head when she finished. "That's just crazy.

Of course, at this point, it's getting to be a whole new level of crazy for everything.

"I spoke with Harry while you were in there. He's secured the base in France. They locked down the gates so that his asshole brother couldn't come back unexpectedly, but they have someone snooping around. He can't head for New Zealand until they take care of them, one way or the other."

Jess sighed. "We have so many things we have to do. I'm not sure we can handle this all by ourselves. We need more people. People that we can trust."

"You need to set up a recruiter on Earth. One that can quietly find people with useful skills. With the base in France, we can get them to where we need them. Of course, if we could find a portable gate that we could set up in the US, it would be better."

"Add it to the list. Until then, I suppose we need to formalize an agreement with Cabot and her people. I'm still not sure I trust them yet, though."

"Having backup plans are good," he assured her, "but you have to work with the tools at hand. From what I hear, she might be able to shed some light on this stuff. Surely that's worth having a discussion over terms."

Jess couldn't argue with that kind of logic. "I'll clean up and make the trip to Earth to see them."

The lifter made it back into orbit, and McCarthy landed it outside the base entrance next to the other lifter they'd brought from *Liberty Station*.

Freedom Express had ships inside, but they didn't know how to fly them yet, and there was no easy way to get them out. The gates they used led everywhere imaginable but not to the surface of the extinct comet, which seemed stupid, so they'd probably missed an external gate. They were still looking for any on the surface of the dormant comet.

Jess left the team to handle the work of unloading everything and made her way inside. She stripped off her suit once the pressure and temperature came up.

She'd take the cat down to the lab and leave it with the team there to examine. Then she'd clean up and go have a long talk with Brenda Cabot.

That plan lasted right up until she reached for the pet carrier and saw a pair of green eyes examining her from inside it.

5

Clayton waited patiently for the scouts Commander Krueger had left outside to report. Their tactical radios gave the special operations team a distinct advantage over the more primitive folk that were coming up the hill, as did the video feed from the small drone that the Americans had brought with them.

Commander Krueger and he watched the feed from it over the operator's shoulder. The slow-moving craft was almost coasting over the hill and had a great view of the string of men climbing a disused and rocky path toward the summit.

Ulysses—the CIA agent—sat glaring at them from a handy shelf of rock. The Navy officer had cut him out of the command loop now that they were no longer on Earth, and he wasn't happy about it. He'd also objected to Krueger accepting their parole.

Clayton knew the type of man Ulysses was. He'd dealt with far too many like him over the years. The bastard would cause him trouble at every turn.

With a sigh, he pushed the toad from his thoughts and focused on the handheld monitor. "What do you suppose they're going to do, Commander?"

The officer shrugged. "Probably look around the general area. The elevation is good for that. They're not going to find the cave, based on the route they picked, so that probably wasn't their destination in the first place."

The men on the hill made their way up to the clearing Clayton and the rest had visited yesterday. The drone was too far away to capture their facial expressions, but based on how far away they stayed from the altar, it wasn't their objective, either.

That said something good about their character, he supposed. The human bones scattered around the slab of stone indicated the owners had some bloodthirsty habits.

The primitive men ended up going to the rough platform the Special Forces troops had found. They either wanted a look at the dead alien city in the distance or something between it and the hill.

"Bring the drone in for a pass with the engine off," Krueger said to the operator.

"Aye, sir."

The officer glanced at Clayton. "The prop is quiet, but without it, the thing is almost undetectable on a close pass. Anyone seeing it will think it's a bird soaring by."

"That assumes there are birds on this world."

"Good point," Krueger said approvingly. "One that I've already verified, but still good thinking."

The operator took the drone around then dove in from the side, capturing the men and the area around them as he soared past. A few people looked over at the drone but didn't seem to pay it any undue attention.

Once the drone was safely back up and away, Krueger had the operator extract the video and pass it on to a second handheld wielded by Gunnery Sergeant Danvers.

The man found a good view of the people on the platform and paused the video. "Those are uniforms but not ones I recognize," the marine said. "I suppose there are some similarities to what was used around the time of the Revolutionary War, but I think that's more a factor of manufacturing methods than design.

"I'm more interested in their weapons, honestly. They share a lot of similarity with muskets of around the same period, too. I'm not a black-powder man, but they don't look like repeaters to me."

"Let me see," Mick Bird said. "I have some friends that are into historical reenactment."

Clayton raised an eyebrow. "New Zealand seems to be quite a stretch for Revolutionary War reenactors."

The young man grinned. "You'd be surprised how many people outside the US have interests in the time period. I'm not one of them, mind you, but I enjoyed shooting the guns. Lots of smoke and a big kick."

The New Zealander examined the image closely. "I hate to disagree with you, Gunnery Sergeant, but that is a uniform from the American Revolutionary War. At least I'm pretty sure it is. One of the State Militias, I think. Couldn't tell you which one, though. And those long guns are definitely of a similar make to the ones I fired."

Krueger frowned. "How can that possibly be? You said the war between the aliens and the humans with bases happened a thousand years ago. The Europeans hadn't even found the New World back then."

Clayton snorted. "I've stopped asking how anything is possible. I've discovered that I'll probably never find out the answer. All we can do is take in the facts and make educated guesses. I'd say that at least one gate exists in the United States and these people's ancestors came through it a few hundred years ago."

"I suppose that's as good a theory as any," the officer admitted. "Take the drone over the camp. I want to see this army. Make the pass high enough to keep the drone looking like a bird."

The drone captured the camp in enough detail to see the layout. There were a lot of tents and campfires.

"It looks as if there are a few thousand men," Krueger said after a long look. "The layout isn't as regimented as I'd have expected."

Something caught Clayton's attention. "There is something at the center of the camp. I caught a bit of the light."

The gunnery sergeant backed up the video. There was a large tent in the center of the camp, and someone was standing outside it. They seemed to be watching the drone through what looked like a long glass—one that briefly flashed in the morning sunlight when the angle was perfect.

"Oh, crap," Krueger muttered. "They've spotted the drone."

Gunnery Sergeant Danvers shrugged. "That probably doesn't matter, sir. It's not as if they know where we are. They might not even recognize what the drone means, even after seeing it."

Honestly, the fact that someone had seen the drone mattered less to Clayton than the person who'd spotted it. The figure below was a woman, based on her generous cleavage, but her clothing was out of step from what he thought he knew about the revolutionary setting.

The image was too distant to make out her features in detail, but the woman looked more like she was dressed up for an Errol Flynn movie than the Revolutionary War.

That actually matched more closely with the seaman's eyeglass she was using and the curved sword strapped onto her hip.

Who the hell were these people?

* * *

HARRY WATCHED the newcomers from his perch high on the hill over the French base. The intruders had parked their vehicle almost a mile away from the remote site and walked in on foot. Sandra had kept watch on them every step of the way via a microdrone.

They didn't look like terrorists, but he knew looks could be deceiving. He wasn't going to take any chances.

He suspected they were associated with Brenda Cabot. She was one of the few people who knew he was back on Earth. He hadn't made it easy for her to keep tabs on him, but she was a former FBI agent. That probably meant she had mad skills when it came to tracking people.

These people were probably French members of her secret organization. It had existed for a thousand years and probably stretched around the globe. He'd be astonished if they didn't have people literally everywhere.

Unbeknownst to their watchers, Rex had taken his team around to keep a close eye on them. The scout had mad skills of his own. He and his people were less than twenty meters away from the concealed men.

A second team had already secured their vehicle. As soon as Rex had them in custody, they'd bring the vehicle closer. Once again, he didn't want to chance anyone finding them with all these dead bodies. That might cause some indelicate questions.

"Rex," he said over the encrypted channel. "Are you in position?"

Two soft clicks indicated he was.

"You are go to proceed," Harry continued. "Remember, take them all alive. We don't want to kill any of our potential allies."

Seconds later, Rex and his men seemingly popped up out of the ground near the intruders with their weapons in their faces. Wisely, the invaders raised their hands. The scout team quickly secured and searched them for weapons.

"Intruders secure," Rex said. "We're on our way back in. By the way, these people aren't terrorists. They actually bathe."

Harry laughed. "Copy that. Get them and their car up here as quickly as you can. Sandra, does the area look secure now?"

"None of my people see any signs of backup," the sniper said. "We'll keep our eyes open, but I think these are our only visitors."

It took Rex half an hour to march his prisoners up to the secret base. As a precaution, he put bags over their heads to keep them from seeing precise details of the base entrance. The builders had hidden the damned thing fiendishly well, and Harry didn't want to lose that advantage.

Harry had selected an empty room on the third level to interrogate them. It had once been a storage room, he suspected.

Rex and the scouts herded the prisoners into the room and closed the door behind them. Two men stood behind each prisoner, holding their arms. Rex pulled their hoods off.

His French was crappy, but Harry had enough vocabulary to get the point across. "Who are you?"

One of the men, a tall thin fellow with a well-trimmed mustache, cleared his throat and spoke in decent English, though with a pronounced French accent. "Please do not harm us. We are associates of Brenda Cabot. She asked us to make contact with you."

That was about what he'd expected, but Harry needed to be sure. "Do you have any proof?"

The man looked at his companions and shrugged. "I'm not precisely certain what form of proof you would accept."

Harry made a mental note to work out a series of code phrases with the former FBI agent. He should've done that right up front.

Since their groups were loosely aligned, they needed to have a secure method of identifying one another's operatives.

"My concern is that you might be associated with the US government," Harry said. "They know Brenda Cabot and I are aware of one another. You need to offer me something that only she or her people would know."

The man seemed to consider that for a moment and then shrugged again. "I find myself at a loss, Mister Rogers. You see, we are not directly part of her family. Our branch is active only in France. Perhaps you could call her. She would vouch for us."

That was a possibility, but one he'd prefer to use only as a last resort. He had a number for her, but the potential for an NSA intercept was high. They'd only be able to speak in generalities, and he'd have to use one of his people as a proxy. They'd be looking for his voiceprint. Hers, too, but she undoubtedly already knew that.

"I assume your family is aware of your location," Harry said after considering his options. "What will they do if I hold on to you until I'm certain of your bona fides?"

The man smiled slightly. "The potential for conflict when we made contact was always there. I have a code phrase that I may call them with to assure them of our safety and inform them that we will be staying here for the time being. My phone was confiscated by your men."

It was always possible the code phrase would mean something entirely different, but their silence meant something, too. It was probably best to take the chance. Whoever had sent them already knew roughly where the base was located.

"I'm going to leave you with my associate so I can take care of other matters requiring my attention. He will also endeavor to verify your identity with Miss Cabot. Once we're sure whom we are negotiating with, we can settle this misunderstanding."

Once the man nodded his agreement, Harry made his way out into the corridor with a gesture for Rex to follow.

He closed the door and spoke softly enough that no one inside would overhear. "Get his phone and let him pass the code phrase along. Use one of the burner phones and call Cabot, too. Don't mention any names, but inquire whether she might have sent a friend or two to visit us. If she says yes, these people are probably legitimate."

"I'll take care of it," the scout said. "What business are you going to be looking into?"

Harry grimaced. "As much as I'd rather let him rot, I need to get to New Zealand and figure out what happened to my father. If the US has him, that's a terrible security risk. We'll have to spring him.

"If he got away, he's either somewhere in the wilderness, down in the New Zealand base, or on a world connected to it by gate. We need to secure the base and keep the government down there from seizing it."

"Good plan. I'll handle my end. We still need to move all the vehicles away from the area. When someone official finally comes looking, they're going to spark a lot of questions. There were a bunch of terrorists involved in this attack, too. Someone is going to miss them."

"We can't control that," Harry said grimly. "So long as we move the vehicles a sufficient distance away, it doesn't matter what anyone does. They won't be able to locate this base. That's the important thing.

"If the terrorists had left word of their destination, we'd have already had more company. How long do you think it's going to take you to relocate all the vehicles?"

The scout shrugged. "If we use every available body and only move the cars forty or fifty kilometers, we should be able to get all of them relocated before dawn. We'll still be on the road getting back here, but we should be safe enough."

It would have to do. "Make it happen. Gather the bodies onto pallets near the gates and move them to *Freedom Express*, too. We'll give them a quiet burial in deep space. Collect all the intelligence you can as you go. We might need to know who their friends are later."

"Copy that. Good luck on your search."

Harry headed up to the surface. He'd take the jet that had brought them to France. With the time shift during the flight, he probably arrived in New Zealand just after dusk, local time.

He had no idea what he'd tell the New Zealanders. Everyone on Earth knew he was on Mars. He couldn't just reappear with no warning. He'd need to pretend to be someone else.

Thankfully, he'd been in his suit when they'd recorded the landing on Mars. His face might not be widely known. At least he hoped it wasn't. He'd find out soon enough.

6

Q ueen stepped off the rolling steps and onto the hot concrete of the airfield. His hat provided some protection against the glare, but he still had to shade his eyes with his hand.

A man in a blue Air Force uniform stepped forward and extended his hand. Silver stars glittered in the blinding light. "Welcome to Area 51, Secretary Queen. I'm Lieutenant General Nick Guthrie, the base commander."

Queen shook his hand but raised an eyebrow. "Isn't that classified?"

The man smiled. "We stopped denying the place existed quite some time ago. We just keep the details of what we do here under wraps now."

He gestured toward a waiting SUV. "Let's get inside before you melt."

Queen climbed inside the air-conditioned SUV gratefully. Once he'd secured his seatbelt and the general had climbed in beside him, he inspected the man.

The Air Force officer seemed young for his rank. Of course, as Queen got older *everyone* seemed younger. He supposed such was the nature of the universe.

"Has this vehicle been scanned for bugs?"

The officer nodded. "I had my people give it a thorough scan right before I came out to pick you up. It's clean, and the driver is cleared for anything we discuss."

"He might have the clearance, but he doesn't have the need to know. We can wait until we're in a secure facility to continue."

The building the SUV pulled up in front of was nondescript except for the hangar adjacent to it. Still, they'd originally designed the base to hide the stealth planes the US had tested here. The best way to conceal critical hangars was to have a lot of them to confuse observers.

The two Air Force military policemen guarding the door saluted the general as he escorted Queen inside.

Queen expected them to take the elevator down into some sublevel, but the general surprised him and hit the button for the top floor. He took a moment to scan the rows of buttons and quickly determined that there was no basement level to this building. None with a button, anyway.

The general raised an eyebrow. "Looking for hidden facilities concealed deep inside the earth?"

Queen allowed himself a smile. "I confess that I was. Too many old movies, I suppose."

The man shook his head. "We do have a number of underground facilities. In fact, we're converting them for project use as we speak. If you like, we can take a tour once we're done with the initial briefing."

The elevator doors slid open, and Guthrie led him to a conference room. The thickness of the doors and walls indicated it was a secure facility. No one would be able to monitor anything discussed within its confines.

Half a dozen people waited for them inside. Two were Air Force officers, and the remainder appeared to be civilians.

Queen recognized one of the latter. Ethan Wagner, the former lead scientist of BenCorp and Kathleen Bennett's scientific lapdog, sat on one side of the table.

To his credit, the man had fallen all over himself in an effort to prove useful. And Queen was willing to admit that the man *was* a valuable resource.

While he was no longer in charge of this research project, they'd continue to utilize his particular knowledge so long as he proved useful. If that ceased, the man knew he had a nice comfortable cell waiting for him at Guantánamo Bay.

General Guthrie gestured toward the chair at the head of the table. "If you'll have a seat, Mister Secretary, we'll get this briefing under way."

Queen assumed the indicated seat and waited for the general to take the remaining open chair to his right before speaking. "Good afternoon, everyone. For those of you who don't know me, I'm Josh Queen, the secretary of state, but the president has also placed me in charge of Project Prometheus and I'm here to learn what the baseline status of our investigation is."

Guthrie gestured toward the two military officers. "On your left are Majors Gregory Durant and Stephanie Mills. They fill the role of security officers for the project. Both have science backgrounds and can competently oversee all research and researchers. On the civilian side, I believe you are already familiar with Doctor Ethan Wagner."

Queen gave the scientist a cool smile. "Yes, we've met before. How are you, Doctor?"

The other man shrugged. "I suppose that depends on what we compare my situation with. Held up to a cell in Cuba, I'm doing wonderfully. Measured against the life I had before this, not so well."

"I suggest you don't use exterior yardsticks to measure how things might have been. You made the choices that led you here. You now have an opportunity to regain the freedom you once enjoyed. Don't screw it up."

Of course, both of them knew that was unlikely. With the critical knowledge the man had in his head, Queen couldn't just allow him to wander around freely. Wagner would always be subject to close monitoring and other restrictions, even if he earned his so-called freedom. Frankly, it would be a lot simpler to drop the man into solitary confinement once this project was well under way and lose the key.

Guthrie continued. "The remaining scientific researchers have all been pulled from other high-classification projects on the base. To your left is Doctor Tran Lee, center is Doctor Benedict Pender, and right is Doctor Astrid Sherrod."

"How much do they already know?" Queen asked.

"Nothing. I felt it best for you to tell them whatever you wanted them to know."

"Excellent. Everyone, I'm about to tell you a story you will have difficulty believing. Nevertheless, I assure you it's true." He glanced at his watch. "We're going to be here late into the evening, so I think it best if we send out for something to eat. Does anyone object to pizza?"

"Pizza is a favorite around here," Guthrie confided. "I know a guy that makes some amazing pie. We'll get that ordered, and it should be ready for us in an hour."

"Perfect," Queen said. "That should just about allow me to lay out the basics. It all starts in the jungles of Guatemala…"

* * *

"I TELL YOU, that cat was frozen solid," Jess insisted. "Ray can back me up."

"It was," the engineer said. "I was there when she found it."

The man blinked and turned to her. "You don't suppose any of those other people are going to come back to life, do you?"

"No. They're dead. The cat, though, appears to be a different story. Something is not as it seems."

She'd gathered her core scientific team—Emily Adams, their computer specialist; Michael and Sierra Crockett, their senior archaeologists; Rachel Powell and Paulette Young, their restoration specialists; and Debbie Callahan, the medical specialist they'd brought on board to deal with any issues in her realm—to discuss the unprecedented reanimation of the frozen cat. If anyone could figure out what the hell was going on, it was this group of people.

Debbie spoke up first. "I performed a brief physical inspection of the cat and the bodies that you brought up from the surface. I can categorically state that the cat is not a biological entity. The bodies are."

Ray Proudfoot scratched his head and leaned back in his chair. "Not a biological entity. It's some type of mechanical device. That's a hell of a thing. It looks *exactly* like a cat."

The physician nodded. "She acts like one, too. Without putting her into a scanning device, I'd never have been able to know that I wasn't dealing with a real cat. She's an amazing replica. Each and every detail is perfectly correct."

Michael Crockett shook his head. "That's crazy. Why would anyone build a mechanical cat?"

"To avoid cleaning the litter box?" his wife, Sierra, asked with a smirk. "And maybe control shedding. Trust me, nothing tastes better with cat hair as an ingredient."

The grumpy scientist laughed in spite of himself. "Those are good points. You could also program them to stop knocking every single thing you own to the floor."

Emily Adams, the third member of their poly relationship on this mission, sighed at her partners. "Context. You have to look at the context. That planet down there—that frozen, impossible Earth—is one big wall-to-wall city. I'd imagine they had enough trouble growing food for themselves, much less supporting the kind of ecosystem that we take for granted. Perhaps cats and dogs are extinct there.

"Hell, we've got enough trouble on Earth with species dropping dead. I can only imagine what it would be like in a few hundred years with the continuing population curves we're seeing now."

Jess shrugged. "That makes as much sense as anything else I can come up with. I suppose we'll have to continue our examination to be sure."

She turned in her seat to face Doctor Callahan. "If this is some type of cybernetic cat, one might assume that it has capabilities that a regular cat would not. Without disassembling it—which I am not willing to authorize—how can we know what we're dealing with?"

The woman shrugged. "Based on everything I've seen, it seems designed to behave like a cat. If it has capabilities in excess of that, it's not showing them. There's no indication that it understands anything I'm saying to it."

"It might have a command word or phrase that puts it into a different state," Ray said. "It's probably designed to be a cat unless someone intentionally places it into a different operational mode. Good luck figuring out what that is without taking it apart."

Jess scowled at him. "I'm not going to hurt that cat to satisfy your curiosity."

The engineer held up his hands in surrender. "The pedant in me wants to insist that it isn't a cat, but I know that's a losing argument. I'm simply stating a fact. Perhaps we can find out where it was made or locate one that's in a nonoperational state as we continue searching the planet."

She rubbed her face. "Talk about looking for a needle in a haystack. Searching that planet is going to be a huge pain in the butt. It's, well, Earth-sized. Obviously. Because of the temperature and vacuum conditions, I can't think of a more hostile environment."

Paulette Young leaned forward. "Rachel and I have been doing some calculations. Based on the size of the connected urban centers, which as you said take up the entire available landmass, that planet could have supported more than one hundred billion people. Perhaps many more."

Rachel Powell nodded at her partner. "With the landmasses fully occupied, all food had to have come from the only available location: the ocean. I'm certain we'll find that they had some scheme for raising and harvesting vast amounts of fish protein—"

A knock on the door interrupted the woman. John McCarthy stuck his head in. "One of the observation teams found something: a massive excavation site in what would be central China on our version of Earth.

"Based on the images I've seen, it looks as if someone was checking out what was down there on a grand scale. And by grand, I mean bigger than Manhattan. It seems they leveled a bunch of buildings and created an open space. The structures that they've raised in the center have the look and feel of Asharim technology."

Jess stood. "As interesting as the cat is, we need to focus on the Asharim presence. Emily, have you found someone we can hire to help you crack into the computers on the station and extract the destination code the ship used?"

"I have," the young woman said. "His name is Kevin McHugh. All I need to do now is convince him to help us. He's a pretty big deal in the global hacker community and can do things with computers that you wouldn't believe. That's not going to translate across to Asharim technology easily, but I suspect that he'll adapt a lot faster than many other people would."

"Make him a generous offer," Jess said. "Cash, alien computer technology, dancing girls, whatever it takes. The sky is literally the limit."

"I'll try not to break the bank. Money and Asharim computer technology will do just fine. I'll hold the dancing girls in reserve."

Jess chuckled. "The rest of you, we're mounting up to go down to the new site. Get something to eat, and meet me at the lock in an hour."

7

Nathan raced out to the room he and his men were using as a command post on the alien ship. The surviving members of his team that weren't out guarding the section of the ship they'd claimed were waiting for him. A number of them gasped and raised their weapons when his mother came into the room.

He raised a hand. "No time to explain. She's okay. We've got to go find out what those bastards have done. Focus on that, and I'll explain the rest when we're done."

With a gesture, Nathan sent the majority of them into the corridor before turning toward his mother. "Stay here. If you start wandering around, someone is going to shoot you." He didn't wait for her reply before following his fighters. Honestly, he still wasn't sure how to deal with her, either.

The strange halls of the alien ship still set his teeth on edge. There was something wrong with the geometry. The corridors were too wide and the ceilings too low. They made him feel squashed.

One of his surviving team leaders was waiting for him at a major cross corridor where they'd set up a defensive fire point. The man gestured toward the rear of the ship. "The noise came from back there."

Nathan hadn't heard a noise. He'd only felt the ship make an unusual move. "What kind of noise was it?"

"I'm not sure. Maybe a small explosion, or something big fell over. It happened right at the same time as something shook the ship. I'm wondering if they damaged the engines."

That would be a disaster. While one of the strange transport gates he and his people had used to get here from France was still intact, they couldn't go back to the abandoned base. It had been full of terrorists.

The ship had originally had three of the gates. Nathan had destroyed two of them, and he wasn't sure how to open the third. They'd used a space fighter to open the gate at the base in France.

Since his asshole brother had managed to get his people out through them, he must've discovered a portable means of controlling the gates. Nathan had collected a lot of gadgets but hadn't had time to experiment with anything. He'd mostly been concerned with finding every weapon left behind after the fight.

"It's time to finish this," Nathan said. "Either we take them out, or we die trying."

He didn't really know how large the ship was, but he understood the sections the enemy controlled. There were four corridors connecting Nathan's operational sector with the Islamic bastards. Both sides guarded them.

The two forces had settled into trench warfare like back in WWI. The two groups sat behind fortifications they'd arranged and waited for any attack by the enemy, occasionally pouring forth to try to overrun the other side.

In order to breach those lines, Nathan needed more force than he currently had available. Oh yes, he had enough men. Unfortunately, he didn't have very much ammunition for the alien weapons.

Over the course of the last few attacks, they'd killed a number of the ragheads. The jihadis' guns had been crap, but Nathan's people had enough ammunition to take care of the remaining foes. It was just going to be bloody.

"Send runners to the other checkpoints," Nathan told the man. "I want everyone except a skeleton crew to this location right now."

The man nodded and sent several people to gather the requested forces.

Ten minutes later, Nathan had the strongest force he was going to get. Together, they advanced down the corridor until they were just behind one of his leading fire points.

Rushing into the face of enemy fire would allow the enemy to kill a number of his people, but so long as he survived, Nathan didn't care. They had to breach the enemy line. Once they did that, they could run amok behind the terrorist fighting positions.

Nathan sent one man with a rocket-propelled grenade launcher to edge into the corridor. The man fired the explosive right before someone shot him in the head. When the explosion shook their position, Nathan sent his men charging forward around the corner, firing at anything that moved.

He followed, emptied his flechette weapon into the enemy position, and stepped back out of sight. Attacking a hardened position was ugly, but inside thirty seconds, they were behind the enemy barricade.

Nathan stalked forward and took the situation in with a glance. He'd lost a dozen men. Some were dead. Some were badly injured. None looked like they'd survive more than a few minutes. The enemy had only lost six. It made him angry.

"Get their weapons and ammunition," he said coldly. "We're moving on."

"What about our men?" the team leader asked quietly.

"We don't have the medical care to save any of them." Technically, he wasn't sure that was true, but he couldn't afford to divert precious resources at a time like this. As Napoleon Bonaparte had said, making omelets meant breaking eggs. Or something like that.

If they continued pushing in the direction they were going, Nathan suspected the enemy would come to them. He was not disappointed.

Filthy men screaming in Arabic came running from several cross corridors, firing wildly as they ran. Their bullets mostly missed, but with no cover or concealment, that wasn't always the case.

His trained people returned fire, killing many of the enemy fighters with their skill. This was going to be a war of attrition. Nathan just hoped they had enough bodies to make this work.

By the time they'd dealt with all the screaming jihadis, he had less than a dozen men still with him. He hadn't seen the enemy's cultured leader, the one who'd cut his mother's toe off, so he knew they still had at least one heavy fight still in front of them.

Nathan had spent enough time on regular ships to recognize that they were moving into the engineering section. The aliens hadn't designed this part of the ship for normal crew or passengers. The amount of equipment was increasing the farther aft they moved.

He hoped no one shot anything critical. If they disabled anything critical, there was nothing he could do to fix it.

One of his men came back from a scouting trip. His left arm was bloody, but the man still seemed combat effective.

"There's another barricade in the room ahead," he growled. "I couldn't see how many people were behind it, but it's going to be ugly. They've got a great field of fire."

One of the men had captured a rocket-propelled grenade launcher. He held up two fingers when Nathan raised his chin.

"Lead with the grenades, and take them down."

The man frowned. "Are you sure we're ready for this, boss?"

"Do we have a choice? If we retreat now, they're going to come after us. We have to end this while we have them off-balance."

The other man sighed and headed toward the forward position without another word.

The assault on the position kicked off with an explosion. Then there was a second one, much closer to Nathan than he liked. It seemed they had a grenade launcher of their own.

To their credit, his men didn't flinch from running into the hail of bullets and explosives. Nathan followed and picked up the grenade launcher from where his man had dropped it when he'd died. It took a moment to fit the final grenade into place, but his people kept the enemy pinned down long enough for him to fire it at the defenders.

Ironically, he hadn't needed to waste the ammunition. The enemy fighter with a grenade launcher raised himself from cover. One of the many bullets flying around struck him in the face, sending him staggering backward. He must've pulled the trigger because the grenade fired straight up.

Normally, a rocket-propelled grenade had to travel a predetermined distance before it armed, but they must've done something to their ammunition. It exploded the moment it struck the ceiling, delivering its lethal payload to each of the defending terrorists.

Nathan and his men advanced and shot anyone that still twitched. He was down to five people, counting himself.

He raised his radio to his lips. "I want every man to move forward and join me. Every single man."

Ten minutes later, his force was back up to just over a dozen men. If this wasn't enough to end the fight in his favor, he was going to die.

They probed ahead and found a large compartment ahead of them. More defenders were waiting there.

"One final chance to surrender," Nathan called out in French. Not that he intended to allow any of the enemy to live.

The cultured tones of the enemy leader came back. "We only surrender ourselves to Allah. Come and take us if you can." He punctuated his demand with a rain of bullets.

"Charge," Nathan said. "Kill everyone."

The final assault was brutal. Even though Nathan held himself to the last position, he found himself flat behind the body of one of his people and shooting at the defenders. It wasn't that he was a coward, but he preferred not to risk his own life. It was the only one he had.

With a wail in Arabic, the enemy rushed from behind their position. His people gave a good account of themselves but were overwhelmed.

Nathan emptied his rifle into the enemy, drew his pistol, and shot several more before finally finding himself with only a knife as a weapon.

In the smoke and confusion, he wasn't sure how many of the enemy remained standing. At least two, since both of them charged him. They must've been out of bullets as well, because they had curved daggers that cut toward his face and body.

A trained knife fighter, Nathan knew the odds of him coming out of this conflict with his blood still inside his body were slim. He dodged to the right, placing one of the attackers between him and the other. The man stabbed at Nathan's face before slashing down.

Nathan resisted the urge to retreat and pushed forward, accepting an intensely painful gash to his arm. The end result was worth it. He jammed his knife into the other man's throat and pulled it brutally out the side. Then he kicked the dying man into his friend, sending both of them tumbling to the deck.

While the second man was attempting to extract himself, Nathan drove his knife through the man's eye and into his brain.

A slow clap accompanied him rising to his feet and looking for new enemies. The only one he could see standing was the enemy leader. He was just walking from behind the improvised barricade. Not the kind to risk his skin, then.

"Most impressive," the other man said. "Though you are an infidel, you are not a coward. I salute you."

Nathan eyed the other man. He held a pistol, but it pointed toward the deck, and the slide had locked open.

"You're boring me," Nathan said. "Let's end this."

The other man smiled and produced a magazine for his pistol. Now that wasn't very sporting. The distance between them precluded Nathan from reaching the man before he finished reloading. A thrown knife was chancy at best. He needed another option.

One presented itself in the form of a rifle dropped during the earlier fight. Nathan had no idea if it was even loaded at this point. He'd just have to take a chance. He threw the knife at his enemy on the assumption it would force him to dodge and disrupt his reloading.

Taking advantage of that hoped-for lull, Nathan threw himself to the deck, grabbed the rifle, and rolled desperately to the side while bringing it to bear. The sights lined up with his enemy, and he pulled the trigger.

Nothing happened.

That's when Nathan noticed his throw had been better than he'd had any right to expect. The hilt of his knife protruded from the other man's throat.

To his credit, the dying man was slowly raising his now-loaded pistol toward Nathan. But it never rose high enough. With a gurgle, the man fell backward. The pistol discharged into one of the bodies just in front of Nathan.

To be safe, Nathan waited an additional thirty seconds before he rose cautiously to his feet. The bolt on the rifle he'd picked up had locked back, but he found another magazine with ammunition to recharge the weapon.

The enemy leader was still alive when Nathan stepped over to him. Barely. He tried to say something, but his ruined voice box wouldn't cooperate.

Wordlessly, Nathan raised the rifle and fired a single shot into the man's head.

Taking the dead man's pistol, he went from body to body and made sure that all his enemies were similarly dead. Unfortunately, all of his allies seem to have perished as well.

It took him more than an hour to finish searching the area for potential hostiles. None remained. The ship was his—and just about his alone. Only his mother remained.

He took the precaution of collecting enough ammunition to fight if he was wrong, but he didn't think he was. These people had fought to the death. They'd almost been good enough to take him out.

He found no signs of sabotage. What he did find was an observation chamber above the engineering compartment. It wasn't very large, but it had a view of the entire ship forward of engineering. What he saw chilled him.

The ship was now in orbit around a large planet. It was definitely not Earth, and the ship wasn't alone. Scattered across his view were other ships.

Or perhaps it would be more accurate to say parts of ships. While there were some large chunks, the ones he could see didn't seem to be whole. There had been a battle here at some point in the past.

That explained the noise and vibration. A chunk of debris had struck the ship. Obviously not disastrously, but with the amount of potential ruin he could see floating around them, that probably wouldn't last.

The victory he'd sacrificed his men for had been fleeting. This new danger was even more of a threat. He needed to get himself and his mother off this ship before something punctured the hull and left them trying to breathe vacuum.

8

Clayton stared at the woman in the image. She was just another question mark in the middle of the mystery people that were dressed as if they'd come from the Revolutionary War.

Commander Krueger leaned in and gave her a close examination. "Is she a pirate?"

"Whoever she is, she's spotted your drone," Clayton said. "They know we're around here somewhere. How is that going to change what we do next?"

"It doesn't change one damn thing," Ulysses snarled. The CIA agent stalked into the chamber and gave them all a withering stare. "They're primitives. It doesn't matter one damned bit what they think or know."

Clayton shook his head and smiled sadly. "Those who do not learn from history are doomed to repeat it. I'm quite sure the British felt somewhat similarly about the Zulu nation back in the day. That didn't turn out as well as they'd hoped."

Ulysses rounded on Clayton, brandishing his fist in the older man's nose. "You shut your mouth, traitor. I've had more than enough of your crap. You're a prisoner, and you don't get a say in anything."

The other man smiled cruelly. "If I had my way, I'd chain your ass to a rock and keep you there until I got you to Guantánamo. And once I did, I'd break you."

The other man's expression changed to one of panic as Gunnery Sergeant Danvers grabbed him by the back of the neck and yanked him off his feet. The noncommissioned officer shoved the CIA agent against the wall. He grabbed Ulysses's right hand as the man tried to go for a weapon.

"I've had enough of you, cockroach," Danvers growled. "If we're going to chain a prisoner to a rock, it's going to be you."

"Call your dog off, Krueger," Ulysses sneered. "We both know who's going to win this confrontation."

"I'm not sure that we do," the Navy officer said. "Frankly, you come across like a congenital idiot and a man born outside of his time. You seem the type of man who'd be much more comfortable working for the Nazis. Probably torturing people for them."

A wave of shock traveled across the CIA agent's face only to be replaced by rage. "If there's an idiot in this room, it's you. Now call him off, or every single one of you gets a room next to Rogers in Hotel Guantánamo."

"I don't think so. Gunnery Sergeant, I'm placing Agent Ulysses under confinement. I'm afraid the situation is too much for him, and his demonstrated instability has become a threat to our mission. Secure him somewhere, and search him thoroughly for weapons."

"Yes, sir!"

"You sonofabitch!" Ulysses screamed. "I'll see you executed for this!"

Whatever else the man had been about to say was cut off when Danvers drove a fist into his gut. The gunnery sergeant threw the CIA agent flat on the ground and planted a knee in the center of his back while other members of the team helped secure their new prisoner. They then roughly hoisted the CIA agent to his feet and hustled him out of the chamber.

Clayton gave Krueger a curious look. "His superiors are not going to be pleased. Frankly, he's probably right. They'll throw you into a cell right next to mine."

The Navy officer sagged a little. "Maybe, but there's only so long I can tolerate assholes. Frankly, Ulysses is the kind of guy that ends up being shot in the back by friendly fire before he gets a chance to report."

"You'd actually kill him before we go home? That's quite a step, Commander Krueger. I didn't think you had it in you."

The other man sat on a handy rock. "I probably don't. It's just wishful thinking. Frankly, Mister Rogers, I'm not certain what I'm going to do. I'm not certain what I *can* do. The information that you've uncovered—the things we've seen on this mission—was probably already going to get me and my men locked away."

Clayton considered the other man for a moment. "I know you've heard a lot of bad things about me. Many of them are true. I've done awful things in pursuit of money and power to fulfill my goals.

"But you also know my son. He's not the kind to work with me on something that doesn't have the potential to help a great number of people. You've only seen the tip of the iceberg. There are greater threats to humanity than you can imagine and the potential to uplift us all to a new level of free society that hasn't been seen in the United States for decades. Hell, maybe a century.

"You've burned your bridges behind you. Allow me to extend a hand in friendship. Don't trust me. Trust my son."

The officer rubbed his eyes tiredly. "I don't suppose I have much of a choice."

"That's not true. You have a very stark choice. You can continue to support an authoritarian regime that Mussolini would be proud of or you could become part of an organization that is trying to secure freedom for humanity."

Krueger considered him for a moment. "At the moment, it's a moot point. We're trapped on an alien world with people seemingly plucked out of history. Until we find a way home, it doesn't matter what I decide."

Clayton smiled more widely. "That's not true, either. It matters very much. If you join my team, I can fill you in on everything we've discovered. Everything we suspect. Then we can work together to find a solution without worrying that the other is going to betray them."

"How do I know you won't betray me?" Krueger asked. "As you say, you've got quite the reputation."

"A reputation for driving a hard bargain and then abiding by it. I'm confident we can work out the verbiage in a way that satisfies you, but we can come to an agreement in principle right now. My son needs as many other trained military personnel as he can get because the alien threat is much greater than even the United States government currently understands.

"If he's agreeable, you could stand at his right hand. You have all the skills one could hope for and probably many contacts that would prove exceptionally useful. Since you have doubts about me, I'm more than willing to allow him to do the negotiation of the details. I assure you that he will confirm everything I'm telling you now."

Krueger sighed. "It seems that events have overtaken our earlier agreement. I'll pass the word to my people that we're releasing you on your own recognizance. You are no longer our prisoner. But we don't work for you. Not yet. I'll do everything I can to get us home, then we'll see. That's the best I can offer."

Clayton extended his hand. "That's more than good enough for me. Allow me to welcome you provisionally aboard. I suppose our first question is what we'll do about the people in that army out there."

The drone must've been hovering uncontrolled this entire time. The stabilized image of the woman showed that others had joined her. In particular, a distinguished-looking man in uniform. He held the spyglass now and was observing the drone.

"It does appear the cat is out of the bag," Krueger agreed. "We can get the drone away, but they'll be on their guard now. If we wish to avoid meeting them, we can huddle inside the cave, and they might miss us."

"But they might not," Clayton argued. "I think the time for concealment has passed. Besides, if we're ever going to learn the lay of the land and find a way back home, we're going to have to talk with these people. We have to convince them that we're friends, or at least potential allies."

He examined the woman in the image again. She was speaking with the man beside her. He didn't know them, but Clayton was a master of body language. The man might be the military officer, but she was his superior.

Perhaps socially. In any case, she was ultimately the one he'd have to convince to help them.

He allowed himself a smile. Well, high-pressure negotiations were his specialty.

* * *

HARRY STARED out of the helicopter as it flew over the wilderness. The New Zealand landscape below was lush and untouched. "It's beautiful."

The pilot—an officer in New Zealand's air force—nodded his agreement. "Sure is. Hell to walk through, though. I feel sorry for the poor buggers wandering around down there."

"Any word on the search?"

"Some. We sent a ship out and confronted the US destroyer yesterday. They refused to let us board, so we forced them to turn back with our jets and ships. Since they weren't in our waters, this has turned into a real international incident."

Harry shook his head. "Sorry about that."

"Not your problem. Hell, it's not even your boss's concern. He came here with diplomatic immunity. America had no right to send soldiers onto our soil, much less kidnap two of our citizens and someone under our protection."

The man sounded grim. If his attitude was widespread—which Harry suspected it was—that boded ill for the US's influence in the area for a long time to come.

"They didn't turn up on the ship once we impounded it, either," the pilot continued. "No one is talking, but based on personal belongings, at least a dozen of their people are unaccounted for. That probably means they're still around here somewhere. We'll find them."

Harry suspected they wouldn't find anyone at this point. The only reason he could think of that the military people hadn't made it back to their ship was that his father had led them into the base. They were either still down there now, or they'd escaped to another world.

Yet one more headache for him to deal with.

"You've confirmed it was an American drone?"

That bit of information had been waiting for him when he'd landed. The US forces had left quite the calling card.

"Oh yeah. A number of our boys have worked with American forces before. One of them recognized the drone as a kind favored by the CIA. No weapons but great cameras. Somebody shot out the engine and it crashed. The electronics were booby-trapped, too. It was American."

"I'm sure that's going to prove awkward when you trot it out as evidence at some future point."

"I hope so," the pilot said. "I bet they cart it to the UN and make a huge stink over it. Not that the UN is good for much except generating hot air.

"We're almost to the landing zone. The search parties are centered on the area where Mister Rogers was camping. Once I drop you off, I'll join the search."

Harry nodded his thanks, even if it wasn't a prospect that filled him with joy. The man might've shown himself to be a human being, but Harry had a lifetime of dislike to overcome. Frankly, he doubted he'd ever change his opinion of his father.

That didn't mean he couldn't work with the man. So long as their goals aligned.

The landscape around where his father had set up camp was gorgeous. It seemed to be untouched by human hands before their helicopter had touched down. He could imagine living out here himself.

The headquarters for the search area consisted of several tents set up near a large flat stone suitable for landing a helicopter on. Just adjacent to that was a larger mesa that Harry immediately suspected housed the New Zealand base.

Not that he was likely to confirm that anytime soon. Several men and a tall woman stood waiting for the helicopter to idle. No doubt these were the people coordinating the search. They'd occupy his time to a much greater degree than he'd like for the foreseeable future.

At some point, though, he'd be able to slip away and examine the mesa for concealed entrances. He just had to bide his time.

Once the rotor blades had slowed, Harry shook the pilot's hand, set his headset down on the seat, and made his way out to meet the New Zealanders.

As he'd expected, the woman stepped forward. "Mister Jacobs? My name is Molly Goodwin. I'm sorry to meet you under these circumstances. We're doing everything we can to find your employer."

He hoped the false name and cover story held long enough for him to find his father. Harry shook her hand firmly. "I'm sure you are. Do you have any idea which direction they went? Were they injured?"

"I'm afraid not. They sent the rest of their party off while they created a distraction. They climbed up on that mesa over there and rappelled down the far side."

Harry looked at the mesa. "If you don't mind, I'd like to take a look up there. Alone."

She gave him an odd look before shaking her head. "That's not going to be possible. They used a large stone to take out the easiest way up."

He smiled. "I served in special operations for quite some time. I have a lot of experience climbing places you wouldn't think people could get to. I assume you've already got a rope hanging down to assist people in getting to the top?"

"We do, but it's not the safest option."

"The important things in life rarely are. I understand that sounds strange, but I need to see this for myself."

She looked unconvinced. "I'll see what we can do."

He didn't feel bad about manipulating her. If that was the last place anyone had seen his father, the odds of the entrance being up top were exceptionally good.

Not that he'd have an opportunity to explore the base right now. The very last thing he wanted to do was tip the New Zealanders off that they had an ancient installation in their backyard. If that happened, they'd seize it.

He'd locate the entrance and perhaps scout it out. Then he'd come back once everyone was asleep and check it out in more detail.

Harry hoped whatever problems his father had embroiled himself in weren't time sensitive. Otherwise, the old man would have to get himself out of them all by himself.

On second thought, he hoped the man wasn't all that safe. The bastard deserved some grief for all the hell he'd caused Harry over the years. Karma was a bitch. He'd settle for pulling the old man's ass out of the fire at the last minute.

9

J ess had to travel to the French base in order to contact Brenda Cabot. She really needed to figure out a better way to communicate with people on Earth.

By the time she arrived, it was dark in the United States. Though it might be rude, she didn't have time to waste. She dialed the burner number that Cabot had given them using a burner of her own.

That number had changed after Harry's people had called to verify the intruders at the base were associated with Brenda. That made sense to her. With the global communications intercept capability of the NSA, they would quickly tag any call in the world that seemed suspicious. And international calls to US citizens *always* made the US government suspicious.

The phone rang twice before Cabot answered. The woman sounded a bit groggy. "Do you know what time it is?"

Jess considered her watch. It was still on GMT. She did a rough calculation in her head. "Late?"

"Early," Brenda said firmly. "Is there a fire? There better be some kind of fire."

"We need to talk face-to-face as soon as possible."

There was a moment of silence. "Give me a half hour to get set up."

"Thank you."

Jess ended the call, removed the SIM card from the phone, and crushed it under her heel. She handed the now-useless burner to Rex. The scout took it and dropped it into one of his many pockets.

In exchange, he pulled out a different phone and handed it to her. Then, to her confusion, he pulled out a third phone and handed it to her.

She glanced at them before giving him a quizzical look. "Is this some kind of social commentary about me talking on the phone too much? Seriously, I'm not a chatterbox."

He laughed. "Not at all. You're holding a piece of brand-new technology, one that can make your life a lot easier. Those are quantum phones. Apparently, Clayton Rogers had perfected the technology and then kept it secret so that the US government wouldn't get it."

Jess examined one of the phones more closely. It was a bit bulkier than her usual one, but not by much. Honestly, some of the carriers had gone ridiculously slim. At least these had enough bulk for her to hold them comfortably. She touched the screen and found that it looked very much like the phone she'd just used. "It seems pretty normal to me."

The man nodded. "And it behaves fairly normally as well. It can connect to any of the regular cellular networks. One positive is that it utilizes software embedded inside the network to generate a false identity for the phone. You don't have to pull out a SIM card once you use it.

"Every call appears to come from a different phone—one already located in the general area that you're in. Apparently it's some kind of backdoor that Clayton Rogers installed before he sold that company to the Chinese."

She had to admit that sounded useful. "Why do I have two?"

"Because it also has a quantum mode. You don't have to use any existing cellular network. You can call other quantum phones directly. I haven't tested the range, but the geek that delivered these said I should be able to call Harry directly without any issues. I figured you'd want one to give to Cabot so you could have secure communications."

"That does sound like a good idea. The last thing we want to do is bring the US government down on her people. They have the only operational gate inside the United States. Did you get one sent to Harry?"

Rex smiled wryly. "They arrived about an hour after he'd left. I paid an exorbitant amount of money to send someone after him. It'll be dark there before my guy lands, but he should be able to get a phone into Harry's hands early tomorrow morning."

"How can it call from here to New Zealand without using a cellular network?"

The ex-military man shrugged. "Damned if I know. I've never even used it."

As an engineer specializing in space projects, Jess knew a lot about science. That didn't mean she understood quantum mechanics. Frankly, she was halfway convinced the scientists that claimed they did were just making things up.

Still, the universe had proven itself stranger than she'd anticipated. She'd do more research and then some real-world testing before she formed an impression.

"Once I'm done meeting with Cabot, I'll get her to send me directly back to *Freedom Express*," she said. "If you've got one of these close at hand, let's get the number in my contact list now."

"Already done. The units are meant for Harry and Cabot, too. As far as I know, that's all there are. These are prototypes. The guy that dropped them off said it would probably be another six months before there is any kind of real production, but who knows what that means?"

"I'll need his contact information, too."

"Will do."

Jess waited until the designated time and went down to the gate. She grabbed the cat carrier that she'd left down near the gate when she'd gone upstairs. The artificial black cat stared patiently at her through the grate.

That made her feel guilty. She knew intellectually that sitting down here for half an hour hadn't hurt the mechanical device, but she should've left it somewhere more comfortable. Somewhere with food, water, and a litterbox.

Once she'd established the connection to Cabot's gate, her end filled with mist and lightning. She waited for it to clear and then walked through.

Cabot and two of her associates were waiting on the other side. Jess wasn't familiar with either of the men.

The other woman raised an eyebrow at the carrier. "Stopping by the vet after your visit?"

Jess smiled. "Something like that. I wanted to know if you have any kind of advanced scanning technology to look at the cat."

The other woman's expression became confused. "I'm not sure I understand."

"Then allow me to explain. You're going to find this fascinating."

* * *

BRENDA STARED at Jessica Cook in shock. She knew her mouth was hanging open but couldn't help herself. "Is this some kind of joke?" she asked. "An artificial cat? Why in the world would the Asharim build an artificial cat?"

"They didn't. It appears that the Asharim were investigating something amazing in the outer system, way out past the orbit of Pluto. They have a station there in orbit around a dead, frozen planet. The cat came from there."

Brenda stared into the cat carrier. The small black cat looked completely normal. Nothing struck her as off.

"Are you sure it's artificial?"

Cook nodded, her expression dark. "It was lying in the lap of a frozen body. Someone who had probably been dead for more than a thousand years. That's the minimum. We found definite signs that the Asharim were exploring the world. The cat was there when the world died, however long ago that was."

"May I? Is it safe?"

The other woman gestured toward the carrier. "It seems friendly enough."

Brenda figured out how to open the carrier and held a hand in. The small black creature delicately sniffed her fingers and then brushed her cheek against them. Brenda could hear a soft purr coming from inside the carrier.

This was unreal.

When she encountered no resistance, Brenda pulled the cat out of the carrier and set it on the table in front of her. It stood under her hand as she petted it, its tail flirting.

"This has got to be some kind of joke. I've never heard of anything like this. Even the Asharim couldn't have built such a perfect replica. You say you found a dead planet. Why would the inhabitants build a replica cat?"

The other woman extended a tablet toward her. "I think I'd best let the pictures explain for themselves. These were taken from the camera on my vacuum suit."

Brenda took the tablet and brought it to life. The first picture was already queued up. It was the exterior of some kind of building with lots of snow piled around it. She felt her hackles rise as she flipped through the images. The sight of the frozen bodies made her heart lurch. Especially the family on the couch. The little girl with the small black cat in her lap.

Her eyes shot up to meet Cook's.

"Humans?"

"Our doctor confirmed it. These people were completely human. What's more, they didn't come from anyone taken by the Asharim." The woman pulled an ID card from her pocket and slid it across the table.

Brenda saw that it was a Virginia driver's license. Then she started noticing the oddities. The birthdate was August 4, 2223.

"That's bullshit!" she said.

"I have proof, if you have some kind of scanning device."

"We have some scanning technology," Brenda admitted. "It's designed for human medical issues. I have absolutely no idea what it would return from a mechanical device. Or a real cat."

Cook smiled. "I suppose we'll find out." She took the unresisting cat and put it back into the carrier.

Brenda looked at one of her men. "Get Granger down to the medical center."

He headed out at a trot.

She led Jessica Cook down to the area they were using as a medical center in their new headquarters building. Five minutes later, Doctor Todd Granger walked briskly into the room.

He smiled at Cook. "Jessica! It's a pleasure to see you again though, I must confess, I didn't expect you to come visit me. You're not hurt, are you?"

His asian looks and deep southern accent made her smile at the discontinuity. Granger had been with Brenda when she'd led a group to meet Harry Rogers and Jessica Cook for the first time. He'd been escorting their prisoner at the time, Secretary of State Josh Queen.

The doctor had a way with people. He got along with everyone. It was all part of his bedside manner and general personality.

Cook smiled more widely as she shook Granger's hand. "It's good to see you again, Todd. Though I still can't get over your accent. It throws me for a loop every time."

That made Brenda laugh. "I've known him since we were kids. It still messes me up. How can somebody that looks like he just stepped off a flight from Japan sound like he came from Appalachia?"

"It's a gift," Granger said with a grin. "What can I do for you ladies?"

Cook hefted the cat carrier. "Agent Cabot says that you have a scanning device that might be able to take a good look at my cat."

Granger raised an eyebrow. "That may be one of the most unusual requests I've had in recent memory. Though I suppose there's some sense to it. You are one of the most wanted women in the world, after all. I'll wager dropping in on your vet might be a poor idea."

"I'm a human doctor, not a veterinarian, though. Perhaps if you tell me what the problem is, I might be able to work something out, but I wouldn't hold my breath." The man bent over and peered into the carrier. "The little thing looks healthy enough. She's a cutie by the way. At least I assume she's female from the size."

Cook set the cat carrier onto the examination table. "I'd rather not lead you down any specific trail of thought. Could you just give her a general examination and tell us what you think?"

Brenda nodded when he glanced at her. "It's actually more important than you think. Be thorough."

"Okay. She doesn't bite or scratch, does she?"

Cook shook her head. "She's one of the friendliest cats I've ever met."

Granger shrugged, took the cat out of the carrier, and began examining it. After a few minutes, he carried it to a hooded machine with a gurney that slid inside it.

"This might look like an MRI machine, but it's capable of several different modes of scanning. As I told you before, I don't know that much about cats, so I don't know if I'll be able to determine anything. Also, if she doesn't stay still, the scan will be useless."

Cook stepped up beside the gurney and squatted so that her face was just a few inches in front of the cat's. "Sit still for a minute."

To Brenda's amazement, the cat promptly sat down and curled her tail around her legs.

"It's almost as if she understood you," Granger said with a smile. "Let's see if we can take advantage of this miracle." He gently pushed the gurney under the scanning hood and stepped back to the controls. A few deft motions and a low hum emanated from the machine.

"All done. Go ahead and get her out, and we'll take a look at what the scan recorded."

To all appearances, the cat was sitting in exactly the same position it had been when they rolled the gurney into the machine. Cook picked the cat up and held her to her chest, petting her. That seemed to be precisely what the creature wanted because it snuggled against her and began purring loudly.

Granger brought up an image on the built-in screen and stared at it. "What the hell?"

To Brenda's inexperienced eye, that didn't look like a cat. She wasn't sure what it was. "What are you seeing?"

The doctor turned and squinted toward Cook. "That cat doesn't have any internal organs. Hell, it doesn't even look biological. What is going on?"

"That's what I was hoping you folks could help us figure out." Cook turned her attention to Brenda. "Is that enough evidence for you to accept what I'm telling you?"

"Provisionally," Brenda said. "I want to see this place with my own eyes. What does this have to do with the Asharim? Hell, if this planet was there before they even visited us, what has it got to do with humanity?"

"I haven't got the slightest idea. We're going to contact someone someone that might help us get into the computer systems on that station. Not only would it be useful to find their research notes, I'd like to unlock the destination that Harry's relatives used to escape in that ship. The longer they're on the loose, the greater the chances that someone we can't deal with is going to come visit us."

"I've already taken some steps in that direction," Brenda said. "I'll have a guy here in the morning who might be able to help you crack those computers. Not only is he one hell of a hacker, he's made a specialty of porting that skill over to Asharim technology. His name's Kevin McHugh."

Jess laughed. "How weird is that? He's the guy Emily Adams wanted me to contact. That's excellent new. In exchange for your help, I'm willing to share everything we find there with you and your people. That world looks like one huge city. A megalopolis spread across every single bit of land.

"We haven't even begun to scratch the surface of their technology. Everything is in a vacuum and frozen. It's going to be in amazing condition, I think. I don't know if they were more advanced than the Asharim, but just based on this cat, I would suspect that they had some areas they were ahead in."

Brenda considered the cat. "It's really damned hard to argue with that. I can already see one aspect of technology that these people had the Asharim beat in. You say this critter was frozen for over a thousand years but came back to life as soon as you thawed it. Smaller Asharim power supplies would've failed long ago."

Cook's eyes narrowed. "I hadn't thought of that. Good point. Oh, and I have another present for you." The woman dug a phone out of her pocket and handed it to Brenda.

"I've got plenty of burner phones," Brenda assured the woman.

"Not like this one. You don't have to destroy this one when you're done. It's linked into the carrier networks with an artificial SIM card. Software in the carrier will give it a different identification every time it's used. Basically, it clones a nearby phone and pretends to be it.

"But that's not the biggest thing. It also incorporates quantum technology. Something that Clayton Rogers had been working on. There are only four of these phones in existence, but when communicating between these units, the transmissions are undetectable. No way that anyone can intercept what we're saying."

"Seriously?"

"That's what I'm told. The range is also much greater. It won't use any of the equipment here on Earth or in orbit, but it should be able to call someone on the other side of the globe. I have one unit, Harry will have one in a few hours, Rex has one, and your group will have the last. The numbers are in the contact list."

Luckily, Brenda had someone who understood quantum mechanics very well. Victor Holyfield had been a doctoral candidate in particle physics. He'd be able to use words small enough to explain what this meant to her.

Even so, she already grasped the implications. They'd built a level of trust with Cook and Rogers that might allow them to become real allies. That was a hell of a lot more valuable than any toy.

She glanced at her watch. "We've got a couple of hours until your hacker arrives. Why don't we have breakfast and go over what you found in more detail? Then we can work on how my organization can do the most to help you leverage what you've found."

Cook smiled at her. "That would be perfect. Please tell me you have blueberries."

"I'm sure we can find some. Thanks for your help, Todd."

"My pleasure. If you ladies don't mind, I'm going back to bed. Somehow, I suspect tomorrow is going to be a busy day."

10

It took Clayton twenty minutes to convince Krueger that they had to meet with the woman and her army. He understood why the man was reticent. Once they revealed themselves, there was no going back.

Yet they didn't have much of a choice. Now that these people knew someone was around, they would look hard to find them. The simple fact that the drone hadn't completely discombobulated the viewers indicated they'd seen its like before. Unless the Americans wanted to be thought of as hostile, they had to create a different impression and soon.

Even though Krueger eventually conceded the point, he'd insisted the contact happen in stages. He'd sent scouts to keep an eye on the army while they put together a group to meet with them.

"Honestly, I think we should send as small a party as possible," Clayton said. "If things go wrong, I'd prefer to leave some options on the table. I think I should meet them alone."

The Navy commander raised an eyebrow. "That's risky as hell. Why would you volunteer to do something like that?"

Clayton shrugged. "Do you happen to have a better negotiator in your back pocket? While I've never dealt with this particular situation before, I don't believe they'll see me as a threat, so they'll allow me to approach. A larger group might come under fire."

"I can see the logic in that," Krueger conceded, "but why not take one or two other people? Having a few extra bodies isn't going to raise the threat level that much. They have an army."

"If I'm going to put myself in danger, why put other people in the pot with me? If these people aren't willing to discuss things in good faith, that seems like the safest move."

The officer shook his head. "And a dangerous one to our eventual chances of getting home. You have a lot more knowledge about this alien technology than anyone else in our group does. I understand that even your insight is limited, but ours is nonexistent. We didn't even know these gates existed until after we'd walked through one. What else don't we know?"

Clayton nodded. "That's a point. Still, my computer has every bit of information I have. If things go sour, you'll be able to study the files. As long as the battery holds out, anyway.

"In any case, time is wasting. We need to send someone before they conclude the drone is hostile. Frankly, they've probably already assumed that. It's going to be difficult for me to convince them that we're harmless. Spending extra time talking with you isn't going to help me do that."

The Navy man sighed. "I'll have someone escort you down the hill. The trail is rough, and no one seems to have used it in a long time. It's not like the one their party took to the crown of the hill. That one has seen occasional traffic.

"Our scouts have been down this one several times, and we've blazed a trail that won't be obvious to any observers. We'll also send a small group with you to provide cover in case you need to retreat."

Clayton cocked his head a little. "You mean like snipers?"

"That's exactly what I mean. I'll give them orders not to interfere unless they believe your life is in danger. If you want to risk capture, I can't stop you. Well, I suppose I could, but I sort of agree with everything you've said thus far.

"Nevertheless, if it looks as if somebody is going to shoot you, one of my people will put a bullet in their head. I hope that my men will be able to give you enough covering fire to retreat if that happens. We'll turn this hill into a fortress if we have to."

Clayton stood and brushed his pants off. "It's my job to make certain we don't have to. Under the right circumstances, you can make a deal with anyone. You just have to understand what they need and come up with a way to provide that in exchange for something you want.

"They have detailed knowledge of this world that we don't. If there's something our technology can allow us to do for them, it may very well be that we can come to a straightforward solution to our problem."

The officer didn't seem convinced. "They're obviously outfitted for war. I'm not sure that anything we can provide will make much of a difference. Yes, our technology is of a higher caliber than anything we've seen them use, but there aren't that many of us, and we didn't bring a lot of ammunition. I was only supposed to make a brief foray into New Zealand and take you into custody, not fight a war."

Clayton smiled. "As you well know, fighting isn't the only thing that can be brought to the table in a combat situation. Gather your men, and let's get this going."

Krueger rose to his feet and summoned several of his men. He gave them instructions in a low voice then came back over to shake Clayton's hand. "Good luck and be careful."

Gunnery Sergeant Danvers led the small group of men that escorted

Clayton to the bottom of the hill. Frankly, Clayton was glad he had the man. He didn't see the trail at all. It just looked like rough hillside to him.

Thankfully, they managed to get him to the bottom of the steep slope without him breaking his neck. Once he was on relatively level ground, Clayton felt a little bit more confident about his ability to move around.

"The army's that way," Danvers said, gesturing toward the forest in front of them. "I've got two guys out front keeping an eye on the area between here and there. As of five minutes ago, the path forward was still clear. We'll accompany you until we get to the edge of the clearing on the far side."

"Thank you, Gunnery Sergeant. I hope I won't require your services to extract me."

The man gave him a humorless smile. "Me, too."

The journey through the rough woods wasn't nearly as difficult as climbing down the hillside, but it still took longer than Clayton would've liked. He was grateful that he'd been dressed for the wilds of New Zealand when he'd come through the gate. The vegetation would've torn his regular business suit and loafers to shreds in minutes.

By the time they arrived at the edge of the clearing where the army had bivouacked, almost an hour had passed since the strangers had spotted the American drone. Just looking at them, Clayton couldn't see any indication that they were overly concerned about coming under immediate attack. Still, he wasn't a soldier. He didn't pretend to know what that type of reaction would look like.

"Be careful, sir," Danvers said. "If we have to start shooting, there's no walking that back."

He clapped the other man on the shoulder. "Then let's not be hasty. I'd prefer it if you only took action under the direst of circumstances."

"Yes, sir."

Clayton sighed, stretched his back, and stepped out into the clearing. No one noticed him immediately, so he continued walking slowly forward.

He'd made it about a third of the way to the nearest tent when some of the soldiers noted his approach. He kept his pace easy and his hands in plain sight. Hopefully, the fact that he wasn't carrying a weapon would preclude them taking any precipitous actions.

Half a dozen men came from the camp with their weapons at the ready. Clayton was no firearms expert, but it certainly looked as though these were relics from the Revolutionary War or based upon them.

When they shouted at him to stop, he did so. He was grateful that he could understand them. That had been one of his worries. If they'd spoken a different language, negotiation would've been almost impossible.

He kept his hands out to the sides at waist height, palms toward them. "I'm unarmed," he said. "I mean you no harm."

One of the men came forward after handing his rifle to one of the others and roughly searched Clayton. Undoubtedly, he was looking for weapons. Clayton's modern clothing seemed to confuse the man. Understandable.

Once the man seemed satisfied that Clayton was unarmed, he grabbed him by the arm and dragged him forward without a word. The other men formed up around them, making certain that Clayton had no avenue of escape.

The people in the camp stared at them curiously as they made their way toward the central tent. The looks weren't overtly hostile, but they weren't friendly, either.

When the group arrived at the large tent, the same group of individuals he'd observed watching the drone came out to meet him.

It would be interesting to see if the woman took a direct role in questioning him or allowed the senior military commander to do so. If these people were indeed from revolutionary times, it was entirely possible that the woman's role was constrained in some manner.

She corrected that notion immediately. "Who are you, and what do you want?"

Her English was excellent, though her accent was quite distinctive. At first blush, he was tempted to say it was Jamaican, but that didn't sound quite right, either. It was definitely something from the Caribbean. Interesting.

"My name is Clayton Rogers, and I represent the people who control the device you were observing an hour ago. We would like to talk. We mean you no harm."

The woman snorted. "Well, of course you don't. Why would you? And what is that accent? I can't quite place it."

He blinked in surprise. This was a turn of conversation he hadn't expected. He wasn't quite sure how to respond. How could a group of armed people not regard a stranger as a potential threat?

She must've found something in his expression amusing because she laughed. "You're an odd bird. Wherever you come from, you must know the fact you are a human makes you our ally. Unless, of course, you're telling me that you're a traitor."

"I'm not, but my story is somewhat more complicated than you might expect. If you don't see me as a threat, perhaps we could speak more privately."

The woman considered him for a moment then gestured for his guards to take him into the tent.

Large tapestries covered the sides of the tent, thick carpets covered the ground, and ornate wooden furniture filled much of the interior. It all looked quite opulent.

The woman sat in a padded chair with armrests. Two of the men brought out a stool at her gesture and forced him to sit. The other men that looked like military officers arrayed themselves against the side of the tent. The woman was *definitely* in command.

She lounged in her chair and considered him at length.

"I cannot say that your clothing strikes me as familiar. To my mind, that means you must come from afar. Perhaps from one of the other colonies?"

Clayton smiled a little. "I'm not familiar with the colonies to which you refer. Are you perhaps acquainted with the gates between worlds?"

"Of course. Hence the colonies to which I refer."

That was interesting information. They had operational gates. Somewhere.

"My companions and I traveled through one quite recently. We're not familiar with your world."

She frowned. "I find that most difficult to believe. Unless, of course, you claim that you have traveled through a gate under the control of our enemy."

Clayton shrugged. "I'm not even certain who your enemy is. This entire world and its peoples are new to me."

"All this dancing around the subject bores me. I refer to the Asharim, as you undoubtedly know."

That made him blink in surprise. From what he knew of the aliens, they were used to gravity significantly lighter than held sway on this world. They'd fallen a great deal if these primitive people were able to fight them.

He leaned forward on the stool. "Perhaps I might be permitted to question. From your accent, I would guess that your people originate from somewhere in the Caribbean. Would that be true?"

Her eyes narrowed. "That is a name I haven't heard in many long years. I find myself wondering how someone unfamiliar with my people would even know it."

"That's simple enough. I've been to many of the islands there."

The woman smiled widely. "Finally, you interest me."

11

Chen had been expecting Secretary of State Queen's summons, so he allowed only mild interest to show on his face as the man's guards escorted him into the American's office.

"You wish to see me, Mister Secretary?"

"You're damn right I do! What the hell do you people think you're doing?"

Chen smiled blandly. "I presume you are referring to our repossessing our property on the Yucatán Peninsula. The spaceport, to be specific. Our government has nullified the sales to Kathleen Bennett. That being the case, you had no right to seize our property, and we won't allow that situation to stand."

Queen surged to his feet. "This is an act of war."

"Your *original* seizure of our property was illegal. Our retaking it is merely seeing justice done."

The other man stared at him for a moment before he apparently mastered the anger inside him. "On behalf of my government, I give you one day to withdraw your forces from the spaceport and release our people."

Chen spread his hands slightly. "I do not need such time. We refuse to relinquish our property. We will release your personnel, however. In fact, that task is already under way as we speak.

"Now it falls to you to decide how our countries proceed. Will you initiate a war to seize property in our possession? Do you believe you can win that fight? We are both aware the United States military is not what it once was. China is ascendant. You would do well to consider your next words *very* carefully."

Queen took a deep breath and let it out slowly. "If you think for one second that we'll allow this situation to stand, you're wrong. Others have misjudged how strong American will is to their sorrow. We bow to no one. That is something *you* should consider carefully.

"Send this message to your masters. We will forcibly eject whatever Chinese forces are still present inside the Yucatán Spaceport in twenty-four hours. If they resist, our soldiers will use whatever force is required to dislodge them. Any deaths will be on your hands."

Chen bowed slightly. "I will pass your message along to Beijing, however, they have already authorized me to speak to this eventuality.

"If your forces attack the Yucatán Spaceport, we will view that as an act of war and will strike at you wherever we choose across the globe. Our navy is better positioned than yours to attack any number of targets. Our ground forces outnumber yours ten to one, and they are better outfitted. Take this moment to save face, or feel our wrath."

Without waiting for a response, Chen turned and walked out of the room. His guards flanked him to the embassy car, and he was on his way back to the embassy a few minutes later.

That had proceeded just about as poorly as he'd expected. Good. He honestly wasn't sure what the United States would do in the face of his country's provocation, but it hardly mattered. Everything he'd said was true. The United States could ill afford a direct confrontation with China. It was a fight they'd lose.

More importantly, it was a fight that would distract them from the critical tasks they had before them. They could hardly exploit the technology that had come into their possession if they were busy fighting a war for survival. That gave the Dragon an opportunity to act if they played their cards correctly.

The expected courier had arrived to collect the information Chen had gathered and to give him specific instructions on how to proceed. The Dragon had its claws into the highest levels of the Chinese bureaucracy. It would dance to the Dragon's tune.

He considered his options as the limousine drove through the gates to the embassy. Once securely on Chinese soil, he felt somewhat safer. The possibility always existed that the United States would violate diplomatic norms, but he personally doubted he was personally in any danger.

His expulsion from the United States was the worst threat facing him. That was hardly something to worry over, though it would make his job more difficult.

No, it would probably be better to have his forces in place before trouble erupted.

The Americans thought they were clever using Area 51 in Nevada to house the research on the Asharim technology. He had to admit it was an isolated, well-guarded facility.

Still, its very isolation provided him an opportunity. It wouldn't do to have a direct conflict here in the United States, but the Dragon had personnel inside the secret base. In fact, one of their operatives was assigned as a senior researcher to this very project.

Doctor Tran Lee had been in place at Area 51 for several decades now.

The Americans trusted her, and rightly so. Her instructions had been precise. She made obvious her distaste for the Chinese government. That wasn't difficult. There was much to dislike about it.

He climbed out of his limousine and sauntered into the embassy. His official tasks concluded, he headed for his quarters. The guards standing by outside his rooms were not only Chinese security, they were also vetted members of the Dragon.

He had no cause to worry that anyone had invaded his privacy, but he still instructed them to do a sweep in case someone had managed to place listening devices anywhere inside. He waited patiently for them to conclude their search.

Once they declared his rooms clear and departed, Chen settled down in front of his personal computer. This unit wasn't connected to any external networks. In fact, he'd paid quite a bit of money to be absolutely certain it was impossible for anyone to connect with it at all.

Everything was encrypted, and the external connections required both a fingerprint and voice recognition for a very specific phrase to activate. Once that was done, the system still logged every action. He checked the file to verify no one had attempted to access it during his absence. No one had.

He activated the external reader and plugged the chip from his pocket into it. A different courier had brought it from Nevada. The woman had met with someone who worked outside the confines of the base. Discreetly, of course.

The deep-cover agent had collected the chip from Doctor Lee in a manner designed to pass muster with the security people that undoubtedly watched her every move. She'd then waited half a day before leaving it in a specific location where Chen's courier had retrieved it.

The courier had then driven to Las Vegas and taken a flight through Texas before changing identities and flying to Washington. It was all suitably spy-like but very effective in making sure his connection to his agent was not compromised. Above all, that could not be allowed.

Once he'd accessed the chip, he'd reviewed the covert images Lee had sent to him. There was no written report, but that was to be expected. Merely taking the pictures in that facility was challenging enough.

Lee utilized an exceptionally miniaturized camera built into her glasses. The security apparatus at the base regularly checked everyone for bugs and other monitoring devices, but these were designed to be virtually undetectable. They were literally part of the frame.

The courier had to recover the glasses themselves in order to read the data from the camera. Lee had swapped her pair for an identical set at the spa.

Once Chen knew what the Americans had, he would determine what level of force would be required to infiltrate the base and destroy the equipment. If nothing was important enough to require retrieval, the task would be straightforward. If there was an item the Dragon required, that would make the task significantly more complex.

He preferred the former case. If he arranged for the destruction of all the Asharim equipment, he would not have to see it removed from the United

States. All that truly mattered in that case was denying the Americans access to the forbidden technology.

Forbidden to them, anyway.

If the United States decided it wanted a military confrontation with the Chinese, Chen suspected the Dragon would use that conflict as an opportunity to destroy the Indian-built Mars craft that the Americans had purchased.

Honestly, that could be the only reason the Americans were making the Yucatán Spaceport into such a flash point. They had to have some means to access their craft if they wanted to contest Roger's ownership of whatever he'd discovered on Mars.

The Chinese government was unaware of the Asharim. The Dragon would prefer to keep it that way for as long as possible, but that wasn't likely to hold for a great deal of time.

The best the Dragon could hope for was to ensure everyone on the Chinese-built craft belonged to their organization. Then, no matter what happened on Earth, the Dragon would reap the benefits of whatever Rogers had found.

* * *

KATHLEEN BENNETT STARED out from the massive viewport over the engineering section of the ship at the debris swirling around them. It was both glorious and terrifying.

The way the ship was oriented, it seemed as if the planet was above their heads. It was obviously not Earth. The colors were similar, and the cloud-covered view of the continents delivered the same impact as seeing images taken from orbit around Earth.

This was quite the counterpoint to the death and destruction she'd witnessed on her journey from her hiding place to the rear of the ship. She'd seen a lot of blood and pain over the years, but never anything like that.

She turned to her son. "Are you sure that you got them all?"

He shrugged. "It's been hours, and no one has turned up. None of the places I checked had any indication there were holdouts. All we can do is shoot anyone who appears."

"What about this junk? Are we in any danger?"

"Probably. Again, I have no frame of reference. If something large enough comes along and smacks into us, it'll rupture the hull. Nothing we can do about that."

That was true, based on what Nathan had discovered in searching the forward part of the ship. The control room—if that was what it was—didn't even have chairs or consoles. Everything seemed to be computer controlled.

That might indicate the computer wasn't worried about the debris. She supposed she'd have to hope this turned out favorably.

"Well, now that we control the ship, we have to figure out what to do with it," she said. "If we can get it back to Earth, we can bring more of our people on board."

Nathan snorted and shook his head. "You're not thinking clearly, Mother. The only way on or off this ship is through that damned gate. Unless you know of one on Earth that I'm unaware of, that means going back to the base in France. You know that one. The one full of terrorists."

It was her turn to smile. "Actually, I do know of another one. Remember how I used the controls of the fighter to activate the gate? I took pictures with my phone. There were two others on that screen. From reviewing the records, I know one leads to the far side of the moon and another one leads to a jungle somewhere on Earth. Probably in South America."

"I hope you know which one is which," Nathan said dryly. "I'd prefer not to open the gate to the moon."

That was a concern, she admitted.

"That isn't our only possible destination," she said after a moment. "There's always that." She extended her hand and pointed. Floating just off to the side of the ship was something she'd at first dismissed as debris, but now seemed to be whole. It looked like some kind of space station.

Nathan considered it for a moment. "Since we don't know what the code is to open a gate to it, I'm not sure how that's going to help us."

"Do I have to think of everything?" Kathleen asked waspishly. "I've already seen an answer to that question, too. Look down."

Her son leaned forward and stared out the viewport. "Is that a—"

"A ship?" she asked, cutting him off. "It looks like one, doesn't it?"

Seated directly in front of the observation area and below it was the nose of what certainly appeared to be a small craft similar to the one she'd stolen from her ex-husband. Only this one seemed to be in excellent condition.

"I'll wager this ship went many places that didn't have gate access," she said. "It only stands to reason that you'd need something to land on a planet with no gate."

"I didn't see any way to access it, but I wasn't looking at every single hatch," Nathan admitted. "Even if we can get inside, what do we do then? It's not as if either of us knows how to fly these damned ships."

"One problem at a time," she said firmly. "If we can't figure something out, there's always the gate. A fifty-fifty chance is better than none."

12

Climbing up the mesa in pitch-black darkness was significantly more difficult than Harry had anticipated. That didn't mean it was impossible, though. Slipping out of the camp in the dead of night was probably the easiest part of this operation.

These people were rescuers. They weren't military guards used to keeping watch. Everyone was sound asleep by midnight. He waited an additional few hours to be sure no one would get back up before starting out.

As the woman leading the rescue operation had explained earlier, someone had tumbled a large rock down the path up the mesa. It was totally blocked. A rope trailed into the darkness above. The moon provided some illumination but hardly enough to offer any margin of safety whatsoever. He needed to go slowly and cautiously, or he was going to fall to his death.

Forty-five minutes passed before he stood on top of the mesa. It was a fairly large swath of territory to search, but this was where his father had been seen last. If there was an accessible entrance to the base, it would be up here.

As he was above the camp, he felt fairly safe in bringing out a light to assist in his search. He was only in danger if he flashed it toward the edge facing the tents. That being the case, he started his search there and moved away from it.

It took an hour, but he found what the other searchers had missed. An opening that led deeper into the mesa. Someone had used brush very astutely to conceal the cave, but once he suspected it was there, it was simple enough to move it out of the way and descend into the darkness below. He made sure to put the brush back in place. He didn't want to chance the New Zealanders finding the base.

It quickly became obvious that the depression was actually a collapsed ceiling above the first level of the base. There was no telling how long ago the roof had come down, but it had been a significant amount of time.

The corridors inside were laid out in a similar fashion to the base in France, but there was no power. The lights were completely dark. There were also signs of combat. Nothing recent, in any case.

The scattered bones and armor of long-dead fighters littered the floor. He recognized the body shape of numerous heavy-worlders. Obviously, they'd found this base and attacked.

There were signs in the dirt on the floor that led him toward the stairs. He knew the gates would be on the lowest level. Since his father hadn't reappeared, the safe bet was that he'd gone through a gate.

Even though the base seemed to be without power, he wagered the gates were still operational. He'd find out soon enough.

The door at the bottom of the stairs was wedged open and led into a corridor. That was different from what he'd seen at the French base. There must have been different floor plans. The corridor led to an intersection.

He chose to go one way and found what seemed to be a large power-generation room. He'd seen one like it at the French base. Huge machines filled with light from massive cubes. The cubes were missing from this room, and everything was dark. That explained why there was no power.

He reversed course and went the other direction. Inside another door, he found the gate room he had been expecting. It was just as dark as the other room, but much larger. It was obviously used for cargo handling, too. A small machine holding one of the blue cubes that powered the Asharim ships sat near one of the arches. Perhaps a makeshift power supply for the gates.

It had a large cable running to the arch, undoubtedly to provide power for its operation, and a second smaller cable that lay on the floor. That one was more confusing. Why did they need the second cable? He shrugged. The question would answer itself if he could figure out how to reopen the gate to its last destination.

Harry pulled out a gate controller from his backpack and brought it online. It found one gate but not the other two. As he'd suspected, this device was providing power for it.

Unfortunately, the gate was locked. Nothing he did released it to his control. He couldn't even determine the last address it had used.

He eyed the cable again. It stretched toward the gate as though someone had pulled it after them. What if they had? If the power supply was jury-rigged, perhaps they'd needed a hardwired controller as well. If so, they might've taken it with them when they left.

If that was the case, he was screwed. They hadn't figured out a way to access the gates directly yet. That was something Jess was eventually supposed to work on with Brenda Cabot. Until they worked a method out, he had no way of pulling the address from the gate's memory.

Well, he hadn't expected this to be easy. His best guess was that his father had retreated through the gate and the American military forces had followed behind him. They were probably trapped on an alien world.

He'd have to circle back to this base once the search ended. That might take days or weeks to accomplish. Harry sighed. It wasn't as if he had a choice. If Jess came up with a solution before then, he could always return here in the dead of night and follow his father. He just had to hope the old man didn't get himself killed first.

* * *

QUEEN WORKED LATE into the evening, gathering every bit of data he could about the potential operation in Mexico. After considering all options, he'd recommended to the president that they wait to take the spaceport back.

Chen was right. A war with China would be disastrous. Congress had whittled the US military to the bone over the last three decades. They were a hollow shell incapable of fighting a serious war against anyone, much less a superpower like China.

As much is it galled him, the United States no longer qualified for that title. Perhaps they would once they'd mastered the technology Rogers had found, but today was not that day.

Far better to focus his country's attention on the more serious prize: the technology on Mars. The Indian-built ship would take months to reach the Red Planet, but once the United States put marines on the ground, that fight would be over. The younger Rogers wouldn't fight other Americans.

That mission was outside the scope of his current duties anyway. His immediate goal was to assess the technology they'd already captured and locate the traitors. Brenda Cabot and her organization were a direct threat to the national security of the United States. Hell, the world.

Thankfully, they'd gotten the captured technology placed securely inside Area 51. The facility was hardened and isolated. There was no way anyone would figure out what they were doing.

The irony that all the conspiracy nuts thought the government used the place to study alien technology amused him. It was certainly true now.

Eventually, he decided that he had to get something to eat. He considered ordering delivery but decided a quiet table at a nearby restaurant would suit his needs better. The low murmur of conversation while he had a good meal and some wine would settle him. It took less than ten minutes to get his security detail in motion. They saw him down to his armored transport and off to the restaurant.

This late, the place was only half-full. That suited his mood perfectly. The maître d' found him a table in the back, away from the rest of the diners. His security detail settled around him as he ordered an appetizer.

The man had barely left his side when an odd noise made Queen look up. The member of his security detail closest to the front of the restaurant was talking to someone.

No. Not talking. Arguing.

That was unusual. Most people didn't screw with armed security in Washington. There were plenty of high government officials that warranted protection, and no one really wanted to mess with that kind of person.

Another of his guards went to back the man up while the remaining one stepped nearer to Queen's booth. No one was pulling weapons, but they were preparing for the possibility of trouble.

Queen finally got a look at the person confronting his guards and realized it was a woman. Not anyone he recognized. Her annoyed expression marked her as someone used to getting her way. Not today. With a huff, the woman turned and stalked off.

He'd barely returned his attention to the menu when a much louder noise sent adrenaline roaring through his system. A gunshot. The guard standing next to Queen's table jerked and collapsed. The other two members of his security detail whirled and went for their weapons. The shooter was somewhere in the back of the restaurant.

Queen rolled under the table and pulled his concealed pistol. He hadn't carried one before but had decided it was necessary after Cabot kidnapped him. Not that it would've helped that time, but it could certainly help now.

The crescendo of gunshots trailed off. Since he wasn't seeing his people, Queen took that as a bad sign. He'd really rather not risk his neck, but if he waited for his attacker to come to him, he'd be at a distinct disadvantage. After taking two quick breaths, he shoved himself out far enough to get a decent look while retaining the option of ducking back under cover.

That move caught the shooter out in the open. The man's attention was focused toward the front of the restaurant, so Queen had a short window to act. He snapped off three quick shots at his attacker and was rewarded by seeing the man dive for cover. Unfortunately, he was pretty sure he hadn't hit the bastard. Queen ducked back inside the booth.

"Damn, but you're hard to kill." The voice was unfamiliar, but that reduced the number of potential attackers down to one: the guy who'd shot him right after Cabot had kidnapped him.

"You'll have to forgive me, but I don't believe we've been properly introduced."

"Nor will we. I'm afraid I really must be going, but I think I'll send you on your way first."

Queen prepared himself again. "Might I inquire what I've done to offend you? I'm sure that we've never met."

"What else? Money. Though I will confess that I'm going to take some small measure of personal satisfaction in killing you. I was sure I'd hit you the last time, but somehow you managed to slip away. Not this time."

Knowing he wasn't going to get another opportunity, Queen rolled out from beneath the table and fired in the direction the assassin had gone. He didn't stop rolling—which was a good thing because the killer had been waiting.

The hail of gunshots partially deafened Queen, but anything that interfered with the other man putting a bullet into Queen's head was a good thing. Unfortunately, all the movement put Queen out into the open. Once the man drew a bead on him, this was going to be over fast.

Of course, that's when the slide on Queen's pistol locked back. He was out of ammunition.

The other man rose from his hiding place and brought his pistol to bear on Queen. "Bye-bye."

The next shot made Queen flinch, but it caused him no pain. That's because the assassin hadn't fired. The guard beside Queen's booth must not have been dead after all. He'd gotten his weapon out and proceeded to fire shot after shot into the killer, even after the man had gone down.

Queen didn't wait to see the results of the man's shots. He leapt to his feet and sprinted toward the front of the restaurant. He recalled the woman who had tried to gain entrance to the seating area and decided that she had probably been an accomplice. That convinced him to grab one of the downed guards' pistols.

It wasn't necessary though. The restaurant was pure pandemonium. Everyone was rushing to get away. No one seemed to have any interest in him at all. He considered running out with them but decided that would be the perfect time to take him down. The woman might be waiting to do just that. He'd let the police come to him.

Queen didn't believe the assassin was still alive, but he hoped he was wrong. Getting some answers about who was trying to kill him would be useful. Stopping them from sending anyone else would be even better.

13

J ess stayed with Brenda Cabot and her people until Kevin McHugh arrived. The young man fit her idea of what a hacker looked like precisely: tall, gangly, and bald. He favored small round lenses on his glasses. Colored purple, of course. His clothing fell somewhere between hip and trendy.

At least she didn't need to explain Asharim technology to him. He already knew far more about it than she did.

"So let me see if I've got this straight," he said as they stepped through the gate and onto *Freedom Express*. "You found the big gate on a space station, and you want access to figure out the address it used to send a ship somewhere else. Is that right?"

Jess nodded. "Exactly. Unfortunately, while we know where the gate is, we haven't found the computers that control it."

He smiled. "That's easy. The computer is in the gate itself."

She frowned. "That doesn't sound easy. The gate is on the outside of the space station."

"Hmmm. That *does* add a layer of complication. Still, it's not impossible. I assume you have spacesuits. I'm not trained to use one, but if you can get me out to where I need to go, I could probably still make it happen."

Jess considered him for a moment. "I think that's a really bad idea. If something goes wrong, you could die in a moment. If you're going to use a spacesuit, we need to train you.

"How about this? We send someone out to examine the gate, and you watch the video feed through the helmet. We've got some expert spacewalkers. Hell, I'm an expert spacewalker."

He raised an eyebrow. "Do you have a technical background?"

"You could say that. I have several degrees in engineering, and I've messed with this technology before."

"That might work. You'll need some tools to open the panels on the gate, but I should be able to provide those. I came prepared."

"The tools need to be large enough for somebody wearing gloves to manipulate them," she warned him. "It would be better if we could attach a strap to them as well. Things tend to float off in Zero-G."

"That shouldn't be a problem, but it'll add a little time to the project. If you want to do this right, I should probably work with a machinist to copy the tools."

"We can do that, but first I want to give you a look at the big gate."

The hacker looked around them at the corridors as they walked. "So this is a spaceship."

"Sort of. It's actually a hollowed-out comet. A dormant one that your ancestors modified for their use."

He didn't ask any more questions until they arrived at the central control room. The view stopped him in his tracks as they came out of the lift. "Whoa!"

The control center had that effect on almost everyone the first time. Hell, it still affected her that way. The lift exited out onto a walkway that was in the precise center of the comet.

That meant that the spherical chamber sat all around them in every direction. The use of artificial gravity meant up and down had very little meaning in this case. Stairs led down to various parts of the control room.

She automatically selected the one that would take them to the pilot's station. "Watch your step. It would be awkward if you fell and had to explain to Miss Cabot why we had to send you back for medical treatment."

"Isn't that the damned truth?" The young man took a firm grip on the handrail, but he didn't let his eyes stop wandering. "I've heard stories, but I never really imagined it looked like this. You know how you get a picture in your head of how something is? I'm not sure what I expected, but this isn't it. This is *way* more awesome."

She gave him a suspicious glance. "Did you grow up in California? I swear you talk just like every surfer I've seen in a movie."

McHugh laughed. "You figured me out! And I'll have you know, talking that way is like a badge of honor there. Even if it does occasionally get me laughed at."

She stepped over to the pilot's console and smiled. "Morning, Lindsay. Everything still looking good?"

Lindsay Waller was nominally the command pilot on *Liberty Station* but was on long-term loan to *Freedom Express*. *Liberty Station* didn't really need a pilot while it was in Mars orbit. If trouble came calling, they'd have months to prepare, and she had very competent assistants.

"We're good," Lindsay confirmed. "Black Jack just took a team down to the new site. I expect to have some kind of report on their general status in about forty minutes."

"Excellent. Lindsay, meet Kevin McHugh. He's one of Brenda Cabot's people, and he's going to help us with the big gate. Can you give us a look at it, using one of the probes?"

The pilot nodded and turned back toward her console. "Sure. We got several of them mapping the surface of the station. It won't take long to relocate one."

The woman's hands moved confidently over the controls. They'd only been in possession of *Freedom Express* for a short while, so the pilot's competence amazed her.

"Wow. You've really got this under control."

Lindsay grinned. "I've been working hard, and I have to admit, the latest iteration of the translation software really helps. Emily has just about got this thing nailed down, I think."

The woman glanced at McHugh. "I'm betting that's because of the help we're getting from your people on the language. That's putting this whole project way ahead of where we expected."

The young man inclined his head. "I can't take any credit for that, but you're welcome. Allow me to second what Miss Cook said. You sure look like you've got this whole thing under control."

Jess made a face. "I'd rather you just use my first name. I'm not that formal."

"Awesome. Call me Kevin."

"Okay," Lindsay said. "Here we are."

The view on the screen was far enough out to show the entirety of the massive gate. The damned thing was huge. Easily big enough to move a spaceship across the universe.

Not *Freedom Express*, though. The comet was too big. Pity.

McHugh leaned forward and examined the image. "I think the access panel we want is down and to the right. Maybe a little lower than the center."

Lindsay made a few deft adjustments, and the image of the section McHugh was pointing toward began to get larger.

He waited until the gate filled the screen to ask her to stop. "Right there. That's the access panel to the computer."

To Jess's inexperienced eye, it looked just like the rest of the gate. "How can you tell?"

"Believe it or not, color. That panel is just a bit darker than those around it. That's how the Asharim denoted access panels. As for knowing where on the gate it was, that was an educated guess. This is where I'd find one on a smaller gate. Well, the one gate that we have anyway."

Jess nodded, still a little jealous of the fact that Cabot's people had a mobile gate. One they could pick up and move wherever they wanted. She really needed to find something like that.

McHugh turned toward her. "Basically, once we open the access panel, I should be able to plug in a computer to pull the data from the controller."

"Well, it's not exactly the controller. Technically, the controller is what sends the signal to the gate, but I call the receiving equipment that activates the gate a controller, too."

"How difficult is it to get the data from the gate? Is it going to be password protected? Encrypted?"

He shook his head. "I don't think so, though I suppose it's always possible. That's not how the Asharim set up their computers. If you like, I can give you a demonstration on a different gate. One of the ones inside."

"I think that would be very helpful," Jess said with a nod. "Lindsay, thank you very much for your help."

"You're welcome, and it's a pleasure to meet you, Kevin."

Getting to the gate room took another fifteen minutes. The young computer expert grinned when he saw the gates built into the side of the cargo room.

"Now *that's* what I'm talking about! I've seen some pictures of the original tech. These are permanent gates, not like our portable one. You want me to pull a destination log out of one of these for you?"

Jess gestured toward the gates. "Actually, I'd like to get destination logs for all three. And once you do, there are a few other gates I'd like to get information from as well: the ones on Mars and the ones at the base we discovered in France."

"I heard about that one. Brenda was pissed. It's been right there all this time, and none of us ever suspected."

"I'm pretty confident we'll find a way to share. As a matter of fact, we believe we know the general locations of several other bases on Earth. If our relationship develops the way I expect, some of those can certainly go your way."

"That would be awesome! Our own secret base. Well, not that our current base isn't secret, but you know what I mean."

Amusingly, she did understand. "Go ahead and get to work. I can't wait to see how you do it."

"You betcha." The young man walked over to one of the gates and began taking tools and equipment out of his pack.

* * *

CLAYTON LEANED back on the stool and waited for the woman to continue. This was her show. He had nothing to gain by rushing her into making a hasty decision. He'd dangled the fruit. Now he'd see if she was hungry.

She seemed content to let the silence drag out for a long minute. Then she seemed to make a decision. She gestured toward the guards, and they filed out of the tent, leaving only the two of them and the officers dressed in military garb.

"Since it seems we have things to discuss, I suppose it would be prudent to introduce myself. I am Susanna Adorno, the civilian commander of this force. These men are my military adjuncts: General Norbert Norris and his assistants Colonel Brock Carver and Major Antonio Logan."

The three men inclined their heads toward him. At her gesture, they stepped away from the side of the tent and arranged seats for themselves.

Adorno leaned forward. "We only have contact with other humans intermittently. Sometimes for years at a stretch, other times only for hours. No one has ever found a way to return to the place we came from. Earth.

"My people and the Volunteers are the most recent immigrants to the stars by many centuries. It has been hundreds of years since we came to this place. I find it curious that you have come through at this particular time. And I'm somewhat confused as to how you managed it."

Clayton shrugged. "Not knowing the specifics of your circumstances, I find it difficult to comment. In the end, I can only speak for my own people and how we found our way here.

"Before I can do that, I want to be sure we don't see one another as enemies. We have no desire to fight your people or to defend ourselves from you. You said earlier that we weren't your enemy because we were human. I'm not sure how seriously to take that statement."

She considered him shrewdly. "You do not know the circumstances away from Earth, do you?"

"In large part, no. We're familiar with the Asharim, though only recently so. My son and people in my employ found discarded items belonging to them only a few months ago. That led us to the discovery of the gates. We are still exploring, but we believe the Asharim have fallen from their pinnacle of technical know-how."

"That latter is true," General Norris said. "The Asharim were no longer wizards when we came to this place, with some limited exceptions. Only the large numbers of slaves at their command prevent us from outright victory.

"Your accent is somewhat strange, but you sound as if you come from the colonies. Might I inquire as to the situation that holds sway there now?"

"Are you referring to the War of Independence? The fight against King George? If so, that ended successfully. The colonies have become a powerful nation in their own right."

The officer gave him a steady look and slowly nodded. "We knew that the fight must have ended long ago, and we took it as an article of faith that our righteous cause would be rewarded. It's good to hear it, though."

The woman shook her head. "I won't bother to ask the situation in the Caribbean. My ancestors knew quite well that their time was coming to a close, and that was probably a good thing. I might count pirates and privateers among my ancestors, but I don't think I would relish practicing their trade."

She crossed one leg over the other knee. "We have no quarrel with your people. This regiment is moving to secure the ancient city just over the horizon. Every few decades it trades hands between the Asharim and us.

"The fighting spills our blood, leaving both sides exhausted for years at a time. Once we recover, the fight begins anew. The city holds the only operational gate on this world. We use it to be part of a wider universe of human colonies. I'm unsure what the Asharim do. Nothing good, I'm sure."

"You said that your people worked with the Volunteers," Clayton said.

"I'm assuming these folk were a militia during the War of Independence, so please correct me if I'm wrong. How did both of your groups find the gate that brought you here? To my sorrow, none of the gates that we have located on Earth are inside the United States."

The general leaned back in his chair. "The United States," he said slowly, seeming to savor every word. "It rings upon the ear, does it not? Oh, I've heard the name before. It was bandied about for long years before the fighting started, but it still sends a thrill up my spine."

Clayton smiled. "The United States of America came into the world as something completely new and turned all the other nations on their head. Through many of the trials and tribulations in the centuries since its founding, it has stood for truth and justice. Sadly, that has changed in recent years, though we hope to reverse the process."

The other man considered that. "I've heard it said that, from time to time, the tree of liberty must be refreshed with the blood of tyrants and patriots. Perhaps such a time has once more come.

"In any case, I cannot tell you the precise nature of how we came to this place. Our ancestors were maneuvering in the wilds of Virginia when we came across a cave. Inside this cave, they found the wonders of the Asharim. We did not know that at the time, because the place was abandoned.

"At some point, they found a way through the gate and brought a number of refugees from the fighting with them. This method is still known to us today, but I am not sure how they learned it. That story has been lost in the mists of time."

"The story of my people is much the same," Adorno said. "They were in Port Royale when a mighty earthquake leveled the city. Many of the survivors were brought to a place near the water that had a gate.

"The people that brought our ancestors there warned of a great tsunami that would likely come. I have no idea who they were. They saw the survivors of Port Royale through the gate just before the wave came. They left us on this world and went elsewhere. Since that time, they have never returned.

"The Volunteers came through many years after us. They were very lucky that my people had seized the city at the time, or the Asharim would have executed them in a grisly fashion."

Clayton considered the strangers but decided he couldn't worry about them now. He had more important and pressing worries.

Adorno pressed her lips together. "If you only recently came to this world, where is the gate? Surely not the one in the city. The Asharim would have dealt most harshly with you."

He didn't see how he could avoid talking about that, so he didn't try to lie. "There's a hidden cave in a large hill nearby. Inside is a gate. Unfortunately, we have no means of controlling it. Once we came through, we were trapped here. I know how to return to Earth, but I must have a way to control the gate to use it."

"I suspected something of the sort. If I am correct about which hill you mean, no one ever had cause to believe there was anything inside it. It's a place where the Asharim conduct unholy ceremonies.

"We have discovered that humans must stand together against the Asharim and their slaves, Clayton Rogers. I look forward to hearing more from you and your people. On behalf of my forces, I invite you and yours to come dine with us tonight in safety."

Trust had to start somewhere. It wasn't as if they had much of a choice. They needed these people's assistance to get back to Earth.

"We would be happy to join you."

14

Nathan found the entrance to the small craft easily enough now that he knew where to look. It was a hatch no different from any other he'd seen on the ship with one exception: it had something written on it in an alien script. That was new.

His mother stopped abruptly in front of the hatch, her mouth hanging open.

"That's not a very elegant look, Mother," he said snidely.

She ignored his taunt, still staring at the hatch.

"Mother? What's wrong?"

She raised an arm and pointed toward the hatch. "What does that say?"

He glanced from her to the hatch and back again. "I have no idea."

She turned slightly toward him. "I do. It says 'shuttle access.' What I don't know is how that's even possible, because it's not in English. Nathan, what's going on?"

He stared at her, dumbfounded. "How am I supposed to know? How could you possibly know what it says?"

His mother rubbed her face. "It had to be the machine I was in. Not only did it heal and make me younger again, but also it put something in my head. The knowledge of what those words mean."

Nathan felt his eyes narrow. If it put that in her head, what else might it have done? Could she be under the influence of the alien computer? Dealing with his mother was already a frighteningly dangerous proposition, but if she was under alien control, that added an entirely new element of uncertainty.

One he couldn't deal with right now. He'd keep an eye on her and see how she behaved going forward. If she became a problem, he'd solve it.

He opened the hatch, and it led into a short corridor with another hatch at the end. He recognized the far hatch as part of an airlock. That made sense. If the shuttle were gone, you wouldn't want to open a door into vacuum.

Thankfully, the operation of these hatches was relatively simple. He turned and found his mother still standing in the main corridor.

"I realize this is unsettling, Mother, but you need to come along. Our time is limited. If something comes and smashes the ship, we don't want to be here."

She shook her head as if she were waking from a daydream. Her face scrunched into a snarl, and she stalked forward. The two of them entered the airlock and then the shuttle beyond. It was *exactly* like the ship they'd stolen from his brother. Only this one seemed to be in perfect shape.

His mother led the way to the front of the shuttle. They settled into the couches set aside for the pilots. She reached out and swiped her hand across the control console. It came to life, and so did the large screens in front of them. Those showed the view of the ship they'd captured. It was an impressively vivid image.

"The researchers showed me how to bring the systems on the other shuttle to life," she said. "Or at least to look at the controls. Beyond that, I'm not sure what I'll be able to figure out."

Nathan wasn't going to be of any help. His use of the alien technology had been extremely limited. If she couldn't figure out something, they weren't going anywhere.

She stared at the control console for a moment. "Weirdly, I seem to know what each of these symbols means. I mean as in what will happen if I touch them." Her eyes swiveled toward him. "We want to go to the station?"

He shrugged. "That seems to be the only place worth visiting, unless there's something on the planet below that would be useful. That said, I'm not sure how much I'd trust you guiding a spaceship during reentry based on information implanted in you by an alien computer. One mistake and we'd burn up."

"I can't argue with that." She reached out and tapped one of the icons, and the console reconfigured into a different layout. Hesitantly, she touched three symbols in sequence.

The shuttle shuddered and came loose from the ship. He could see them rising in the screens.

"We've separated from the ship," his mother said needlessly. "Let's see if I can guide us toward the station."

He hoped she could. They were committed now.

She tapped a few more controls, and the ship reoriented itself and began moving toward the station. Thankfully, not very quickly.

"What about the debris?" he asked. "If we get hit by a piece of wreckage, we're done."

"The shuttle seems to have taken that into account. It's marking the courses of everything that might come near us. I have it adjusting course to miss anything flying in our direction. I can't say that's going to keep us safe, but it's the best I can do."

The situation unsettled him significantly more than he'd prefer to admit. Trusting his mother's strange new knowledge and skills was against his nature.

The station slowly grew larger in front of them. Nathan had no frame of reference, but he thought it was large. Very large. It didn't seem to have taken significant damage, either. Which was odd considering how much debris still floated in the area.

That made him wonder. How could there still be debris left over from some event that must've taken place centuries ago? Perhaps even a thousand years ago. Even at the time of the event, shouldn't the debris have floated away? Something wasn't right here.

His mother brought the shuttle around, and he saw places dotted across the hull that looked as though they had massive hatches. She seemed to have one of them selected as a destination. He hoped she could get it to open.

Thankfully, it began sliding ponderously open as they approached. His mother guided the shuttle through it and into a dark cavern beyond.

Overhead lights snapped on, revealing they were in a massive hangar filled with numerous small craft similar to the one they were in and many others besides.

She brought the shuttle down onto an open area on the deck. "I've signaled the hatch to close. According to these instruments, there's air outside. We can go see what's out there."

"Forgive me if I seem confused, but how could there be air outside when we just opened the door?"

His mother shrugged. "I have no idea."

"Why would they even bother to have airlocks if they had a means of keeping air inside? Or did the air come in after we did?"

"I have no idea," his mother snapped. "Stop asking me questions I can't answer."

Nathan was tempted to keep badgering her, but he knew he had her right on the edge of outright rage. He'd rather not have her come after him.

"Sorry, Mother," he said soothingly. "What should we do now? Is it safe to leave the shuttle?"

"I suppose there's only one way to find out."

She stood, walked back into the main body of the shuttle, and tapped the control by the airlock. The inner door slid open. She turned toward him. "Are you coming?"

He'd have really rather not, but he supposed he didn't have a choice. He rose to his feet. "Let's go see what we've found."

* * *

Harry made it back to camp with plenty of time. He was sitting at one of the campfires when the people tasked with cooking breakfast rose for the morning.

He hated that he needed to stay here while the searchers scoured the area. Particularly now that he knew there was no chance they'd find anything. That galled him.

The list of things he needed to do was ridiculously long. He couldn't afford to be tied up waiting for them to declare his father lost. Worse yet, if he did find a way to activate the gate, he'd need to lead the force after his father. He couldn't just sit here waiting.

Well, he supposed some "dire emergency" could call him away. It wasn't as though he didn't have enough of those on his hands. Thankfully, the locals didn't know his true identity. As an employee, he could slip away.

Molly Goodwin rose just as the sun peeked over the horizon. She got herself a cup of coffee and sat down in a folding chair beside him. "You're up early, Mister Jacobs."

"I had trouble sleeping. I must confess that I'm concerned you haven't managed to locate any of the missing people yet." He held up a hand to forestall her response. "I'm not implying that you aren't doing everything you can. It just seems as though some sign of them should've turned up already."

She sipped her coffee and nodded. "That worries me, too. The terrain around here is very rough, so that makes it hard to spot them, but it also means they can't have gotten very far. Mister Rogers should have been able to flag down a helicopter. He should've realized by now that all the aircraft in the area are friendly."

She considered him for a moment. "I wanted to bring up another issue before the day really gets started. Perhaps you could help me understand something."

"I'd be happy to try," Harry said.

"We'll see how happy you are once I've asked my question. Is your name really Jacobs? I think the answer is no because I'm almost certain I saw your face on the news. Mister Rogers."

Well, this was awkward. Did he attempt to lie his way out of it, or did he confess that he'd snuck back to Earth? He probably should've sent Rex in his place. Coming had been a mistake. He wasn't sure what he'd been thinking.

He took a long drink of his coffee to give him a moment to consider his options. In the end, he decided that it really didn't matter. His father had bought the land in order to claim the New Zealand base. The place was a wreck. Maybe the gates could be salvaged and relocated elsewhere, but he wasn't even sure of that. The government of New Zealand would seize the place in a heartbeat.

Still, that might work to his advantage. Up until now, they'd been operating in the shadows. Only the US government had a clue what was going on. Perhaps it was time to widen the circle.

"I prefer to keep that to a limited number of people," he said softly. "I recognize that you're going to have to report my presence, but I'd rather not have it become general knowledge."

She shook her head. "I can hardly believe it. You were on Mars, weren't you? Was that all some kind of trick?"

"You mean like the conspiracy theory that the moon landing was faked? No. It was real. I was on Mars."

"That's been one of the main features of the news for the last several days.

Your spaceship or space station, whatever you want to call it, is still there. How could you possibly be sitting here next to me?"

He grinned. "Aliens."

A bark of laughter escaped before she could clap a hand over her mouth. "I'd say that's not funny, but it obviously is. You're not going to be able to get away with laying this at the feet of mysterious aliens you found on Mars."

"Let me ask you a question, Miss Goodwin. Do you work for the government of New Zealand?"

"In a manner of speaking, yes," she said. "I act as coordinator in cases where people have gone missing in the wilds. I'm not a policewoman or anything. And I'm also not a government bureaucrat. I actually work for a living."

"That's good to hear. I'm going to tell you a story that you'll find very hard to believe. I can prove it, though. Once everyone is up and about their business, if you'll accompany me to the top of the mesa, I can show you how I got here. Honestly, you wouldn't believe me if I told you without proof."

She stared at the mesa in the early dawn light. "You're going to have some kind of alien ship land on the mesa? Is this going to be like a scene out of *Close Encounters of the Third Kind*?"

"Something like that. I promise there won't be any probes."

The woman laughed again, not trying to hide it this time. "I can't imagine what kind of story you're going to try to sell me, but I need to have some breakfast before I think about it.

"It seems the cooks have wrapped up their preparations, so let's get something before everyone stampedes them. You haven't seen how searchers go through food. They'll eat everything in sight and then come back for another pass. They're like locusts."

He rose with her, his stomach already grumbling from the delicious scent of the bacon. The next few hours could go very badly, so he'd eat well and hope for the best.

15

J ess floated in space outside the station using her maneuvering thrusters to stay near the access panel Kevin McHugh had identified on the big gate. She'd watched him open a number of access panels on the smaller gates, so she felt confident that she could do the same here.

"Yeah," he said over her radio. "That looks right. You remember how I showed you to open the panel?"

"I remember. It's just this one is a little larger than the others."

That was certainly true. This panel was the size of a hatch on the lifter. If it proved difficult to move, she wasn't sure how she'd gain the leverage to make this happen.

Well, no time like the present to figure this out.

She found the recessed grip that allowed for movement of the access panel. On the smaller gates, either a screwdriver or fingernail would do the trick. On this one, she needed a pry bar. Thankfully, she'd come prepared.

First, she used the special tool to unlock the panel. It was a special kind of screw, acting almost like a key. She'd worried that it would be different on the larger panel, but it was thankfully the same as the smaller gates.

With that done, she pulled the bar off her belt slowly so as not to tangle the cable keeping it attached to her. The fit of the head was a little loose when she put it in place. If she ever had to do this again, she'd bring a bigger bar.

Since she was in Zero-G and had no grip, she used her suit's maneuvering thrusters to apply pressure, and the access panel popped open. Like the ones on the smaller gates, this one was attached so that it only swung open rather than flying off into space.

Unlike the smaller gates, the larger version shielded a lot more equipment. She had no idea what most of it did.

"Wow," McHugh muttered. "That's a lot of stuff. Look around for a port like the one I showed you. There has to be one that will accept the cable."

It took about fifteen minutes of examination before she found the small port. At least it looked like the one Kevin had shown her. "Is this it?" she asked.

"I think so. If it's not, it should be no harm no foul. Just plug the comp in and see what you see."

She took the time to reattach the pry bar to her belt before she pulled the comp from its pouch. It only took a few moments to seat the plug into the port. "Here goes nothing." Jess tapped the icon on the comp just as Kevin had shown her. A new window opened, and a series of codes began scrolling by. They were the same twenty-character codes she'd seen on the smaller gates.

"You did it!" he said. "The comp will have them saved in its memory once you come back in."

Jess was relieved, but this didn't solve all her problems. Having the code that Harry's family had used was useful, but unless they knew how to activate this larger gate, it wouldn't do them any good. She'd already tried connecting to it with a standard hand controller. The device didn't even see the massive gate. There had to be something else required to link with it.

They'd try to use one of the smaller gates to link with the code Nathan and his mother had used, but she personally doubted the smaller gate would link with the larger one. There had to be some type of safety mechanism. After all, one wouldn't want a massive starship trying to come through a small gate. The reverse might work, but it seemed as if the systems would be radically different.

Once she had the codes, Jess detached the cable and put the comp away. She maneuvered herself around to the other side of the access panel and used her thrusters to push it slowly closed. She couldn't hear any noise when it sealed, but it didn't pop back open.

She gave it a good thump with her fist just to be sure. Having this come open and be at risk for micrometeor damage was unacceptable.

"I'm on my way back in," she said. "We can go over the numbers once we have everything in the lab."

"Roger that. See you in a few minutes."

Jess jetted back to the lifter that was waiting for her and closed the airlock behind her. As the pressure began rising, she considered her next move. They'd already pulled all the codes off the gates on *Freedom Express*, the Mars base, the French base, and the gate rooms they discovered on the station.

She was sure there were plenty more gate rooms on the station that they hadn't discovered, but the exploration was still in progress. The place was bigger than Manhattan. It was going to take a lot of time to look into every single compartment.

Meanwhile, she'd finally spoken with Harry. The delivery of the quantum phone right before she'd gone outside for this job had allowed her to give him an update on the situation.

To her astonishment, they were able to communicate from this great distance with no time lag or loss of signal. These new communication devices were finally going to allow them to coordinate their actions.

The next thing she wanted to do was test how far they'd really reach. Being able to communicate across the solar system was absolutely worthwhile. Yet if it worked at interstellar range, that would be even more impressive.

Once the pressure in the airlock came up and the temperature had risen to the normal range, she popped the helmet off her suit and opened the inner door.

Black Jack McCarthy grinned at her from the pilot's couch. "I was listening in over the com. Everything went well. That's awesome." The ex-marine pilot waited until she'd strapped herself in and then turned the lifter to head back toward *Freedom Express*.

"It did, but that's only a start. There are so many other things we need to do. Including being able to get someone down to where Harry is in New Zealand. He's going to need this comp to pull the gate codes."

The man nodded. "I suppose we can send it through to France and have them fly it out to New Zealand. That's going to take a while."

"We could do that, but I have a better idea. One of the biggest issues in travel we've had is the fact that we can't get any of our lifters to the gates. There are ships down there, but we don't know where to send them.

"There must be some way to get them to the surface. Probably a gate stashed somewhere on the side of a mountain or something. If we could find one of those, we could get the ships out and use them."

He shot her a considering glance. "And you want me to fly one of them?"

"Do you think you could?"

"I've been working with Lindsay Waller quite a bit, learning how to fly the big ship. If the controls are similar, I think so. You know, you've been pulling codes out of gates, but you've missed an angle. The ships need to open gates that are useful to them. That means they've gone places that will accept a fighter flying out. We should get into one of them and see if we can access the codes *they've* used."

Jess smacked herself on the forehead. "Crap. I've been so focused on the gates that I forgot the ships probably act as controllers. If we look for codes that are the same on both the ships and the gates, we'll find the best potential places to send a ship through."

She gestured toward *Freedom Express*, which was growing larger ahead of them. "Let's get this thing landed and head down to the gate room. I want to start working on this right away."

* * *

QUEEN WASN'T able to get away from the restaurant. Even his high position in the government hadn't shielded him from having to answer to the police for the violence that had taken place.

At least there were enough people present that no one believed he'd instigated the attack. It had quickly become apparent to all that he was the victim here.

He hated playing the victim card. It made him feel weak. Nevertheless, it got things moving in a productive direction in fairly short order.

All three of his guards had died in the attack. Apparently, the one that had killed the assassin had been almost gone. Queen was genuinely sorry for that. They'd been good men.

He tried to get the police to give him information about the assassin, but they'd kept their mouths shut. He'd have to see about alternative methods of identifying the man.

There were no cameras inside the restaurant, unfortunately. It was well known for its discretion. That meant identifying the woman was going to be difficult. The police would look at cameras in the area to see if they had an image of her, so it was always possible they'd have another thread to follow.

They'd spent hours questioning him over who might want him dead. He'd laughed. With his work, there were any number of people that might want him to bleed out on some floor. Nothing he could tell the police would narrow their suspect pool. Only enlarge it.

In any case, he was fairly certain that he'd figured this out. The first attack had come during the investigation on Kathleen Bennett. If he were a betting man—and he was—then he'd wager she'd paid quite handsomely to have him eliminated. He'd proven to be quite the thorn in her side.

With her in hiding, she'd probably thought eliminating him would simplify her situation. She was probably right. Other people in government might make a deal with her. Not him. Not now.

He'd come to see her as the worst actor in this little play. Her ex-husband was no winner, but he wasn't in her league.

Her son, Nathan, was more like an evil force of nature. Harry Rogers was mostly honorable, which was something Queen could use against him.

Jessica Cook was a mystery. He still didn't know quite what to think about her. She should've been a mousy little scientist, but she had a spine of steel. Harry Rogers deferred to her. That had to mean something.

Brenda Cabot and her group were a wildcard. Still, she'd saved his life the last time the assassin had struck. He could safely remove her from the suspect list on this one.

With the assassin dead and a description of his accomplice spreading across the city, he really needed to turn his focus to dealing with Cabot. Unfortunately, just about all the useful organizations were in disarray due to the search for moles.

Sadly, it hadn't taken long to find people who had been doing questionable things. Investigators were tugging on strings to see if they connected to Cabot's organization, but Queen wasn't sure he could trust what they found.

If he were on the other team, he'd frame people to take the fall while leaving his own operatives intact. They could still watch everything that took place and direct the investigators to people who would not harm their organization.

The investigators would find some people to question, but he doubted anything would come of it. Cabot's spies would still be in place. After all, they'd already passed every lie detector test required for their sensitive work.

That probably had something to do with the technology they had access to. Some type of alien machine that made it so they could lie their asses off about being traitors.

That annoyed the crap out of him. His only option was to continue the search for people involved with the organization. Eventually, they'd find something.

His phone rang. He brought it up to his ear. "Queen."

"Guthrie here. I need you to call me on a secure phone."

Oh, that couldn't be good. "Give me ten minutes."

He disconnected and walked over to the detective in charge of the scene. "I have to step out to my car. Something has come up, and I need to use the secure phone."

The man in the rumpled suit turned to Queen with a look of annoyance on his face. "We'll be done with you in another half hour, Secretary Queen. You'll just have to wait until then."

Queen smiled coldly. "That's where you're wrong, Detective. I'm going outside right now to take this call, then I'm leaving. We're done. If you need any further information from me, you can contact my office."

The detective scowled. "Don't try to pull that crap with me. You might be the secretary of state, but you aren't above the law."

"We've already determined that I'm the victim here," Queen said calmly. "All you're doing now is being an ass. You can do that on your own time. Push this and you'll find out how much of an ass I can be in return."

The two men glared at one another, but the detective eventually nodded brusquely. "Fine, but don't think this is over. I'm going to figure out who is behind this. If you're connected to them in any way, you're going down, too."

"I can say with a clear conscience that I had nothing to do with that man. No illegal dealings whatsoever. You're not going to find anything that worries me. Good day, Detective."

Queen stalked out toward the parking lot. He wasn't completely certain the detective would find nothing. It was entirely possible that some of the alien knowledge would seep into this investigation, in which case the federal authorities would have to quash it.

He smiled at the thought that they might have to take the detective into custody. That would serve the bastard right.

New guards surrounded him as he exited the restaurant and saw him safely into the armored limousine he was using for transport. Once he had the door closed, he picked up the secure phone and dialed the number for the general.

"Guthrie."

"Queen here. What's the problem?"

"There's been an incident at the lab. An explosion of some kind."

The words made Queen sit up abruptly. "How bad is it? What's the damage?"

"Total. It had to be sabotage. There was nothing in that lab capable of producing that kind of blast. Someone managed to sneak something past security or rigged something up with materials in the labs themselves.

"I'm afraid that either the explosion or the fire that followed has ruined every bit of technology you brought here, Mister Secretary. Worse, it killed a lot of researchers, including Doctor Wagner and the guy doing the forensic work on the bodies. They're gone, too. Everything is gone."

16

C hen leaned back in his chair, pleased at the report that had just arrived. Doctor Lee had successfully escaped Area 51 before the explosion.

One of his remaining operatives in the zone indicated the blast had been even stronger than anticipated. Odds were very good that it had destroyed everything in the lab. Frankly, based on images of the building, the lab itself was gone. The attack had undoubtedly eliminated many of the researchers as well.

His operative had manipulated the exterior security logs, so it was entirely possible the Americans wouldn't realize that Doctor Lee had escaped.

That would be the perfect outcome, but he couldn't count on that. Chen would settle for a less than optimum result so long as all the equipment was gone.

News from China itself was also good. The Dragon had successfully sunk its claws into the Mars mission. The fact that they would need to contest with armed personnel for control of the Red Planet had finally convinced the Chinese leadership to go with an all-military mission.

That had always been one of the options, so there were suitable personnel already trained. The Dragon had made certain that many of them were already loyal. In the aftermath of the events leading up to the confrontation with America, they had replaced any unaligned soldiers.

The rest of the world believed the Chinese Mars mission would leave in three weeks. He knew that date was a ruse. Much like Clayton Rogers had done with his so-called space station, the Chinese Mars mission would leave early and had engines more powerful than anyone would expect.

Not as strong as the ones that pushed the space station to Mars in a matter of days. No. It would still take them weeks to arrive, but they had a nuclear power source, too. The UN and America would undoubtedly wail. Let them.

Harry Rogers would expect the mission's arrival. There was no way to conceal the fact that they were on the way. What the man wouldn't be ready for was the level of weaponry they had outfitted the Chinese ship with.

The Chinese had always intended to arm the vessel. They would never allow any other nation to contest with them while they were unarmed. They would take those weapons with them, but the Dragon had used technology of their own—salvaged from ancient Asharim equipment—to create devices that were even more potent.

Chen wasn't cleared for the details, but those he'd spoken with seemed confident the forces of the Dragon would have no difficulty in securing the Red Planet.

Since they would control every aspect of communication from that world, they didn't need to worry about leaving evidence behind. They could destroy *Liberty Station* and every person they'd brought with impunity.

His contact had indicated the mission would depart soon, but he hadn't known the precise time due to mission security. He also hadn't been able to shed any light on what steps the Chinese government intended to take against the only other spacecraft in orbit.

If the official government decided not to directly act against the Indian-built ship owned by the Americans, the Dragon would surely arrange some suitable sabotage to remove them from the game. If that sparked a greater conflict, so be it.

The soft rap at his door caused him to frown. He'd left strict instructions not to be disturbed. He secured his computer, rose to his feet, and unlocked the door. One of his bodyguards bowed when he looked out.

"Deepest apologies, Ambassador. Your secretary indicates you have a visitor that you should see without delay."

That surprised Chen. His secretary would not interrupt this moment unless there was need.

"Send the visitor in at once," he said. He returned to his desk and resumed his seat. This should be quite interesting.

Another rap at the door a few moments later preceded the entrance of the guard and a short man with blond hair. An American by all appearances.

The man waited until the guard retreated and closed the door before he bowed deeply. "Ambassador Chen, my name is Arthur Hyde." The man then uttered a long code phrase that only an operative of the Dragon would know.

That intrigued Chen. He'd thought he knew every operative inside America. Obviously not.

Chen gestured toward one of the chairs in front of his desk. "Please sit, Mister Hyde. I'm told your news is quite urgent. Perhaps you'd care for a drink to ease your story."

The man smiled. "I wouldn't turn down some whiskey, but I believe it can wait until I'm done, sir."

"Proceed then."

"As you probably surmised, I'm embedded inside the United States government. Something has come to light that is important enough to warrant I reveal my existence to you.

"I work for the CIA at a high level. There have been meetings taking place between my superiors and others in senior leadership that I believed revolved around what was taking place with Clayton Rogers and his spaceship on Mars. That much turned out to be true, but there was more.

"The United States government is, of course, aware of the Asharim and their technology now. The new factor is that Secretary of State Queen was kidnapped briefly by an organization familiar with Asharim technology, operating inside the United States—an organization that is not connected with the Dragon."

Chen slowly straightened in his chair. "Are you sure of that?"

The man nodded. "I've now confirmed it independently with two sources that were present at the meeting. Queen briefed the president and others on the existence of this group.

"A former FBI agent named Brenda Cabot kidnapped Secretary Queen and took him through a gate to a location where they met with Harry Rogers and Jessica Cook. I presume that location was Mars. Possibly an old resistance base there."

That was quite the revelation. Someone here on Earth had access to a gate, the Holy Grail of Asharim technology. How could the Dragon not have known about them?

"I see," Chen said coolly. "This is indeed explosive information. Have you determined anything else about her group?"

The man shook his head. "I'm afraid not, sir. It's entirely possible that more information has been shared but has not yet made its way to my ears."

"I assume that you have instructions for me," Chen said.

"That's correct. I'm to continue assisting you in every way possible. I have many assets inside the various arms of the US government. Those are now at your disposal.

"Our superiors are willing to risk anything to gain access to that gate. I feel confident that a courier with instructions to that effect is already in route."

That wouldn't surprise Chen at all. For possession of a gate, the Dragon would set China against America in a heartbeat. Millions of dead was a small price to pay for the universe.

With a smile, Chen rose to his feet. "This is indeed momentous news. Allow me to pour you one of the finest whiskeys in my bar. We shall toast to the success of the Dragon."

* * *

IT TOOK QUITE a bit of persuading to convince Commander Krueger to come out and meet their new friends. He was rightly concerned there would be some type of betrayal.

Clayton had to admit there was a risk. None of them truly knew the people of this world. Despite what he believed, the sacrificial altar on the top of the hill might belong to the very people they were going to dine with tonight.

It was with that in mind that Krueger decided Gunnery Sergeant Danvers and his best people would take up positions watching the camp. If there were any shenanigans, the frighteningly competent man would settle it.

Mick Bird and Penny Cash—his civilian employees trapped on this unplanned adventure—would accompany Clayton. This was an all-hands-on-deck sort of event. Those not directly involved in watching over them were going to have to socialize and learn about their new hosts. Every additional pair of ears might hear a critical piece of information.

Krueger took in the camp as they walked closer. "Perhaps it's just me, but it sure looks as if they're a little lax with their security. We have people in the woods watching them. They should have sentries out to make sure that doesn't happen."

Clayton could see the logic in that. He wasn't sure why they didn't. Perhaps he should ask.

In a very similar fashion to when he'd approached the camp the first time, soldiers came out to meet them. Thankfully, they didn't feel the need to point their weapons at him or his companions. They merely formed up around the group and escorted them into camp.

He did note that the soldiers were eyeing the modern weapons carried by his friends. They were radically different from the long rifles the Volunteers carried. The Volunteers might not even understand that the weapons were multi-shot, much less fully automatic. That would be a truly unpleasant surprise for them if things went badly.

That set him to wondering why the technology for weapons had not improved here over the last several hundred years. Had their population been so low that they had no time? Or was this some kind of ritualized behavior?

An anthropologist would have a field day here, but he didn't have time to worry about it. He made a mental note to see about sending one if he ever got home.

Once again, Adorno and her military companions waited for them outside the large tent. Unlike last time, the sides were raised and the contents had been rearranged. It seemed to be set up for a party gathering now.

Clayton bowed toward the woman as they approached. "Susanna Adorno, allow me to introduce the military leader of our expedition, Commander Karl Krueger. He's a Navy special operations officer."

Krueger mimicked Clayton's bow. "Ma'am. It's a pleasure to meet you."

The woman eyed his camouflage clothing and strange gear. "Commander. I confess that I thought Mister Rogers dressed strangely, but your adornment is even more unusual. I barely know where to begin asking questions about it."

The officer smiled. "Wherever you like, of course."

Clayton cleared his throat and introduced Mick and Penny then allowed Krueger to name his people. Adorno did the same for her senior officers.

With the introductions out of the way, she gestured for them to proceed under the tent. "Meal preparation is always a challenge in the field, but we've done what we can to provide some palatable food. I do hope it is to your taste."

"I'm certain it will be fine," Clayton said. "If I might ask: Commander Krueger was somewhat concerned that you didn't have sentries posted along our route of approach. Aren't you concerned that the Asharim will come upon you unawares?"

She smiled. "We do have sentries out but not so close to camp. They are set up some distance away along all the avenues of approach that the Asharim might use. If they detect enemy forces in any number, they'll send word back here quickly. We are in no danger."

Krueger didn't seem convinced. "With all due respect, ma'am, it's the enemy's job to do inconvenient things at the worst possible moment for you. If they know how you have your sentries set up, they might be able to slip around and surprise you."

"My military commanders disagree. I suppose the possibility exists, but we would surely hear the fighting if they tried to overrun any of our lookout posts. There is no method they can use to slip past so many observers with any force at all."

"I grant you the possibility that they may scout our position, but they won't pose any danger to it. Their strength lies in their defenses in the city. They know that. They'll wait there for us."

"The perimeter is my responsibility," Major Logan said. "I take that duty quite seriously. You may trust that we are in no danger tonight."

"If I might ask, what manner of weapon is this? As a rifle, it seems quite short. Its accuracy must be terrible at anything more than a few dozen yards."

Krueger's smile widened. "Appearances can be deceptive, Major. I can hit a man-sized target at quite a distance with this weapon. Perhaps, if circumstances permit, I might demonstrate it for you tomorrow."

"That would be very interesting," the officer agreed. "I see a particular pattern in your clothing would make it difficult to see you in the foliage. That's quite clever."

"I wish I could take credit for it, but some bureaucrat in Washington probably figured it out."

The man frowned. "Washington? Did you perhaps mean some bureaucrat with General Washington? I would have thought him long dead."

Clayton allowed himself a smile. It seemed he and his people weren't the only ones that had some adjustment to do.

"That's a very long story," he told the officer. "One that I'm convinced we can expand on at length. However, the food will be getting cold. Perhaps we should sample it before we settle in for a long night of conversation and getting to know one another."

Adorno nodded. "Quite right. Please, step this way. Our beer is perhaps not the best, but it is palatable."

Late-night parties weren't exactly Clayton's thing, but he'd spent more than enough time at such events. Tonight was important. They had to learn as much as possible about the world they were trapped on.

He'd learned one never got a second chance to make a first impression. Tonight, he would make these people his friends.

Clayton hoped Commander Krueger was wrong about the danger. He had no desire to fight anyone, much less at night. With any luck, Krueger's fears would prove unfounded.

17

Kathleen stepped out into the wide bay and stared around in amazement. The damn place had easily four or five times as many vessels as she'd seen inside the base in France. The designs were different, but she wasn't sure what that meant. Honestly, she wasn't sure it really mattered. Alien ships were alien ships.

Nathan stepped up beside her. "It looks as if you score another point, Mother. We do indeed have air to breathe."

She shot him a look of annoyance. Even though his words hadn't been offensive, his tone was. "Your attitude is wearing on me. I suggest you try to be less of an ass."

He took two steps away and turned back to consider her. "You've known who I am my entire life. Hell, you've had a big part in making me the person I am. If there's any considering to be done, I suggest you consider how our circumstances have changed."

"What the hell is that supposed to mean?"

Nathan gestured around them. "Does this look like your corporate headquarters? Oh, that's right! You don't have one of those anymore. Not only that, you don't have any people, either. The government took everything. The only things we have are on our backs."

He drew his pistol and pointed it at her head. "I have nothing to lose by shooting you, and you'd best begin remembering you're not the boss of me."

The sight of the deadly weapon pointed at her did indeed frighten her, but she wasn't going to show fear to the likes of him. Once people knew someone was afraid, they'd come back again and again to take what they wanted.

She reached out, grabbed the barrel of his pistol, and pulled it to her forehead. "Pull the trigger and then figure out how you'll get off this stupid station. Can you fly the shuttle? No? Do you know the gate code for Earth? No? That's unfortunate."

Kathleen pushed the pistol away in a safe direction and planted her knee in his crotch. That was a fairly risky maneuver. There was a chance he'd shoot her for it. Still, it was a chance she had to take. Her dominance must be absolute.

The blow doubled her son over. Thankfully, he didn't shoot her. Rather than provoke him further, she strode away without looking back.

Inside, she was trembling. She'd never been in as weak a position as she was right now. Nathan was correct. Her only possessions, her only advantages, were what she carried in her mind.

She needed to find a way to turn this around. If she could find a way to get these ships back home, she was certain she could use them. Perhaps reducing the nation's capital to rubble would convince Queen to surrender.

An airlock similar to the one they'd found on the ship, only much larger, stood in front of her. It opened at her touch. In fact, both doors did. A wide corridor sat beyond it.

She frowned and looked at the deck. Everything was so clean. Shouldn't an ancient facility like this be coated in dust? Perhaps there were machines that kept everything in working order.

Right now, her only concern was determining who controlled this facility —if it was occupied at all. It seemed as though anyone here would know the shuttle had arrived. Hell, it should know the ship was sitting out there in space near it.

A glance over her shoulder showed her son hobbling along behind her, his pistol once again in its holster. Good. He'd learned his lesson. Too bad it wouldn't last.

The idiot would continue challenging her unless she acquired enough power to keep him in his place. At this moment, he had no choice but to follow her orders. That would change the moment they had a way back to Earth.

He'd always been a problem for her, but he'd had his uses. Now she thought that time was coming to an end. To keep things tidy, she needed to acquire muscle of her own and then eliminate him.

As she'd told him just a few weeks ago, she didn't need to have him to create grandchildren. She could do that in a lab. With the right amount of money, she could hire a suitable woman to bear her grandchildren. Yes, that was sounding better every day.

The wide corridor led deeper toward the center of the station. It seemed sensible to place critical facilities inside the deepest part of the station. She wasn't sure what those looked like, but until she explored the area, she couldn't be sure. The center of the station would be an excellent place to start.

What she found when she got there confounded her. The center of the station appeared to be an atrium. The wide-open space was perhaps one hundred meters across and a dozen levels tall. Based on her relative position, she seemed to be in about the middle.

Running from the top of the chamber down to the bottom was a thick cable. She couldn't tell what it was made of, but it didn't seem to be metal.

Perched on the cable was a huge cylinder that filled the atrium completely. It rested at the very top. The only reason she could tell it wasn't the roof was the gap that went around the edge. It was deep enough for her to see that the cylinder was a separate object.

She considered the strange setup for a moment but wasn't able to determine what it could be. Perhaps a massive elevator for moving things from one level to the other?

Kathleen watched her son walk around the circumference of the central area. Only when she was sure he was far enough away did she step near the railing. It would be just like Nathan to try to throw her over the edge and damn the consequences.

The floor of the atrium seemed to be made of clear material. She could see it was longitudinally split, almost as if it were a massive hatch that closed around the cable. Considering that she could see the cable continuing down toward the planet beyond the edge of the station, that didn't seem to be a stretch.

This tickled the edge of her memory. She'd read something about this kind of technology before. Was this a space elevator? A way of cheaply transporting a large amount of goods from the planet to orbit?

If it was, she wondered why the aliens used it. They obviously had spaceships. They even had small craft capable of entering an atmosphere. Why build something so radically different?

Kathleen shook her head. She wasn't going to find her answers standing here wondering.

It took her a moment to locate the stairs about a quarter turn to her left from the atrium. "I'm going to see what that is," she told her son. "Are you going to continue being difficult?"

He gave her an angry stare. "No. You've won again. For now."

That was so like him. He couldn't keep his thoughts to himself. She wasn't going to miss that at all.

Without waiting for him to respond, she turned and headed for the stairs. If that really was an elevator, she might see if it could take them down. The station was obviously unoccupied. Any answers would probably come from the planet.

* * *

It took several hours before Molly Goodwin was ready to accompany Harry up to the top of the mesa. She was leading a rescue effort, after all. He couldn't very well tell her he knew where his father had gone. Not yet.

When she finally had everyone performing their tasks, she set her assistant to keeping an eye on things and accompanied him to the path leading up to the top of the mesa.

She stared up the path at the huge rockfall. "What a mess. If there wasn't already a rope there, I wouldn't believe it was possible for anyone to get past that."

He smiled at her. "It all depends on the level of training. I went up last night."

Molly gaped at him. "Are you serious? It was as black as a pit last night. How could you possibly have climbed over that?"

"I won't say it was easy. Have you ever done any rock climbing before?"

"A little."

"Then this is going to be a piece of cake. Basically, we'll climb directly up the face until we get to the top of that big boulder. It's a lot easier on the other side."

She didn't seem convinced, but she was ready to give it a try. Moving carefully and slowly, he assisted her on the climb until they stood on top of the mesa.

When they were away from the edge, she stared back down. "I can't believe we just did that. Worse, I can't imagine going back down. Whatever you brought me up here for better be worth it."

She gave him a smile, probably to take any sting out of what she'd just said.

"I think you'll find it fascinating."

He led her to the depression and pulled the brush out of the way. "We're going down there. I brought lights for us."

"You brought me up here to go spelunking?" she asked incredulously. "I don't want to find myself wedged in some tight crevice I can't get out of."

"It only goes down a few meters and opens up almost immediately. Trust me."

With seeming reluctance, she sighed. "I hope to God you're not just a nutter."

"The jury is still out on that."

He clicked his light on and went down into the passage. Once he'd reached the bottom, he turned and shined the light back up. "See? Just come down right to here."

She made it about two-thirds of the way down before the ground slid beneath her feet. She shrieked as she came the rest of the way down.

He caught her arm to steady her as she came to a stop. "Are you okay? No twisted ankle or anything?"

She shook her head. "I'm fine. Now what is this place? A cave?"

He helped her to her feet then turned his light down the corridor.

"Bloody hell!" she said. "This is artificial! No way straight lines like this happen in nature."

"This may be hard to believe, but somebody put this here before New Zealand was colonized. I'm not joking. When I said aliens, that wasn't an exaggeration or a joke. Human beings associated with them dug this mesa out and constructed a facility inside of it."

He took a few steps and gestured for her to follow him. "Let me show you a few things I found last night. I'm afraid some of this is a little grisly."

Harry had already identified several of the skeletons as heavy-worlder. He wasn't interested in frightening her with the bones, but the dead warriors had left armor and weapons scattered about as well.

It only took a moment to find one of the latter under a thick layer of dust. "See this? You'll note that I haven't disturbed it. It's been here for a very long time."

Taking care not to scatter choking dust all around them, he raised the weapon off the floor and shook it a little. The power pack was undoubtedly dead, so there was no danger in allowing her to examine it more closely.

He put his flashlight between his teeth and extended the weapon on his palms.

Molly stepped closer and examined it. "I've never seen anything like it, and most of my family likes to shoot. So do I."

"Let me give you the nickel tour. Once I show you the bottom level of this facility, you won't doubt me any further."

"I don't need to see any more to believe you. This is tremendous. Momentous. Is that what your father was after when he came here? Is that why the United States sent military people to take him into custody?"

She wiped her face with a hand. "You know I have to report this. I can't possibly keep my mouth shut."

He nodded. "I suspected that would be the end result when you figured out my identity. Come on. If you're going to report this, you'll want to see everything I have."

Harry took her down to the very lowest level and showed her the engineering room and then the gate room.

Molly stared around in awe. "You weren't joking about aliens. Even in decrepit condition, I can tell this was high technology and it's been here a *very* long time."

She turned toward him and put her hands on her hips. "I want to hear the full story. I deserve to hear it all."

"I'll tell you everything you want to know, but I think I should mention the glowing square right there is powering the arch on the wall. I can't control it yet, but that isn't a solid wall.

"It's actually the entrance to a quantum tunnel. One that leads to other worlds. You're not going to find my father or anyone else you're searching for. They went through that. They won't be coming back unless I figure out how to go after them."

"Even having seen all this, I find that hard to believe. You mean like Mars? Did you get back here with something like that?"

"Exactly. We found a base in much better condition on Mars. Honestly, I've been to other star systems already. I'll be happy to show you once I get it working.

"The aliens that designed this technology had a civilization that spanned some unknowable distance and probably included thousands or tens of thousands of star systems. That gate right there is the key to the universe."

Molly made a slow turn, looking at everything around her. "This is going to change the world. This is what America wanted. They'll probably do anything to get this technology.

"Hell, so will my government. Do you realize you've just started a mad scramble to possess this technology? Wars have happened for far less."

Harry nodded grimly. "That's why we have to keep this quiet for as long as possible. Do you want China coming here to take it? They will. How far away are they, and what is their relative military strength?"

It was her turn to pale. "Bloody hell."

18

"We got some codes that might interest you," Kevin McHugh said to Jess.

She looked up from the screen on her desk and raised an eyebrow. "Oh?"

"I went with your friend Colonel McCarthy to the base in France and looked at the ships before he started bringing them back here. There was one open when your people got there, and it had a code that led to the ship you guys are looking for. I'm betting that's how your bad guys got in."

"We knew it had to be something like that," she said glumly.

"We found something else interesting," he said. "It seems the person who used the fighter as a controller also viewed a couple of videos of the fighter using the gate. That stood out to me, so I took a peek.

"It turns out that the fighter used two different sets of coordinates that I think you'll find very helpful. One of them opens up on the far side of the moon. I can't tell you where, but it's definitely the moon.

"The second one opens a gate on the side of a mountain over a jungle. The night sky looks familiar. Though I'm no expert, I think it might be South America."

"That's great news," she agreed. "I don't suppose you have any ideas on activating the big gate?"

He shook his head. "The people you assigned to examine it found a few more access panels, but the equipment isn't familiar to me. I'm still working on my vacuum certification, so I can go out and see for myself.

"I'm not too hopeful, though. I might not be able to figure out what it does in a short period of time. Anything that I can access, I could probably work out. Sealed components are another story."

She'd been afraid of that. Well, there was nothing she could do to speed the process along. "Do the best you can. We appreciate it."

He bowed his head. "You bet."

Once he was gone, she considered her options. The exploration of the Asharim site on the planet below was going well but slowly. It might yet prove to be a gold mine, but she was tempted to focus her attention elsewhere.

The latest update from Harry indicated he was going to discuss the situation with the government of New Zealand. No doubt that would stir up a whole bunch of new trouble.

Up to this point, their people had controlled the gates, except for the one Brenda Cabot and the Families had. Of course, no one wanted to reveal their existence to the world at large, so they wouldn't be broadcasting the knowledge.

Bringing one of the alien spaceships out into the light of day was a different story. That would prove to be a huge deal for everybody. The United States knew about the Asharim. No one else did. Not yet.

Once that became common knowledge, it would start a mad scramble to possess the technology. That would inevitably lead to war.

With the number of people learning about what was going on, that day wasn't far off, either. Would it be better to control the method in which they revealed what they'd learned? That was something to discuss with Harry.

In any case, it wasn't going to stop the government of New Zealand from taking control of the ruined base. That was a given. Based on what she'd heard about its condition, it wouldn't do them a whole hell of a lot of good. If Harry took the power cube from the gate, they wouldn't even be able to use it.

Of course, to do that, he had to get what he needed from it first. Unfortunately, the damned thing seemed to be locked up tight.

For the next few minutes, she considered the various options and made her decision. Things were about to spin out of control, so she might as well make some friends down under. They'd need allies against the United States and possibly China.

New Zealand wasn't powerful enough to deter China from invading. Its military just wasn't up to the task of defying a superpower. If she could bring Australia into the deal, and possibly Japan and South Korea, that would change the equation.

She thought about adding India to the list but rejected them. That was too risky. While they weren't as volatile as Pakistan, they had elements inside their government that would be much more problematic than she'd care to deal with.

Her mind made up, she rose to her feet and headed for the gate room. As expected, McCarthy was looking one of the ships over. The room held more than the last time she'd been there. The new ones must be the ones from the base in France. Room was limited until they figured out a way to get the ships outside, but the information Kevin had provided might be the key.

She was pleased to see the pilot working inside the same class of small craft as the crashed cargo ship. It had room for Kevin McHugh and some military types.

Jess walked through the lock and up to the front of the ship. "Everything working on this one?"

McCarthy shrugged a little. "That's what the automated systems are saying. I don't know enough to double-check anything."

"Excellent. We're taking it to New Zealand. Harry needs Kevin as soon as we can get him there, and he found a way to make that possible. He found gate codes that supposedly lead to the moon and possibly South America. The moon would be better, I think."

The ex-marine nodded slowly. "Probably. Are you sure this is the best idea? If something goes south, we'll be a long way from any kind of help."

"I think we have to. Time is growing short, and I want to make the biggest impact I can on our potential allies. We're international pariahs and need some governments in our corner."

"You're the boss," he said agreeably. "I'm ready to head out whenever you are."

"I'll get everyone together."

That took almost half an hour, but they finally had everyone in the shuttle. McHugh sat behind the pilot's couch where Jess could look back and see him. She'd taken the copilot's seat, of course.

Five of Harry's men took up the remaining seats. They were armed for bear, so to speak. All had advanced body armor and flechette rifles. She devoutly hoped they didn't need that kind of firepower today.

"We're ready," she told McCarthy. "Open one of the gates."

They'd held off testing the addresses because she couldn't be sure of the conditions on the other side. Honestly, she wasn't sure the gate would stop a vacuum from sucking all the air out of the chamber and wanted all her people away before they made the attempt.

"Here we go," Black Jack said. He tapped a control on his console, and the gate activated, filling the arch with mist and lightning that quickly cleared.

At first, she thought it had opened to another chamber, but she finally picked out the stars. She was looking through the gate at open space. Jess checked her console and found the chamber still had an atmosphere. It seemed as though the gate was somehow keeping the air from rushing out.

"At least we know we can have people in here next time," she said. "Let's see where that is."

McCarthy lifted the shuttle into the air and edged forward. Moments later, they'd slipped through the gate and into space. The sky opened up as soon as they were through, and she saw they were in a crater.

He took the shuttle up, and Jess got her first good look at their surroundings. It sure looked like the moon. That would be great news. It was a lot closer to Earth than any of the other external gates they'd found.

McCarthy pointed at part of the sky in the new screen. "I recognize that constellation. Virgo. It looks just right, so I suspect we're still in our own solar system. Let's take a trip farther up and see if we can determine where."

He brought them up high enough to see the curvature of the body they'd emerged on. That brought the planet it was orbiting into view. Earth. The gate had indeed opened on the moon.

She grinned. "This is perfect! We need to make note of where the gate is so that we can create a base there."

McCarthy glanced at her. "How do you know there isn't one there already?"

Jess blinked. "I guess I don't. We'll have to send through a search party to make sure. We still have radio contact with *Freedom Express*?"

"Sure do. The gate is still open. I'll pass word back for them to do that."

Jess looked at the Earth hanging in front of them as he murmured into his headset. Once he finished speaking, she continued. "It looks like we're in a good position for a trip to New Zealand. I can see it right there. Do you have the coordinates for the base?"

At his nod, she pointed. "Then let's get going."

"Aren't you worried they'll detect us?"

She shrugged. "If China isn't aware of what we've found yet, they will be soon enough. They have to have spies all through the American government. Still, I take your point.

"Let's not make a production out of this. Keep our speed to a reasonable level, and maybe they'll dismiss us as some type of aircraft once we get down into the atmosphere."

He seemed to consider that for a moment. "I'll take us in over the deep ocean. From there, we can come in low and fast. Radar is good, but if we're on the deck, they probably won't spot us."

"You're the pilot. Make it happen."

She spent the next half hour worrying someone was going to come after them, but they made it down to the ocean without anyone raising alarm. At least she didn't think they did. At least no one sent any jets after them.

Once he was down into the atmosphere, Black Jack McCarthy leveled the shuttle and increased its speed until they were flying across the water at an insanely low altitude. The waves seem to be lapping just below her feet.

"Do you think you could pull up just a little?" she asked.

The ex-marine test pilot grinned at her. "Feeling a little nervous? Don't worry. We've got plenty of space. There's at least ten meters of open air between us and the water."

"Somehow, that doesn't make me feel any better."

He laughed. "I'm scanning far enough ahead to pick up any ships. Unless we have a rogue wave, we should be okay. Frankly, I should see that far enough in advance to hop over it, too."

That didn't stop her from feeling as if they were about to crash-land on the water. The only thing she could do was close her eyes and cross her fingers. And her toes.

Twenty minutes later, McCarthy cleared his throat. "We're coming up on New Zealand. I've edged around so we're coming into a relatively unpopulated area. If somebody calls the government and complains about a plane flying low and fast, they'll send someone to check it out. I'd rather avoid that."

So would she. An armed confrontation was something they could probably avoid, but she'd rather not take unnecessary chances.

It seemed to be taking longer to get to the landing area than it had taken to get to New Zealand, but she imagined Black Jack had slowed the shuttle down a little.

"We're almost to the mesa," he said half an hour later. "I'm picking up some aircraft off to the south. I think they're helicopters out in the search pattern. They don't seem to have spotted us."

Jess sat up and watched the approach on the screens in front of her. The land around the mesa was beautiful—wild and untamed.

Black Jack waited until they were almost to the mesa before he lifted the shuttle higher and brought it to a hover over the rocky top.

That's when Jess noticed the area wasn't completely empty of people. Harry and an unknown woman stood several hundred meters away. Her partner waved while the woman gawked at them with her mouth open.

"Set us down somewhere close to them," she told McCarthy. "It's time to meet the neighbors."

19

Brenda woke when someone knocked on her door.

"Just a minute," she called out groggily as she sat up. A glance at the clock on her nightstand told her it was just before dawn. She pulled her thoughts together, stood, and threw a robe on. If someone wanted her this early, she probably didn't have time to get dressed before she heard their news.

Victor Holyfield stood outside her door. The large man bobbed his head. "I'm sorry for waking you. They need you downstairs. It's urgent."

If they were sending for her at this hour, it had to be. "Do I have time to get dressed?"

He nodded. "I'll wait out here."

She closed the door, dressed quickly, and stepped out to join him. "Give me the rundown."

"It was my turn on the night shift. Cyrus just sent a runner over with information I think you'll want to hear directly."

"Is there a reason you didn't just call me down? We have these new devices called telephones."

The young man gave her a smile as they climbed into the elevator. "I suppose I could've done that, but he wanted to be discreet. The walls up here are pretty thin. If your phone rings, other people wonder what's happening."

That was one thing she didn't like about their new accommodations. The building could do with some serious renovation.

The elevator opened onto the lobby of their building. In a higher-class neighborhood, it might have a doorman. Not here. In fact, everything still seemed to be closed up for the night.

Appearances could be deceiving, however. One of the rooms just off the lobby housed the security group tasked with making sure their living arrangements remained secure. If they determined hostile forces were moving into the area, they'd see that the building began evacuation before things became too dangerous.

Not that she expected that to happen anytime soon. Every federal agency was searching for her and the Families, but she hadn't given them anything to indicate she was even in Washington, DC. Admittedly, every ordinary criminal probably thought the same of the police.

If she'd had her way, she'd have moved their headquarters to one of the states surrounding the district. The capital wasn't the safest place for them at the moment.

She made a mental note to look into that again. There had to be a better way to balance security and convenience.

Victor rejoined the other security man monitoring the cameras and left Brenda with the courier.

She recognized him as one of Cyrus's junior assistants: Danny Benoit. He rose from his seat at the table and inclined his head. "Miss Cabot."

"Morning, Danny. What have you got for me?"

He pulled the data stick out of his pocket and handed it to her. "There was some type of major sabotage at Area 51. That's where they moved all the captured Asharim technology. From what we hear, the loss was total. It's all gone."

That set her back on her mental heels. "Seriously? Are we sure it was sabotage? Maybe they had the mother of all lab accidents. The technology can be dangerous."

"We're pretty sure. Someone figured out the US government had it and decided they shouldn't. That's my read on the matter."

She took the data stick, walked over to one of the computers, and sat down to review the report. There wasn't much to it: two communications intercepts and what looked like a few long-range pictures using a telephoto lens from a great distance, so they lacked a lot of detail.

The intercepts were more interesting. They were both brief and appeared to be phone conversations. Someone had said something on an unsecure line that one of their people was monitoring—or probably one of their programs, if she was being honest.

The NSA would be horrified if they suspected the capabilities the Families possessed for intelligence gathering. Which, now that the US government was aware of them and the Asharim, was probably the case.

It only took her a minute to read the entirety of both conversations, and she saw what Danny was talking about. One of the callers was a military officer of some kind contacting a superior at the Pentagon. He never mentioned the Asharim by name or what had happened, but he stressed several times that this wasn't an accident.

The other call sounded significantly more suspicious. It mentioned the Asharim by name. Or rather, someone in the background mentioned them loudly enough to be audible on the call. The woman doing the speaking immediately instructed the other person to be silent in Chinese. That was doubly interesting.

"Do we have any idea who this person is?" she asked.

"The voiceprint isn't on file. If you think it's worth the risk, we can have one of our people at the NSA run part of the call against their databases."

Brenda immediately shook her head. "It's not worth the risk. Everything there is already under a microscope. We can't chance drawing undue attention to our people or ourselves. I'm operating on the assumption the call was made from a burner phone. Is that correct?"

"Got it in one. The destination number was also a burner, but we isolated the cell tower it used. This may come as a shock to you, but the Chinese embassy here in Washington uses that cell tower."

"So do a ton of other important people," Brenda said. "I don't want to assume anything. Did the recipient say anything?"

"Just a couple of words. Hardly enough to recognize who it was without utilizing the NSA databases."

She rubbed her face tiredly. She really needed coffee. "We have to assume the Chinese government is aware of the Asharim now. With the heightened tension between the two governments, this greatly increases the opportunity for unfortunate occurrences.

"I think the best course is to monitor every communication in the area around the Chinese embassy as closely as we can. I realize the NSA is doing the same, so keep an exceptionally low profile. Start capturing voice files for every caller that uses that cell tower. I'll also want our audio for these calls."

"You'll have it within the hour. Cyrus has already increased the monitoring of that cell tower and is capturing logs and voiceprints for everyone that uses it. If we get a hit on the guy, we'll let you know immediately."

Brenda let him go and made her way back up to her apartment. She wanted to take the time to prepare and eat breakfast alone while she pondered her next actions.

She was tempted to do something exceptionally risky. The thought made her smile. As if everything they were doing wasn't dangerous enough already.

Well, there was dangerous and then there was *dangerous*.

By the time she'd fixed herself a simple breakfast, eaten it, and fully woken up, she'd decided to proceed with her crazy plan.

The morning traffic leaving the building was in full swing when she made her way back to the security room. The majority of the residents here didn't realize they even had a security room. They just thought it was the area the building manager used.

Victor was preparing to hand responsibility over to his relief when she walked in. He raised a hand and stepped over to her. "You need me for anything?"

"Did Danny send over some audio files for me?"

The big man nodded. "We got a data stick right here."

"Pull the call to the Chinese embassy off it and see that a courier gets it into the hands of someone Secretary of State Queen trusts. Make sure the courier can't be traced back to us. I'm going to write out a note to go along with it."

Victor raised an eyebrow. "Are you sure that's the best idea? The guy kind of hates you."

She smiled coolly. "Then he's really going to love me after this."

* * *

CLAYTON ENJOYED the strange food more than he probably should have. He was used to eating the very best of everything, so even moderately decent food tasted better than usual after the military's MREs.

They'd talked late into the night about these people's situation here on this world and the Earth from which they departed centuries ago. Susanna entertained him with stories both of this world and the last.

He had to admit he was a sucker for pirate tales. He also had to admit she was a consummate storyteller. She'd obviously practiced her timing and delivery to enhance the stories she wove. Perhaps not professionally or even intentionally. It might be that she simply had style.

The amount of beer he'd consumed might also have had something to do with it. The quality of the brew had been good when he began his meal, but continued consumption hadn't hurt his appreciation of it.

She was in the middle of telling them something one of her ancestors had recounted about Port Royale when Commander Krueger leaned over and whispered into his ear. "We really need to call it a night."

Clayton slid his eyes momentarily over to the other man. He'd trained himself not to look at his watch when meeting with other people so as not to seem hurried, but realized it must be quite late.

When Susanna reached the end of her tale and they'd shared their appreciation, he cleared his throat. "As much as it pains me to say, I believe we really should be bringing our evening to an end. My companions and I are tired, and I'm sure you have important things to do tomorrow."

"Indeed," she replied. "Allow me to share my appreciation for your indulgence of my theatrics. One of my uncles was an inveterate storyteller, and he infected me early. I've never been able to resist an audience."

Commander Krueger quickly got his people into order as Clayton bowed over Susanna's hand. "If you have no objection, I'll accompany Commander Krueger back to speak with you again tomorrow. We still have many things to discuss."

"I'll send Colonel Carver and Major Logan to escort you back to your hill. It's been a pleasure hosting you and your compatriots. You've been perfect guests. I think we shall get along famously."

"I hope so. Until tomorrow, Miss Adorno, General Norris."

The buff military officer extended a hand to Clayton. "It's been a pleasure, Mister Rogers. I look forward to our continued conversation."

Major Logan preceded them out and quickly arranged for a group of soldiers to escort them into the woods.

"I must say that I've learned quite a bit about your people and perhaps even about my own ancestors," the officer said as they made their way into the open field. Several of the soldiers held lanterns up to light their way. He supposed that was so they did not fall into a burrow dug by some local creature.

"As did I," Clayton said. "I hope we have an opportunity to visit the land the Volunteers currently call home. I think that seeing how you've developed from revolutionary times will be singularly interesting."

The soldiers around them reached the tree line and proceeded under the canopy.

Clayton knew that somewhere around them Gunnery Sergeant Danvers and his people were probably watching them. He suspected the men weren't going to reveal themselves until the Volunteers had departed to maintain their security.

"I think that would be interesting as well. It saddens me that such a visit won't occur."

Clayton was just beginning to frown at the officer when the man pulled a pistol out of his belt, aimed it at Colonel Carver, and pulled the trigger.

There was a slight hitch of time between the ignition of the primer and the firearm going off. It wasn't nearly as sharp a sound as a modern pistol, but the boom of the weapon still deafened him.

It did much worse to Carver. The shot took the other officer in the side of the head, and he went down without a word, dead before he realized he was betrayed.

The soldiers all around them quickly turned their weapons to cover the Earthmen.

"I suggest you keep your hands far away from your strange weapons," Logan said with a smile. "We wouldn't want any further misunderstandings, would we?"

Even though he already knew the basic answer, Clayton felt the need to ask the question. "What the hell are you doing?"

"Your presence has vexed my original plans, but I'm staging a coup. Or perhaps betrayal would be a better word. The Asharim are certainly going to enjoy having strangers like yourselves join that bitch of a Privateer in their little ceremony on top of that hill."

The man was selling them out to the aliens. The aliens that liked ritually sacrificing human beings. That filled Clayton's blood with ice.

20

Harry heard Molly Goodwin's inhalation of breath, turned, and saw the Asharim shuttle rise over the edge of the mesa several hundred meters away.

He had to admit that he was more than a bit surprised. The thing was utterly silent. Since he doubted the aliens had just dropped in, Jess must have figured out how to get one of the alien ships out of the bases. Or his brother Nathan had come to eradicate him. Not likely, but possible.

"Oh my God!" Molly gasped. "It's true!"

"Told you," he said as he raised an arm and waved at the shuttle. It slid further over the mesa and settled to the ground a few dozen meters away.

The airlock slid open a few seconds later, and Jess waved back at him as she hopped down to the ground.

"I decided to drop in for a surprise visit," she said with a grin.

"So I see. Meet Molly Goodwin. She's leading the search for my father. Molly, this is my partner Jessica Cook."

Jess extended a hand to the other woman. "Just call me Jess."

Molly hesitantly took Jess's hand. "Harry told me about the aliens, but I confess I didn't believe him. Not completely, at least until your grand entrance."

"That's how I roll." Jess focused her attention on Harry. "I decided it was time to reveal ourselves to the government here in New Zealand. I probably should've told you ahead of time."

"That's quite the reveal," he said dryly. "As it happens, I came to a similar conclusion myself. Hence me telling Molly about the base and giving her a tour."

"Great minds and all that. I brought you a present." Jess turned back toward the shuttle.

Harry's soldiers had exited the shuttle and were watching the perimeter. Black Jack McCarthy was just escorting an unknown man out of the craft.

"Harry Rogers, meet your new best friend, Kevin McHugh. Kevin is a hacker specializing in Asharim technology. He's managed to access the gates and get their destination codes.

"I thought he might be able to control the gate down in this base. If so, you can just go right on through and rescue your father."

Harry shook his head. "You used to work for my father. You know nothing is ever that simple with him. If it were, he'd have already come back through. No. Something's gone wrong on the other side. We just have to hope it's not too bad."

Black Jack escorted the young man up. "Harry."

He held his hand out to the pilot. "It's good to see you living up to your reputation, Black Jack. So you're flying alien ships now?"

The ex-colonel grinned. "You know me, always taking advantage of new learning opportunities."

Harry smiled and focused his attention on Brenda Cabot's man. The guy was young with very hip, round purple lenses on his glasses and a shaved head. "It's a pleasure to meet you, Mister McHugh. I find myself deeply needing your services. I hope you brought your equipment with you."

The man patted a satchel after he shook Harry's hand. "Got it right here, Mister Rogers. Can you tell me what I'm looking at?"

"Call me Harry. There's a gate down below, running off a temporary power supply that seems to have a missing controller. It won't respond to the handheld I brought with me.

"I suspect whoever set it up locked it to a specific controller. One that's not here anymore. Honestly, I think my father probably took it with him. That might be why he hasn't returned."

"I've never tried to do anything like that, but I'll do my absolute best to get it unraveled for you." The man held his hand out to Molly Goodwin. "Kevin McHugh."

Molly shook his hand. "Mister McHugh."

"I think you should stay with the ship, Colonel," Harry said to Black Jack. "It might be necessary to move quickly if someone gets excited."

"Got it covered."

Harry gestured to his men and started toward the depression. "We'll go back down and see if we can open up the gate. If we can get in and find my father waiting on the other side, we'll bring them back over.

"If not, we'll make sure that the gate works then meet with the New Zealand authorities before proceeding. Do you have any objection to that, Molly?"

"I think that makes perfect sense. I'm sure some bureaucrat is going to disagree with me, but that's my judgment. They can just suck it."

Getting back down to the bottom level only took a few minutes. Jess looked around in shock. "Wow. This place is in worse shape than any of the other bases we found."

Molly blinked at her. "You've found other bases?"

The orbital engineer nodded. "Sure have. A big one on Mars and a mobile one buried in a comet. We even found an abandoned space station out beyond Pluto. All of them were in much better condition than this."

Harry noted that she didn't mention any other bases on Earth. That was good. They needed to keep some secrets to themselves.

Once they arrived in the gate room, Kevin McHugh examined the device sitting in front of the single operational gate. "Yeah, it looks as though somebody rigged up a temporary power supply. This cable right here probably went to the handheld controller. One rigged up to interface directly with the gate through the power supply. That's clever."

The young man pulled a comp out of his satchel and messed around with connectors until he was able to seat the cable to the power supply. "There we go. Yeah. It's not locked out, not in the way you mean. This isn't a security feature. More like an accidental bug. I've got the interface to the controller now.

"There are a number of destination codes in here, but it looks as if the gate accessed only one the last few times. I'll wager that's where your father went. Do you want me to activate the gate?"

"Do it."

His men gathered and raised their weapons as the gate came to life, filling with mist and lightning. It cleared to reveal a dark tunnel beyond.

"We're not going to be able to open the gate from the other side," Harry said. "Keep it open. We might be coming back in a hurry." He led the way through the gate.

* * *

NATHAN STARED at his mother as she led him into the massive chamber at the center of the atrium. What was she doing? What was this place? His eyes narrowed as he watched her begin manipulating a control panel as if she knew exactly what it did. The strange knowledge made him extremely uneasy.

If the machine she'd slept in could change her physically and manipulate her mind, it might be able to control her. In fact, this might not be his mother at all. Just because the woman resembled her didn't make it her.

After all, what was more likely? A machine capable of regenerating a human body or one that created a mechanical device that was similar? He couldn't be sure what he was dealing with.

Obviously, whatever this was, it had his mother's memories.

His eyes narrowed. Or did it? He hadn't really pushed for any specialized knowledge from her. He'd been too busy trying to save their lives.

"What are you doing, Mother?" he asked in an even tone.

She spared him an irritated glance. "There's obviously no one on this station. Any idiot can see that. If there had been, they would've come looking for us immediately. The fact that we have been unmolested means we're alone. That means we need to go where the people are."

"That's a lot of words to say nothing. What *exactly* are you doing?"

She tapped a couple of controls and swiped her hand across the screen. The floor beneath their feet shook, and it felt as though an elevator were going down. That wasn't a bad analogy. The large chamber they stood in was dropping to the bottom of the atrium. This was going to be a very short trip.

"We could've just walked down the stairs," he said dryly.

"Really? Well then, I'm so sorry to have wasted your time."

Looking through the transparent floor, he watched in awed consternation as the bottom of the atrium split apart and separated. The chamber continued through where that barrier had been and took them into space.

Now he could see the cable hadn't stopped at the bottom of the atrium. It continued on toward the planet below.

What the hell were they in? The universe's biggest elevator?

The large chamber continued along the cable at a growing pace. He wondered how long it was going to take them to reach the surface at this rate.

"That's quite clever," he finally admitted. "Climb into a large room on the surface, press the button, and go into space. Any idiot can do it."

"Apparently so," his mother said. "The only thing we don't know is what we're going to find down there. With all the wreckage in space, civilization may be gone.

"Or perhaps not. In any case, we'll undoubtedly come across people hostile to us back on Earth. We need allies."

"We didn't need allies until you started us on this harebrained trip," he said. "We could've stayed on the ship and figured out a way to get home. The ship brought us here. It could still take us back. It's by far the most valuable artifact we've found so far. One that might allow us to crush all our enemies."

When she didn't answer, he considered what to say next. How far could he push her before she snapped? Far enough to find out who she truly was?

"We haven't had time to talk since you got out of that machine. What did it do? Make you young again?"

She walked to the edge of the chamber and sat on a handy bench. "I don't know." Her voice sounded tired.

"Well, you have to know something."

"Do I? Maybe I'm just accepting that I've changed. This alien technology can do all these other wondrous things, why not regenerate an old woman's body?"

"Or create some kind of strange duplicate," he said coolly. "How do I know you're really my mother?"

The corner of her mouth quirked up in a cold smile. "Even if I answer that question, how do you know it didn't just copy my mind? That's a slippery road you want to walk down."

"Oh, I'm not the one walking," he said as he sat near her. "You are. I'm just trying to decide what to do about it."

She sat up a little. "Before you get all excited, you should remember that I have you completely in my power. Could you take this space elevator back up to the station? I doubt you can even read the language. The aliens below probably don't speak English, either. How's your Asharim?"

That was annoyingly astute of her.

He shrugged and eased his weapon over until it pointed even farther from her. "I can't know anything for sure. Perhaps you should convince me that you're really my mother."

"When you were six, you wanted a dog. I was allergic, so I said no. Anyone might guess something like that, but I'll wager you remember my exact words. 'If you want a dog, you can move out of my house and live on your own.' That's what I told you. Remember it?"

He could hardly forget. Even after all this time, it still enraged him.

The smug satisfaction in her voice also confirmed this was undoubtedly his mother. Only she would get so much pleasure from being a bitch like this.

The floor under his feet shuddered just barely enough to be noticed. He looked out through the windows and saw clouds. They were already down inside the atmosphere. Unbelievable.

He'd expected something traveling such a long distance along such a slender cable to travel slowly. Well, he supposed aliens could do what they wanted when it came to physics. They could manipulate gravity, so he supposed this was related.

Rather than goad his mother any further, he stared at the floor to see if he could discern their destination.

After a short time, the last of the clouds cleared away to reveal a wide city stretched out below them. From this height, he couldn't tell what condition it was in, but he was willing to bet it was abandoned or had fallen into ruin.

He'd find out soon enough. With their luck, the space elevator would reach the bottom to find the building collapsed and kill them both. If it didn't, they'd probably find man-eating aliens.

21

Q ueen was tempted to fly out to Area 51 but knew it wouldn't do him any good. All his presence would do was distract the people trying to determine what had happened.

Hell, he already knew what had happened. Someone had gotten wind of the Asharim technology and decided they couldn't afford to let the United States have it.

This was a disaster, pure and simple. They'd been on the edge of achieving something that would've changed the face of the world forever. Someone had taken that from them.

He even knew who had to be behind the attack. Very few people knew about the aliens, and fewer still had the resources to get into such a secure location. That made the suspect list incredibly short.

It was Cabot. It had to be. The bitch had figured out where they'd taken the captured equipment. As a former FBI agent that had actually seen it, the woman knew everything.

Her damned secret organization probably had people embedded in Area 51. They were probably so established it would take weeks or months to figure out who he needed to be suspicious of.

That was what was so frustrating about this damned illuminati business. Even in cases where the secret organization wasn't involved, he'd be seeing their shadowy hands in everything.

A knock at his door pulled him out of his deep funk.

His assistant cracked the door and looked inside. "A courier dropped something off for you, sir. I think you should take a look at it."

He frowned. "What is it, and who sent it?"

"The sender is listed as Brenda Cabot."

That shocked him. Then it pissed him off.

Had she sent something just to taunt him? He'd have thought somebody with FBI training was smarter than that. It would only make him more determined to bring her down.

Queen made a gesture for his assistant to bring the delivery in. The man set a manila envelope on the desk and stepped back. "Security already looked inside. There's a handwritten note and a thumb drive."

"Bring me a laptop. One that we can afford to lose if this has a virus. Make it snappy."

He emptied the contents of the envelope onto his desk. It was as described: a folded note on a regular sheet of paper and a thumb drive. He unfolded the paper and began reading.

Secretary Queen,

I rather expect this contact comes as an unexpected and unwelcome surprise. I'm not sending this message in order to gloat, as difficult as that may be for you to believe. Rather, I felt the need to give you a warning.

We heard about the attack you suffered at Area 51. I want to tender my personal regrets for any injuries or deaths. Based on the images I saw, there must've been more than a few of each.

As difficult as this will be for you to believe, neither I nor my people had anything to do with this. In fact, I believe a third party is involved. One I was previously unaware of.

The data stick I sent to you contains a call my people intercepted that we believe was made by people involved in the attack. Since it does not suit my ends to allow another group to upend the applecart, I'm forwarding this information so you can deal directly with the people who are attacking you.

As unsettling as this will undoubtedly be, if you want to talk about this I'm more than willing to do so under conditions that will assure my safety. I'm not going to be silly enough to give you a phone number that you can trace to me or the area where I'm located.

If you want to talk, all you need to do is post a note to that effect on your social media account. No need to be coy. Just say that you wish you had more of a chance to talk with an old friend from the FBI. My people will see it, and I'll contact you.

Because I know you're a man who likes to nurse grudges, I'm going to say this again. Neither I nor my people carried out this attack against you. We are not enemies of the United States, regardless of what you think. Honestly, the vast majority of my people are fervent patriots.

It's still possible we will make common cause at some point. My people only want to keep humanity safe from the Asharim. Keep that in mind.

Brenda Cabot

Unbelievable. She honestly expected him to buy that load of crap? What kind of idiot did she think he was?

He reread the note and found it just as stupid the second time through.

His assistant came in, carrying a small laptop, which he set on the desk. "This isn't connected to any of our networks and doesn't have any work-related files on it. It should be safe to use."

"Where did it come from?"

The man shrugged. "It belongs to one of the junior assistants. There's no telling what kind of crap is actually on there, but I assume you're not searching for his porn."

That forced a chuckle out of Queen. "No. I could care less what his perversions are."

He plugged a thumb drive into the laptop and looked at the folder that opened. There were two files: one audio and one text. He turned the speaker on and played the audio.

The man receiving the call had a voice he found tantalizingly familiar. He played it several times, and his certainty grew. It wouldn't stand up in a court of law, but he knew that voice belonged to Ambassador Chen.

The text file containing information about the cell towers involved with the call and the phone numbers. He could confirm much of that information with the NSA, and he would.

In fact, he'd have them thoroughly vet everything and try to get the same information without telling them one damned thing about the file.

If Brenda Cabot was telling the truth—and that was a *big* if—the United States might be in even deeper trouble than he'd imagined.

Should the Chinese be aware of the Asharim and their technology, that put a sinister twist on the military confrontation that was growing between the two nations. It also made their possession of the Yucatán Spaceport *much* more troubling.

If they'd decided this technology was connected with the rogue Mars mission that Clayton Rogers had launched, they wouldn't be sending scientists to explore the Red Planet. They'd be sending soldiers.

Not that he cared one bit about what happened to the bastards that had tricked him. His only concern was what they might have found there.

Hell, not might. Had. He'd seen more than enough to accept they had a treasure trove of advanced technology at their fingertips.

He unplugged the thumb drive and pushed the computer away from himself. "Get that scrubbed. I want to make absolutely certain there's no chance it has any information left on it. Give the guy who owns it a large bonus for his trouble. And this might happen again, so pick up a machine at some random box store for us. Just in case."

The man picked up the laptop and nodded. "Will there be anything else?"

Queen smiled coldly. "Summon Ambassador Chen. I think it's time he and I had a heart-to-heart chat. Then get me the president. I'm going to need authority to do what needs to be done."

* * *

Clayton opened his mouth to say something—he wasn't sure what—to dissuade the man, so he got a mouthful of blood when Major Logan's head virtually exploded in front of him.

Other shots rang out from close by, and the Volunteer soldiers threatening Commander Krueger and the rest staggered or collapsed. That gave an opening for the men on his side to pull their pistols and end the threat.

Clayton was still trying to spit the horrible taste out of his mouth and wipe the blood from his eyes when Krueger grabbed him by the arm and pulled him deeper into the forest.

"We need to get moving. They won't be alone."

While that might be true, Clayton dug his heels in. Literally. "No. We have to warn Adorno. She has to know they've been betrayed."

"They're going to find out soon enough," Krueger said grimly. "Logan wouldn't have acted if the trap wasn't already closing. He was in charge of the sentries. If the Asharim aren't all around us, I'll eat my boots. We need to get up the hill."

"No, dammit. They're going to be slaughtered. Being inside the hill isn't going to do us one bit of good if we're surrounded by an ocean of enemies. We have to warn them so they can fight."

Krueger took a deep breath and visibly gritted his teeth. "Shit. Danvers."

The gunnery sergeant materialized out of the darkness. "Sir?"

"Get Mister Rogers and the rest back to the hill and dig in. I'll take two men and warn the Volunteers about the ambush. Keep an eye out. We're probably going to be coming back under fire. We'll need you to clear a path for us."

"Aye, sir." The marine grabbed Clayton's arm and pulled him forward.

Clayton knew better than to argue at this point. The man had his orders, and he was going to carry them out. If Clayton didn't want to end up over the marine's shoulder, he was going to have to trust that Krueger would take care of business.

The marines all around him had extinguished the lights. It was as dark as the devil's armpit. They had to be using night-vision goggles.

He made a mental note to get something like that in his gear going forward. Hell, he was going to have to have his assistant completely update his bag. His needs and the threats he faced were significantly different than they'd been six months ago.

They reached the hill unmolested. That was actually one hell of a shock. Clayton had been sure the Asharim were going to prevent them from reaching safety.

Unfortunately, he could hear fighting in the distance. The unmistakable booms of black-powder weapons and the sharp, controlled bursts of automatic weapon fire. The Asharim had sprung their ambush, or the Volunteers had found more traitors in their ranks.

Danvers pushed Clayton, Mick, and Penny into the cave entrance. "Stay inside. We don't know what type of weapons they have. I won't have a sniper picking you off."

Clayton stopped just inside the cave. "We need to know what's happening."

"We've already got a drone in the air. We should have information in a couple of minutes. You can look at the screen. Inside. The. Cave."

Since he'd done exactly that earlier, Clayton really didn't have any room to complain. He wasn't sure why he felt the need to observe the fighting personally.

Maybe it was his innate need to control his own destiny. That was a weakness he'd realized he had years ago. Or perhaps weakness was the wrong word. He did revel in overseeing important work.

One of the marines had a tablet out and was reviewing information from the drone as he walked into the chamber. Clayton didn't know much about reading a display at night, but it didn't look as if the Volunteer army was alone.

"Tell me what I'm looking at," he told the marine firmly.

"This is an IR image, sir. The group at the center is at the camp you just came from. There are large groups to the east, northwest, and southwest. They've encircled the camp. The temperature looks a little off, so I'm not certain we're looking at human beings. I've never seen an alien in infrared."

"What do the relative numbers look like? Can they hold them off?"

The other man shrugged. "I have no idea if they can hold out, sir. I'd say the friendly forces are outnumbered at least two to one. Perhaps three to one. The defenders are going to have an advantage, but if they don't get out of the pocket, they're probably going to get slaughtered."

Clayton cursed. "And you don't have enough ammunition to spring them. Hell, you don't even have enough ammunition for us to hold once they come for us. What are we going to do?"

"Under those circumstances, I'd call for reinforcements," a voice said from behind him.

He turned in surprise and found Harry standing at the entrance to the tunnel leading to the gate. He held a rifle and had several armed men stood behind him.

22

———————

Jess turned to Kevin McHugh as soon as Harry was out of sight. "What's the address of this gate? Can you get me that?"

The young hacker nodded. "Sure. The address for a specific gate is locked in when it's created. That prevents any possibility of having two gates with the same address."

He tapped his comp a few times. "Got it. What do you want me to do with it? Link it to your phone?"

She raised her eyebrows. "You can do that?"

The bald man snorted derisively. "Please. I can do that in my sleep, even if you didn't give me the number first. Let's do this the easy way." He held out his hand.

She considered the security implications, shrugged, and handed him her phone. It wasn't as if Brenda Cabot didn't already have her number.

While the young man worked, Jess turned to Molly Goodwin. "This must all seem so strange to you. If it helps, you'll adjust quickly."

The other woman laughed a little. "If you say so. As I told Mister Rogers, I'm going to have to inform my superiors. I probably should do that now. Can I get someone to escort me back up to the surface so I can make that call?"

Harry had left the three of them alone. If anyone were going to escort Molly up, it would have to be her or Kevin. She wasn't sure she could trust the young hacker not to get sidetracked down some passage, so she'd have to take care of that herself.

A shout came up the passage from the other side of the gate. Jess couldn't quite make out what was said, but she recognized the urgency in the man's tone. Her hand darted down to her waist, and she pulled the pistol she'd begun carrying. Something was wrong.

One of the guards she'd brought with her from *Freedom Express* came tearing down the corridor and skidded to a halt just on the other side of the gate.

"We found them, but there's some type of military crisis involving other bad guys. I figure we have maybe twenty minutes. We need reinforcements. As many as you can get. Have them bring extra weapons and ammunition."

He didn't wait for Jess to respond before he turned and ran back the way he'd come.

"So much for having enough time to do everything nice and slow," Jess muttered. "I'll need that phone, Kevin."

He handed her phone back. "I stuck the address in a text to yourself."

"Thanks."

She called Rex. He answered after a few rings. "Jamison."

"I need the best fighting force you can gather ASAP. I'm going to call *Freedom Express* and get the troops they have on their way first. Be ready. I'll text you the gate address."

She disconnected and scrolled through her contacts until she got one of the gate addresses for *Freedom Express*.

Jess gestured for Kevin to hold up his comp so she could see it. She killed the gate, and the connection to the alien world vanished, showing nothing but a plain stone wall.

Reading from the phone, she entered the address for their mobile base. The gate reconnected, and she saw armed personnel standing in the loading bay.

"Get every single person that can fight in here right now," she shouted. "I'd prefer people that have fought together like Harry's forces, but I need everybody that can shoot.

"I'm going to disconnect the gate connection and get the forces Rex has under his command. Be ready to go as soon as I reconnect the wormhole."

Once the woman nodded, Jess killed the connection and dialed the French base.

Rex was standing just on the other side, outfitted for war. He had several dozen men standing behind him carrying backpacks and extra weapons. They rushed through as soon as the gate formed.

In as few words as possible, she filled Rex in on what she'd been told and what she suspected.

She connected the gate to *Freedom Express* as soon as she finished. Those forces boosted Rex's numbers to about five dozen.

Jess wasn't a trained warrior, but she grabbed one of the flechette rifles and checked it. She'd used one before and was trained well enough. At least she hoped she was.

She turned to Kevin. "As soon as you connect with where Harry went, I want you to take Miss Goodwin back up to the surface. Tell Colonel McCarthy he's to take her down to the camp then return to *Freedom Express*. If we run into serious trouble, we're going to go back there directly."

The hacker nodded, his face pale. "I should probably call Brenda. She'll want to know what's going on."

As soon as the hacker opened the gate back to the dark stone tunnel, Rex led their scratch fighting force forward. Jess followed them. She posted one annoyed man to stay behind and hold onto the comp controlling the gate.

The tunnel twisted and curved a little bit but quickly led them to a chamber where Harry was already directing Rex to head farther up the tunnel.

She saw Clayton Rogers standing beside his son. There were a couple of civilians and what looked to her like some marines nearby.

Her eyes narrowed, and she edged the barrel of her weapon toward what she assumed were the men that had kidnapped her boss.

The elder Rogers raised a hand. "Peace. These men aren't our enemies. We've settled our differences. Mostly.

"Jess, meet Gunnery Sergeant Danvers. He has tactical command of the American forces here. Less than a dozen men. His commanding officer, Commander Karl Krueger, is out trying to save our allies. Which is what we need to help them do."

She felt her eyes narrow. "Gunnery Sergeant *Jacob* Danvers?"

The man's eyes widened. "I'm not sure how you knew that, ma'am."

Jess lowered the barrel of her weapon a trifle. "It seems we have friends in common. I don't know if you knew, but Michael and Sierra Crockett are working for us. So is Emily Adams."

The man blinked in surprise. "I knew they had a classified project they were working on, but I didn't realize it had anything to do with Mister Rogers. Well, that's awkward."

"I couldn't agree more," she agreed.

"As unexpected as this might be, we need to focus," Clayton Rogers said. "We've got two armies just outside the cave. The Asharim—who are apparently devolved from their higher technology selves—are leading an attack against humans friendly to us with a lot of what we're told are slaves. Probably also not human. The people we're trying to save somehow got here around the time of the American Revolution."

Harry shook his head. "We've got a few dozen people. Even modern weapons won't stop thousands. Not if they're determined."

Gunnery Sergeant Danvers held a hand to his ear. Based on the way he was frowning, someone was saying something into an earbud.

"Copy that, sir. We'll be ready."

He looked at Harry Rogers. "That was Commander Krueger. The Volunteer army has broken out of the ambush. They're coming to us, and they have hostiles all over them."

"Then we better get ready," Harry said grimly. "Let's go set up a warm welcome for the Asharim."

* * *

CHEN STEPPED into Secretary of State Queen's office with a smile on his face. He felt certain he understood the true reason he'd been called here so abruptly. It had to be the attack. Somehow, the US government suspected that the Chinese were behind it.

Good luck to them in proving it.

Once the assistant had closed the door behind Chen, he bowed slightly. Somewhat less than a person of Queen's rank was entitled to, but more than enough to seem as though he wasn't slighting him.

"You wished to speak with me, Mister Secretary?" he inquired politely.

The other man glared at Chen. "You're damned right I do. I want to know what the hell you think you're doing."

Chen raised an eyebrow. "I'm afraid you're going to have to give me a little more information to go on, Mister Secretary. Precisely what do you *think* I'm doing?"

"I want to know why you attacked our facility at Area 51."

Chen spread his hands slightly. "I'm afraid that you're under a misapprehension, Mister Secretary. My government has conducted no such operation. Was there an incident?"

Queen slammed his hands down on the top of his desk and stood. "Don't play innocent with me. I heard the recording of your phone call. I heard your voice when they told you the attack had gone off just as you wanted."

That last bit sent a chill down Chen's spine, but he didn't allow his expression to change. The Chinese as a people were well-known for their ability to conceal their emotions, and he was better than most. One of the best, actually.

"Many voices sound similar to the ear, but I can assure you I did no such thing, Mister Secretary. I realize that our governments have placed us into conflict, but I urge you to seek restraint. Don't allow external events to color an already-difficult situation. Don't make accusations that you have no proof of."

"Ah, that's where you're wrong. I *do* have proof! You're probably aware that the NSA captures metadata from all calls that take place into or out of the United States. That includes calls within our boundaries.

"You probably feel fairly confident that we can't save every single scrap of audio data, and you'd be right. Unfortunately for you, I do have audio of your conversation. My government is quite capable of comparing that audio to the voice print we have on file for you."

Chen maintained a mildly curious expression when Queen paused expectantly but said nothing.

After a few moments, Queen continued. "Since you're going to make me tell the entire story, I suppose that I should just get on with it. The voice in the recording matches yours to greater than ninety-five percent. That's enough for an actual conviction in a court of law. I'd call that proof, wouldn't you?"

Chen spent a few moments considering his options and then shrugged. "I, of course, deny all of that. I don't understand why your government would forge evidence in such a fashion, but it hardly matters. I have diplomatic immunity. This farce serves no real purpose."

Queen sat back down and leaned back in his chair. "I expected you to say that. While I can't arrest you—as much as I want to—I can have you take a message back to your country for me.

"The United States hereby revokes permission for you to be here and declares you persona non grata. In fact, we're expelling the entire staff of your embassy. We consider this event to be an act of war."

Chen smiled slightly. "Don't you believe that is taking measures a little out of scale? Did someone blow up one of your cities? I have not heard of any occurrence that would constitute an act of war."

"So that's the game you're going to play? Fine. You're quite aware of what my government came into possession of. You took steps to make certain we didn't retain it. I regret to inform you that your actions were less than total, as many critical pieces are still in our possession.

"That doesn't negate the fact that you attempted to destroy them on our soil. When added together with your seizure of the Yucatán Spaceport, it's obvious that your country seeks direct conflict with us. I gave you many opportunities to step back from the abyss, but you chose to push this fight. Now you have it."

"Critical pieces of what?" Chen asked with false curiously. "If you want me to transport a message to my government, you're going to actually have to say it out loud. Use your words, Mister Secretary."

The other man snorted bitterly. "We *know* you know about the Asharim. I'm not sure how long you've been aware of them, but you're not going to be able to keep that knowledge to yourself any longer.

"Even as we speak, our ambassador to the United Nations is making a presentation to the Security Council. This is all going to be out in the open now.

"That's not going to change your fate, however. I want all Chinese diplomatic personnel out of my country within twenty-four hours. Every last one of you treacherous bastards. If you're still here by sunset tomorrow, I'll arrest you no matter what your status is. Is that clear enough?"

Chen bowed only an insulting fraction of the distance Queen would normally be entitled to, not bothering to pretend at any real respect. "As clear as spring water, Mister Secretary. I cannot wish you luck in your endeavors, but I hope that your regret is brief. Now, it seems I must go pack. Good day."

23

Kathleen felt a lot more uncertainty than she allowed her face to show as the chamber slid into a large building where the space elevator anchored to the planet. Once it stopped moving, she lost all control over events. She would be at the mercy of whoever ruled this place.

The floor vibrated as the chamber came to rest and the large hatches set along the outer walls all opened at once. Her son held his weapon at the ready and turned slowly, looking for threats.

None materialized.

She picked one of the exits at random and strode through it. The room outside was at least a hundred times the size of the chamber itself, though that was hard to see in the dim light cast through too few windows. Overhead, the domed roof soared into the darkness.

Parts of the space held what had likely been cargo at some point. It had collapsed into piles of rubbish. It was obvious that this place had not been occupied in a very, *very* long time. While that added to her safety at the moment, it was a negative in the long-term. Allies would be better.

"This place is as deserted as the ship," Nathan said, lowering his weapon.

"Perhaps," she conceded. "Perhaps not. It may just be that no one was close enough to the building to get here before we did. Or they wanted to have more numbers at their back when they did. We don't know the situation here, so we'd best not assume anything."

"What are you hoping to accomplish here, Mother? Do you really expect to find anything useful? We could've just tried one of the two gate codes that you have in your phone. Once we get back to Earth we can—"

"We can what? Scurry around like mice in the dark, hoping that no one finds us? Don't be an idiot. We need weapons and allies. It's entirely possible this place can provide both."

Nathan looked around meaningfully. "It doesn't seem that way, does it? Anyone that still lives in this place is probably a gibbering savage."

A flicker of movement to her left caught her attention. "I'd keep that opinion to yourself. It seems we have visitors."

She couldn't see where they were coming from because it was behind a large pile of debris, but she could hardly miss the people that walked brazenly into view. They didn't seem the slightest bit worried that she or Nathan posed a threat to them.

The first thing she noticed about the new people was that they were human. Built wider and a bit squatter than she would expect of a normal person, though. Each of the men looked as if he could break them both in half without any effort whatsoever.

Kathleen would hardly call their clothing modern, but it wasn't primitive like a savage's might be. They also carried Asharim weapons.

They surrounded Nathan and her at a distance of about a dozen meters and stood there silently, as if they were waiting for something.

She took a deep breath before stepping forward.

The men directly in front of her raised their weapons, but one of them held a hand out to his comrades. Perhaps he was their leader. He considered her for a moment then said something in a language that she was unfamiliar with.

No, that wasn't quite true. As she considered the noises he'd made, she was able to extract meaning from it. Perhaps it was another of those implanted memories, but she could understand what he was saying if she focused.

The real question was going to be whether or not she could answer him. "My name is Kathleen Bennett, and yes, I did come down from the sky." Astonishingly, it seemed she could speak the alien language.

From the man's expression, he hadn't been expecting her answer. Or perhaps he just hadn't believed she'd understood him.

"You do not look like any of the images of the Masters we possess," the man said, his voice a deep rumble. "You look more like us. Weaker, though."

"That is true," she admitted. "We are not the Asharim. Have you been waiting for them long? Or have you hoped they'd never return?"

The man's weapon lowered slightly, and he allowed himself a brief smile. "Depending on who you ask, some of both. I now know your name, but I do not know who you represent. The fact that you have come from the sky frightens my people. Explain yourself."

She could imagine what the unsaid "or else" might mean for her and her son. "We do not serve the Asharim."

Kathleen knew she was taking a very large risk with that pronouncement, but she was fairly good at reading body language. In her position, she had to be.

"Then who do you serve?"

"I come from a planet called Earth. The home of humans like ourselves."

The man seemed to consider that for a moment. "Humans. I don't believe that I've ever heard the word before. It's not Asharim nor is it one that the People use among themselves."

She could hear the capital letter in the word 'People.'

"That's a very long story," she said. "The short version is that I come from the place they took your ancestors from."

He nodded slowly. "How did you use the sky bridge?"

Kathleen assumed he was talking about the space elevator. "I have some knowledge of the Asharim technology. It would be helpful for me to know who you serve. Are you still loyal to the Asharim?"

The man shrugged. "That is a complex question. Some elements of the People still long for the return of the Masters. Others are pleased that we have lived on our own for so many lifetimes. If you had been the Masters, I am uncertain whether your arrival would have caused celebration or war."

He stared at her for a moment more. "I believe that we shall start with celebration. My name is Kerrick Vidar, and it is my honor to lead the People.

"I declare you our honored guest, Kathleen Bennett. We shall arrange a great celebration to herald your arrival. Meanwhile, it might be best if we meet privately to discuss the true reason for your visit and what it means for the People."

She suspected that if her answers didn't please him, there wouldn't be a celebration. At least not one where she was the guest of honor. Was the prisoner at an execution considered the guest of honor? She'd really rather not know the answer.

Kathleen inclined her head. "We have much to talk about. I assure you that I have no ill will toward your people. In fact, it may be that we can help one another."

"Perhaps. Perhaps not. In any case, we shall come to know one another shortly. Come."

She gestured for Nathan to follow her and the men formed up around them as they led them away from the space elevator. If things went badly, she knew she'd never see it again. She'd have to use her very best negotiating skills to make certain that didn't happen.

* * *

HARRY FOLLOWED the somewhat bemused Gunnery Sergeant Danvers out of the cave and onto the side of a tall hill. It was night out, but that didn't stop him from seeing or hearing the fighting. The small flickers of muzzle flash were like little lightning bolts off in the distance.

Basing his guess on the distant rumble of the shots, he suspected the fighting was at least a kilometer away. Perhaps a bit more. Most of the shots had an odd timbre.

"Do we have a better idea of the situation?" he asked Danvers. "What are the weapons in play down there?"

"The natives use low-technology weapons. Black powder. Though I suppose 'native' might not be the right word. There are apparently Asharim on this planet. At least that's what your father called the aliens. This might be their world."

Harry shook his head. "The Asharim favor low gravity, maybe sixty percent of what we have on Earth. Of course, if they lost their technology, they might not have much of a choice.

"That's actually a lucky break for us. Reloading black powder is a lot slower than our modern firearms. Once they come into range, we should be able to force them back without too much trouble."

"It depends on how fanatical they are. A dozen men with clubs can take down a man with a gun. We're low on ammunition, so if they want to take this hill, they're going to be able to do it. They just have to be willing to pay the price."

"I assume you're using standard NATO ammunition. My guys brought as much of it as we could carry. That'll help."

"Your numbers are going to help more. Trying to fight off an army with less than a dozen men was a losing proposition. Particularly if we're covering the retreat for thousands of others."

Harry stared out into the darkness. It looked as if the fighting was coming closer. At this rate, they might have visitors inside half an hour. Sooner, if they'd send out scouts to secure the way, which is what he'd have done.

"I want you to pair one of your people with each of my teams," he told the marine. "You know who the friendlies are, we don't. We absolutely don't need any blue on blue casualties."

"Roger that," the man said with feeling.

Harry watched as the marine spoke softly into his microphone. It was hard for him to accept that he had to be careful of the man beside him and his comrades. He'd fought beside many people just like them for a third of his life.

Yet these folks had come to take his father into custody and drag him back to the United States for what was probably going to be a secret trial and incarceration at Guantánamo Bay.

Clayton Rogers didn't seem perturbed, but Harry wasn't going to allow Queen to get his hands on any of them. He hoped that didn't mean he had to fight these men, but he'd do it if necessary.

"I've got men assigned to each of your teams," Danvers said. "We're spreading out around the side of the hill to get good fields of fire to cover the retreat. We'll be able to shoot at the enemy before they start climbing, if they're packed together tightly enough. One of my snipers might be able to cause a little chaos at longer range, but this is going to be a brutal, ugly affair."

Unfortunately, Harry agreed with that assessment. A team of snipers might've been able to make a difference fighting during the daylight. At night, there just wasn't sufficient time to locate and eliminate the right kinds of targets.

Danvers reached up and touched his ear. "Copy that."

He glanced over at Harry. "The lead elements of the Volunteer forces have arrived at the base of the hill. There's a path up. I had one of my folks mark it with luminescent sticks so they could find their way without being escorted.

"We've got thousands of people headed our way. There's no way we can fit them all into the cave, so they'll have to go up to the crown of the hill. Once we start spreading our forces thin trying to cover every approach, the enemy is going to be able to breach our lines."

Harry smiled. "Then we have to make sure that's not a possibility. Send them through the gate. The base might be a dead pile of shit, but that beats getting shot. Once we have everybody on the other side, we can figure out how and where we're going to relocate them."

"Thank God that's above my pay grade," the marine noncom said. "I suppose you have a way of using that gate to go other places."

"Indeed we do. We'll let my partner handle the relocation while we take care of slowing the enemy down. Once we're certain we've gotten as many people through as possible, we'll retreat into the cave and bring down the entrance with explosives. I'd like to deny them the gate."

"Considering the fact that they might come after us, I think that's an excellent idea."

When he finally saw some of the humans from this planet, it was hard for him not to shake his head in amazement. They looked as if they'd just come from a Revolutionary War reenactment.

The trickle quickly became a flood. Even as their numbers increased, Harry heard his men opening fire. The enemy must be in range. That's when he spotted several men in the flow of people dressed in modern combat gear. He recognized the man in the lead.

He smiled at Karl Krueger and extended a hand. "It's been a while, Commander."

"Let's not stand on ceremony, Harry," the officer said as he took it. "I'm damned glad to see you."

The man gestured toward a woman standing beside him dressed in what appeared to be pirate garb. "Harry Rogers, meet Susanna Adorno. She's the leader of our allies. Susanna, Harry is Clayton's son and a very skilled warrior. He leads the people who have come to rescue us."

Considering the timeframe that these people had come from, Harry had to fight to keep the surprise off his face. While he expected to see women in leadership positions in the modern day, that didn't hold true several hundred years in the past.

He wasn't sure whether he should extend his hand to shake hers or attempt to kiss it.

She solved his conundrum by reaching out and taking his firmly. "I am most pleased to make your acquaintance, Harry. Your timing is excellent.

"Without your help, we would never have been able to hold the enemy at bay until dawn. I am still uncertain as to how long we can hold out against them, but your assistance is greatly appreciated."

Harry cleared his throat. "Actually, I've decided that the simplest way to solve our mutual problem is to send everyone through the gate inside this cave. It will take us all back to Earth. We'll use explosives to bring down the entrance.

"I realize that might seem to be a major setback, but I didn't bring enough force to take on an army, even with my superiority in weapons. We can come back at a future point in time, but if we want to live, we're going to have to go."

The woman's expression was similar to that of someone who'd bitten into something sour. "I cannot say that your assessment surprises me, but I greatly dislike being forced to retreat, much less abandon our world. We all have family and friends here. I must insist that steps be taken to see we are able to regain our footing here quickly."

Thankfully, those kind of negotiations were outside his realm of authority. "I'll leave the details of that between my father and you. In the short term, if we want to survive, we have no choice."

Susanna sighed. "No, I don't suppose that we do. Well, I've always dreamed of seeing Earth. The stories told by those who saw it with their own eyes have been passed down from generation to generation."

The ruined base in New Zealand was going to be a terrible disappointment, Harry was sure. He hoped that he could make it up to her later.

24

Brenda knew every trip into the city was a risk, but she was going stir-crazy. She was one of those people who had to be out doing things. She couldn't just sit on her butt and let other people do all the work.

Not that she was working at the moment. She was off to the deli, getting food for those who were. Which was an adventure in and of itself.

She'd never been to this particular place before, and there were a number of dishes that caught her eye. Trying new food was always a high point in her week.

Her preference was to have a meal herself and then take her friend's food to go. She loved to eat hers hot and fresh while people watching.

Today was shaping up to be a decent day. The sun was out, and the temperature was actually bearable. Some low clouds on the horizon threatened rain, but it was still a ways off.

The neighborhood they'd picked for their hiding place was a little south of middle-class. It wasn't a poor area by any means, but it was dedicated to working-class folk.

That kind of homogenization was useful in spotting people that didn't belong. The men and women they had watching the cameras were looking for people that didn't fit in, either in dress or action.

As a trained FBI agent, she noticed anything that was out of place. It was almost a subconscious process at this point. She was even better at it when she focused on a particular subject.

For example, she'd been watching the crowds as they made their way along the street in front of the deli. To one degree or another, most people fit in to the area in which they lived or worked.

Oh, there was the occasional person that stood out. The woman in the high-class outfit stalking along on stiletto heels was a good example.

Brenda considered the woman as she walked by and wondered what her story was. She didn't think the woman was suspicious. Just being dressed differently wasn't enough to set off her Spidey Sense.

The woman could be anything from a business owner coming down to check on something to a highly paid escort on the way to work. Hell, in Washington she might be a diplomat. There was no telling.

What Brenda could see of her as she waved down a cab was that the woman had no interest in anyone around her. Not even the guy who was angling to steal her purse.

Part of Brenda wanted to get involved and stop the crime that was about to occur right in front of her, but that would draw undue attention. The woman was about to learn a painful lesson in situational awareness.

Better a snatch and grab than something darker. Perhaps this would save her from walking blithely into a much worse assault some night.

The thief timed his attack perfectly. He waited until the woman was reaching for the handle on the cab door to make his move. His hand lashed out and snagged the woman's expensive-looking handbag as he sprinted away down the street toward Brenda.

The woman screamed at him to stop and took off after him. She was surprisingly fast on those tall heels. She'd never catch the man, but she was making a credible effort.

Brenda watched the thief run with interest. Was he going to duck into another vehicle or run down an alley? There was always the possibility that one of the bystanders would attempt to stop him, but the odds of that were actually much lower than most people thought.

It was all in the reaction time. It took seconds for people to realize what was going on and even more to decide if they should act or steer clear. By then the thief would be past them.

Unless, of course, someone in front of the thief figured it out and decided to intervene. Such as the large Asian man in the dark coat who stepped from a business just as the thief reached it.

The man extended one bulky arm directly in front of the sprinting criminal and clotheslined him. The runner somersaulted into the air and slammed facedown into the concrete.

Brenda winced. That was going to leave a mark. The Good Samaritan planted one large foot in the center of the man's back, pinning him to the ground just as effectively as a pin held an insect for study.

She watched the large man and felt a warning run down her spine. Something wasn't right about him.

The woman ran up and retrieved her purse, kicking the thief hard in the ribs and profusely thanking the man. Brenda couldn't hear his response, but it seemed low-key.

By now, other bystanders had gathered around and were restraining the thief. Someone had undoubtedly called the police, so it was time for Brenda to go.

Still, she couldn't dismiss the large man. She considered what it was about him that made her feel he was different while she waved down the waiter and asked for her to-go order and a box for her excellent food.

The answer occurred to her as the waiter returned with everything. It was the man's build. He looked just like Victor Holyfield. The proportions were *exactly* right. That man was a descendant of heavy-worlders.

The realization set her to looking for any possible companions. If he was an operative, he probably wasn't working alone.

While it was conceivable that the man had absolutely nothing to do with her and perhaps didn't even realize his own heritage, there weren't that many people with heavy-worlder genes on Earth.

Her ancestors had rescued four heavy-worlders after the fighting a thousand years ago. They'd kept excellent records of their genealogy since. They'd had to.

Victor might look like a bodybuilder, but his strength exceeded anyone's wildest expectations. He was designed to live on a world with three times the gravity anyone here faced.

The young man declared himself out of shape every chance he got, but there were limits on his lower-end body strength. She was sure he could flip a car. That kind of physical prowess stood out.

The Families had decided long ago that they couldn't allow those genes into the wild. They would raise all the wrong kinds of questions. So who was this fellow?

Brenda pulled her phone out and made a show of taking pictures of the ruckus. That brought her no extra attention because *everyone* was doing it. Social media consumed everything these days. Videos of this scene would be all over the Internet by now.

The man had finally disentangled himself from the grateful woman and was looking for a way out of the spotlight. That gave Brenda the perfect opportunity to snap a close-up of his face.

He turned and went back into the business he'd come from moments later.

Following a hunch, Brenda picked up the bag with her takeout and made her way around the block to the alley behind the row of buildings. Without seeming overly curious, she walked briskly past the alley and glanced down it.

As she'd suspected, the man had exited the rear of the business and was getting into a car. Three additional men with similar builds were joining him.

So much for coincidence. While she didn't know every person in the Families, there wouldn't be four people with heavy-worlder genes in one place like this accidentally. The fact that all four men were of Asian descent also struck her as odd.

She paused as soon as she passed the alley and stuck her phone out just enough to snap a few more pictures. At the very least, she'd get a license plate to run.

Moments later, the car came out and sped past her. She'd resumed walking and turned her head down to stare at her phone like everyone else around her. The car never even slowed down.

The events at Area 51, the call to someone at the Chinese embassy, and these men had to be connected in some way. The good news was that she now knew about the threat. The bad news was that they suspected she was in the area. That was the only answer that made any sense. Someone was onto them.

* * *

ONCE THE VOLUNTEER soldiers had begun making their way into the cave, Clayton made the decision to return to Earth with them. Someone had to be there to decide their eventual settlement.

He made certain that Mick Bird and Penny Cash were right there with him. They were his responsibility, and he'd see them safely home.

Clayton had to admit that even the destroyed base looked good after the situation they'd found themselves in. Part of him hadn't expected to make it home.

Jess followed him to a handy corner of the large room. "This isn't going to hold everyone, is it?"

He shook his head. "No. We're going to have to see them taken to other floors while the gate is open. Once everyone is here, we can move them to the surface. This is only temporary."

"I have a better plan. We've got full control of the gate now, so perhaps the base in France would be a better choice."

He had to agree, but if they had access to any of the other gates, there were better choices.

"I'm not sure that's the best choice in the long run," he said. "France is a very unstable country. If anyone discovers the base, there will be a lot of awkward questions or hostile actors making moves to seize it."

Jess seemed to consider that for a moment. "Perhaps we could use France as a staging base while we prepare *Freedom Express* for housing more people? Hell, the station in orbit around the frozen planet has more than enough space to hold everyone."

He raised an eyebrow. "The what? What frozen planet? Which station?"

She smiled. "That's right. You missed out on that. It's a long story, but we found something big out past the orbit of Pluto. Maybe even the reason the Asharim came to our system in the first place.

"But we don't have time to get into that yet. There's also the base on Mars. We have life support working there. It's probably big enough for this kind of influx, too."

Her expression took on a hint of unease. "We'll need to get them out of here as soon as possible, though. I made the decision to notify New Zealand's government that this place existed."

He frowned. "Why in the world would you do any such fool thing? That's going to greatly complicate our lives."

"Because it needed to be done," she said firmly. "It's only a matter of time before someone other than the United States learns we have this kind of technology. We need allies with clout in the international community."

"Such as New Zealand? It's a beautiful place but a little small, don't you think?"

"Yet it's very close to the Republic of Nauru. And let's not discount Australia and Japan. With China being so close to us, we need friends in our back pocket."

Clayton sighed. The island he'd literally bought control of was very close indeed. "Well, I suppose it's a little late for me to complain if you've already begun the process. Have you?"

Jess nodded. "I explained the basic situation to the leader of the team searching for you. She's seen the inside the base and is aware of the gates. She's up top right now, probably calling her bosses. We can expect company before too much longer."

"Then I suppose I should join her and begin making some calls."

She pulled the phone out of her pocket and handed it to him. "This is one of your quantum devices. Apparently it doesn't need cell towers."

He smiled. "Ah, I'd wondered when these would become available. If you'd be so kind, please make certain someone escorts our new friends as they go to the other floors. I don't want anyone becoming lost. If they wander away before we leave, they might become trapped."

"The buddy system. Got it. I'll make sure everyone stays in sight of everyone else."

Clayton watched her walk back over to the growing crowd and begin calling for their attention. He didn't pay specific attention to what she was telling them, though. His mind was racing with other thoughts. Trying to consider what options made the best sense.

Obviously, he'd have to stay here in New Zealand. He had to be here in order for the surrounding governments to trust him. He'd rather not have revealed the existence of this base, even in its ruined condition, but he supposed that would play out better in the long run.

The sad thing was that the government of New Zealand would probably invalidate the sale of the sheep station he'd bought here. That was a real pity. He truly loved the land around this base and wished it could remain among his holdings.

Well, there was no use crying over spilt milk. The first person he needed to call was his assistant. Clayton was going to need a lot of help to make sure the situation didn't spin out of control. The man could send as many bodies as he needed to talk to the various bureaucrats and elected officials.

In fact, he made a mental note to snag Penny to assist him before they arrived—and after. She was very astute and knew many of the local players.

He'd take her with him to the top of the mesa as soon as he finished this call. It was now their job to delay anyone from going below until Harry had seen everyone into the base and sealed that damned cave from the Asharim.

Jess would then take them all to the base in France. They'd go elsewhere after that, but Clayton wasn't in a position to make decisions relating to that. Not until he'd been briefed on everything he'd missed.

With any luck, the authorities would get this wrecked base but none of the people inside it. If Jess took the controller he saw attached to the gate with her, the entire thing would be useless.

But was that what he really wanted?

Perhaps Jess was right. If they went out of their way to show the surrounding governments what they had access to, those people would strongly defend this area. If he made a deal to share some of the technology, they would protect his interests in the region as well.

Yes, that was probably the best course of action.

The call he'd just dialed went through, and his assistant picked up. Clayton immediately launched into a list of what he needed and where he needed it. Time was critically short.

25

Kathleen Bennett stared curiously at the ruined city around them as their party exited the massive building that anchored the space elevator. The lines of the surrounding structures were distinctly different from what she was used to on Earth. Much like the inhabitants she had met, the buildings were tall and wide.

Even though they were standing, the buildings were no longer being maintained. That much was obvious. Some had huge cracks along their faces, and others were missing windows that made their sides look like empty skulls. Still, the fact that all the buildings hadn't collapsed spoke to the technical capabilities of the builders.

Their hosts—or perhaps their captors, depending on how one viewed their circumstances—led her son and her through wide boulevards that did not seem designed for ground traffic.

Even though long overgrown, it was obvious the spaces between buildings had been meant for growing things. Perhaps the entire city had once sported wide parks between the skyscrapers. She imagined it had been quite beautiful in its heyday.

Kerrick Vidar noted her gaze. "Do you not have cities such as this on your world?"

She shrugged. "Yes and no. We have large cities, but the buildings are not as tall and strong. On the other hand, ours aren't empty, either."

The man seemed to consider that for a moment as they walked. "Our people once lived in the city, or perhaps I should say near it. The Masters and their favored servants were the true occupants. My people either served in ships in orbit or lived and trained at military bases in the surrounding lands."

"And that changed when something befell the Asharim?"

"War. The Masters found themselves in a conflict with another species.

The time between the discovery of these others and the war that followed was short. The Masters tried to prepare and use the forces they had available, but they suffered greatly."

Kathleen didn't need to look around to see that was true. "Did they win?"

"I assume not, since they have never returned. Neither do I believe they lost. Surely those who sought to replace them would not have left us unmolested. The priests insist the Masters will one day return."

She tried to imagine what must've happened in the city around them and failed. "If the Masters and their trusted servants lived here, where did they go?"

"They used their gates to depart when things began turning against them. They left others to command us. Then they locked their gates and trapped us all here."

"Why haven't your people used the elevator to go to the station in orbit around your planet? You do know there is one up there, don't you?"

He shrugged. "Our ancestors did, hoping to find a way back to our home. Some great battle had taken place around this world, and all the ships were gone. Only wreckage remained. Once that was known, there was little need to return."

"Forgive me, but this world seems more like my home world than one where someone of your strength would be from. Did you come from here before the war?"

He shook his head. "The stories tell of a world with much more gravity. One that held us to her bosom so that only the strong thrived. The People likely still live there, but we have no way to return. This world is now our home."

Rather than engage him in further conversation, she let some time pass in silence. They quickly exited the center of the city and found an area cleared of buildings. It didn't appear there had ever been buildings here.

"What was this originally used for?" she asked.

"A large park, I believe. The city had many."

"I thought the areas between buildings were parks."

He shook his head. "Not precisely, but the vegetation in the parks expanded to fill that space as well."

Part of the area ahead of them was being used to raise crops, Kathleen noted. Other sections held relatively primitive buildings, like rustic villages back on Earth.

Men, women, and children waved cheerfully at the group as they passed. The men were built much like her new friends. The women, oddly enough, were more slender, though still stocky.

"Why are your men so much larger than your women?"

He laughed. "Because we were designed that way. As warriors, the men had to be very, very strong and imposing. Intimidation of our foes before the fighting began was one method to win. The Masters understood that.

"The strength of our women is quiet, subtle. Do not mistake that for weakness, though. They are as strong as the men, in their own way."

He let that sink in for a moment before he continued. "Tell me how you came to our world. Obviously, you came from the station above. You have a ship, then?"

Unsure of how much to tell the man, she glanced at her son. As he couldn't understand any of the conversation, he seemed just to be watching the area around them as they walked. His expression told her he was very unhappy at their current circumstances. She couldn't blame him.

Rather than consult him, she made the decision to be honest with their host. Not completely honest, of course. Only a fool did that. Yet, the best lies were ones planted in beds of truth.

"Yes. We arrived in a ship that is still in orbit around this world. We've come seeking allies in a war to control the home world. The place the Masters took you from."

The news didn't seem to disturb him, but it didn't seem he was very interested it, either. He walked in silence beside her for the next few minutes, and she let him stew.

Finally, he spoke. "While it is not my place to make that kind of decision for the People, I would still know more of the enemy you face. You have just arrived, and the People do not know you."

She gave him her most practiced open smile. "I'll tell you everything when the time is right. Who makes decisions like those for the People? Your priests?"

He nodded. "Anything involving the Masters must be decided by the priests. While you are not the Masters, you come from off world. They will see your presence as a sign. All that remains is for them to determine if it is for good or ill.

"When the time for fighting comes, I lead. Thankfully, the art of conducting war is one we still practice. The priests insist it remain so, since one day we may have to serve the Masters again."

"Tell me about the priests. What kind of people are they?"

Vidar shrugged. "The ways of priests are not for common folk like me. They spend their lives in contemplation of the Masters. I warn you that they do not have much in the way of humor about them. They are very single-minded in their goal to see the Masters returned to rule over us."

She could tell he didn't feel very enthused about that prospect. He was giving lip service to the Asharim, but Vidar would probably be pleased if they'd been exterminated. Personally, she shared his opinion.

So, the key to gaining allies on this world were the priests. If she could convince them that helping her take Earth would be a step toward returning the Masters—their gods, she imagined—to power, then she might be able to get them to provide military force that no one back home could resist.

Inside, she smiled. Finally, something she could manipulate to her benefit. These rubes should be a piece of cake.

* * *

Jess's stomach was rumbling by the time Harry ushered the last of the refugees through the gate and onto Earth. There'd been a lot more of them than she'd expected. She wasn't certain how much of the abandoned base was occupied now, but it had to be a lot.

There'd been a loud explosion and then the unmistakable rumble of falling stone just before he and the Navy officer came through. She'd known his intent to collapse the cave entrance, but the noise was far too similar to the cave-in at the Mayan pyramid for her taste. That still gave her nightmares.

He shut the gate down and entered the code for the French base as she held up her phone for him to read the address. Once the wormhole stabilized, he turned to the woman dressed like a pirate.

"The base on the other side of this is in our hands. We still haven't finished cleaning it up or exploring it. My brother—who is not a nice person, by the way—fought some other bad people there recently, so be warned: there's still blood on the floor."

Jess suspected the warning had been meant for her, too. It must still be pretty bad.

"I have seen battle before," the woman said. "What remains of the dead and dying is never a pretty sight, but we shall persevere. When will we be able to return to our homes?"

Harry shrugged. "We've got to give them time to back off. It'll also take a little while for me to gather enough men with modern weapons to take and hold the terrain around the hill. Once we can do that safely, we'll bring your people back through."

"I note you do not give the estimate I requested. I understand your uncertainty, but are we speaking of days, weeks, or months? I have my people to consider. If we are gone too long, the Asharim will strike at our homes. They are well defended, but without this army, our families are in unnecessary peril."

"Days," Harry said firmly. "A week at most. I can't imagine it being any longer than that."

"And I accept that circumstances may alter your intentions. Man plans, and God laughs."

Jess understood that sentiment. She stepped over to the gate and motioned for them to follow. "Let's get you set up inside the other base. Once we have everyone across, I'll see about getting food and supplies. We'll have medics come in to help the injured."

She knew for certain they had many of those. The fighting to get to the hill must've been ugly. Some of the humans from the other world had been shot.

A glance at the makeshift sick area told her that not everyone was going to make it. Some had already died. Standing around thinking about it wasn't going to help them, though. She needed to get this in motion.

Getting everyone moved through the gate they'd just come through took longer than Jess would've liked. She supposed the lack of people shooting at them sapped some of the urgency this time.

In the end, it took almost an hour to get everyone into the French base.

Thankfully, it was much easier to move people around here with the power on. Though the concept of elevators seemed like sorcery to the newcomers.

Sandra Dean and her sniper team had come inside the base to assist with triage for the wounded. They'd used one of the other gates to connect with *Freedom Express* and bring in every doctor and medic they had there. As soon as the triage was complete, they'd move the wounded to *Freedom Express* to expedite their treatment.

The floor and walls of the large gate room had splashes and dried pools of blood. The bodies had been removed, but the evidence of carnage was everywhere. The smell was terrible.

She added cleaning supplies and hands—willing or not—to her list of things to bring in.

The Volunteer military officer, General Norris, stepped over to her as soon as things were well in hand. "Someone called this place 'the French base.' Does it in fact belong to our old allies?"

Unlike far too many Americans these days, Jess had studied her history lessons hard. The French had been allies in the American rebellion against King George.

"Not precisely," she said softly. "The base is inside France, but the people here are unaware of it. Hardly anyone on Earth knows about the Asharim.

"That's going to change in the relatively near future, but for now, we're keeping the location of this base a secret. And unfortunately, the France you've heard about in your stories is a much different place these days. Do you know about Islam?"

The man shrugged. "I've seen it mentioned in our writings. None of its practitioners came across with the Volunteers."

That surprised her a little, but she really didn't know how many Muslims had been in revolutionary America.

"Like many religions, most Muslims are good people. Unfortunately, in the world we live in today, there are far too many using Islam—or rather its perversion—as an excuse to commit mass atrocities and murder. France has a large Muslim community.

"Again, mostly good people that just want to live their lives in peace. Yet the nonbelievers have been targeted by radicalized militants intent on overthrowing the French government and forming a caliphate.

"They, of course, want to take over the entire world in the process and murder anyone who doesn't agree with their ideas. The French people—Muslim and non—are fighting back against them, but I'm not sure how this is going to turn out."

The man looked crestfallen. "Oh, how I wish our people could lend them the same help that they offered us in our hour of need. Yet if you, with your own powerful weapons, are unable to stem the tide, I'm uncertain what we can do.

"I shall speak of this with Susanna. We must consider our options carefully. If there is some way that we can return the great boon the French people once gave America, then we must work diligently to discover it."

That was a lot more help than modern America seemed willing to give. They'd become isolationists, turning their backs on the world.

That would probably change once the mad scramble for the Asharim technology began in earnest, but she wouldn't hold her breath that things worked out well for the French people. That was something far beyond her control.

"Let's get everybody settled in and start bringing food for them," she said. "It's probably been a long time since you last ate. It probably won't be long before Harry comes looking for you, either. There's someone he wants you to meet."

26

It was after dinnertime when Brenda's people located the unknown heavy-worlders again. They'd moved to a restaurant on the other side of the neighborhood. Or perhaps they were just having something to eat and not using the place as a base of operations. Until they watched the men for a while, it would be hard to tell.

The heavy-worlders had no reason to suspect that anyone would recognize their genealogy on sight. Hell, they probably had never even suspected there were others of their kind on Earth.

Their kind. That wasn't exactly fair. They were as human as the people around them. Just enhanced.

She still wasn't sure what the men were looking for. Did they have a description of her? She wasn't sure how they'd have gotten it, unless they'd stolen it from the US government. She was at the top of the most wanted list, after all.

That made the most sense. If they knew about the Asharim technology—which they did—then they knew about her. Worse, they knew about the Families.

Maybe not by name, but the US government understood there was an organization of some kind associated with her. They'd almost certainly underestimated her people's numbers and reach, even after everything she'd told them.

If these men were descendants of the heavy-worlders that had been present in this system a thousand years ago, they had fully integrated into society. Most likely in China, based on where the clues were pointing and their own appearances.

The Families had never been active in China—not until recently—and their reach was still very limited there. Until a hundred years ago, the damned place had been closed off from the outside world in every way that mattered.

She wondered how much of that had been the doing of these people and their ancestors.

Now that she had eyes on them, she wanted to be absolutely certain they didn't realize they'd been made. They still thought they were operating in complete secrecy. Even the information she'd passed on to Secretary of State Queen didn't mention them, since she hadn't known what she was facing at the time.

She wondered whether or not she should tell Queen about them and their ancestry but decided against it. He was smart enough to figure that out on his own. Her speaking slowly and clearly, as if to a five-year-old, wouldn't be helpful, though it might be satisfying.

The sight of the four men on the monitor mesmerized Victor. With the number of heavy-worlders being limited inside the Families, he'd probably thought he'd known every one of them on the planet. This had to be a great shock.

"What are you thinking?" she asked him.

He shrugged. "I'm not sure what to think. These people are like bogeymen from the past. If they're the descendants of heavy-worlder fighters that never converted to supporting humanity, they're probably enemies. That's a whole new level of screwed up."

She clapped the young man on the shoulder, feeling his tense thick muscles under the skin. It was like slapping a brick wall. "At least you'll have somebody to arm wrestle with now."

He laughed. "I suggest you keep your day job. Comedy isn't in your future."

The phone Jessica Cook had given her rang. She stared at it for a moment, certain that this couldn't be good. Then she answered it. "Talk to me."

"I'd like to see you in person," Harry Rogers said. "Events are in progress that you need to be aware of, and I've got some interesting people for you to meet."

His idea of 'interesting' was probably a lot different than hers. Still, based on everything she'd seen, it wouldn't be boring.

"Give me ten minutes to get down to the gate room and power it up."

She disconnected the call and pocketed the phone. "Victor, keep an eye on those guys, and let me know if anything changes. If they lead you back to their hiding place, I want to know about it before you make a move."

"You got it, Boss."

Brenda sauntered out into the lobby and waited for the elevator to be clear. Once she could get into it alone, she hit the button for the basement. The button blinked three times and she knew it was reading her fingerprint.

That was a security measure to keep any of the curious residents from going to take a peek for themselves. Anyone not cleared for the knowledge would just think the button was broken.

Once she made it to the makeshift gate room, she gestured for the man at the table to power it on. They'd started keeping the power cube disconnected so that no one could open a connection without letting them know ahead of time.

Not that she expected Rogers to betray them. It was just common sense. That's also why she had four heavily armed men on duty here at all times.

A few minutes later, the wormhole formed, and Harry Rogers walked through with two of the most outlandishly dressed people Brenda had ever seen at his side.

The woman to his right was dressed like someone out of *Pirates of the Caribbean*. All that was missing was a gold hoop earring and a parrot.

The distinguished gentleman on the other side of her ally had seemingly stepped out of the painting of George Washington crossing the Delaware. In fact, he bore a striking resemblance to the first president.

Brenda spent a moment assessing everyone before she focused her attention on Harry Rogers. "When you say interesting, you mean it. Who are your friends?"

"Brenda Cabot, meet Susanna Adorno and General Norbert Norris. I found them on the planet my father recently visited. He's safely home, by the way.

"I thought you might be interested in how they made their way off Earth. They left from our side of the pond either before or during the Revolutionary War."

That surprised her. Her people hadn't had access to a power supply for the gate, and while she knew that Harry Rogers and his people had located several bases on Earth, the Families hadn't been aware of any them, and none of the ones he'd mentioned had been inside the United States.

"You have my attention now," Brenda said. "Miss Adorno, General Norris, it's a pleasure to meet you."

She extended her hand to the woman first. Rogers had introduced her before the general, so she was making the assumption the woman was the man's superior.

Susanna Adorno's grip was firm. "Mistress Cabot. Mister Rogers has spoken very highly of you. The allies of my allies are my own as well."

The woman's accent was like what Brenda imagined someone from the Caribbean would sound like.

General Norris shook Brenda's hand a little less forcefully, for which she was grateful. It was never a good thing when a man wanted to get into a hand-crushing contest to show how big his balls were. As an FBI agent, she'd met all too many men who wanted to do that.

"Mistress Cabot," the supposed military officer said.

"The current form of address favors Miss rather than Mistress," she said with a smile. "General, if I might say so, you look rather like paintings I've seen of George Washington."

The man nodded. "I've been told my family and his are connected in some way. It's a great honor to be a distant cousin of the great general, of course.

I've never seen a painting of him. If the opportunity presents, I would be deeply appreciative of the chance to do so."

"I'll see what I can do. Perhaps the three of you would care for something to drink while Harry fills me in on what's going on."

Ten minutes later, they were seated around the table in her small kitchen. The homey room made the two people from off planet seem even more out of place, if that was possible.

She'd brewed them all some tea. As she might've expected, the strangers wanted theirs hot while Rogers and she took theirs iced.

After taking a sip, Brenda focused her attention on Susanna. "If you don't mind, I'd rather let you tell me your story in your own words, without asking questions. There's plenty of time for me to do so when you're finished."

"A sensible plan," the other woman said.

Brenda listened to what she'd have considered a tall tale under other circumstances. Yet the woman's very existence argued it was true. There had once been a gate in the Caribbean, just outside of the infamous Port Royale.

More amazingly, it had been under the control of humans that both knew how to use it and were unknown to the Families. That was shocking, really. Who had these people been? Why hadn't they sought out others here on Earth?

The mysteries just kept rolling in.

The general's story about the Volunteers was even more interesting. A gate hidden deep in a cave somewhere in Virginia. How the hell had it gotten there and why? Who'd activated it and sent them through to this other world?

Since her instructors at the Academy had verbally beaten the concept of coincidence out of her, she was certain they must be the same people. Why else send both groups to the same location?

The fact that the two events had taken place almost a century apart argued that these individuals were still present on Earth today. The Families hadn't seen or heard of them in the intervening centuries, but she couldn't take the chance that they'd just vanished somewhere.

Odds were now good there was another player in the games afoot. One that none of them had considered before and one with aims that no one could guess at. Still, she'd best make sure before they assumed that these newcomers hadn't met the Chinese players.

"Tell me, do the old stories of your journey indicate the people running these gates were from the Orient?" Orient wasn't commonly used today, but she hoped it was recognizable to these folks.

"No," Adorno said. "The tales don't mention someone of exotic appearance. My assumption is that the men in the Caribbean look like everyone else around them. I have always seen them as dark-skinned in my mind."

General Norris seemingly agreed with her thoughts. "The volunteers believed the people running the gate were very much like themselves. There were colonists with dark skin—some brought unwillingly, to my personal distaste—but the people of the stories were of the same skin tone as myself, I believe."

The man leaned forward. "I am making an assumption, based on my limited observation, that you are not a slave. The Volunteers made the choice when we founded our society that that institution had no place in decent human company. Is that also true here?"

She nodded. "It wasn't as cleanly done here, and the repercussions of slavery are still felt in America today. No, I'm not a slave and no one in America has been for almost two centuries. Sadly, that still doesn't mean everyone is seen as equal."

The man shook his head and sighed. "It is always a great disappointment when the icons of one's youth have feet of clay. On behalf of my ancestors, I apologize."

"We all have our burdens to bear," she said philosophically. "Thank you for your concern."

Brenda suspected that the people running the two gates hadn't looked like one another. The ones in the Caribbean had probably been much darker than the ones in Virginia. That spoke of a somewhat larger organization, since she refused to believe there were two separate groups using the same destination code.

"By any chance, do you happen to know in which part of Virginia this cave is located?" she asked the man.

"That's actually what we're hoping you can assist us with," Rogers said. "If we can locate this base or gate, if it's just stashed somewhere deep inside a cave, it would give my people a way to access locations here in the United States that doesn't rely on traipsing through your hidden base."

Brenda shook her head firmly. "If there's a base inside the United States, my people want it. You already have more than enough. We can provide you with the portable gate in exchange, but if there's a permanent facility, we deserve it. So long as it's in good shape."

The man smiled. "Somehow I suspected you'd say something like that. I'm willing to be reasonable. I don't particularly care how this works out. If we find a fully operational base—or anything close to it—that you can take over, you're welcome to it in exchange for your portable gate."

She nodded decisively and extended her hand to him. "Then you've provisionally got a deal."

If they could locate an old base like he'd already found, the amount of equipment inside could be a game changer. The Families had been operating without the kind of technology their ancestors had once had. They'd be willing to deal if they could regain it.

Assuming the previous owners weren't still in charge of it, but that was an entirely different situation.

"Let me bring up some maps on my tablet, and we'll see if we can narrow down the location," she said. "I can also show you a picture of General Washington.

"Actually, I should say President Washington. I'm not sure you know, but he was elected the first leader of our country. This is the United States of America, by the way."

General Norris smiled. "I did not know of his election, but it cheers my heart. I've heard the name of our parent country before, but we were still fighting for it when the Volunteers left this world. There is so much history that my people do not know about this nation. What a wonderful time in which to live."

Brenda couldn't argue with that. She retrieved her tablet and began searching for maps from the Revolutionary War. Those would look more familiar to the man, she suspected. With any luck, they might be able to put a search party in motion tonight. Things were starting to look up.

27

Nathan was getting tired of listening to his mother and the stranger jabber on in the alien language. He wanted to know what the hell they were saying to one another. Yet he could hardly complain about the muscular bastard not being able to speak English.

Which did absolutely nothing to improve his mood.

The group was arriving in a large village on the far edge of the wilderness zone inside the ruined city. The wilds seemed to stretch out in a radial fashion from the center where the space-elevator building was located. Perhaps there were others villages like it spread out through the damned thing.

They'd passed through several clusters of dwellings, but this one seemed larger than the rest. Not any better constructed than the previous ones, but this one had more people living inside it. And there was a building that seemed more important than the rest. Or perhaps more *self-important*.

This one was at least four stories tall—two more than the buildings around it—and was covered with what appeared to be religious carvings. Something related to the aliens, he believed.

The beings shown in bas-relief were as tall and willowy as the ones they'd heard about in relation to the aliens. Ugly bastards. Why anyone would want to show any reverence at all for them made him shake his head.

A number of men dressed differently than the ones who'd captured them came out of the building. They weren't dressed for doing everyday tasks in those long obstructive robes. Just considering how unwieldy their hats were, this had to be some type of ceremonial regalia.

These had to be priests or something. Great. Religion never improved a situation, it just made things worse. With his luck, human sacrifice was next on the schedule.

The leader of the group who'd captured them led his mother up the wide steps to stand before this group of self-important bastards. He spoke in that same indecipherable language that he and Nathan's mother had been using.

The man standing in the center of the group at the top of the stairs—the one with the tallest, stupidest looking hat—stared down haughtily and responded sharply.

That didn't seem to disturb the man who'd brought them here, but he bowed slightly from the waist and took two steps back. That left Nathan's mother standing alone.

Nathan took the opportunity to head up the stairs and stand beside his mother. It almost made him laugh when they both shot him mirrored looks of irritation. It seemed he could offend family and aliens at the same time. It was a gift.

The Grand Pooh-Bah said something to Nathan. When he shrugged back, the man repeated the words more slowly and in a louder tone. Yeah, that was going to make him understand an alien language more easily. Idiot.

Nathan made a show of smirking at the man and then shrugged elaborately. "Sorry, asshole. I don't speak your idiotic language."

"God dammit, Nathan!" his mother said sharply. "Shut your stupid mouth."

"Why? It's not as if he can understand me. I can say anything I want, like how retarded his hat looks. Like a giant penis on his head. Maybe I should call him the Grand Dickhead. That's perfect!"

Apparently, comprehension wasn't strictly required to determine when someone was being insulting. The man in front of Nathan grabbed him by the throat and lifted him off his feet with one hand.

Nathan kicked him while he used his hands to beat at the man's arm, but it was like hitting a concrete wall and a steel bar. None of Nathan's efforts even made the man wince. This wasn't good.

His mother said something in the alien language using an imploring tone.

The man stared coldly into Nathan's eyes for a moment then tossed him to the men standing nearest the entrance to the building.

Even as Nathan sucked in great drafts of air, the other men gripped his arms and legs roughly and carried him inside.

He'd been kidding about the human sacrifice part. Seriously.

Nathan shouted for his mother to stop them, but she didn't answer. She was leaving him to his fate. Bitch.

If anything, the inside of the building was even more garishly decorated than the outside. Certain sections of it were well lit, highlighting works of what looked like precious metals and sculptured stone.

His captors' rough handling prevented Nathan from seeing anything clearly, but he thought many of the objects were shaped like the aliens. That was just screwed up.

The men quickly carried him to a room in the rear of the building and down some narrow steps. Unlike the rest of the building, the room at the bottom had advanced equipment in it. Just based on the layout and shape of the consoles and machines, this was Asharim technology.

There was a wide chair sitting in the middle of the room with an extensive headset perched above it. The men slammed him into the chair and held his arms and legs in place while others secured thick straps around them. No amount of struggle did him the least bit of good.

Someone strapped a band around his forehead, brutally yanking his neck back as they tightened it. When they were done, Nathan couldn't move at all. Then they lowered the complex-looking headset down over his head.

No, this wasn't menacing at all.

The Grand Dickhead walked slowly down the stairs and into the room. He set his giant penis hat on a handy console and said something low and menacing to Nathan.

Nathan would have shot him the finger, but part of him was afraid the bastard would chop his hand off. There were limits to his insolence after all.

Another man ran down the steps with some kind of book in his hands. It was large, with gold inlay on the dark leather cover. He held it up so that the Grand Dickhead could flip to a specific page and see it clearly without having to bend over.

After consulting the displayed page for a few moments, the Grand Dickhead walked to one of the consoles and brought it to life. The book carrier followed him faithfully.

The Grand Dickhead manipulated the display and then stared at Nathan. With a cold toothy grin, he pressed something, and intense agony shot through Nathan's skull.

Nathan heard someone screaming and only belatedly realized that it had to be himself. He wanted the pain to stop, but there was nothing he could do about it. He was completely within their power.

It might have lasted five minutes or five hundred, for all he knew, but the pain eventually ceased. Nathan sagged, panting hoarsely. Based on the stench, he'd soiled himself. Oh, the bastard was going to pay for that.

The Grand Dickhead was standing in front of him with his hands planted firmly on his hips. His smile, if anything, was even wider than before.

"I'm going to kill you," Nathan muttered roughly. "When you least expect it, I'll plant a knife in the center of your back and leave you to bleed out."

"You're not the first to want me dead, and you'll hardly be the last," the man responded with a laugh.

Nathan gaped. "How did you learn English?"

The sonofabitch laughed harder. "Fool. It is below my dignity to use any language other than that of the Masters, which is what you are now soiling with your impudent mouth."

What? That couldn't be right. "How is that possible?"

When Nathan focused on the syllables coming out of his mouth, they were definitely not English. "Who the hell are you?"

"My name is Jedan Louvan, and I am High Priest of the Masters." He slapped Nathan so hard his head rang. "That is for your earlier insolence. Prepare him."

Nathan spat blood and tried to slow the spinning room. "Prepare me? For what?"

"What would be the fun in telling you that?"

* * *

HARRY LOOKED at the map on his phone then squinted into the early morning sun. He hadn't wanted to wait to start looking, but darkness had been too close yesterday. Now they had time to search. They'd pulled over to the side of the road in an attempt to reconcile the rough—very rough—map they'd settled on to the actual terrain.

Automobiles had shocked Susanna Adorno and General Norris. They both sat in the back of the SUV, where the tinted windows helped conceal their terror from the general public.

Harry and Brenda had talked the two into changing clothes so they didn't stand out like sore thumbs. Not that they looked comfortable in the modern garments, but at least they weren't drawing the eye of every single person they came across.

Their fear didn't spring from the strange technology so much as the speed with which it traveled. It seemed horses hadn't made the trip to the new world, so foot power was the fastest mode of transport they'd ever seen before.

He had to admit they were being good sports about it, though. They'd swallowed their unease and clenched their handrests until he feared for the plastic but had still taken it all in stride.

"It's hard to believe this is the Virginia out of legend," Norris said after they'd driven a ways. "Even here, far from the bustling metropolis that is our nation's capital, there are so many people. It is difficult for me to imagine how you can farm enough land to feed them all."

"Technology helps with that," Harry said. "Some of the best farmland in the US hadn't been discovered when you left Earth. Now it grows enough food for our nation and also provides a surplus that feeds the hungry around the world."

Susanna gestured out the window. "And all of it is covered by roads such as this? Each person has a vehicle such as this one?"

"Pretty much," Brenda Cabot said from the driver's seat. "Oh, the vehicles differ from person to person, but most people have one. Only the very poorest in our society get by without one.

"We couldn't travel across the country, or even the city we live in, without one. Though they have buses, like the one I showed you as we drove out of Washington. Buses help those without automobiles get from place to place inside major cities. Out here in rural areas, though, things are a lot different."

"It is difficult to believe that so many people can live in a single location," Susanna said. "While it is not the same as the ruined city of the Asharim, it is still immense in scope."

"You should see New York," Harry said with a grin. "It's starting to come into the same scale as the Asharim city. And the residents are even ruder."

That left the two newcomers sitting in silence trying to process what that might look like.

Harry used the opportunity to bring up a map of the area on the SUV's console. After a few minutes of study, he gave up trying to reconcile the old map with reality as it existed today.

He turned in his seat and gazed at the rest of them. "I think we're about as close as we're going to get without actually walking into the woods. Frankly, it's amazing that there's even a road this close to the general area where you think this cave is located.

"I think you're right that the line of hills just off the road is probably where the cave sits. The terrain is suited to something like that. The problem is going to be locating it. If it was in plain sight, someone would've stumbled across it by now."

"I may be able to assist with getting past that stumbling block," Susanna said. "Over the years, I've heard many different versions of this story. A few speak of a specific outcropping that resembles the rising sun. Surely such a unique feature will aid in finding a concealed entrance."

Harry did a quick search of the web and came up empty. If such an outcropping existed, it wasn't public knowledge.

"Do we have any idea who owns this property?" Brenda asked. "I'd like to avoid getting shot for trespassing or having the police come ask us some very awkward questions."

"This is actually public land, believe it or not," Harry said. "I have no idea what they intend to use it for—or even if they intend to use it at all—but we have as much right to be here hiking as anyone else."

Brenda stared out at the rough brambles on the side of the road. "I don't think we'll find many people hiking through here."

"Maybe not," he admitted. "It's a good thing we put on good boots and jeans."

"These boots are exceptional," Norris agreed. "I should like to keep them, if you have no objection. They are more comfortable than any I have ever owned and seem most sturdy."

"Feel free," Brenda said. "Does the map show a place we can park?"

He considered the map and nodded. "There's a side road about a quarter mile ahead. We can leave a note on the dash that says we broke down and will be back for the car. It's not as likely to get stolen out here."

"It's a long walk back if it is," Brenda said with a note of resignation in her voice. "Still, that's better than anything I can think of. Let's go find a hidden cave."

28

Clayton stood with Molly Goodwin on top of the mesa and waited for their incoming visitors. Thankfully, due to the isolation of the area, it had taken quite a while to convince anyone he was serious about needing to speak with someone with real authority.

That had allowed plenty of time for the people displaced from the Volunteers' world to make it to the French base. Now there was no one below to be caught up in any trouble.

In fact, the only people here that were in potential trouble were the American military group. That was particularly true now that the CIA weasel they'd imprisoned was free.

The entire time they'd been in the Volunteers' world, they'd stashed Agent Ulysses in a side cave. Clayton suspected Gunnery Sergeant Danvers had gagged the man. Two of the military personnel still held the idiot with his hands secured behind him. Only now, his mouth was free to rave.

"You're all going to prison," Ulysses said, his mouth actually frothing. "Starting with you, Rogers. You're going straight to Guantánamo Bay. The rest of you have Fort Leavenworth in your future."

Molly shook her head as she stared at the disagreeable man. "What makes you think you're not in trouble? You came to New Zealand and kidnapped our citizens as well as those under our protection. It's you that's going to jail."

Ulysses laughed harshly. "Don't be naïve. You're not going to lock up a representative of the United States government. We'd squash you like bugs. In fact, by the time this is all over, we'll be in possession of this facility, and you'll be thankful for it. Only we can protect you from the aliens."

"It's almost as if he's a caricature," Clayton said, still not really believing the man's performance. "All he needs is a mustache to twirl and some railroad tracks to tie someone to."

The woman chuckled. "He seems more like one of those people suited to a goatee. One that he strokes while revealing his wicked plan."

"Laugh while you can," Ulysses sneered. "Once our ambassador becomes aware of what you're doing, this all comes to an end. Enjoy it while you can."

Clayton pulled Molly a little farther to the side. "I've spoken with Mick and Penny. We truly don't hold anything against the military personnel. I'd prefer to see them released to their ship. None of these unfortunate circumstances was of their doing.

"I realize the whole 'I was just following orders' bit doesn't excuse everything. Still, I would like to see everyone's wrath focused on someone actually calling the shots, such as the CIA agent in charge of the operation.

"If your government could find it in their hearts to slap these gentlemen's wrists and send them back to their ship, I will cheerfully pay for any damages they have inflicted. I'm also certain that I have other information and equipment to offer as a sweetener."

Molly shrugged. "That's outside my purview, but I'll pass everything along when the authorities get here. It won't be long now. I'm more concerned about you."

"Me?"

"You were looking for a hidden alien base when you bought this property. I haven't got the slightest idea what laws you might've broken, but I suspect there's something they're going to hold against you."

Clayton smiled. "Then I suppose it's a good thing I have diplomatic immunity. Personally, I'm going to miss this place. It's very beautiful."

"It sure is," she agreed. "This mesa would've made an excellent spot for a grand home to look out over the wilderness."

About that time, he heard the low thrum of a helicopter in the distance. It sounded as though they were about to have company. Time to put on his game face.

"No matter how this turns out, I'd like to thank you and your people for coming out to search for me. Very few people recognize what good folks like yourself do for those in dire straits.

"I've already made an arrangement with my assistant to make a large donation to all of the groups involved to show my deep appreciation. In addition, I'd like you to accept a personal gratuity."

"I can't," Molly said. "I'm a government employee. That bars me from accepting anything that might look like a bribe."

He chuckled. "I've given far more bribes in my life than you could possibly believe. Trust me when I say that I can come up with a gift that is not a bribe but one that you will appreciate."

Off in the distance, he saw the approaching black dot of the helicopter. It rapidly covered the distance and began circling the mesa. Probably to make sure everything seemed safe to land.

A minute later, it settled to the rock about fifty meters off. Clayton could now see it was a military aircraft and that it was full of armed troops. They'd come expecting trouble. Good.

The helicopter doors opened, and all those soldiers came fanning out to cover everyone. The US military personnel had already taken the precaution of stacking their weapons off to the side. There was no need to invite trouble, after all.

The next person to exit the helicopter was a distinguished-looking gentleman with wavy gray hair and a suit that was both well styled and extremely out of place in the wilderness.

The man looked everyone over before he walked to Clayton and extended his hand. "Mister Rogers. I'm Isaiah Vaughn, assistant to the prime minister. I'm glad to see that our searchers located you. I confess that all too many folk who wander off into the wilderness back here don't have such a happy outcome."

Clayton shook the man's hand firmly. "I'm pleased to have come out of this intact, Mister Vaughn. I'd like to thank you, your government, and all of the searchers for the efforts you put out to ensure my safety. They are greatly appreciated, and I will, of course, reimburse all costs related to it."

"You're very welcome."

The official turned his attention to the US soldiers. His expression grew grim. "You gentlemen are far less welcome. You are illegally operating on the soil of New Zealand, and there are going to be grave consequences for each and every one of you."

Ulysses laughed coldly. "Please. Blah blah blah. You're not going to do anything to us, so let's not even pretend. Get on with your speech so we can get back to our ship.

"And if you know what's good for you, you'll send that traitor with us with the little show of resistance you no doubt have planned. The consequences if you don't are going to be extreme."

"I don't believe you know what extreme consequences are," the New Zealander said coldly. "I can think of a number of very serious crimes you've committed on our soil. If you see the outside of a cell in the next two decades, I'll be astonished."

Clayton cleared his throat. "I believe it would be in our mutual interest if you secured Agent Ulysses somewhere we don't have to listen to him rant. It become less pleasant by the minute."

Vaughn gestured toward Ulysses. Several of his men roughly secured the CIA agent and shuffled him off toward the helicopter. He resisted and shouted dire threats, but that did him absolutely no good.

"Take the rest of them as well," Vaughn said.

Clayton smiled and held up a hand. "If I might have a few words first, I think that action might be a bit precipitous."

The other man gave him a quizzical look and gestured for his soldiers to pause. "I'm not sure I understand. Aren't these the men who tried to kidnap you? Unless I miss my guess, they were going to take you to some black site where no one would ever see you again."

"Indeed. Still, we've come to an arrangement."

"That may be, but you're not the one to make those decisions."

"I was under the impression that Miss Goodwin told you what we found here."

"All I've heard are a lot of tall tales and frankly unbelievable stories that I'm inclined to blame on the great stress you've been under. Why she felt the need to tell anyone something like that on your behalf, I have no idea."

Clayton pulled his phone out and dialed a number. "Come get us."

The Asharim shuttle rose from the forest about a kilometer away and flew quickly to the mesa. It hovered silently above them.

He watched with a smile as the government official and the soldiers with him gaped at the impossible ship over their heads.

"Some versions of insanity come with props. Mister Vaughn, everything you've heard is completely true. More, it's only the tip of the iceberg. These soldiers are the very least of your concerns. Trust me on that."

* * *

CHEN ARRIVED at his new office with mixed emotions. Being thrown out of the country in which he'd resided for so long had an emotional impact, after all.

To balance that out, he was only just south of America's border. The Yucatán Spaceport would serve his needs quite well.

There was also some pleasure in being able to sit in something his enemies desired more than anything else. Something he'd taken from them.

Oh, not directly. Rogers had sold the Yucatán Spaceport to the Chinese government. Yet Chen had urged them to use force to take it back when the Americans seized it.

Without a spaceport, the Americans wouldn't be using that pretty little ship they'd forced the Indian government to sell them. Well, they weren't going to be able to use it due to other actions, but this was just icing on the cake, so to speak.

The loss of the Asharim artifacts was only the first of the Americans' setbacks and not the most painful. Now that the Dragon knew there was a base inside the caldera of Olympus Mons, they couldn't allow even the potential for any other group to travel to Mars.

Today was the day they made certain the Americans never left the surface of the Earth again. That single move would cement the future in the Dragon's favor forever.

The office that Chen had taken over was well appointed and had probably belonged to Clayton Rogers at some point. That was fitting, too.

He didn't know where the old man was at this point, but Chen suspected he'd turn up eventually. Dealing with Rogers and his son was going to be significantly more complicated than stopping the Americans from reaching Mars. The man's company was already in orbit around the Red Planet, after all.

Worse, those forces would know the Chinese spaceship was coming weeks before it arrived. The only saving grace was that the Dragon would make sure the Mars mission they sent was more than capable of eliminating any threats they might meet.

Chen settled himself at the desk, picked up the phone, and dialed his superior's number.

"Wu."

"Minister Wu. I have arrived at the Yucatán Spaceport. Might I inquire as to the status of my suggestion?"

Coming with the backing he'd had, his "suggestion" that the Chinese government use military force to seize or disable the Indian-built Mars ship was actually an order. All that remained was to discover which choice of options they'd taken.

"Ah, Chen. It's good to hear your voice. I'm pleased you've relocated successfully. Indeed, they have decided upon a course of action. One that will have permanent reverberations across the globe.

"Even as we speak, we are preparing one of our concealed satellite weapons. Very soon, the only other ship capable of reaching Mars will no longer exist."

Chen smiled. "That is indeed good news, Minister. I take it that that also means our ship is prepared to depart. I fear the Americans will retaliate in kind if it does not."

"Then lay your fears to rest. Our ship will depart before we take action."

"Am I to communicate our intentions to the Americans before our strike takes place?"

"No. The decision was made to allow the strike to speak for itself. So far as we are concerned, the Americans initiated this war by seizing the spaceport in which you sit. All we are doing is making certain our assets are in no further danger and repaying their temerity."

That wasn't quite the smartest play, Chen thought, but it wasn't his call to make. Indeed, it hardly mattered what the Americans did in response to the Chinese provocation. The world order was about to change, and change favored the Dragon.

"I understand, Minister. I will await your instructions."

Once the call was done, Chen leaned back in his comfortable new chair and considered the future. Oh yes, things were about to get very interesting indeed. All he had to do now was wait.

29

Jess didn't think the French base was going to be a good place to house the Volunteers over the long-term. Even having worked for years in space, the artificial corridors would drive her nuts over time. She could only imagine how someone used to living out in a nature setting would react to that kind of confinement.

Still, this didn't have to be a permanent thing. Once Harry managed to gather enough force, he could return to their world and clear out the zone around the hill. Once he did that, all of these people could go home.

Meanwhile, they were making themselves useful. The battle between Harry's brother and the Islamic extremists at the base had made quite a mess. The bodies were gone, but the bloodstains remained. Extra hands for cleaning duty were most welcome.

As soon as she found time, she pigeonholed Kevin McHugh. As expected, he was examining one of the gates when she cornered him. He'd gotten a comp to replace the one he'd left with Clayton Rogers and had plugged it into a gate.

"I thought you'd already checked these out," she said as she stepped up beside him.

"I did. I'm looking at something else now. There has to be a way to restrict outside access. I mean, the Asharim had these things in their homes. Surely you don't want to have a door that anyone can open from the outside in a place like that."

"I can help with that. I found it on *Freedom Express*."

She found and showed him the screen with the orange knot that locked the gate.

"This part is easy," she said. "What might be more useful would be the ability to authorize only certain gates to connect or restrict them to certain times of the day. It seems like that would make sense."

"Exactly what I was thinking. If I can locate the subroutines that authorize that kind of behavior in the computer, I can lock these gates down so that only friendly people can connect rather than completely sealing them off."

He gestured meaningfully around at the people cleaning the room. "I'd sure like to avoid having the people that caused all this mess come back for a repeat performance."

Jess couldn't argue with that kind of logic. "You look for that while I do something else. We had two addresses that looked like somewhere a small ship could go. We figured out which one was the moon. I'd like to know where the other one lets out."

She walked over to the next gate and brought out a handheld controller. After consulting her phone, she entered the address that led to the mountain range she'd seen in the video they'd recovered from the fighter.

The gate cycled through and opened onto a late-night view of what looked like the same mountainous area. The full moon bathed everything in silver.

Being careful to only extend her upper body through the gate, Jess checked that this wasn't a sheer cliff. It wasn't, but that didn't mean she had a lot of room to maneuver. The gate sat on the side of a mountain, all right. It was inside a relatively enclosed space, but she wouldn't call it a cave. It was more like a massive divot.

The floor of the arca seemed natural enough and extended out from the gate about ten meters. Being careful of her footing, she stepped through the gate and edged up to the opening.

There was a breathtakingly sheer drop into the dark jungle below. The light from the French base gave her enough illumination to see the entire area around the gate.

There was no base here. This was just an exit for small ships. Pity. With a sigh, she went back through the gate and killed the connection.

She was just working herself up to helping clean up the bloody mess when Sandra Dean came into the room. The sniper immediately altered course and headed right for her.

"Good," the other woman said. "I was hoping to find you."

"Why is that? Nothing good I'm sure."

"My, haven't you turned into a pessimist? I wouldn't call this good news, but at least it's not overtly bad."

Jess smiled wryly. "Lay it on me."

"One of my people is monitoring the local police bands. They found the cars we moved away from the base. That's got them buzzing."

After the fight between Nathan and the Islamic militants, there had been no survivors left at the French base. Thankfully, it was isolated enough that no one had noticed all the vehicles they'd left behind.

It had taken Rex and his people all night and several trips to move the vehicles fifty kilometers away. That was still a bit close for her comfort, but they'd only had one night to make it happen.

"You're right. That's not good news. What do you think the odds are they're going to trace any of the activity back here?"

Sandra shrugged. "I have no idea. Rex and I have worked out an evacuation plan to get everyone to *Freedom Express* if someone comes sniffing around. They're not going to come in guns blazing. We'll have plenty of warning."

Jess supposed that was true, but she'd hate to lose this facility. Of all the bases they'd found on Earth, this was the only one in operational condition.

"If trouble comes knocking, we're not going to be able to move our refugees in a timely fashion," she said after a moment. "We need to start relocating them if we even suspect we're going to have company."

"And on the flip side, since we don't have a means of locking the gates so only we can use them yet, if bad guys come calling, we need to be able to get everyone up to the surface and away from danger. We have to keep them unlocked for Clayton to execute his plan."

Sandra considered that and nodded slowly. "If Nathan Bennett and his thugs come back, we'll give them a hot reception, but that means innocent bystanders stand a very good chance of being hurt."

Jess turned toward the gates. "He hasn't come back yet. After the ship he and his mother were on went through that massive gate, we haven't heard a word from them. Maybe they didn't make it."

"Last we saw, they were trapped on that ship with a bunch of hostiles," Sandra said. "It's always possible they lost that fight, but we can't take that for granted. That's why Rex has those men over in the corner. They'll give any hostiles an extremely warm welcome."

Jess sighed. "Christ. I hate not knowing what they're doing. I'd rather they'd just make their move and be done."

* * *

Kathleen put her best face on as she sat waiting for the high priest to return. She was more nervous about Nathan's fate than she cared to admit to herself.

Yes, the little weasel had gotten himself into this trouble. And yes, she'd made the decision that her life would be a lot simpler without him. That still didn't make this process easy. She was a mother, for God's sake.

She'd rather not be the one *directly* responsible for his death. It would be a lot better for all concerned if he managed to go out in a blaze of glory because of his own idiocy. Perhaps that could be arranged if she played her cards right.

About an hour after he'd departed, Jedan Louvan returned. He stalked into the room where she waited without bothering to knock.

Kathleen rose to her feet, hiding the irritation she felt at his rudeness. "Were you able to teach my son how to speak the language of the Masters?"

The man grunted. "Yes, but that does not make him any less of a savage. He is rude, insulting, and uncouth. Blasphemous, too, though I must overlook some aspects of his behavior, as he is not aware of the full scope of the Masters."

"That's true of everyone on Earth. A year ago, we had no idea the Masters even existed. You're the first person we've met that could explain them to us. We have a lot to learn."

He sat, waving to one of his acolytes. "Bring us drinks and cakes. Veristar juice."

Kathleen noted he didn't ask what her preferences were. Apparently, she was getting what he wanted.

The high priest of the Masters considered her for a moment. "You claim to come from a world filled with people like ourselves. Rather, like the beings we were before the Masters changed us. Do I understand that correctly?"

"You do. For example, you saw how my son was unable to resist as you took him to educate him in your language."

The man held up a warning finger. "Not my language. The language of the Masters. Never forget that."

"The Masters," she agreed. "As I said, we know virtually nothing of the Masters. No one on Earth does. And there are people there who, now that they know the Masters exist, are working hard to make certain they can never return."

The man sat up abruptly. "What blasphemy is this? Explain yourself swiftly or face my wrath."

Kathleen made a show of shrugging. "Sadly, the leaders of the forces arrayed against the Masters on Earth are my ex-husband and other son. I can't begin to tell you what great disappointments they are to me. I'm fighting against them, but at the moment, they have the upper hand."

The high priest's eyes narrowed. "Tell me the story from the very beginning. Leave nothing out."

She gave thanks to the gods that she was a skilled liar. It took her almost no effort to morph the truth of recent events into a story that suited her ends.

Clayton and Harry became the enemies of the piece. She became the hero. Nathan was an inconvenient sidekick and fool.

The tale she told twisted everything into seeming as though she'd left the home world searching for the Masters. Looking for their aid in reestablishing their rule on Earth. By the time she'd finished, Kathleen was almost ready to cheer herself on.

Louvan seemed less than convinced. He sat there staring at her with one of the most skeptical expressions she'd ever seen.

"As High Priest of the Masters, it is my unfortunate duty to correct the faithful when they stray. I've heard many lies in my life. Some crude and others as smooth as a child's skin. I've gained some skill at sensing deception.

"I sense great deception in you, Kathleen Bennett. Oh, some aspects of your story are undoubtedly true. Perhaps even most of it. The part I doubt is your motive. That is always the place where a liar conceals the harshest of truths."

Kathleen was impressed, but she didn't let that emotion make it to her face. Instead, she showed him a gentle sadness.

"I understand your skepticism. In your place, I would feel much the same.

Yet, I can prove all of these things. Whether I am telling the truth or lying, you would still stand to gain from working with me."

An acolyte walked into the room with a tray holding a pitcher of liquid, two glasses filled with ice, and some kind of small snack cakes. The man set it on a low table between the high priest and Kathleen before departing.

Louvan poured them both glasses before sipping from his and nibbling on a cake. "The juice is from a local fruit you might find interesting. It is sweet but comes with an almost shockingly sour aftertaste. It is quite good. The cakes serve to clean the palate and are also quite tasty."

Kathleen worried for a moment that he intended to poison or drug her but set it aside. A certain level of trust would serve her cause well here. Besides, they'd have to eat sooner or later.

She sipped the drink and found it was indeed just like he described it. An initial rush of sweetness like apple juice gave way to an almost lemonade flavor. It was refreshing. The cakes were sweet and light. She set herself to trying more as her stomach grumbled.

"If I were to work with you, what goals do you see us sharing?" he asked.

Kathleen smiled. The hook was set.

"If you want to bring the Masters back, then you need to suppress any who do not accept them. The forces of my ex-husband are already hard at work to make certain humanity never kneels to the Masters.

"I saw warriors among your flock. You could take some of them back to Earth where you could fight our shared enemies and establish new homes to use as bases for converting the rest of humanity to serve the Masters."

The man grudgingly nodded. "Fighting the enemies of the Masters is always worthwhile, and I agree that bringing servants who have lost their way back into the service of the Masters is also a desirable thing.

"What I do not understand is how that will benefit you? You do not know the Masters, Kathleen Bennett. They have not touched and shaped your life down to the very genes inside your body. What do you hope to gain?"

"Nothing too much," she assured the man. "Unless you have greater numbers than I am aware of, you will need the willing assistance of unmodified humans on Earth.

"I intend to enter this agreement as your partner. One can serve the Masters and still rule the land on which they live to some degree. Much as you do here. I want the same on Earth."

He considered her a moment without saying a word. Then he inclined his head.

"I cannot argue with the logic of your statement. While the People are great warriors, our numbers are not what they once were. Food was more difficult to produce after the Masters departed, so it served our needs to allow our numbers to fall.

"Yet when we fight, we still have the technology of the Masters and are unbeatable. Do not think yourself capable of betraying us. Once you enter the service of the Masters, you cannot change your mind."

Kathleen could see the fire of belief in the man's eyes. He was a fanatic. He meant every word he said.

She wasn't sure she could finesse this situation completely, but she still had faith she would win in the end. All that mattered now was securing the best outcome for her. If she ended up being a servant of the so-called Masters, so be it. They probably didn't even exist anymore.

"I'm in agreement," Kathleen said. "All that remains is getting us back to Earth. I assume you have gates here."

The high priest scowled. "We do, but they have not worked since the Masters departed. That is what causes me the most shock about your arrival."

Kathleen smiled. Her mind had promptly provided information on how the Asharim would have locked the gates. With access to a controller, she could undo it from this end. Physical access was key.

"How long will it take you to gather a strong raiding party?" she asked. "There is a base on Earth that should be easy to secure if we strike quickly."

The man seemed to consider her words for a moment before nodding. "We can gather enough men before dark. I agree that we should strike as soon as possible."

She was almost certain the man intended to betray her, but she knew that, once she reached Earth, she could turn things around. She had knowledge from the Asharim computers that this man didn't.

If things truly went badly, she could lock the gates down on that side and deal with the people that came with her. As long as they captured the base in France, this was going to work out in her favor. One way or the other.

"We have a deal."

30

It had taken far longer to gather officials from New Zealand, Australia, South Korea, and Japan than Clayton had wanted. Not that he'd allow them to see his impatience. That would never have done.

Still, he'd finally convinced people with sufficient authority that he was telling the truth. Or at least something important enough to require sending someone to report back.

The prime minister of New Zealand was put out that Clayton had contacted the other three governments. He'd much rather have kept it a close secret, no doubt.

The senior government officials from Japan, South Korea, and Australia had only just arrived at the ruined base. The Asharim shuttle had wowed them, but now they were all staring at the gates with skepticism.

Yoshida Sato, an extremely powerful ally of the Japanese prime minister, walked boldly up to the center gate, staring down at the blue cube powering it. He spoke briefly with the translator he'd brought with him, and the woman turned to face Clayton.

"Minister Sato asks what form of power is resident inside this device. Is it dangerous?"

Uncertain if this was somehow related to the man's possible feelings about nuclear power, Clayton shook his head. "The specifics of how it generates energy are something of a mystery. I can say that it isn't based on nuclear energy."

Reginald Baker, the Australian prime minister's brother, walked past the small group and into the gate depression itself. "I'm not seeing the big deal," he said bluntly. "Just a glowing cube that probably has something painted on the inside and a hole in the rock."

Clayton smiled. "If you'll step back out and away from the gate, I believe I can demonstrate what the big deal is."

Once the man had rejoined them, Clayton picked up the comp Kevin McHugh had left attached to the power device. A few taps on the screen brought up the address for the French base. He activated the gate.

Everyone stared at the roiling mist shot through with lightning that suddenly appeared inside the gate. Once it cleared, they could all see the interior of the French base.

The room on the other side was very much like the one they stood in, but it was well lit and filled with people. First and foremost among those was Jessica Cook. The engineer had known Clayton would be opening the wormhole and had been standing by.

She smiled and walked into the ruined base. "Hello, everyone. My name is Jess Cook. As you can see, this gate linked to another place.

"In this case, it's a base we have at a secret location. Basically, matter transportation via a wormhole. These gates can link to one another across the planet, across the solar system, and across the galaxy.

"They were seeded by an alien race called the Asharim. Not nice people, but they seem to have gone down in a war about a thousand years ago. Earth has a lot of catching up to do, and we can't allow any one government to do it alone. That's why we summoned you here."

"Even seeing it with my own eyes, I can't believe it," Isaiah Vaughn said slowly. "This is just too crazy."

Jess's expression turned sympathetic. "Imagine how difficult it was for those of us that actually located the equipment and made it work."

"Did you find something on Mars?" Park Sung-min, the South Korean minister of Science and ICT—information and communications technology—asked in almost unaccented English, asked. "I remember seeing something in the news about your people landing on some big volcano there. Is that what you found?"

She smiled at the man. "That's exactly what we found. A fully operational base filled with technology beyond our dreams."

"I do not understand why you are telling us this," Sato said through his interpreter. "You are Americans. Surely the American government will be angry that you revealed it to us. Why are they not your partners in this endeavor?"

Clayton took that verbal slow ball and swung for the fences. "The government of the United States isn't what it used to be. It's become more closed-minded, more corrupt.

"The name of the company we formed to exploit the technology is called Humanity Unlimited for a reason. These discoveries need to belong to humanity as a whole, not to one government bent on using it as a club against its enemies—or even its allies."

Kevin McHugh picked that moment to walk through the gate from the French base. He edged over to Jess Cook and spoke softly in her ear. Jess excused herself and headed back through the gate while Kevin remained standing beside the power supply.

Clayton hoped there wasn't some kind of serious trouble brewing. Even if there was, however, he needed to get on with the demonstration.

He cleared his throat. "I have one other location I'd like to show you. My son inadvertently discovered this place by transposing two characters while exploring the gate system. Pure chance, you understand."

He disconnected the connection the French base and used his phone to look up the address to the world Harry had discovered. The gate connected once he'd entered the correct code and revealed a sparkling beach with plants very similar to palm trees underneath a sky with two suns.

That got their attention.

"From everything we've been able to discover, it's perfectly safe. The island is relatively small and located in the tropical zone of a world thousands of light-years away. No dangerous creatures have been identified."

Vaughn stared through the gate. "Are those palm trees?"

Clayton shrugged. "I don't believe so, but I can't rule out them being related in some way. The similarity is striking."

He stepped through the gate and into the bright sunlight. "As far as we've been able to determine, this was a resort at some point. There are no buildings on the island, just serving areas. Old tables and chairs that are just about to come apart.

"The kitchen and serving areas must've been at a different gate address. Frankly, we're told that that was a common practice for the Asharim. The wealthiest in their society would have homes with separate rooms in different locations connected by gates that were never turned off. Basically, their homes were distributed across the galaxy."

Vaughn shook his head as he stepped through and stared out over the waves. The rest of the dignitaries followed suit. Clayton said nothing, content to allow them to take it in at their own speed.

Five minutes later, even though no one had said a single word that indicated they were ready to finalize a deal, Clayton knew the inevitable outcome. They couldn't shield their body language well enough to pretend they hadn't already come to a decision.

The Republic of Nauru, New Zealand, Australia, South Korea, and Japan would have a pact for mutual protection and exploitation of the technology by the day's end.

* * *

NATHAN BURNED INSIDE. The bastard had raped him. He'd quite literally restrained him and forced something into his mind. Then, after compelling him to learn their language, the bastard hadn't asked him a single question.

And his mother had let it happen. Hell, she'd thrown her own son to the wolves. Oh yes, she was going to pay for that. Only right now wasn't the time.

His mother and the Grand Dickhead had been strategizing for the last hour on the specifics of an attack plan for the base in France. They intended to seize it from the Islamic assholes.

Nathan didn't have any objection to that. Those sorry bastards deserved to die. He just didn't want to risk his own neck to make that happen. Not when he was certain he'd never see any reward for his efforts.

The only problem was that he didn't imagine he could opt out. He needed an exit plan from this fiasco, but he'd have to execute it once he got back to Earth.

If he could arrange to separate himself from the attacking force, he could make his way to Paris and use the resources his mother and he had around the globe to set himself up.

His mother wouldn't be pleased with that. Teach her to make him do all the work. He knew where everything was.

It was at that point the conversation between the Grand Dickhead and his mother turned to him. The three of them were seated at a long table in the temple, along with the buttmunch that had captured them at the space elevator.

His first inkling that they finally wanted his input in their stupid plan was his mother's imperious instruction to tell them everything he knew about the base in France. She'd seen enough of it that he couldn't outright lie about the layout. Pity. That would've been amusing.

He sketched a verbal picture of how the gate room was at the bottom of the base, the number of floors that sat above it, and the landscape surrounding the facility. He then described in rough detail the capabilities of the jihadis.

The Grand Dickhead dismissed that last with a wave. "These savages barely qualify as combatants. Our forces will sweep them aside."

The man who'd captured them didn't look as convinced, but he seemed disinclined to argue with his leader.

"So how do we do it?" Nathan asked. "Find a local gate and push through enough force to seize the other end?"

His mother's expression became irritated. "It seems the Masters did something to the gates here that I can't figure out how to undo. They won't turn activate from this side. We'll either have to use the gates on the station, if there are any functional, or transport people to the ship and use the one there.

"Once we get to the other side, I'll use a gate there to connect with one of the gates on the planet here. I'll lock it open, and they can bring through as many reinforcements as they want to take the base."

That was going to restrict the number of people they could send through for the initial assault, particularly if they had to transport them to the ship on that little boat.

He allowed himself to nod. "That sounds fine. When do we go? Tomorrow?"

The warrior shook his head. "We cannot allow the enemy to consolidate the gains they have made. Even now, they might be bringing reinforcements to this base.

"We leave as soon as this council is complete. I've already gathered a large force. Most will wait here while we strike, but I'll take my best men with us."

And that's what they did. The level of general planning horrified the professional inside Nathan. They were just going to take a gamble that they had enough force, push it, and hope they had what it took to open a gate back.

They'd gathered about a hundred fighters armed with alien rifles. He'd seen how potent such weapons could be and knew the men were devilishly strong, so maybe this wasn't as weak as he'd feared.

As the group marched back to the space elevator, Nathan edged close to his mother. Thankfully, the Grand Dickhead was leading the way, giving them a little bit of privacy.

"Are you sure this is the right thing to do, Mother? Once we get to Earth and open the gate back, these people are going to be in control."

She gave him a withering look. "I don't see where we have much of a choice. The entire damned planet is arrayed against us back home. We need allies."

"I can't imagine how you see these people as allies. They're going to be our masters."

"You never could see the long game, boy. Sometimes you have to do things you don't want to in order to position yourself for future success. Just trust that I know what I'm talking about."

So much for forcing her to see reason.

The force they'd gathered barely fit inside the space elevator, and the trip up seemed to take forever. The view of the approaching space station through the clear ceiling was spectacular.

As he'd expected, the gates on the space station proved to be unresponsive. Why would they be any different from the ones on the planet? That meant they had to do this the hard way. It took forever to ferry the men across to the ship. More wasted time.

The warriors they'd brought dutifully lined up in an attack formation in front of the operational gate, ignoring the ripe bodies scattered around the gate compartment after the fight with the Islamists.

Nathan set himself at the rear of the column. It appeared that the Grand Dickhead and his mother were going to wait on the ship.

The religious nut had several of his acolytes guarding them. In that particular, they didn't look much different than the warriors. They were armed and tough.

When the gate finally formed, the fighters rushed through and began shooting people. To Nathan's surprise, the people shooting back were not Islamic nut jobs. They looked like Harry's people.

Even better.

He raised his rifle and charged in, shooting as he went.

31

J ess gaped at the heavy-worlders rushing through the gate for a moment before dropping behind the closest cover—in this case, a pile of crates holding supplies from *Freedom Express* for the refugees.

Christ, the refugees. She pulled her phone out as she huddled there and called Rex. He was somewhere upstairs with Sandra.

"Go," he said moments later.

"We're under heavy-worlder attack through the gate. Get the refugees out and bring help."

"Crap. On it."

She set her phone beside the nearest crate and drew the pistol she carried at the small of her back. With the number of enemies pouring into the base, she didn't have nearly enough ammunition to stop them. Not even to delay them.

What she could do was take one down and upgrade her weapon. The downside of that plan was that she'd draw an immediate hostile response when she opened fire, and those flechettes would be deadly.

Well, it wasn't as if she had much of a choice.

Jess raised herself just enough to see what the situation in the gate room was like. It wasn't good. The heavy-worlders' attack had caught everyone by surprise, even the people who were there to defend against just such an incursion.

The defenders had taken significant casualties and fallen back to the reinforced positions. They were taking a toll on the enemy, but they hadn't escaped unscathed. The bodies of far too many of her people littered the floor.

Thankfully, they'd done a real number on the heavy-worlders, too. That left several flechette rifles lying tantalizingly close to her hiding place, and the enemy was focused on the forces arrayed in front of them.

She'd have one chance to strike from the rear. She'd better make it count.

Jess raced from cover toward the nearest of the fallen. She'd made it almost halfway to the weapon she'd had her eye on when Nathan Bennett stepped through the open gate and spotted her.

She snapped several shots at the man as she threw herself down beside the dead heavy-worlder. Harry's brother had seen her and ducked behind one of the fighters. She was pretty sure she'd missed the rat.

Apparently, her shots hadn't missed everyone, though. She saw another group of about half a dozen heavy-worlders on the other side of the gate. These were dressed in robes and wore odd headgear. Half of them were clustered around a sagging man at their center, and the remainder were looking at her with blood in their eyes.

Perfect.

She emptied her pistol at the new threat before dropping it and snatching up the fallen flechette rifle. Thankfully, she'd had the opportunity to practice with weapons just like this one.

Bennett hadn't shown himself, so she exchanged fire with the heavy-worlders on the other side of the gate.

They weren't idle or cowardly, though. Some of them charged toward her while the remainder opened fire. Their dead comrade was not going to prove much of a barricade against the flechettes coming her way.

Her initial burst took down the three heavy-worlders charging toward her. Unfortunately, that gave the three on the other side of the gate time to zero in on her.

She flattened herself behind the bulk of the dead man as flechettes ripped his body to shreds. The man's bulk miraculously stopped most of them but not all. She felt a sharp pain in her gut then another in her left leg. She'd been hit.

Jess didn't let that stop her. She exposed herself just enough to empty her flechette rifle at the enemy. Several of them went down. Not all of them, though. One was still on his feet and heading her way.

She ejected the spent magazine and tried to pull a fresh one from the dead guy's belt. Her hands felt so clumsy. She couldn't seem to focus. Her vision was narrow, and she felt so cold. That probably wasn't good.

Before she could fit the new magazine into the rifle, the heavy-worlder kicked the weapon out of her hands. He shouted something at her in an alien language and raised his weapon to finish her.

His head exploded, and he dropped like a stone. That meant he fell right on top of her, driving the air out of her lungs.

Jess struggled to roll him off, but he barely moved. The irony of being suffocated before the gunshots could kill her would have made her laugh, if she had the air.

The weight vanished as someone rolled the body off her. She sucked in blessed air and saw Nathan Bennett grinning down at her.

"Well, well, well," he purred. "We meet again."

She did laugh then. It sounded wet and horrible. She could taste blood in her mouth. A lot of it. "I think you're a little late to do anything to me now."

He scowled at her body. "No! You're mine, dammit! You can't die now!"

Then he grinned. "I have a brilliant idea. You'll hate it."

She didn't imagine the dead hated much of anything, so she wasn't going to worry about it. She'd focus on the regrets flooding over her. She'd never explore the universe and never see her friends again. That was almost worse than the physical pain.

Nathan snatched her up off the ground, threw her into a fireman's carry, and raced through the open gate.

Jess wanted to fight him, but her dying body didn't have the strength or coordination. She had no idea what he thought he could do to save her, but she knew it was doomed to fail.

She'd caught a glimpse of her body as he picked her up. Her torso was covered in blood, and she actually saw her intestines through the rip in her flesh. Her left leg had been opened to the bone, too.

She'd bleed out long before he could do anything to her, and that was just fine. Better death than being his prisoner.

The dizziness had almost overwhelmed her when Nathan carried her past the dead heavy-worlders on the other side of the gate. She saw something she'd missed in all the excitement. Harry's mother had been standing off to the side.

Somehow, she'd survived where they'd died. No, it wasn't her. It was a young woman that looked something like her. Odd. The blood loss was affecting her in some really strange ways.

Jess saw the unknown woman manipulate a gate controller, and the gate to the French base closed.

Nathan didn't slow down as he raced through the corridors. She recognized the layout and realized they were on the ship that had once been in the Sol system. The one Nathan and his mother had escaped in.

Her world had shrunk to almost nothing when he set her down on a cold metal surface and grinned down at her. "Still with me, I see. Good. We'll talk again real soon."

She wanted to spit in his face, but she couldn't focus well enough to make it happen. She was barely alive enough to see some kind of metal lid slide across above her.

She had just enough time to realize that she was in a sarcophagus before her world went dark and she died. That seemed appropriate, somehow.

The last of the light vanished and she knew nothing more.

* * *

HARRY TIREDLY OPENED the passenger door to the SUV. As he'd more than half expected, they hadn't found anything. If there was a cave out here that held one of the quantum gates, it was exceptionally well hidden.

Or perhaps it had just collapsed over the intervening years. There were enough rockfalls that could've concealed it out here. Without bringing in equipment and doing a search that would undoubtedly draw the wrong kind of attention, there was no way to know for sure.

If anything, Brenda was even more annoyed than he was. Understandable. After all, she considered this her backyard.

"What do we do now?" he asked as he handed bottles of water to the other three. The two from off planet examined theirs curiously. He showed them how to twist the plastic caps off. They made faces at the taste of the water.

"We go back into town," Brenda said. "This was a good reconnaissance, but we're going to need a lot more bodies to do this right."

They'd almost made it back to Washington when his phone rang and he saw Rex's number. "Go, Rex."

"Heavy-worlders just opened a gate into the base, and they're pouring through," he said. "We're pushing back, but Jess is down in the gate room. We're moving the Volunteers up to the surface."

"Crap. Do the best you can, and I'll be there as soon as possible." He disconnected. "We need to get back to the gate as quickly as possible. The bad guys found the French base. We're moving all your people up to the surface, Susanna."

The ex-FBI agent accelerated the SUV and turned on flashing lights and a siren.

"Won't this draw a little too much attention?" he asked dryly, trying to keep from worrying about Jess.

She grinned. "Have you ever seen a cop stop another cop? No. Does it sound bad?"

He nodded, his stomach roiling. "Real bad. I'd better call my father so he doesn't accidentally walk back into the firefight."

Harry dialed his father's number.

"I'm a little busy right now," the old man said quietly. "Can this wait?"

"That depends on how much you value your skin," Harry said bluntly. "The heavy-worlders are attacking the French base. Don't open a gate to it."

The other man swore. "Jess is there. Is she okay?"

"I don't know. Now doesn't seem like the right time to call and ask, either. We're going to have to force our way back into the gate room. Rex has virtually all of my security forces at the base, thank God."

"Is that going to be enough?"

"I hope so. I'll call you back when I know anything else."

He checked his watch. It would take them a while to get to the building holding Brenda's gate. Everything would probably be settled by the time he got there. He felt incredibly helpless. Things had gone wrong so quickly.

* * *

CLAYTON QUICKLY EXPLAINED the situation to the dignitaries. Needless to say, his news put a damper on their enthusiasm for the pact they'd just agreed to.

"That's bad," Vaughn said roughly. "Will you be able to contain them?"

"Probably. The real trick will be stopping them from bringing in too many people to overwhelm before we get more people in place. To do anything about that, we need to get soldiers there as soon as possible."

"I have an idea," Kevin McHugh said.

"Trot it out, young man," Clayton said when the boy paused. "You have my complete attention."

"Did you ever see the original *Stargate* movie? It has gates similar to the Asharim ones. The fictional US government in the franchise sent a nuke through the stargate to make sure no one could overwhelm the people protecting it if things went bad."

Clayton hadn't seen the movie, but his assistant had explained it in a general way. "That does sound like a capital idea, but I'm a little short on nuclear devices. I suspect our friends are in similar circumstances."

"True, but you have a US warship impounded here in New Zealand. Tell me they don't have portable nukes locked up on board."

That gave Clayton pause. He had no idea if they did or not, but it sounded like a reasonable possibility. They also had trained soldiers.

By now, Commander Krueger and his people were back aboard their ship. Clayton had convinced the New Zealanders to only make an example of Ulysses and let the rest go.

If anyone could save their bacon now, it was Krueger and his people. Unfortunately, they wouldn't be able to lift a finger to save them without orders.

"I'll try to get their assistance, but I'm not hopeful," he said after a moment. "To do that, I need to convince Secretary of State Queen to assist us. That seems… unlikely."

Well, unlikely wasn't impossible. He'd give it his best shot. Jess's life might depend on getting more people into the French base fast. Hell, all their lives might rest on stopping the invasion in progress.

He pulled out his phone and dialed information. "I need the main number for the State Department," he told the operator.

32

Queen rubbed his tired eyes. He'd thought things couldn't get any worse, but he'd been wrong. The damned Chinese were mobilizing all around the globe.

Not only had they blown up the lab full of alien technology, they seemed intent on making an issue out of the Yucatán Spaceport. They wanted war. That wasn't a big shock, he supposed. This day had been coming for years. Their timing sucked, though.

It had to be the damned Mars mission. They assumed—as did he—that Rogers had found the mother lode on Mars. They wanted all the marbles for themselves, and they were willing to kill as many people as needed to make that happen.

That made the next call he received inevitable but infuriating. He took it as soon as his assistant told him who was calling.

"You have a lot of nerve calling me," he snarled into the phone.

"I'm sure," Ambassador Chen said cordially. "My superiors didn't want me to do so, but I feel that we shouldn't make the same mistakes as our neighbors a century ago.

"China views your actions against us as an act of war, and we are responding to them as such. You will no doubt receive word of military action in the very near future. Regrettable as that is, you precipitated this action yourselves."

"Liar," Queen said bluntly. "You already knew about the alien technology, so don't try to spin this as anything other than a power grab. You want what Rogers found on Mars."

Chen chuckled. "Of course we do. How could we not? We shall have it, too."

"We'll see about that."

His assistant stuck his head in and started making frantic gestures.

Queen muted the call. "What?"

"Something just blew up the Mars ship we bought from the Indians. It's gone."

He sat there, stunned for a moment. "Damned Chinese. Did they fire a missile at it?"

The man shrugged. "Our national defense assets would've seen something like that. Maybe something from their ship?"

"Or a satellite already in orbit. Can we strike their ship?"

The man shook his head. "It must've already boosted from orbit. I got word of that just before they blew our ship up. It happened on the other side of the planet, so we only just got the notice."

Even if Queen called the president for authority to fire a ballistic missile at the Chinese ship, it was going to be too far away to do any good.

"Crap."

Chen had been blathering in his ear all this time, but Queen hadn't been paying attention. He cut the man off. "You bastard. You blew up our Mars ship. We had people up there."

"Casualties happen during war," the other man said urbanely. "The loss of life is, of course, regrettable. You will recall I did deliver our declaration of war before hostilities began, however. It is all as required by international law."

"Screw you, and screw your declaration. We'll burn you to the ground." He slammed the phone down hard.

Now all he needed was a way to hurt them. He had to call the president and tell him what was happening. The military needed to get into a more aggressive posture and make the bastards pay for this.

His frazzled assistant stuck his head back in. "There's another call you need to take. Line two."

"Dammit, what now? Are the Russians shooting at us, too?"

"It's Clayton Rodgers."

Perfect. The bastard had probably called to gloat.

He snatched up his handset and pressed the button for the active line. "I'd say you have a lot of nerve calling me like this, but I'm busy. What do you want?"

"The situation has changed and not in a good way," the old man said. "The Earth is in danger."

"No shit. If this goes nuclear, millions could die."

There was a long pause from the other end of the connection. "Do you have me bugged? How could you possibly know I was calling because I need one of your nuclear devices?"

Queen opened his mouth to say something offensive then realized he had no idea what the man was talking about. Obviously not the Chinese.

"You need to start over," he told Rodgers slowly. "I'm talking about the Chinese declaring war on the US and destroying our Mars ship. What crisis are you talking about, and why would you possibly need a nuke?"

"Someone activated a gate to Earth and is attacking Harry's people. They're the best, but he doesn't have many of them. If these heavy-worlders get a hold on Earth, they might pour millions of soldiers through with advanced weapons. Hell, they might have the Asharim right behind them."

Queen buried his head in his hands. "Christ. You led them right to us."

"I seriously doubt that. If anything, Kathleen and Nathan did. We never had control over them. They were on the ship that the Asharim left watching our system that jumped out through the gate in the outer system. They had the address to the base in France."

"What gate in the outer system and what base in France? How many gates and bases do you have?"

"That hardly matters, and we don't have time for me to explain in detail. I'm in New Zealand, where you tried to kidnap me, standing in the remains of another base.

"I'm sure Commander Krueger is briefing his commanding officer about the gate here as we speak. He's on his ship. The one the New Zealanders impounded.

"I want to get them back here with every man they have available, and I want them to bring one of the portable nuclear devices I suspect all US ships carry nowadays.

"They can turn the tide in France and secure that gate before it becomes a beachhead. If we don't act soon, it might be too late. The Chinese are not the biggest threat on the board right now."

This was absolutely the worst time for this kind of distraction, but Rogers was right. An alien invasion trumped a conventional war. The Chinese could be dealt with. Hordes of high-tech aliens were a completely different story.

Queen rubbed his face. "I can't just send them in. The New Zealanders would never allow them off the ship, particularly with a nuke."

"Even if I could, you don't get my help for free. Your monopoly of the alien tech is over. The Chinese ship is on its way to Mars. You have to cut America in, or there is no deal."

He had absolutely no idea if any deal he struck—even if Rogers agreed to it—would make it past the president and Senate. Still, the bastard needed help, and this was the best time to make him give up control. Besides, if what the man said was true, time was running out for all of them.

"I agree in principle. Humanity Unlimited doesn't have the forces or the knowledge to deal with the aliens. As to the latter, you need to make your peace with Brenda Cabot and her group. They know far more about the Asharim than either of us."

Perfect. One more enemy he had to bring to the table. Yet, now that push came to shove, he knew he had to do that, too. He couldn't afford a world war with an enemy like that buried in his government.

"I also agree, in principle," he said tiredly. "I can probably get hold of her in a few hours."

"Would having her call you right now help?"

He snorted bitter amusement. "I suppose that shouldn't surprise me. Yes.

Give me fifteen minutes to call the ship and give them orders. Rather, to call the admiral in charge and have her make that call. I'll have to get the New Zealanders to buy in, too."

"Make your call. I have an assistant to New Zealand's prime minister standing right beside me. He's already gotten the go ahead to let your people off the ship with the weapon so long as they don't detonate the bomb on their soil."

"This changes everything, Rogers," Queen said slowly. "We've been acting like kids pushing each other around in the schoolyard. As much as it pains me to say, the United States is going to have to step back in time and become the leader it once was. You and your people can help us or hinder us. I hope we can find the right path forward to save us all."

"So do I, Mister Secretary. So do I."

Queen disconnected the call without a word of goodbye. He had a lot of calls to make and some serious convincing to do.

* * *

Harry ordered every man and woman who could handle a weapon to move to the base in New Zealand. The only break in his nonstop planning sessions was while Brenda Cabot negotiated a ceasefire with Queen.

He couldn't believe they had to work with the damned stuffed shirt, but he saw the logic, as much as he hated it. They just couldn't turn back an invasion with the forces he had at hand.

If they survived, everything was going to change. He wasn't sure how yet, but that was inevitable. The American government was going to try to take over, and he'd have to work with Jess to stop them or at least slow them down.

That started another round of worrying about the engineer. Rex hadn't heard from her since the fighting had started. That meant she was hidden somewhere in the base, captured, or dead.

He hoped for the best, but deep down he knew the chances of her still being a free agent were low. He prayed she was still alive. Losing her would be devastating both personally and professionally.

Listening to Brenda fill Queen in on what she suspected about a separate group of people from the Asharim conflict a thousand years ago was educational and distracting, too.

He immediately connected the Chinese conflict with that group. Brenda's certainty that they were heavy-worlders made the likelihood of them being loyal to the Asharim—even after all this time—too great to simply dismiss. There might even be a possibility they had some connection to the attack in France, though he didn't see how.

If they were as deeply embedded in society there as Brenda claimed her people were in the US, these people were probably manipulating their government. Or they'd placed their own in charge over the intervening centuries.

It made him wonder about the Communist takeover a century ago. Had the heavy-worlder secret society been behind that?

If they were in control, the conflict wouldn't end easily. These people probably thought they had a lot to gain and very little to lose. It also meant that the Chinese ship probably had a crew of their choosing. One that likely had some kind of Asharim tech along to even the odds.

Thankfully, he had a few weeks to worry about that problem. Assuming he survived the next few hours, of course.

Rex had done the best he could, but the enemy had forced him into withdrawing from the gate room. They were steadily forcing their way up, and it wouldn't be long before he had to abandon the base entirely. At least the Volunteers had finished evacuating.

Harry couldn't imagine what the French authorities would do once they figured out they had fighting on their territory. It probably wouldn't be good. Yet another thing to worry about.

They made it back to Brenda's building a few hours after dark and raced down to the gate room. Her people had already opened a connection to the ruined New Zealand base, and he stalked through it while she finished gathering those of her people who might be able to help.

His father was talking with Karl Krueger. They both turned to face him as soon as he stepped into the room.

"Perfect timing," the commander said. "I've been going over the basic situation with your father. It doesn't sound good."

Harry looked around the room at all the people they had gathered. His people made up about a quarter of the hundred or so people in the chamber. The US forces were of a similar number. The remainder wore camouflage uniforms of an unfamiliar make.

"It's looking better than I expected. Where did you come up with so many people, and who are they?"

"A quarter of them are mine. Not all Special Forces, but they have some combat training. The rest are the best New Zealand could gather on short notice. We have enough to secure a bridgehead on the far side, so long as we can do it quickly. My team will form the point.

"The basic plan is to open a gate and launch a heavy weapon to clear the floor on the other side. If the chamber is the same size as this one, it won't do the job completely, but it will cause enough shock and awe to get our people through.

"Then we hold while we take the package through the gate to the hostiles' home base. If it seems appropriately bad there, I have the green light to set the thing on a short timer and leave it while we withdraw. It's nice that cutting off the gate means we go from having a backpack nuke in our laps to being a long way away in a few seconds."

Harry nodded. "Damned straight. What about our people on the other side? I don't want to lose a single person, but I'm concerned about one in specific. Jess Cook isn't just my partner. She has irreplaceable knowledge of everything we're doing. We need to get her out alive if we can."

Krueger sighed. "We'll do what we can, but we have to protect our forces first."

That wasn't what Harry wanted to hear, but he knew it was a hard truth. This was going to be difficult no matter how they sliced it.

"What if they've closed the gate down?" he asked.

"That's where I come in," Kevin McHugh said from nearby. He must've slipped up while they'd been talking. Brenda stood beside the bald man.

"How so?"

"I can access the gates to read their most recent incoming and outgoing addresses. It'll take a few seconds, but I'll be able to recreate the connection. It would be useful to guess which gate up front, though. I don't want to waste time on the wrong one."

"When will we be ready?" Harry asked the navy commander.

"We're ready now," Krueger said. "Give us a minute to get into final positions and we can kick this party off."

The fighting forces were gathered on either side of the gate. That made sense. If someone shot through it at them, they'd be out of the direct line of fire.

They'd set up some kind of portable missile launcher a bit back from the gate with its tubes angled to fire into the small area. Harry hoped none of them missed, or they'd destroy the gate and probably kill a lot of people in an ugly blue on blue incident.

His people were closest to the gate and held satchel charges. They'd throw them through as soon as the gate stabilized. That would clear the immediate area of threats as they charged in.

As soon as everyone was ready, Harry gave the signal, and the gate came to life. The fight to protect the Earth began now.

33

To say the battle began with a bang was insufficient, Clayton thought. Even covering his ears, the explosive charges Harry's people threw into the French base deafened him.

Then the missiles fired, roaring through the gate and detonating so strongly that he feared the ceiling would collapse. The pressure wave actually made him stumble.

The soldiers seemed unperturbed and rushed through the active gate. There must've still been an active threat on the other side because they immediately opened fire.

He stuck close to Kevin McHugh as the young hacker raced into the other chamber and was momentarily stunned at the devastation.

Rows of Asharim ships had become blasted, burning wrecks in seconds. Bodies littered the floor, and someone at the far side of the huge chamber was actively shooting at the friendly forces. Neither of the other gates was open.

The hacker had his comp out and was tapping the screen as he huddled behind what was left of some crates. Oddly, the thing that stood out to Clayton was the phone lying just out in the open. It was the duplicate of the one in his own pocket. It had to be Jess's.

He resisted the impulse to reach for it when flechettes slammed into the crates.

"Got it!" McHugh shouted. "Dialing now!"

The gate to their left rear came to life, and men began pouring through it from their side. There were a lot of bodies in the room on the other side but no active resistance. The stench was incredible. No way those were from this fight.

Harry's people led the way in, their weapons up. The SEAL team followed closely behind. Commander Krueger held a large case that Clayton assumed had the nuclear weapon.

"Are you sure this is the right place?" Harry asked McHugh. "I'd have expected resistance."

"This is the only gate to open since the attack started. It has to be the right place. Hell, the dead guys kind of point that way."

"I suppose so. Wait a second."

Harry turned and frowned at the gates. "I know this place. This is the ship Nathan stole. He blew up the gate and cut that one guy in half."

"So what do we do?" Krueger asked.

"We make sure this area is clear while Mister McHugh checks the gate for a different destination. If they aren't here, they used the ship as a waypoint. Maybe my mother and brother didn't want to reveal Earth's address directly to these people."

The armed men spread out, setting up at the entrances to the room. One of them called back. "I have fresh blood here."

Clayton stayed back from the front, content to let Harry and Krueger lead the way. If they found anyone looking for trouble, they'd be the ones to give it to them.

The blood drops were numerous and frequent. If they were Jess's, the young woman was in a bad spot.

Krueger sent men out at cross corridors to search. That cut their numbers down, but they needed to make sure no one came at them from the sides or from behind.

Harry stopped when they reached a closed hatch where the blood ended. "Get ready," his son said before opening the hatch and heading in with his weapon up. Others followed him in.

Once they called out that the room was secure, Clayton went inside. The compartment was fairly nondescript. The only odd thing about it was what looked like a large piece of equipment that resembled a technological sarcophagus. The blood drops led up to it, and there was some smeared across one side.

"What is that thing?" he asked Brenda.

"I think that's some kind of healing unit," she muttered as she walked around it. "Some of the oldest stories talked about how the Asharim could miraculously heal themselves and their most trusted allies. Kevin, can we see what's inside it?"

"Maybe. Let me find a port and check."

He opened panels until he found something that made him grunt. "Here we go." It took the man a few minutes to plug his comp in and tap into something. Then he swore.

"What?" Brenda asked.

Kevin turned the comp and showed them the video feed he'd tapped into. Jess Cook lay there, pale as death.

Clayton opened his mouth to curse, but automatic weapon fire from outside the room cut him off.

* * *

THE SHOTS MADE Brenda almost jump out of her skin. She'd been in fights before, but this was a whole new level of pressure. The FBI hadn't trained her for war, and her Glock felt a little underpowered.

"See if you can get her out of the thing," Harry said. "We need to get the hell out of here." He ran out the door before she could argue.

What if they couldn't? What if Cook was too badly injured to move? "Talk to me," she ordered Kevin.

"Hang on. Accessing medical telemetry now."

The man's face went pale. "I'm no doctor, but even I can tell we won't be able to move her. It looks like something ripped her intestines apart, and she's lost a lot of blood.

"It says she's alive but in what amounts to extremely critical condition. If we pop her out, she'll die before we even get back to the gate."

Brenda rubbed her forehead. "Is this portable or connected to the ship's power supply?"

"It's connected to the ship, but it might have some contingency for emergency power. Let me look." The man gestured for the other techs to come help, and they started pulling panels.

Brenda stood near the door with her weapon out. Two men guarded the hatch from the corridor, but she wanted to be sure no one came in while she wasn't looking.

Clayton stepped up beside her. "This isn't going to have a happy ending, is it?"

"Most likely not," she admitted. "I'm sorry."

The older man shook his head. "What a tragedy. She was the brightest, best person I've met in far more years than I can count. She was the hope for humanity."

Part of her wanted to tell him things might still work out, but she couldn't make herself mouth the pat phrase. His partner was almost certainly already dead. She just hadn't finished dying yet.

"There's a slot for a power cube," Kevin called out.

"Too bad we don't have one," she sighed.

The man's eyes darted toward his backpack. "Well, I happened to find one in a partially disassembled ship at the French base. I hope you don't mind that I borrowed it, Mister Rogers."

The old man barked out a laugh. "If you save Jess, I'll give you a whole damn ship. Thank God for sticky fingered hackers."

The man pulled out a glowing cube about ten centimeters across and slid it inside the device. He checked his comp. "It's on backup power now. We can disconnect the unit from the ship."

"Work fast," Brenda ordered. "We might have to pull out at any moment and I don't want to leave her behind."

The sounds of fighting outside were getting louder. Someone was pushing the friendly forces back toward them. Time was running out.

* * *

Harry sent a burst into the heavy-worlder in front of him. The man stumbled and went down. The man behind him fired a storm of flechettes that turned the two New Zealanders in front of him into hamburger.

They were outgunned here. They'd lost almost all of their people and were still getting pushed back. They needed to get off this ship.

"Slow them down as much as you can," he told the remaining soldiers. "We need a fighting retreat to the gate room."

A Marine Corps gunnery sergeant threw a grenade up the corridor to give them time to break contact. "I'll stay here and make sure no one gets by. Good luck."

"Don't be a hero, Jacob," Krueger said. "You have a family waiting for you."

"Aye, sir."

Harry and Krueger retreated back down the corridor.

"Realistically, they won't be able to give us more than a few minutes," Harry said.

"Gunnery Sergeant Danvers will give us the time we need. I only hope you get good news on your partner."

They arrived back at the room just as the techs were pushing the sarcophagus out into the hall.

"We're good," Brenda said. "Let's go!"

They'd almost made it back to the gate room when someone ahead of them opened fire. They all hit the deck, but none of the shots seemed to be aimed at them.

To his amazement, someone in the gate room laughed. "I'd stop resisting if I were you. We found something important." It was Nathan's voice.

"Oh, crap," Brenda said from where she crouched beside the box with Jess inside. "We sent the noncombatants ahead with the other two soldiers. Everyone except Kevin."

Harry edged forward until he could peek around the corner. Sure enough, his brother Nathan stood grinning beside the gate. He had a pistol to his father's head.

Kathleen Bennett stood beside her son. The techs were gathered into a small knot off to the side, and the two soldiers lay sprawled in pools of their own blood.

"You can come out now," Harry's mother said. "This fight is over."

Harry came out slowly, his weapon aimed at the three. Nathan only seemed to have a pistol, and his mother was unarmed. Still, they didn't need much when they had his father.

That's when he noticed how young his mother seemed. Unnaturally so. She could pass for someone in her twenties. "You're looking good, Mother. New skin cream?"

She smiled coldly. "It's been a long time, Harry. You never call or come to visit. Don't you love me?"

"Let him go, and I'll let you go," he said, aiming his rifle at his brother's head. The shot was tricky, and he'd be almost as likely to kill his father, but he might have to take the shot.

"Don't be ridiculous," she scoffed. "We have the trump card now. Lay down your weapons."

His father laughed. "Now who's being ridiculous? We all know you and Nathan can't be trusted to keep your bargains. Nathan would ignore you and kill Harry for sport even if you *did* mean it."

His mother cocked an eyebrow and slowly nodded. "I suppose you have a point. That poses a bit of a problem since we have no intention of releasing you."

"Then don't. Let them go and keep me."

"Screw that," Harry said. "I might not like you that much, but that's a death sentence."

His father shrugged. "Making a deal is all about the art of the possible. Right now, I don't see a way where you get out without me staying.

"Take Jess, and go back to Earth. You might figure out a new angle and turn this around."

Nathan bristled. "You can't have her. The woman belongs to me."

His mother held her hand up. "I wish I could tell you all to screw off, but your father is right. My options are limited. That means I'm willing to make a onetime deal.

"Leave with the woman. I couldn't care less about her. I'll keep Clayton as a consolation prize. We have so much to talk about."

"Done," his father said before Harry could reject the offer.

He lined up the shot only to have his brother duck even farther behind his father. He really, really wanted to take the shot.

His mother and brother seemed to realize that and started edging toward the other exit from the gate room. With no clean options, he had to let them out of sight.

"Crap," he said. "McHugh, take my phone, look up the address for *Freedom Express*, and open the gate. I'll keep you covered."

Commander Krueger and Gunnery Sergeant Danvers used their weapons to cover the corridor behind them as Brenda and the rest pushed the sarcophagus with Jess inside into the gate room.

As unsavory as it was, the others had to drag bodies out of the way to get to the gate. The machine had almost no clearance.

Reinforcements poured through as soon as he opened the gate. Harry was tempted to go after his father, but he knew these people were not trained soldiers. If they ran into more heavy-worlders, it would end in disaster.

With a sigh, he stepped through the gate last and made the gesture for McHugh to close the gate.

His mother and brother had won.

* * *

CLAYTON HEARD the gate shut off and knew he was alone with his ex-wife and murderous son. This wasn't going to be pleasant, but it gave Harry a chance to prepare.

Nathan shoved him back into the gate room after he peered in to make sure it was clear. "I can't believe you let him go, Mother. Worse, you gave him my woman."

"Grow up, Nathan," Kathleen said. "You can always get her back when we take over the Earth. I'll have to go back to the base in France and open a gate directly to the planet. Thank God I got the address. We can throw assets at your brother until we win."

"At least the Grand Dickhead is dead," his son grumbled. "They know the ship's address. Can you disable the gate until we get some more bodies?"

She pulled out a controller and did something to it. "Done. I also have the address they just went to. We can visit Harry and pay our respects very soon. Take dear Clayton back to where you had me locked up. We'll leave him there while I take the shuttle to the station."

Nathan shoved Clayton roughly up the hall but stopped when he saw something up ahead. "What is that?"

Clayton smiled as he recognized the open case. Commander Krueger had left the nuclear bomb behind.

Oh, this was absolutely perfect. Hollywood couldn't have come up with a better ending. The only thing that could improve on it was timing.

Nathan pushed Clayton forward, and he saw a digital counter. Nine... Eight...

"It's a nuclear bomb," Clayton said.

His son raised his weapon to shoot it, but Clayton planted a fist in the brat's groin and sent him to the floor.

He hurled Nathan's gun down the corridor and turned toward his ex-wife with a grin. "Looks like we get a karmic ending after all. I'll *literally* see you in Hell."

Her mouth was only starting to open when the counter hit zero.

* * *

JESS SAT BOLT UPRIGHT. Fear flashed through her as she looked around for Nathan. She was sitting in the same box he'd put her in, but the room had changed.

This looked more like a basement with a bare concrete floor, cinder block walls, and a decrepit-looking elevator off to the side. A portable gate sat nearby. Brenda's gate?

"She's awake!" a voice said from behind her.

She turned her head and saw Kevin rising from a folding chair beside a table filled with equipment. He dropped the phone receiver and raced over to her.

"You're safe," he said. "You're okay."

She looked down at the ripped, blood-soaked blouse she wore and doubted that. Yet her questing hands found only healthy skin. The pain was gone. It was as if it had never happened.

A black cat—probably the mechanical one—rose from where she'd been curled nearby and walked up the bed to be petted.

"What's going on?" she asked as she stroked the purring device. "What happened? They're trying to capture the French base."

"Slow down," he said with exaggerated softness. "It's been two days. We poured people into the base, and they finally surrendered."

She blinked at that. "Two *days*? How? What about Nathan and his mother? We need to stop them, too."

Even as she said it, she knew they must've already done something. They had her, and Nathan didn't.

"Harry got you out. His brother and mother aren't a problem anymore."

His sad expression filled her with dread. "Something else happened."

Kevin nodded. "It's a long story, and I know Harry will be pissed if I tell it before he gets down here. He's almost been living here when he hasn't been negotiating with about a billion other people.

"He just went upstairs to grab a bite to eat and take a shower a few hours ago. Give him and Brenda a few minutes, and they'll tell you everything."

She heard the missing part of his statement. "Where is Clayton Rogers?"

The bald man sighed. "I'm sorry, but he didn't make it. If it's any consolation, he got the most *spectacular* Viking funeral in history. Harry said he went out exactly the way he'd have wanted.

"Harry buried an empty casket for him yesterday. He put a quote from Thomas Jefferson on his tombstone. 'The tree of liberty must be refreshed from time to time with the blood of patriots and tyrants.' He said his father was a bit of both, so it felt right."

Her eyes teared up, and her throat tightened. Clayton would have liked that his son had embraced him at last.

"Now lay back until Doctor Granger gets down here," Kevin said. "If I let you hurt yourself, he'll have Victor hold me over the edge of the roof again."

Jess lay back in a state of shock. She had so many things she'd never have the chance to say to the cantankerous old man now. How could he be gone? He'd been such a force of nature, how could they go on without him?

This must be eating at Harry. He'd never liked his father, but no one lost a parent and just shrugged it off. What could she say to him? How could she help him?

She had no idea. Her mind was swirling with loss, and she couldn't seem to swim out of it. It was like a whirlpool trying to suck her down.

Well, she'd deal with it like any other problem. One moment at a time.

The elevator dinged, and she knew that process was about to start in earnest, whether she was ready or not.

She'd get her answers and do what she had to do. The Earth was depending on her.

BLOOD OF PATRIOTS

BOOK FOUR

Harry and Jess thought they had enough on their plates: genetically altered humans bent on world domination, interstellar aliens that thought humans made decent slaves, and a government determined to arrest them for treason.

Then the universe said, "Hold my beer."

With war brewing over the alien technology, a secret society determined to betray Earth, and a head-to-head fight with the aliens on the horizon, they gather both enemies and allies alike to fight for humanity.

If their shaky alliance fails, humanity faces slavery or extermination. They must not fail.

1

Jessica Cook stared at the stars twinkling far above the Washington, DC, rooftop and sighed. Those distant stars had once brought her such peace. When she was little, her father had taught her the constellations, and they'd wondered what amazing things awaited humanity out there in the depths of space.

As it turned out, a lot of pain and violence.

Those days had been some of the happiest of her life. She missed both her father and the wilds of rural Maine deeply. She also missed the innocence that she would never know again.

The light pollution in Washington washed out the beautiful view and made seeing the dimmer stars impossible. Only the brightest stellar objects had a chance of shining through the photonic fog.

She tugged her borrowed coat close and stepped over to the battered metal rail four stories above the dirty pavement. At four in the morning, the city was asleep. That would change in just a few hours.

Even bundled up, the chill breeze still made her shiver, but it also brought hints of life from around her. The stink of the city still bothered her. They were nothing like what artificial structures in space smelled like. Give her wilderness or space, not crowded cities.

The scent of baking bread from down the street made her mouth water and her stomach grumble. She could almost taste the light, flaky bread slathered in butter.

Jess pivoted her gaze across the city. They weren't in the best of neighborhoods, so the buildings were grimy and dingy. The streets below had a scattering of trash that never seemed to get picked up. Even up here, she got occasional whiffs of stench that fought to ruin the glorious scent of the bread. That was a true war of light verses dark there.

The roof access door behind her opened with a low squeal of rusted metal. She turned just enough to see Harry Rogers step out into the dim light. He raised a hand in greeting and walked over to her.

"Couldn't sleep?" he asked softly.

She shook her head. "No. I suppose dying does that. I can't stop thinking about what happened."

"Doctor Granger doesn't think that you actually died."

She snorted. "You know that old saying about how close only counts in horseshoes and hand grenades? Well, it's appropriate for near-death experiences, too. I closed my eyes inside that machine knowing that I'd probably never open them again, and I can't get that out of my head."

No matter how she looked now, she'd taken a fatal wound in the fight with the heavy-worlders at the abandoned base outside of Paris. They'd come pouring through the gate, catching everyone off guard.

Armed with advanced Asharim weapons and strong enough to live and work in an environment with three times Earth's gravity, they'd been almost unstoppable. The few guards that she'd had in the gate room couldn't hold them back for long.

In the fighting, someone had shot her in the gut and leg. Harry's evil brother Nathan had snatched her up and carried her back through the gate to the Asharim warship they'd stolen from Harry and her.

He'd placed her inside a strange machine and promised that he'd see her later. No doubt he'd intended to rape and torture her. She'd closed her eyes expecting never to open them again.

Much to her surprise, not only had she woken up later, all signs of her injuries had been healed. It was as if she'd never been hurt in the first place.

Hell, she was actually in better condition now. The scar on her stomach where they'd taken her appendix as a girl was gone. She was more than willing to bet that the appendix was back in there, too.

Doctor Todd Granger had thoroughly examined her once the machine had finished. Two days had passed since her injury. In that time, the strange device had seemingly repaired every flaw in her body. Even her fillings were gone.

As a member of the Families—the descendants of humans that fled the Asharim—Granger had access to technology far beyond what the Earth possessed. He could see the interior of her body in greater detail than the most advanced medical technology she'd ever seen.

Her mind shied away from the details of what he'd told her. She couldn't quite decide if the machine had healed her or rebuilt her. She felt like herself, but there was a niggling little doubt in the back of her mind about whether this was her original body or a creation that the machine had somehow transferred her mind into.

And that troubled her far more than she cared to admit.

She was also younger, physically. Everyone else could be excused from recognizing the change, but he had to have noticed. Not that she hadn't kept herself in shape, but the change from her mid-thirties to her mid-twenties was impossible to ignore.

Giving her the space to accept what had happened meant a lot, but she knew that they really didn't have time for her to dither. The list of problems facing humanity was long, and far too many of them were immediate threats. So many of them, in fact, that she wasn't quite sure how they could address the most dangerous ones while dealing with the rest of the crap.

She firmly put her worries aside and turned to face her partner. "I suppose that once we have breakfast, we'll need to figure out what to do next. What's our biggest problem right now?"

He scratched the stubble on his chin thoughtfully. "That's a tough one. On general principles, I'd say it has to be the war between China and the United States. Thankfully, wiser heads have prevailed so far, and no one has used weapons of mass destruction yet. An exchange of nukes would be impossible to stop.

"On the other hand, the heavy-worlders are a serious problem, too. Their access to advanced technology and their warlike nature means that they could come back for another pass at us. We don't know where every gate is on Earth, and that could kill us.

"My father managed to stop my mother and brother, though he paid the ultimate price in doing so. The portable nuke that Commander Krueger left on the Asharim ship destroyed the only link between the heavy-worlder planet and Earth, if the prisoners are to be believed."

A combined force of Harry's troops, US military, and New Zealand military had defeated the heavy-worlders in the abandoned French base. Fewer than a dozen prisoners were taken, including the wounded heavy-worlder military leader.

If he was to be believed, the gates on his home world were locked down. Harry wasn't in such a trusting mood, and neither was she.

"We don't know any of the gate codes to get there and see what the situation is," she said after a few seconds. "We have the gate code for the station there, but that's for ships, of which we have none. And that's even if the nuke didn't take out the station when it destroyed the ship your parents were on."

He nodded. "True enough, though I bet Kevin McHugh could trigger the big gate manually. Then we could take small craft through and scout. If we can fit that into our busy schedule."

"I knew some of this, but I have to confess that I still haven't really caught up with what's happened over the last few days," she admitted. "How are you holding up?"

He smiled a little. "You mean about my father? It was a shock, but I never really liked the man. Still, it hurts a little, which leaves me conflicted. As for my mother and Nathan, I'd have shot them down myself if I could have. They were mad dogs."

She nodded and took his hand in hers. "Even so, this is going to be in your mind. If you need to talk about it, I'm here for you."

"I appreciate that, but we have plenty of time to sort out my emotions. The same is true for you, you know. You almost died. That's going to mess with your head. So will the other physical changes."

Jess stared out over the city. "The others haven't said anything, but I've lost about a decade of physical aging. None of the people here know me well enough to have seen it, or they just haven't said anything yet. What happened to me?"

Harry turned to face her. "You didn't see my mother. She was physically the same age as you are now. That sarcophagus is the fountain of youth, it seems. We'll want to keep that aspect of it quiet, at least until we understand it better."

"Probably even after," she agreed. "That kind of thing could be a damned bombshell. We probably need to talk with Brenda Cabot and Doctor Granger about it. They have the best understanding of Asharim technology, after all."

"I wouldn't count out others from guessing," he said. "Karl Krueger saw my mother. He'll have reported to his superiors about her and Nathan. He won't know that was my mother, but Queen will probably guess."

Secretary of State Josh Queen was a weasel, but Jess had to admit that he was probably canny enough to catch that. "He's got a lot on his plate, too. Maybe it'll slip by."

Harry laughed. "When have we *ever* caught a break on something like that? If an author tried to slip that kind of thing by, his readers would complain about *deus ex machina*. Count on Queen figuring it out, even if he doesn't make a point of telling us he did."

Then he sighed. "We should get inside and get some breakfast. Not only do we need to get all our ducks in a row, I have an early appointment with my father's personal assistant. You'll want to be there, too, now that you're awake. I have no idea what the man wants to discuss, but it probably has something to do with my father's estate."

She frowned. "I'm sure that has nothing to do with me. Your father's will probably includes an inheritance for you, but I was just an employee."

"You were his partner," Harry stressed. "He'll have something in there for you."

She shook her head. "He had to have had that will drafted years ago. He wouldn't have made any changes since we found all the Asharim stuff."

"Then you don't know him nearly as well as you think. He'll have considered everything we've found and made adjustments. He has a staff to handle the details and to remind him if something needs doing. Trust me when I say that this wouldn't have slipped by him, even with everything else that was going on."

She rubbed her face. "I don't want anything from him. It feels ghoulish. He was my boss for so long that I hadn't even gotten used to him being my partner in Humanity Unlimited. Everything happened so fast."

Harry clapped a hand on her shoulder. "Look at the bright side. With you around, he probably didn't leave that much to me, so one of us is coming out of this in good shape."

Jess laughed. "You're terrible. I hope he left everything to you. Hell, he probably did."

"There's only one way to find out. Let's go down and see if someone can go get some takeout breakfast. We don't dare show our faces in DC."

She raised an eyebrow. "You don't have to worry about that anymore. With the gate downstairs, we can go to *Freedom Express* and get breakfast with everyone else."

He shook his head and grinned. "Nothing against the cooks there or at the Mars base, but space food isn't nearly as good as what we can get down here on Earth. I'll trust that Brenda and her people know where the good stuff is. Hell, the way Victor Holyfield eats, he *has* to know what to recommend."

Victor was a big man, she had to admit. The heavy-worlder genes he'd inherited made him short, squat, and extremely well muscled. He needed to eat like a weightlifter.

"Let's do that, then," she said. "The sooner we get into motion, the sooner we can see about stopping World War III."

2

J osh Queen slammed his palm against the surface of his desk hard enough to make his subordinates stop squabbling amongst themselves. They were meeting so that they could help him formulate his response to both the Chinese aggression and the revelations of the Asharim and their alien tech.

"Enough!" Queen said into the startled quiet. "Running around like chickens with our heads cut off doesn't help us. Take a deep breath and focus on things we can do that will actually *benefit* us. The president expects solid ideas, and I'm counting on you to help me come up with them. Focus!"

The three people sitting around Queen's desk were all assistant secretaries of state, focusing on different aspects of US policy around the world. That fostered a sense of competition in them that he liked. He'd rather have them in competition with one another than plotting to supplant him one day.

Darryl Dickman—otherwise known behind his back as Darryl the Dick— scowled. "We've got too many hot potatoes flying around to focus our attention on so many things. Obviously, we have to honor the threat and give the Chinese our primary attention. We're at war, dammit."

That comment only made sense for someone who'd been focused on Asia for the last seven years. The man had a dislike for the Chinese and their bullying that Queen didn't disagree with in the slightest.

Under other circumstances, he'd have agreed with the man at once. Now, things were a lot more complex. He didn't need simple answers. He needed complex solutions.

"That fight is the military's to run now," Lana Bohannon said coldly, almost sneering. "They've started shooting, so we'll be talking through the barrel of a gun for now. We need to turn our attention to the *alien invasion!*"

Lana had never been a fan of the military. That trend had grown in popularity in the bureaucracy over the last few decades, and she was far from alone in her feelings. Unfortunately, their distaste left the United States in something of a bind now.

They needed the military, and Queen was regretting every spending cut he'd helped foster over the years. They'd all been badly mistaken about how desperately they'd need a strong military, him most of all.

"Sure," Darryl drawled with a sneer. "You say that *now*. How's that wall funding you supported keeping *these* illegal aliens out?"

"Oh, for Christ's sake," Phillip Judge, the last person in the conference room, said. "Who gives a flying squirrel what policies we supported in the past? We have to face the problems with what we have, not what we wish we had."

"If you'll recall, I supported the wall funding as well," Queen said. "That was for a different problem, and Phillip is right. We have to use the tools we have.

"I'll concede that dealing with the Chinese now is primarily military, but we have to have some policy recommendations for the president. The Chinese won't come to the table unless the military can stop them, and we have to be ready for that moment."

"Why start a shooting war?" Lana asked. "Yes, they blew up the Mars ship we bought from the Indian government. Tell the Indians we hadn't taken possession yet and get our money back and back off from the fight."

"We lost half a dozen astronauts on that ship," Darryl snarled. "We can't let that pass."

"If it suits our interests, we *can* and *should*," Phillip said, taking a sip of his water. "Do we want to fight them now or when we're ready?"

"What about the Yucatán spaceport?" Darryl countered, sticking his chin out pugnaciously. "Are we just going to let them humiliate us in front of the world?"

"Diplomacy is the art of saying 'nice doggie' while hunting for a big stick. Isn't that what Will Rogers said? We should follow his excellent advice, and before jumping off a cliff to show how tough we are."

That advice stuck in Queen's craw, but it had some merit, he admitted grudgingly. If they could delay the onset of hostilities until Jess Cook and Harry Rogers followed through with what the late and unlamented Clayton Rogers had promised, they might be able to bring alien firepower to bear on the Chinese and improve their odds considerably.

"That *might* be a workable recommendation," Queen said before the other three could fall back into arguing about it. "Not for long, mind you, but we can use the public relations angle to damage Chinese standing around the world while we try and get more of the alien tech to use against them."

Darryl looked as if he'd bitten into a rotten apple but held his tongue. Lana and Phillip nodded, with varying degrees of agreement.

"Let's say that keeps them from attacking our forces in other ways," Lana said. "How do we know that these Humanity Unlimited bozos are going to give us the alien tech? They could've just said they would, and now that the heat is off, they'll go on their merry way. It's not as if we can compel them to do what they promised."

Queen shook his head. "I've met the woman in charge. Unlike Clayton Rogers, I think she'll honor the commitment. After the reports that we received from the Navy forces that participated in the attack on the base they claim is in French territory, they know how little they have in the way of troops.

"Not to say the quality of Harry Rogers's special operations mercenaries is low. I've seen the reports, and he has a solid group of people. They even have access to alien weapons. The problem is that there are so few of them. Our intelligence reports say less than a hundred front-line operators.

"Faced with a whole universe full of hostile bad guys, they'll get wiped out in no time flat. Hell, if we hadn't sent that vest-pocket nuke on the last mission, they'd have died and we'd be fighting a *real* alien invasion right now, on top of a war with China."

Queen rubbed his hands across his face. "No, I think she'll play ball. I think I can secure the base in France for our use too, if I play my cards right. Now all I need to do is get them to actually let me talk with her."

Lieutenant Commander Karl Krueger, the man leading the SEAL team sent after Clayton Rogers, was in DC now, and Queen had spoken with him at length last night. Jessica Cook had been badly injured in the fighting and was undergoing medical care by that traitorous FBI agent, Brenda Cabot, and her illuminati group.

He hated the idea of dealing with the woman who'd kidnapped him, but he'd sent an encrypted message to the email address she'd given him, asking about Cook's condition. He'd come into the office this morning to find a reply stating Cook was on her feet and would be contacting him shortly.

Queen wasn't sure if that meant this morning or simply today. It galled him to be at the beck and call of others, but he'd grant the woman was convalescing. Cabot and her people had healed him of a gunshot, so he wasn't going to make that an issue.

"I'm going to send another message to Cabot," Queen finally said. "Did we get anywhere trying to trace the known members of her organization?"

"We found a few, but they've gone to ground," Lana said. "One is Victor Holyfield, a doctoral candidate in physics at MIT, as well as a star on their wrestling team. He hasn't been to class since you met him, and at this point I don't think he'll be back."

Queen nodded. That wasn't a surprise. The man was *very* recognizable. They probably hadn't initially planned on Queen seeing the young man.

"What about Doctor Todd Granger?" he asked. "An Asian man with a Southern accent has to be somewhat unique."

She nodded. "We pegged him too, but he left general practice years ago and fell off the radar. There's no way to use him to trace back to them. The FBI is following up on both of them, and Cabot too, but I'm not expecting a lot."

"Is Special Agent in Charge Pembroke leading the investigation?"

At her nod, Queen smiled. "He has a lot of reasons to work this case very hard. If anyone can track them down, it's him."

He leaned back in his comfortable leather chair and considered the place they'd found themselves in for a minute. His staff knew his ways and let him think. Finally, he sat up straight and nodded.

"I'll recommend to the president that we hold off on hostilities with China at this time. I want each of you to write up any diplomatic measures that we can use to make China look bad in the international community, as well as any covert actions we might take against them that will hinder their operations anywhere in this solar system. Dismissed."

They got up and filed out, already bickering by the time his door swung closed.

Queen brought up his email program. It was time to have a sit-down with Jess Cook and Harry Rogers. For that to happen, he needed to carefully word a promise of temporary immunity. He'd threatened a lot of legal charges against the pair, after all.

He rather suspected they'd prefer to meet him off planet, but he had no intention of surrendering himself to their custody again. They could come to him under a flag of parley. That would have to do.

* * *

HARRY HAD a lot of work to do but got into the panel van when it was ready at the building's loading dock. Seeing his late father's personal assistant wasn't something he was looking forward to, but the man had given his life so that Jess and Harry could live. That kind of sacrifice commanded respect, no matter how Harry felt about him.

People from the Families made certain that no one was in position to see them get inside the windowless van, and they were shortly on their way. The address the assistant had given them wasn't more than twenty minutes away on a good morning. So, with his luck, it would take twice that. Or get them stuck in a traffic jam for a few hours.

Jess's head was down and her eyes introspective, so he left her in peace. She'd gone through something more traumatic than almost anyone alive could claim. She'd been killed in a firefight. The miraculous recovery the Asharim sarcophagus had managed for her took nothing away from feeling her life drain away, he was sure.

Honestly, he didn't know if that was something even he could just shrug off. Hell, she was holding up better than he might in her place.

He'd be there for her when the crisis came, but he knew that he wasn't the best person to be at her side at a time like this. He'd called for Sandra Dean to come as soon as Jess had woken up. She'd be here today, as soon as she'd done her part to get the captured heavy-worlders secure and get the Volunteers safely back into the French base.

Miraculously, no one seemed to have noticed the thousands of people flooding out into the rugged rural area near Paris. He'd been expecting the

French authorities to come knocking over the last forty-eight hours, but there'd been nothing.

He'd have suspected Brenda Cabot's people of using their influence, but she'd told him that even though they'd been ready to do exactly that, no one had reported anything out of the ordinary. That was one piece of good luck that they'd certainly needed, since he'd have had to abandon the base if they'd come calling.

The van came to a halt, and the side door slid open. Harry flipped the hood on his windbreaker up, stepped out, and held out a hand for Jess to join him. She had a hat over her blonde hair to help conceal her identity. Two men from the Families got out with them.

The building they stood in front of was in significantly better condition than the one they'd just left: taller, cleaner, and better maintained. A glance around showed the building was located in a much better neighborhood. No surprise there.

They entered a door on the first level. The interior was set up with a reception room in the front and offices to the rear. There were no paintings on the wall and very little in the way of furniture. Harry guessed this office had been vacant yesterday.

The young man behind the front desk wasn't his father's assistant, but he did look familiar, so he must've been on the man's staff.

"Good morning, Mister Rogers, Miss Cook," the man said in a polite British accent. "Mister Weller is waiting for you in the main office. Your associates can wait here. I have donuts and either coffee or tea for them."

The man's accent cemented Harry's memory. "We've met, haven't we? You're Mister Weller's assistant... Anthony?"

The young man smiled. "You've got an excellent memory, Mister Rogers. My name is Anthony Brighton-Jones. I've been with Mister Weller for five years. Would you care for tea or coffee?"

"Hot tea?" Jess asked. "Please."

The man rose to his feet and went to a small table set up just out of sight of the door and began pouring some steaming tea.

Harry took the opportunity to make himself coffee and give their escorts a nod to signify it was safe to stay here. Based on how they were looking at the donuts, there wouldn't be any left by the time the meeting ended.

When Jess and he were armed with hot drinks, Anthony escorted them down a small hall and gestured toward the door at the back of the office. "Mister Weller is in there waiting for you. If you need anything at all, please don't hesitate to have him call me."

Harry nodded his thanks and rapped his knuckles on the indicated door. At the muffled call to enter, he opened the door.

Gregory Weller, Clayton Rogers's personal assistant, rose from a comfortable seat that had almost certainly been moved in just for this meeting, as the rest of the room was bare, other than two identical seats for Harry and Jess, as well as small tables for their drinks.

"Mister Rogers, Miss Cook," Weller said, shaking their hands. "Allow me to extend my deepest condolences for your loss. If there is anything I or my staff can do to lessen your burden, you have only to ask."

Once he'd shaken the man's hand, Harry sat and placed his coffee cup on the provided table. "I'm sure that we both appreciate that, Mister Weller. I think the best thing we can do for now is see what my father wanted. I assume this has something to do with his last will and testament."

The older man nodded as he sat. "Indeed, it does. Your father employed me as his assistant for the last twenty years, so I count myself as one of the few people in the world that can state with any confidence at all that they knew his mind. I'd like to start this meeting with some personal observances, if I may."

Harry picked up his coffee and took a sip. It was, of course, excellent. "I'd rather not spend too much time out in the open where our enemies can find us."

"Then you can rest easy. We have lookouts for blocks in every direction, and the basement here connects with an old sewer line that can see you to a getaway vehicle that the police—or any other kind of adversary—won't be expecting. If someone were to come knocking at the office door, young Anthony will discourage them."

"With tea and donuts?" Jess asked, a smile ghosting across her lips.

"With the automatic weapon under his desk, more likely. Anthony is former British SAS. He's quite the talented warrior. I'm sure that your escort would also serve to delay any pursuit."

"I see. Well, then, please go on."

"As I said, I knew your father's mind in many things, and though he wouldn't have said so, he deeply regretted the rift that his lifestyle caused between the two of you. While I have no intention of bridging it, I felt it best for you to know that even through the worst of times, he still loved you."

"Not enough to change," Harry said, still moved a little. "I'll accept that, though it changes little for me. He gave his life to save people I care about, so that washes away his sins in my mind. Let him rest in peace."

Weller nodded and smiled. "He'd have been satisfied with that, I believe."

The man pulled a briefcase off the floor and placed it in his lap before opening it. "I have here several sets of documents. Two for you, Harry, and one for Miss Cook. You'll want to have a lawyer of your choice look everything over, but I can explain the basics to you."

Jess took a manila envelope from Weller after Harry had his two. Unlike him, she opened hers. "What am I looking at, and why would I need another lawyer? Can't you do that?"

He nodded. "I can, but as Mister Rogers the elder would often say, trust lawyers sparingly. It's always best to have an uninvolved third party make certain that any documents say what you're told, unless you know the lawyer quite well and trust him. He trusted me, but you don't know me all that well. Get another set of eyes to look them over. Someone you trust."

"I have someone that can do that."

"Excellent." The man turned his attention to Harry. "Aren't you going to read them?"

"I'll let you give me the overview, and then I'll talk to my company lawyer."

"Make absolutely certain the second packet gets a much more thorough vetting than the first. It comes from a source that is both unexpected and concerning.

"The first packet is your father's will. He had it updated when the scope of the discoveries you were making became clear. Virtually all of his fortune was poured into Humanity Unlimited, but he did have some things that were not part of his corporate holdings. Many went to others, but one in specific he wanted you to have.

"He bought a sheep station in New Zealand, the one with the ruined base inside its borders. While that will no doubt end up in the hands of the government there, they've already agreed to not only leave the property in your father's ownership but to expand the purchase around the station to further isolate the base."

Harry frowned as he considered that. "So they're basically keeping him on as the owner of record to conceal the base while they run things? That makes sense, I suppose. It'll keep other nations from guessing too much. But don't the governmental leaders he met from Japan, Australia, and South Korea already know where it is?"

"It seems not. They came in an enclosed helicopter and had no electronics. They even wore blindfolds when being taken into the base. No one other than a select few in New Zealand know precisely where the base is located.

"They believe that the façade of your ownership and expansion will continue to help conceal it from all but the most determined searcher. Your father spoke of building a large house on top of the mesa above the base. New Zealand's prime minister thinks that's a capital idea and has already started the process. It provides excellent cover for moving in everything they need to open and repair the base as well as they can."

Harry had to admit that the raw, untamed wilderness made for an attractive location for something like that and provided ready access to gates that could take him anywhere.

"I suppose if he had to leave me anything, that makes more sense than most. Is that it?"

Weller shook his head. "Not quite. There are some other smaller mementos that are detailed in packet one. Nothing of great monetary value but of personal import to him. He also left you 39% of the shares in Humanity Unlimited, bringing your stake to 49%. He felt that Miss Cook might make for a better senior partner but wanted your shares to be of similar value.

"The packet in your possession has the 11% ownership stake in Humanity Unlimited that I mentioned, Miss Cook. You are now the majority shareholder with a 51% stake in the company. The entity is chartered in the Republic of Nauru, and the laws governing things there do not require any kind of inheritance tax, so the shares pass cleanly to you, as does the title of chief executive officer."

Jess rubbed her face. "I've got a lot on my plate. Can I delegate that?"

"Of course. I've taken the liberty of compiling a list of suitable candidates for that position, as well as for the slot you currently hold, chief operating officer. I suggest you pick people that will provide oversight on one another. Perhaps even select a chief financial officer that will ride herd on the company and other executives.

"The elder Mister Rogers always wanted people on the lookout for top leaders manipulating the company for their own ends rather than the good of the shareholders, whether that was himself or the general public.

"A strong board of directors can also assist in that, so I've compiled a second list of industry movers and shakers with the kind of experience that would benefit Humanity Unlimited. That should allow you to focus on the important work you're already doing."

Frankly, Harry was happy with that. He really didn't care who called the shots or how much money was earned. After a certain point, it was just keeping score. Like Jess, he just wanted to do what needed doing.

"And the second packet you gave me?" he asked.

The other man's face wrinkled in distaste. "That's far more problematic, I'm afraid. I feel that I should warn you I see the contents as being as dangerous as a nest of cobras. That is your mother's last will and testament."

Harry almost dropped the second envelope on the floor and leapt to his feet, but he settled for slowly setting it on the table. "Why do I need something like that?"

"Your mother was far less fastidious in updating her will," Weller said. "In fact, she last changed it over three decades ago. Both you and your brother were small children at that time, I believe.

"Boiled down, she left everything to be split between you and your brother Nathan. Should either of you predecease her or die at the same time, the whole would go to the survivor. In this case, that means she left all her worldly possessions to you, Harry.

"Your brother's will is also in there. It left everything to his mother with no codicil about her predeceasing him. In fact, it explicitly makes his holdings part of hers and dictates that it be disposed of by her or her heirs."

There was a long silence in which no one said anything.

"Based on the enmity between you," Weller said softly, "I'd wager that the possibility his mother would leave you anything at all never entered his mind. Whoever wrote the wills was competent, and I expect them both to pass muster. In fact, the only person with standing to challenge them is... you.

"The state of your mother's businesses is in flux, as the US government is attempting to seize much of it. She purchased your father's Rainforest holdings, so I foresee extreme volatility in the inheritance and challenges from several governments."

The other man smiled sadly. "I'm afraid even with all the pressing matters on your plate, it's going to become a sinkhole of your time, Harry. If you'd like, I would be pleased to offer my services as an assistant to help in these and other matters. I'm quite good and come with an excellent set of references, and a very competent staff."

Harry's head spun at the unexpected grenade that had landed in his lap. What a nightmare. He shook his head, trying to clear it. "I think I speak for both of us in saying we'd welcome your assistance."

Weller started to respond, but a sharp knock at the door preceded it abruptly opening. Anthony Brighton-Jones stuck his head in. "My apologies for interrupting, but several of our lookouts are reporting suspicious individuals moving into the area. They express doubts about them belonging to the police. May I suggest a well-ordered withdrawal before these new people get into position to do whatever it is that they have in mind?"

Immediately after his words, Harry recognized the unmistakable sound of a helicopter coming close. Too close. Without looking out the window, which might be dangerous, he knew that someone was about to put people on the roof.

Harry jumped to his feet. "It's time to go down that rat hole of yours, Mister Weller. The enemy—some enemy—has found us."

3

J ess wasted no time handing her envelope back to Mister Weller so that he could secure it with Harry's and following Brighton-Jones out of the office. She knew Harry would be bringing up the rear and making sure that Weller was right behind her.

She drew the pistol she'd put into a holster at the small of her back as she moved. It was one of two on her person today. She'd been caught unarmed too many times and had vowed that that wouldn't happen again.

She kept the muzzle low because the pistol was one of the Asharim flechette weapons and so was extremely dangerous. It wouldn't be much use to her if the people trying to get to them were the police or FBI, because she had no intention of shooting innocent people, but Brenda Cabot had made note of other people at play.

The Chinese had blown up Area 51 and the US government's cache of Asharim tech that they'd seized from Kathleen Bennett and her company, BenCorp. There was also the unknown group of heavy-worlders seen in the area, no doubt searching for Brenda Cabot or her base. Those people had also been of Asian appearance, so they might very well be connected to China as well.

Whoever they were, they'd be inside shortly, based on the noises coming from the roof. The helicopter was hovering there above the building, probably dropping armed intruders near the stairs. It would likely only be moments before someone broke in the front and rear doors as well.

"Down here," Brighton-Jones said as he stood beside a nondescript door, aiming a lethal-looking rifle back toward the front of the building. "Go straight down and keep any noise to a minimum."

Jess was happy that there was a light on as she descended the narrow stairs.

After having the Mayan pyramid collapse on her and Harry, she'd not done so well in dark, confined spaces.

The stairs let out into a wide, dimly lit, cluttered room with a bare concrete floor and rough brick walls. It looked decades older than the building above it and seemed not to have been cleaned in about the same amount of time.

The brick walls in particular could've done with a few good scrubbings and a liberal application of bleach. Even that might not have killed off the green stuff growing on them, but maybe it would've cut it back some.

Harry and Weller came out from the stairway next. The older man headed unerringly behind the stairs themselves, motioning for them to follow him. There was a large hole in the wall just out of sight from the basement proper. From the lack of bricks nearby, it had probably been opened some time ago.

He picked up one of four flashlights sitting beside the hole, turned it on, and handed it to Jess. "Go in and take the right-hand turn at the sewer."

"You first," she said. "I'm armed, you're not."

"We don't have time for this," Harry said, pointing at Brenda's people. "You're up front with Mister Weller. Anthony, Jess, and I will bring up the rear."

The two men looked as if they wanted to argue but didn't. Especially after hearing a muffled thump from upstairs.

At almost the same moment, the bare bulb that had been illuminating the basement went out. "That was me," Brighton-Jones said as he came slowly into the light, probably so that someone didn't shoot him by mistake.

"I took the liberty of locking the office door," he added. "That noise would be a breaching charge taking it down. It won't take them long to realize that we've flown the coop."

Weller and the two men from the Families led the way into the tunnel. Brighton-Jones gestured to a wooden frame with a paint-splotched canvas thrown haphazardly over it.

"Help me move this over the breach. It will make them have to search harder for where we disappeared to."

Rather than get in the way, Jess stepped back and provided light for them to work.

It only took them a few seconds to pull the cover over the tunnel. It wouldn't fool anyone for long if they were really looking, but it was enough to fool a casual observer.

Harry grabbed the last of the flashlights and motioned for Brighton-Jones to lead the way. He and Jess followed closely behind.

The tunnel itself wasn't new. The slime on the walls was ample proof of that. She wondered who had built it and why. She was also curious how Weller had known it was here for them to use. Questions for later, she supposed.

Whoever had built the tunnel hadn't been concerned with making it neat or pretty. The stones in the walls were of odd shapes and often protruded from the surrounding stones. The mortar between them was crumbling too, so the engineer in her wondered about the long-term stability of the structure. Definitely not professional work.

Thankfully, it was good enough to get them to the sewer. It was an arch of stone that rose almost two meters over her head, had a channel in the middle of the flow to carry the noisome sludge, and concrete walkways on either side.

It also had the stench of something dead that was strong enough to just about knock her over. She clapped her free hand over her mouth, but that hardly helped, as she still had to breathe.

Weller and the other two men had turned right, and she could see the two lights bobbing ahead, so she turned and followed them, praying that the source of the disgusting odor was behind her.

No such luck. The smell grew stronger until she saw the dead animal in the middle of the trough that carried the sewer water. It was too far gone to determine what it had been, and that was probably a blessing.

A muffled shout from far behind them told her that the enemy—whoever they were—had found the hidden exit from the building. So much for their ruse delaying the pursuit long enough for them to get away. She sped up her pace, trying to balance the need to get clear with not slipping on the moisture-slick concrete.

Everything around her seemed to jump as something exploded ahead of them and the pressure wave shoved her back. The loud noise made her ears ring.

"If they're blowing a sewer entrance, it isn't the police or FBI," Harry shouted, his voice sounding oddly muffled to her ears. "Be ready."

A burst of automatic weapons fire cut both of Brenda Cabot's people down without warning. They'd been right in front of Mister Weller, and their bodies shielded Weller and herself from the hail of bullets.

Jess grabbed Weller by the shoulder and threw herself to the left. Her intention had optimistically been to jump over the disgusting contents of the channel, but her foot slipped on the slimy stones, sending them both tumbling into the sewer.

The cold, filthy water covered her head for a moment, but she came up to her knees and found it was only a foot or so deep. She brought her pistol around and opened fire on the man who'd killed their Family escorts.

Harry and Brighton-Jones were already shooting at the man and had him pinned down behind a corner ahead, but Jess's angle let her put several flechettes right into him. He fell into the water with a splash, still twitching after one of the darts shattered his skull.

"Keep them pinned down," Harry yelled, racing ahead toward the connecting tunnel.

With no choice in the matter, Jess kept up a regular fire of her weapon until he reached the dubious safety of the corner, stuck his pistol around it blindly, and opened fire.

Brighton-Jones was right behind him, so Jess stopped shooting, switched out the partly used magazine for a full one, and helped Weller upright, though she kept him in the water. He'd somehow managed to retain his grip on his briefcase. She hoped it was waterproof.

If she looked anything as bad as Weller did, she would need seventeen hot showers to ever feel clean again. And a tetanus shot. Maybe two.

Even though there was still fighting taking place ahead of them, she faced to the rear and stayed in the water. When the bad guys came, she wanted them to miss seeing her at first.

Disgustingly, that meant she had to use the dead animal as cover. The dead, maggot-covered carcass that stank like nothing else she had ever smelled in her life. Make it thirty-six hot showers, three tetanus shots, and a course of antibiotics.

Weller knelt behind her just as half a dozen men in dark suits and bulletproof vests came pouring out from the makeshift tunnel and into the sewer. She immediately realized they were heavy-worlders, at least genetically speaking, though they were dressed in perfectly ordinary clothes.

A momentary flashback of one shooting her in the gut at the French base washed over her, and then she was firing at them. Her flechette pistol made little sound and had no muzzle flash to reveal her position, so the enemy must've thought the fire from Harry and Brighton-Jones was what was taking them down. Maybe they were, but she was firing single shots like a metronome, taking the hostile men down one after another.

In seconds, the sewer was silent, though her ears were ringing from the normal weapons' fire. The enemy behind them was down, some on the concrete and others in the nasty water with Jess. She waited a beat to see if more of them would come pouring out of the tunnel, but they seemed to have stopped for the moment.

"Let's go," Harry shouted. "We don't have much time before more of them get here. Where to next, Mister Weller?"

"Keep straight on and take a left at the next intersection. That will lead to a similar tunnel in the wall that ends up in a warehouse. We have a van inside it."

Jess stood and determinedly put the putrid sludge that covered her out of her mind. There'd be time to throw up later.

"Tell me there's a hose to wash the worst of this off," she begged. "Please."

"Sadly, no," the man said. "At least I'm not sure if we can find one in time. We're just going to have to tough it out."

They stopped long enough to empty the pockets of the dead, friend and foe alike. Then they hurried off down the sewer, Brighton-Jones in the lead, Weller behind him, and Harry behind her.

"Good shooting back there," Harry said as they walked. "I didn't think you'd be that good a shot with an unfamiliar weapon. Or perhaps weapons in general, since you don't have a lot of experience with shooting."

She half turned her head. "What do you mean?"

"The flechettes leave distinctive wounds. I could tell where you hit verses where we did. You took out four of them. Five counting the man ahead of us. All with head shots."

That news made her blink. Had she? How? She wasn't that good with guns of any kind, much less the alien weapons, which she'd only fired a few times, never with much luck.

So what he was saying was impossible. Yet, as she ran her mind back over the fight, she knew it was true. How could she have done that?

The thought kept eating at her until they arrived inside the warehouse. The ever-resourceful Brighton-Jones managed to locate a water hose and sprayed her off as well as possible in thirty seconds. It would have to do.

While he was giving his boss the same treatment, she joined Harry in the back of the van. "They were heavy-worlders. Not the ones from off planet, but the Chinese ones Brenda told us about."

He nodded. "I agree. No off-worlders would have the insight to even be looking for us, much less be able to find us."

"How did that happen?" she asked. "Is the safe house compromised?"

"I rather doubt it," Weller said as he climbed into the front of the van. "Sadly, I expect that they followed me, even though we took every precaution we could. I wasn't in hiding, after all."

Brighton-Jones opened the exit leading into the alley, drove the van out, and then closed it before climbing back behind the wheel. "We'll go nice and slow. With all that ruckus, the police are going to swarm the area. Where should I go?"

"Out of DC," Harry said. "I'll make a call and get Brenda to come for us."

"What if they have a tracking device on them?" Jess asked. "That would lead them right to us."

"We checked, but I suppose that's always possible," Brighton-Jones admitted.

"Pull over and switch places with me," Harry said. "Both of you in the back with Jess. Strip down to your tighty whities. Keep your wallets, keys, and other personally identifiable things, but check them to see if you find anything suspicious. We'll dump everything we can in a dumpster on the way out of town.

"I realize that's an indignity, but we can't risk them tracking us back to the safe house. They cannot be allowed to get their hands on a gate."

Jess was glad she wasn't going to have to strip. The way her luck had been going, that hadn't been out of the question. Though, she supposed her new and younger body would've been an improvement if she'd had to get down to the skin.

In the end, they managed to get out of the neighborhood without drawing any undue attention, though, as predicted, the police were out in force. She didn't imagine that whoever had sent the attackers was going to be pleased with their failure or the fallout.

Better them than her. She had her own problems to worry about. Like her sudden skill with guns.

It had to have something to do with her near-death experience. One more thing the sarcophagus had done to her. One more mystery to solve.

4

Chen Jian, formerly the Chinese ambassador to the United States of America before they expelled all of his country's diplomatic staff, slammed his phone onto his desk, smashing the screen.

How had the targets escaped his team? How had they killed most of his men? He'd seen the report. It was just a few civilians, one mercenary, a scientist, and a few guards.

He'd sent a combat team of Dragons. Their heavy-worlder genetics and combat training should've made the outcome inconceivable. Yet the primary team was dead, and the bodies were in the hands of the American authorities, and the only lead to his targets had slipped his grasp.

Chen sighed and regretted smashing his phone. It would take time to get him a new one and move his data over. The rage was acceptable. The violence was not.

If the man seated in front of him cared about the show of emotion, he was wise enough not to show it. Arthur Hyde, a short American with blond hair, showed only a mildly interested expression and said nothing. A wise decision from the Dragon's lead agent in America.

"I apologize for my unseemly display of emotion," Chen said, putting his ruined phone into a desk drawer in his appropriated office at the Yucatán spaceport. "The loss of our agents is regrettable. The failure to capture any of the people with access to the Asharim technology, though, is unacceptable. How did that happen?"

"It seems there was a preexisting escape tunnel built into the sewers that we had no reason to expect. Once the point team discovered this, the surface teams went down through breached manhole covers, and they surrounded the targets.

"Unfortunately, the confrontation went poorly. As none of the Dragon warriors returned, and the transmissions from the video cameras in their gear was blocked by being underground, I can't say with any certainty how they died. Only the helicopter pilots and the vehicle drivers and lookouts had escaped.

"While I hesitate to suggest this, as it smacks of making excuses, it's possible the targets prepositioned fighters in the sewers. Our people could have run into an ambush that was strong enough to end them, even with terrestrial weapons."

Chen nodded slowly. "That's possible, since we have no insight into how familiar they were with the area. The man we traced there was at one time Clayton Rogers's personal assistant. He is known to be canny, so it's possible that he knew exactly what was there and used it to his advantage."

Leaning back in his seat, Chen half turned and stared out his window at one of the lifter gantries in the distance. Even though the ownership of the place was still being contested, possession, as they said, was nine-tenths of the law.

This spaceport had once belonged to Clayton Rogers. The man had sold it to the Chinese to avoid having the American government seize it along with the rest of his assets when they found out the man had built an interplanetary spaceship with a nuclear powerplant rather than a space hotel.

Quite the trick, Chen had to admit. A worthy play in the great game.

The Chinese in turn had sold it to Rogers's ex-wife, Kathleen Bennett, with the sure knowledge that they could maintain control in the end while replenishing their coffers. The US government was already in the process of seizing her property, so the Chinese government would simply void the sale and keep her money as well.

What was she going to do about the crime, after all? Particularly if the rumors of her death proved accurate. The same was true of the United States. They could scream all they liked, but so long as he controlled the spaceport, they had no other recourse.

The chaos those actions engendered suited the goals of the Dragon admirably. No one outside his organization suspected the Dragon even existed. Descendants of the heavy-worlder attack teams that had assaulted the human resistance's bases in this system a thousand years ago made up the core of the Dragon, and they'd been manipulating the Chinese people and government ever since.

That had held true until recently. Now he was certain there was another group of people playing the great game from the resistance side. His spies had identified a former FBI agent named Brenda Cabot as a leader in this organization, and they were apparently in league with the company Clayton Rogers had formed to exploit the Asharim technology: Humanity Unlimited.

The man's son, Harry Rogers, had led the flight of the illegal ship that they'd named *Liberty Station* to Mars. He'd undoubtedly found an old resistance base there. The evidence was incontrovertible, as he'd appeared back on Earth without his ship returning.

That meant they'd found and activated one of the Asharim gates of legend. The portals that could take a person across the galaxy in a single step. And the key to the Dragon once again finding the Masters and serving them.

The Asharim had transformed the heavy-worlders into their warriors. Each of them trapped on Earth longed to fight once more at their sides.

Which only made capturing Harry Rogers and his female companion more critical. Or Brenda Cabot, as Chen was certain she had control of the gate Rogers had used to return to Earth.

Chen forced himself out of his reverie and turned back toward Hyde. "The original goal of this attack was to capture Harry Rogers or any of his companions, but the secondary goal was to trace Brenda Cabot. He has to be staying somewhere near her, and she is in Washington, DC. Did you have any luck tracing the van that Rogers arrived at the site in or capturing the driver?"

Hyde shook his head. "We captured the driver, but he perished from wounds inflicted during the fight."

Chen grimaced. "A pity. We need to focus on Cabot and Rogers. At some point, they will once more come within our grasp.

"The police will recover the bodies of our people and much evidence from the scene of the attack. I want you to arrange a raid tonight to retrieve them from the morgue and to destroy the crime lab. Also, send a third team to cleanse the sewers with fire. No evidence pointing back at the Dragon must remain in soiled hands."

The man rose smoothly to his feet and bowed. "It shall be as you say. No one will be allowed to discover our secrets." With that, the American left his office.

Chen returned his gaze to the launch gantry in the distance. The battle had barely commenced its opening stages, yet he was hopeful. If they couldn't get a gate on Earth, he'd seize the one on Mars.

Rogers's makeshift ship would not be able to stand against the Chinese Mars vessel. It had weapons aboard that the American would never dream of. If he returned to the Red Planet to fight in its defense, his body would be left moldering on the frozen surface of the desolate world.

The ascendance of the Dragon was within his grasp, and he would not falter. Victory would be his, no matter how many people he had to kill to achieve it.

* * *

HARRY HAD FINALLY STARTED to relax when their van met up with the one Cabot sent to pick them up. The vehicular trade took place in a parking garage, so while there were witnesses, there weren't many, and no one seemed to pay them any particular attention.

Her people put Weller and Brighton-Jones into the back of the van after relieving the latter of his weapons. They also scanned everyone for tracking devices, which was a good idea since he was certain that the attackers had followed Weller to the meeting. They'd found nothing, so the tracker must have been in the clothes they'd discarded.

It was an open question whether the attackers had understood who the man was meeting. If Harry had to guess, he'd have said they'd followed Weller hoping to get Cabot. They'd had no reason to expect him or Jess. So far as everyone on Earth should have known, they were on Mars.

Harry gave Jess a covert look as Cabot's people drove them back to the hideout. She'd been a little off since her brush with death. A lot more introspective than usual, though that was probably inevitable.

Her recent improvement with the Asharim weapon was more inexplicable. She hadn't had time to practice, yet she'd acquitted herself more than admirably. That was a mystery he'd have to invest some time solving later.

The van pulled up behind the hideout, and the guards hustled them all inside. Weller and Brighton-Jones went into seclusion until Cabot either approved of them being there or sent them packing.

"Let's go talk with Cabot," Harry told Jess.

She shook her head. "You go ahead. I need to shower and then go see Doctor Granger. I still have one more checkup, and I have a few questions for him."

"Okay," he agreed, sensing her evasion but willing to let it pass. "I'll fill Cabot in and see how she wants to proceed while you get checked out."

Once they'd parted ways, he took the elevator down to the basement and found Cabot exactly where he'd expected, sitting at a table, going over some of the recovered Asharim technology.

She stopped what she was doing as soon as he entered the room and marched resolutely over to him. "What went wrong? We lost the driver we sent with you when some people attacked the van. I'll assume it was the same people that attacked you. Who were they?"

"The heavy-worlders you told us about, I think," he said. "We got down into the sewers, but I'm afraid they got the men you sent with us as well. We killed them all, and I recovered what I could from their bodies."

He put their wallets, keys, and other objects on the table. "Your people scanned us for tracking devices, and these came up clean. If I had to guess, they were tracking my father's personal assistant, hoping that his visit to Washington had to do with meeting you. We dumped their clothes early."

The woman grunted as if someone had punched her in the gut. "Three good people gone. Dammit."

She rubbed her face and started going through the licenses. She stopped at one. "I know this guy. He and his crew were searching this neighborhood when I first spotted them."

"Do we have any idea who they are?" Harry asked. "Better yet, how did they know you were here? Are they still in the area?"

Cabot shrugged. "My guess is that they're of heavy-worlder descent and that they're based out of China. My ancestors must have missed a few of the heavy-worlder guards that were sent to suppress the human resistance.

"I'm not sure how they tagged this area, but we've tightened up our security and signals control. Whatever it was, they seem to have moved on to other locations. I'm not sure where they're based, but you can bet your ass I'm going to be looking for them a lot more aggressively from now on. No one kills my people and gets away with it.

"Thanks for getting this identification. It's almost guaranteed to be fake, but it gives me a place to start."

She gestured for Harry to come over to one of the cleared tables and sat down. "What did your father's assistant want with you? Something to do with your inheritance?"

Harry took a few minutes to fill her in on what he'd been told. She simply nodded her head until he got to the part where he'd inherited his mother's and brother's assets. Then she laughed.

"Wow, that's some serious karma. All the crap they pulled and then, because they didn't update their last wills and testaments, the guy they were trying to kill gets it all. That's hilarious."

He grunted, unamused. "You're not the one that has to try and make any sense of it. It's not like the US government is trying to confiscate everything out from under *you*. Though, technically, I suppose they are. Frankly, I don't care what they owned. If it all vanishes, that doesn't mean anything to me."

Cabot nodded. "What are you going to do about your father's assistant? Did you decide to hire him?"

"So far as I can tell, the man has always been a rock that my father could count on. With everything we've got going on, I'd be an idiot not to accept his help. So, yeah, I hired him. Jess did too, so I suppose he works for Humanity Unlimited rather than me."

"You've spoken about his competence," Cabot said. "What about his trustworthiness? Is he someone that we can bring completely into what we're doing and trust that it's not going to get out to anyone else?"

Harry considered that for several seconds and then nodded. "My father trusted him implicitly. He wouldn't have done that if the man didn't have what it took."

They sat in silence for a few minutes before he broached the next subject on his mind. "I'm concerned about Jess. Almost getting killed really screwed her up, and today she displayed a talent that I never expected to see out of her: she used one of the flechette pistols like a professional. Way better skill than she'd exhibited with one in the past."

That caused Cabot to frown slightly. "I've heard a couple of stories— legends, really—based around the kind of healing device that we found her in. Humans in general didn't know anything about how they worked, but at least a few of the old stories speak of the people being healed having skills that they'd never had before once the process was complete.

"The skill I'm thinking of wasn't fighting, but since we found this device on a heavy-worlder ship, perhaps a fighting skill was more appropriate than language."

Harry felt his eyebrows rise. "Are you telling me that that machine could implant something in her mind to give her the skill to use the flechette pistol? Seriously? And what do you mean by language?"

Cabot grimaced a little. "This is a very old story, so don't hold it against me if it doesn't turn out to be accurate. What I heard was that the machine was able to teach others how to speak the Asharim language. She hasn't shown any indication of that sort of thing, but it's not as if we've exposed her to anything that would reveal it."

A chill washed through him. "If it could mess with her brain, could it do other things? Turn her against us?"

"I don't think so," Cabot said firmly. "Nothing in the legends ever said anything about it altering someone's personality or allegiances. It wasn't a way to brainwash someone. It was a healing device that might have had the added capability of teaching someone something that's programmed into it. Let's not get carried away and start down the path of paranoia."

"How do we know what it did?" he asked. "If it taught her how to speak Asharim and shoot a pistol, what else might be in her head now?"

Cabot smiled slightly. "We do it the old-fashioned way: we give her a series of tests that she's absolutely going to hate. I suggest we get Jess to see Todd Granger, and then we'll see if we can figure out what's really going on."

Harry rubbed his face. "Just what I need, one more thing on my to-do list. I need to be striking items off it rather than adding them on."

"Welcome to leadership," Cabot said with a laugh as she rose to her feet. "The first thing you learn is that you'll never clear the decks. No matter how much you do, the list of things you still have to get to just keeps getting longer.

"Be glad you've got a personal assistant now. Maybe he can get your life organized and take some of those action items off your plate. But for right now, we need to check on your partner."

Harry reluctantly agreed. No matter how many other things he had to get to, if Jess wasn't in a good place, she deserved his full attention. The rest of the world was just going to have to wait.

5

"Hey," a female voice said, causing Jess to turn. Sandra Dean was exiting the stairwell and headed her way. Fast. Even though the other woman wasn't the most demonstrative person, she pulled Jess into a tight hug.

She then pushed Jess back out and gave her a thorough looking over. "You're looking good for someone that bled out."

"Thanks, I think. I thought you were still in France working on the heavy-worlder prisoners and the Volunteer refugees."

"We moved the Volunteers to *Freedom Express*," the brunette said with a slight smile. "We've got plenty of room for them there. The heavy-worlders are down in New Zealand. The dead base there makes a decent holding area, now that we have the lights on and basic supplies in stock. The gates are dead, other than the one that's locked down, and the only way out is through the cave in the top floor, so we have them penned in pretty good.

"But I'm not here to give you an update on that. I want to see how you're doing now that you're out of that box. Harry said there'd been something weird, and I want to hear all about it."

"I suspect that you weren't supposed to mention that part to me," Jess said dryly.

"Life is too short to talk around the important things," the sniper said firmly. "What's happening?"

"We got into a fight down in the sewers. I shot some people."

"Succinctly put, but that doesn't sound at all outside the realm of normal events these days."

Jess sighed. "I was using a flechette pistol, and I shot it way better than I should have. Way, *way* better. Now I'm worried that sarcophagus did something unexpected to me."

"Other than bringing you back from the brink of death? How will you know?"

"Doctor Granger is going to run some tests, which I'm now late for. Come on."

Jess went farther down the hall and rapped on the doctor's door. His muffled voice told her to come in, so she did.

The room on the other side was larger than the door might lead one to believe. They'd removed a few walls to make a single large room where several had been before. The space was filled with a mixture of Asharim technology and Earth medical gear. The largest object present was the sarcophagus that had healed her.

Doctor Todd Granger, a short man of Asian descent in a white lab coat, stepped over from the alien device and gave her a considering stare.

"You're looking okay," he said at last, his voice jarring her with its deep Southern accent. He'd been raised in Georgia, and the accent was wildly outside her expectations, even though she'd known him for a while now.

"Looks can be deceiving," she said, closing the door behind Sandra. "Something odd is going on, Doctor. Something more than we've already seen."

"Come over to the chair, have a seat, and call me Todd, like I said last time. What have you noticed?"

She sat in the indicated seat and crossed her legs. "I'm younger than I was before. I keep in good shape, but I can tell the difference between my mid-thirties and my mid-twenties. Also, I can now shoot a flechette pistol like a damned champ. I was never that good with things like that before, so I'm really at a loss there."

"The latter does seem a little off," he admitted. "I suspected the age difference based on what Harry told us he'd seen with his mother. She looked as if she were physically in her mid-twenties when he last encountered her as well."

Jess felt her lips compress. "Don't you think you should've mentioned that earlier?"

"I'm trying to get a handle on this too," Todd said somewhat defensively. "Her age change was dramatic, where yours was more subtle. Those people that don't already know you well probably wouldn't have picked up on it."

He held up a hand before she could speak. "And before you rip my head off, I was going to tell you in the next day or so. We're just trying to keep word of a fountain of youth to a minimum. Right now, only a couple of people know about Kathleen Bennett's change.

"Even out of the people that saw her at the last fight, we suspect most of them didn't know her well enough to even realize who she was. We wanted to let things settle out a bit before I called you back in for a more thorough examination."

Jess sighed. "I want to know about changes to me when you do. It's not fair to make me guess that something is wrong. You wanted to do some tests. Let's get that started."

He nodded, picked up a clipboard, and handed it to her. "Tell me what you see here."

Jess examined the paper there and frowned. The writing wasn't in English. The letters were in the Asharim script. She'd seen enough of them on *Freedom Express* that she was familiar with the shapes, if not the content.

Frighteningly though, she now understood the alien text. It was a set of instructions for opening the sarcophagus. The knowledge that she was reading something in the alien script frightened her deeply.

"What the hell is going on?" she asked, waving the clipboard at him. "How can I read this?"

"I wasn't sure that you'd be able to," he admitted. "The legends we have about this device are sketchy at best. The Asharim only used it on themselves and their most trusted slaves. The old stories spoke about miraculous knowledge but didn't give many details. They did say you'd be able to read the Asharim language, so that was a good start for my testing.

"What we don't know is how deep the knowledge goes. Can you only read it, or do you have other hidden knowledge, too? It seems you have familiarity with flechette pistols. What about this?"

He reached behind the sarcophagus, pulled out one of the heavy-worlder battle rifles, and handed it to her.

The first thing she did was flip it over so that the muzzle wasn't pointing at anything important and check to see if it was loaded. It wasn't. And only then did she realize she had no idea how she'd known to do that.

"What the hell is going on?" she asked in a whisper.

Todd reached over and took the weapon from her, placing it back where he'd gotten it. "I think the device implanted some skills to go along with the language lessons. The fact you know about the heavy-worlder weapons tells me that it was angled to be useful to their warrior slaves. Perhaps the last setting was what they used on one of them.

"Or maybe it was set to drop everything in its memory banks. I don't speak Asharim, and I'm still working my way through what I'm seeing. I've got some other tests to run, but at this point I'd say you're going to have a lot of surprising moments over the next few months where you realize you can do something new."

"Well isn't that just peachy?" Jess asked rhetorically, annoyed in spite of the potential upsides. "Are we sure that I'm still me? That's what you were worried about, weren't you? That the machine changed me."

He waved away her concerns. "No. We knew you were you right away. Even the old legends don't talk about the process changing people like that. Don't fear that you've got secret programming in your head. That didn't happen.

"On the other hand, we're going to be testing you on a lot of different things over the next few weeks. I can't imagine what you know that we don't, but it could be the spark for a number of breakthroughs with recovered equipment."

"That's all fine and good, but she needs time to recover from the shock," Sandra said firmly. "Enough poking and prodding."

"I haven't even *started* poking and prodding," Todd objected mildly.

"And it can wait," the sniper snapped. "She has to have time to get used to this. Besides, I want her to come back to the French base with me. I've got to see her shoot for myself."

Jess rolled her eyes. "I don't have time to play, Sandra. Maybe later. For now, let's see if I can figure out how to get some information out of the sarcophagus. I want to know what it did to me, and that means finding the settings it used and deciphering them."

* * *

BRENDA CABOT WALKED into the small park, even though she damned well knew that Queen had people watching it. Meeting him was a calculated risk but one she had to take. The situation was too dire to let paranoia convince her that he was lying about the parley.

Besides, if he screwed with her, she'd have her own people on hand to extract her. Trust only went so far.

The trees were pretty this time of year. The green leaves were bright, and the scent of new growth was in the air. It was nice.

As they'd agreed, he was sitting alone on a bench, watching the birds curiously. He hadn't bothered to clear the park of visitors, so there were a lot of mothers and kids around.

And a few FBI agents. She spotted them by the way they moved. After all, until just recently, she'd been one of them.

She set her bag on the ground beside the bench and sat next to Queen without speaking.

"I can't remember the last time I sat and watched the pigeons," he said, sounding somewhat bemused. "Sky rats, my mother used to call them. She wouldn't let us feed them. Said that would only make them hound us for more."

"Seagulls are like that, too," she responded with a nod. "Only more demanding. Thanks for making the time to meet with me. And not having Agent Pembroke arrest me, since I know that he's in the plumbing van up the street listening in. Seriously? A plumbing van? Cliché much?"

Queen raised his gaze to her face and smirked a little. "That's going to piss him off. He was certain that you'd miss him."

"Not in that van. Seriously though, I know you have no reason to trust me and plenty of other trouble on your plate, so I appreciate you offering to parley."

"I had to look up the legalities of meeting with a wanted felon," he admitted. "'Parley' is an interesting word with Medieval implications that the law doesn't quite cover. Enemies meeting on the field of battle to negotiate a truce or surrender. Are you giving up, Agent Cabot?"

"Hardly, but neither one of us needs an additional enemy right now. You have China on your plate, and I have the heavy-worlders."

Queen quirked an eyebrow at her. "The heavy-worlders are done. You moved them to New Zealand, according to the people I have there."

He made it sound as if he had people with authority on the ground in the South Pacific nation, but she knew they had the only US Navy ship impounded there, and the New Zealanders had only allowed some of the ship's crew to stay in the base as observers after Lieutenant Commander Karl Krueger and his people had helped to fight the heavy-worlders.

Not that she intended to rub that in his face, true though it was.

"They were only the first of many, unless I can stop them at the source," Brenda said sourly. "We think we've locked them out of the base in France— which I also know you know about in general terms—but there are other bases on Earth that no one has found yet. If they come through in force before we can secure them, humanity is toast."

"We'd be happy to assist you with that."

"I'm sure you would, but trust is earned, not given. Thirty years ago, I'd believe the US government would have the best interests of the human race at least somewhere on their radar. Not now. It's an oligarchy in everything but name.

"Still, neither Jessica Cook, Harry Rogers, nor I believe we can do this alone. So, that being said, we're going to reach out a hand and hope you have enough enlightened self-interest not to bite it off."

"How is Miss Cook?" he asked, a genuine look of concern on his face. "Commander Krueger said that she'd been critically injured, but I know that you have access to miraculous healing technology. My compliments again to Doctor Granger, by the way. If I didn't know that I'd been shot, I'd never have believe it after he healed me."

"She's up and about. Good as new. In fact, her exploits are one of the things I wanted to talk with you about."

She relayed how Harry and Jess had met with Clayton Rogers's personal assistant and how they'd been attacked. She left out any mention of the other woman's strange new capabilities.

Queen nodded as she spoke but held his comments until she had finished. "I heard about the attack, though I had no idea who was involved, and the FBI is assisting with that. I was sure it had something to do with the Chinese. Why are they interested in Rogers or Cook?"

"I'm not sure they are," she said slowly. "I think they might have been looking for me."

That made the secretary of state blink. "Why would the Chinese be looking for you?"

"Those people Rogers killed during the escape seem to be of heavy-worlder extraction. We think there is a group similar to mine based in China, only they are descended from survivors from the other side of the fighting a thousand years ago.

"We had no idea they existed, and they didn't know about us. Now they do, probably from having spies in the US government like we do. They're probably the ones behind the attack on Area 51, though they had to have had Chinese government sanction. Hell, they're probably pulling the strings over there."

Queen grunted as if he'd been punched in the gut. "That's an unpleasant bit of supposition, but I suppose it can be verified easily enough. Some of Krueger's troops came back with blood on them, so we can do a DNA screen for heavy-worlders. Shit, we should do it in all critical areas to flush out spies."

"I wouldn't count on all the spies being of heavy-worlder extraction," she cautioned. "They can probably recruit as well as we can.

"In any case, they're almost certainly the ones blocking you from getting into space. They want the tech because they almost certainly don't have a portable gate or access to a permanent one. We've got to keep things that way, too."

"Well, they certainly aren't going to get anything from us," he said, disgust obvious in his tone. "Not after they blew it all up. I told their ambassador that a lot survived, but in truth they got it all. Some of the scientists survived, but all the hardware is gone.

"I assume that means they're on the way to Mars with a lot of technology that we can't match and that they intended to take the Mars base Rogers found inside Olympus Mons."

That was a guess on his part, she was sure, but not too big a leap. Might as well throw him a bone.

"Yes. The base inside the Olympus Mons caldera is huge and filled with functioning tech. We're sure that the Chinese spacecraft is manned by people from this heavy-worlder group and that they have tech with them that will make it hard to deal with them in space, using what Harry has there. That means we're going to have to deal with them before they arrive and hope we can take them out before they blow up *Liberty Station*."

The interplanetary spaceship that Clayton Rogers had built was in orbit around Mars and had no weapons at all, much less any that could deal with Asharim tech. They'd have to run away if they wanted to avoid an engagement that would see them destroyed. At least the Humanity Unlimited ship was far faster in space than the Chinese one.

"Once again, I might be able to help with that, in exchange for some consideration," Queen said.

"Harry might accept that, once it's negotiated in front of witnesses," she said. "He's going to return to New Zealand to deal with the mess his father left behind. He's also going to take the opportunity to talk with the alliance there. I suggest you have someone that can speak for you present. Someone that the New Zealanders respect."

"You mean Commander Krueger. He's not a diplomat."

"You say that as if it's a flaw. If he says something, they'll be much more inclined to believe him than one of your regular weasels. Oh, and be aware that the UN is sending a representative to examine the base. Word is going to get out about all this soon."

"Perfect," Queen muttered. "As if I don't have enough on my plate with the Chinese."

"How would you like to see them on their heels in the public spotlight?"

His gaze sharpened. "What does that mean?"

She related the news about the meeting with the senior Rogers's assistant, including Kathleen Bennett's will.

His eyes narrowed. "I'm not sure what you mean about it being bad for the Chinese. Bennett didn't have a pot to piss in, and neither did Clayton Rogers."

"So you've been saying. Is that the story you want to relay to the world when this goes wide? Or would it better suit your public image to have the inheritance go through? Harry doesn't need the spaceport in Mexico. He does want his ship. Why not trade? Take it out of Chinese hands in a big show that leaves them looking like idiots."

Queen sat back and stared into the distance. "Let Rogers have it all and make the Chinese look like thieves. And allow Miss Cook to have what would more appropriately go to the company. That has some appeal, and as you say, the mundane property is of far less interest after everything that's happened."

"We'd want something in exchange, though. A real technology transfer, including knowhow. An actual agreement on how everything is divided up, including control of these gates. We can't just have people running all over the universe when the Asharim and their minions are out there somewhere."

"That can be worked out in New Zealand," Brenda said. "I'll want something similar for my people. We actually love the US and have no desire to fight you. I'll even make a down payment on my end right now to show good faith."

With that, she picked up the bag she'd brought with her and handed it over.

He opened it up, and blue light from the power cube she'd stolen when she'd kidnapped him washed over his face as his eyes widened.

"We'll also hand over some other tech and someone you already know to help you with it. Victor Holyfield is on your radar, and we know you've been asking questions about him. Why don't I assign him as your liaison?"

Queen considered her for a long moment and then nodded. "We'll have some hard negotiation on the details, but I'll accept the offer provisionally. If it doesn't work out, we'll turn young Victor back over to you rather than holding him."

"I can live with that," she said. "Welcome to the big leagues, Mister Secretary. Let's see if we can't screw those Chinese bastards over."

6

———————

arry stepped through the quantum gate and into the ruined New Zealand base with Jess and Sandra beside him. Tearing his partner out of Doctor Granger's clutches had proven surprisingly challenging. His friend had put up a spirited argument before he'd worn her down.

Molly Goodwin, the woman who'd been leading the search and rescue operation for his late father, was waiting for them, standing beside Kevin McHugh, Brenda's Asharim gate expert.

"I don't know if I'll ever get used to that," Molly admitted in a hushed tone.

The tall, gangly, bald man with purple-tinted, round-lensed glasses standing beside her grinned. "It's wild," he agreed. "Wait till you can see some of the other cool stuff out there."

She gave the man an odd look. "I don't see myself wandering all over the universe. I'm not even sure how I ended up being my government's representative here."

"That's because you're in the know," he confided. "They're not going to tell just anybody about this place if they don't have to. The fact that you're already clued in makes you the perfect person to interface with us."

"If you say so."

She turned to face him. "Welcome back to New Zealand, Mr. Rogers. I'd ask if you had a good trip, but that seems kind of redundant when it only took a fraction of a second for you to get from the United States to here."

He shook her hand. "You'd think, but it's still good to be back in New Zealand. I feel like someone is hunting me when I'm in the United States, probably with good reason. How are our unwilling guests doing?"

The woman shrugged slightly. "As well as one could expect, I suppose.

They haven't caused us any trouble, but that's not lulling us into a false sense of security. We still have them under heavy guard.

"That mainly means using the soldiers from that U.S. Navy ship, and the few of our own people that we brought into the project to fight them.

"We cleared out a couple of levels in the middle of the base and have them blocked from getting to the stairs. We've set up a heavy weapons emplacement on the top floor to keep them from escaping, as well as one in the corridor outside the stairs on this level to keep them from reaching the gates."

She looked around the dark room. They'd brought in portable lights that could tap into the same 10-centimeter blue cube that powered the gate, but the gate room still seemed abandoned and forlorn. Until and unless they got some of the large power cubes to bring the base's power generation systems back online, this facility wasn't going to ever be functional. Maybe not even then.

"So, what's the plan?" he asked. "I understand that Secretary of State Queen intends to use Commander Krueger as his point man. Is he here?"

"He's in the camp where we were during the search for your father. My condolences on your loss."

Harry wanted to tell her that it was fine, that he really hadn't cared for the man anyway, but politeness didn't allow for that. He wasn't even sure it was true. His emotions had been conflicted since his father had sacrificed himself to take down Harry's murderous mother and brother.

"Thank you," he finally said, settling for a polite, noncommittal response.

"I'm going to want to talk with the heavy-worlder leader," Jess said. "He and I have to try and work out a way we can walk back from this conflict. If I had to guess, Kathleen Bennett manipulated him, but making him see that might not be so easy."

Molly nodded. "I'll drop you off on the way up. Sorry, but I have instructions not to leave anyone unescorted inside the base. That means you too, Kevin. Grab your bag and come along."

Harry smiled a little. "If you're worried that we'll take something interesting, you needn't worry. We have more equipment to go over than I could possibly manage in a few decades."

"I suspect that you'll need to work that out during the negotiations," she said with a nod. "Isaiah Vaughn, the assistant to our prime minister, is waiting up there as well. He's acting for the alliance and was involved in the treaty your father worked out, so it'll just be the two of you to settle accounts."

"Then I supposed I'd best be about it," he said with a sigh. "This was one thing I was more than happy to leave to my father."

Molly escorted them up the stairs, dropping Jess and Sandra off with the guards at the level holding the heavy-worlders.

He was pleased to see that they'd cleared the remains of the dead from the top-level corridors. They'd been nothing but bones and armor, but the dead should still be treated with greater respect than time had shown them.

As for the entrance, the New Zealanders had opened it up and smoothed the rockfall into a ramp. He approved of the braces they'd added for stability. Those would go a long way to making sure there wasn't another cave-in.

The bright light of the early morning sun made him use his hand to shield his eyes as they stepped out. The surface of the mesa was as undeveloped as it had been before. That made sense. No need to advertise what was going on to anyone with a satellite.

It would still be better to get some power on in the base and find the hidden door that led out to the slab of rock that had once served as the base's landing pad. Then no one in the sky would see what was going on if they were careful in how they put a tent up there to block the view.

"What is the excuse for you still being out here?" he asked Molly. "The search is over. Aren't people going to wonder what you're doing with so many people coming and going?"

"We're building a rescue station out here, with the permission of the owner of the property, of course," she said as she let the way to the narrow path through the rocks that led up to the mesa from below.

His father had effectively blocked it with a large rock rolled from the top, but they'd cleared things out nicely. Getting up and down still required a rope and some climbing skill, but he was pleased to see that Molly was much more confident in putting on a rope harness and clipping a ring to the dedicated line. Someone had given her some training, and she'd gotten some practice.

He followed suit and preceded Kevin down. Once on the ground, it was a relatively simple process to get to the camp that was set up on the massive stone slab. There were easily a dozen people moving around the camp, but Harry spotted the people he was looking for in chairs near the campfire that was burning cheerily inside a circle of stones.

"Thanks for the escort, Molly," he said. "I've got it from here. I'm sure you and Kevin have more important things to do besides minding me."

She shook her head. "With this joker? Boring."

The computer specialist scowled at her. "I'm not boring."

"No, but what you do is," she countered as they turned to make their way back up the rock face. "All I do is stand around while you plug your slate into things and chatter on about this or that incomprehensible thing."

"I can prove that's just work," he said. "Have dinner with me and I'll show you how charming I really am."

They were too far away for Harry to hear her answer, but he was rooting for the other man.

Karl Krueger rose to his feet at Harry's approach and extended his hand. "Good to see you again, Harry. How was your father's funeral?"

"More trying than I expected," he admitted. "Still, not as difficult as dealing with all the chaos he left in his wake."

"I only knew him a short while, but I could tell he was a complicated man who was playing his own game," the Navy officer said with a smile. "What he did was nothing short of the bravest thing I've ever seen. He stayed behind so we could live, knowing that I left the nuke on a short timer. Even though none of us will ever know, I hope he had a pithy one-liner saved up for the very end."

The idea of his stodgy father tossing off a line like in some action movie made Harry chuckle. "I'm sure he got in the last word. He always did."

Harry turned his focus to the other man, who had also risen from his seat. Isaiah Vaughn was a politician and wore a suit, even out here in the howling wilderness.

To his credit, the man held a battered metal mug filled with coffee, which he moved to his off hand as he extended his primary toward Harry. "I knew even less of your father than that. Accept my condolences as well, and my understanding. I never saw eye to eye with my own father and imagine I know something of what you had to deal with. Join us in some of this amazing coffee."

Once he was seated in the third chair, Harry picked the metal percolator off the grate and filled a battered blue tin cup with steaming black liquid. A sip confirmed it was excellent.

"This is good," he conceded. "Someone has good taste."

"Your father had it in his belongings," Krueger said quietly, bringing a momentary pause to the conversation.

"In any case," Harry finally said, "I'm told that you are empowered to speak on behalf of the United States, Karl. Brenda Cabot said that Queen was willing to bury the hatchet so that we can all focus on the important things. Why don't you lay it out for us?"

"I'm no diplomat," the special operations officer said. "Just keep that in mind. All I'm doing is passing along what he told me to say and operating within the bounds he's allowing me. Don't take this personally.

"He gave me a lot of wordy crap to say up front, but why don't I save us all a lot of time and indigestion? Queen has the Chinese as his most immediate problem, but the secret society of heavy-worlders he thinks is pulling their strings is his real worry."

"Mine too," Harry admitted. "I'm pretty sure that's what's on the way to Mars right now in the Chinese ship and they're probably armed to the teeth with Asharim weapons. I have to count on them having antiship weapons, too."

"And let's not forget the heavy-worlders that attacked your other base," Vaughn said. "The survivors of which we have here. Or the aliens on the world your father was trapped on."

Harry made a dismissive gesture. "The Volunteer world is a lot less worrying to me. They're using small forces and not even that much high tech. Those Asharim have devolved. That doesn't mean I won't have to deal with them so that we can visit the other human colonies that Susanna Adorno told us about."

"And I'm sure that you remember your father promised to get them back there in days not months," Krueger said.

Harry nodded. "I'm far more concerned with the problems we're facing here on Earth, some of which you don't yet know about. Not a threat, but more of a mystery."

He was referencing the frozen version of Earth that Jess had found way out beyond the orbit of Pluto. The one that had either come from the future or an alternate universe, he had no idea which. Neither, he suspected, had the Asharim who'd been studying it before their war had brought them low.

Krueger nodded, but Vaughn held up a hand. "We need to know what that means. Not right this very second, but soon. We can't help with problems we know nothing about, and we're partners in this thing."

"Agreed," Harry said. "I'll get a briefing put together and present it personally. I don't want to let records of it out yet, so we'll do it on *Freedom Express*."

"That's the asteroid ship? I'm fine with that."

"Back to Queen and his offer," Krueger said. "He wants into this partnership you've formed with the nations around here. That's not negotiable."

"You'll forgive me if I'm not that trusting of him or his motives," Vaughn said coolly. "He sent you and that jackass from the CIA to kidnap someone from this very spot. Neither my government or any of the others in this arrangement have any desire to see more of that high-handedness."

Krueger nodded. "I can't blame you. Still, Queen insists we'll be providing the majority of the armed forces, and we did already commit a nuke to the deal."

"Not willingly," Harry said. "And the US has a much bigger military threat to deal with, so we're not talking large numbers of troops. There's no way the US is more than a junior partner. One that has to follow the decisions of the other nations involved, but one that still gets to share in the technology we're finding."

"Only once we agree that it should be shared," Vaughn added. "The alliance has five senior members. Three of them have to agree to share technologies, both those with military applications and those without."

The alliance consisted of New Zealand, Australia, Japan, South Korea, and the island nation of Nauru that Harry's father had bought outright. Jacob Thomas, formerly the vice president of island operations on Nauru, was now acting as the actual vice president, and Harry held the ridiculous title of president.

"Consider my position fought for tooth and nail," Krueger said. "And I had to reluctantly settle for that. Man, this diplomacy stuff is easier than I thought."

Harry laughed. "You say that now. Just don't let Queen know you gave in so easily, or he'll assign you to Antarctica. What do we get in exchange for allowing the US to play ball?"

"The military assistance I mentioned, as well as letting your inheritances stand, with one exception. We want the Yucatán spaceport in exchange for *Liberty Station*."

"Done," Harry instantly said.

"We also want some of the smaller ships you found," Krueger added. "We want a way into space."

"Frankly, I think that's a mistake," Vaughn said. "The US government has not shown that they can be trusted, and the very last thing we want is a space race where the US is trying to find ways around the technology restrictions you just negotiated.

"We have to have a clearinghouse for the information. If we start fighting among ourselves, we're doomed. It is the view of the alliance that Humanity Unlimited is that entity."

"How about military tech that doesn't give us a boost out of the atmosphere?" Krueger asked. "Guns, armor, other battlefield tech that might help us make up the ground against the Chinese."

Harry considered that and then shrugged. "I can agree to that. If the US wanted to use conventional forces against anyone in the alliance, they already have more than we could counter. The people under threat are the Chinese, and it seems like they deserve the attention. I'm in."

Vaughn nodded. "We can live with that."

"There are a lot of little things the secretary wanted to talk about, but that's the big stuff," Krueger said. "Let's finish our coffee, and then we can hash them out. As far as I'm concerned, the hard part of these negotiations is over."

Harry wasn't sure the man's boss would agree, but that was hardly his problem. As far as his issues went, Jess's talk with the heavy-worlder leader was the big issue for today. He couldn't care less about his inheritance.

He'd have to make a call while he was here to the attorney in Australia and see what the salvage case looked like, but he was fairly sure the alliance could smooth those waters. Then he could take Krueger and Vaughn back to *Freedom Express* and show them the wonders of the universe while Jess tried to make peace with the real killers in the fight.

7

Jess spent a few minutes getting her head into the game before she had the guards lead her and Sandra to a room that could be used to talk with the heavy-worlder leader. Like the rest of the base, it had been abandoned a thousand years ago and smelled sour, though someone had done their best to clean it up.

They'd also managed to scavenge a table and a pair of battered chairs more suitable for camping than an office. The table wasn't in much better shape than the chairs, frankly. Still, it would have to do. Sandra lounged against the nearest wall, her hand close to what was probably a weapon.

Jess wasn't sure how she would bridge the language gap, but Kathleen Bennett had done so. She considered the possibility that the heavy-worlder leader could speak English but rejected it as being a low-order possibility. Maybe they'd communicated by writing in the Asharim tongue.

While she was still trying to imagine how this was going to play out, the door opened again, and a massive man stepped through with four guards behind him. They'd found manacles that fit around his wrists, but Jess didn't have a whole lot of confidence in how well they'd hold up, considering how strong she knew people like this man were.

The man wasn't much taller than Harry but was significantly broader and more muscular. She'd met Victor Holyfield, and Brenda Cabot's associate was notably smaller. This man would have significant difficulty passing unnoted on a public street, where Victor could blend in.

She gestured toward the other chair but suddenly realized that he was probably far too heavy to sit without breaking it. Obviously realizing that already, the man smirked and stood unmoving. One of the guards shoved him, and the man barely rocked and didn't move his feet at all.

"That's okay," she told the guard. "Just let him stand there."

"It's not safe, Miss," one of the men said with a distinct New Zealander accent. "If he makes a move from a standing position, he could get to you before we shoot him. He has to at least go over to the wall.

"You can sit by the door and we'll cover your retreat if we have to. Trust me, you don't want to have to fight one of these buggers."

The guard must've been in the fight at the French base. The one where she'd fought the heavy-worlders, killed some, and almost died of her wounds.

Wordlessly, she allowed the guards to make their will known to the prisoner, and he eventually moved to the indicated spot, only when it was clear that he was doing so because he was ready to.

Jess moved her seat so that she was sitting next to the exit with a clear path to bolt if the man attacked. Sandra stood beside her, and the guards arrayed themselves to either side. They kept their weapons ready to fire, but she hoped it never came to that.

There had been far too much blood and death already. Kathleen Bennett and her son Nathan were dead. Let this conflict die with them.

She also had the flechette pistol that she'd proven to be so unexpectedly adept with. They hadn't had much time to see what else she could do because of this trip, but perhaps that would be enough.

"Could one of you get me a notepad and a pen?" she asked.

They gave her an odd look but did as she asked, one of the men returning with the requested materials.

Using them would be a challenge if she was going to stay away from the prisoner, but she could at least test the theory. Jess had no idea how the sarcophagus had implanted the knowledge of how to read and write Asharim into her head, but it was just as straightforward as using English.

That didn't mean it didn't have its own pitfalls. The concepts didn't always match up well with things in English, and finding a suitable word for something on Earth could prove unexpectedly complicated.

This should prove simple enough to use for a test. She wrote out a single sentence in Asharim that asked if he could read what she'd written. She then had one of the guards put it on the table.

The heavy-worlder glanced at it and then his eyes shot back toward it, widening in a classic double take. He picked up the notebook, seemingly read it again slowly, and then stared at her intently.

"You write the language of the Masters," he said, his voice a deep rumble. "Can you speak the language of the People as well?"

That hadn't been English.

"Did you guys understand that?" she asked the guards, already knowing the answer. She was unsurprised when they shook their heads.

"Sounds like how they talk among themselves," the guard that had been doing the talking said.

Jess nodded and focused her attention back on the intent heavy-worlder, not exactly sure how she could try to speak the language rather than English. It didn't prove that difficult in the end. She simply said what she wanted with the intent that it be in his language.

"Is this the language of the Asharim?" she asked, marveling at how the words felt so natural. She saw the guards tense as she spoke.

"No," he said. "It is the tongue of the People. Who are you, and how have you come to speak our language? Are you an ally of Kathleen Bennett?"

Jess felt her expression harden. "No. Until her death, she was my deadliest enemy. She and her son Nathan. She brought you here to Earth, didn't she?"

The man considered her for a moment and then slowly nodded. "She convinced the high priest to bring us to war. I am Kerrick Vidar, leader of the People. Who are you?"

"Jessica Cook."

"Then you lead the people of Earth." It had been a statement rather than a question.

"That's a lot more complicated than you can probably guess," she said wryly. "Let's just say that I'm the leader you'll be dealing with. I have some questions for you, though I can guess many of the answers already. Why did you attack us?"

"You would have to ask the high priest," the man said with a shrug. "He commanded that we attack, so we attacked."

"Did he by chance wear a really tall hat?"

The man's eyes narrowed. "He did. I had assumed that you had kept him and his associates separate from me and my men. That isn't the case, is it?"

Jess shook her head. "All of your people that we captured are in the area where we're holding you. He didn't survive the fighting."

Unexpectedly, that made Vidar smile. "Good. I never liked him anyway. Arrogant fool. I would be pleased to meet the warrior that killed him and made my life better in doing so."

Well, she supposed this was as good a chance as any to test that statement. "I killed him."

The large man blinked. "You did?"

"I did, and five or six of his companions, at the base you attacked. Someone else killed the last of them." The idea of having killed someone still made her insides tremble, but those men hadn't been the first, and they almost certainly wouldn't be the last.

Vidar stared at her for a few seconds. "I confess that surprises me. We have female warriors, but I did not take you as such."

"I'm not," she conceded. "I was in the wrong place at the wrong time. I was wounded and almost died in that fight."

He raised an eyebrow. "You seem quite hale now."

"Perhaps you can explain that as we proceed. You came from a ship when you used the gate. The one Kathleen Bennett came to see you in. How did you get there?"

"She came down the sky bridge to our world. We used it to return to the ship and use its gate when she was unable to activate any of those on our world."

"What is a sky bridge?" she asked, settling back in the uncomfortable chair.

"A cable that reaches into the heavens. A large compartment rises from the building on the ground and goes to a sphere in orbit around our world. Her ship was near it."

Then it wasn't there anymore. The nuke that had destroyed the ship had almost certainly taken out the top of what was probably a space elevator when it had detonated. She wondered grimly how much of the area below it had been crushed under the falling cable.

As an engineer, she longed to ask about the space elevator, but she restrained herself. The makeup of the cable—probably some form of carbon nanotubes—would have to wait.

"That ship held a large box that healed those put inside it," she said. "I was healed in just a few days, and now I have the ability to speak your language. I can do other things like shoot a flechette pistol better, too. I have no idea what it did to me."

The man's eyes widened. "You have been elevated. The Masters once used devices like that to reward their most loyal servants, as well as to maintain their own good health. I have heard the legends."

He frowned. "That would explain many things about Kathleen Bennett. She could fly one of the small ships used by the Masters, as well as understand the workings of the gates, though that was a problem she was unable to solve.

"I suspect that the Masters would have been most displeased to find either of you using the device, but they aren't exactly here to complain. What is it that you want of me, Jessica Cook?"

"Peace," she said. "Or perhaps even just a ceasefire. We have not offended your people, yet you attacked us. I would see our situation returned to what it was before this fight."

"Were it up to me, I would agree in a moment," he said. "With the high priest dead, as well as his most trusted assistants, the decision falls to those he left behind. I confess that I do not know who that is, though the high priest only had a handful of men training under him. If you would have peace, you must come to my home and plead your case before the priests that remain."

She felt her eyes narrow. "I don't have such a high opinion of your priests. What guarantee of safety would I and my party have?"

"None," he said, opening his arms wide. "The priests could overturn my assurance of safe passage with a word. Yet if you would have peace, there is no other way forward."

Harry wouldn't be pleased to hear that. Then again, no one else could speak the man's language. In any case, she had no choice but to try. These people had almost invaded the Earth, and she had to stop that from happening again.

Yes, with the spaceship Kathleen Bennett had used blown to plasma and their gates turned off, they couldn't easily get here, but she only had his word on that. No, she'd be going to his planet and making certain that they were either trapped or friendly. There was no other sane decision.

"We've still got a lot of talking to do, but I have a proposal for you," she said. "I'll take your safe passage even with the caveats you've added, simply to get past your fighters so I can speak with your priests. If we can make peace, I'll return your people we hold here."

"And if we do not make peace?"

"Then you'll be our guest for a significantly longer period," she said bluntly. "I have no idea what Kathleen Bennett told you, but I have a number of problems on my plate, and if you prove to be one of the more complicated ones, I'll set you aside for later."

He chuckled at that. "I would offer you some advice, then. Bring warriors aplenty. The priests may hesitate to order an attack if you are well protected.

"Also, I would advise you to meet with them soon. As it is, they do not know that they now need to select a new high priest. That will leave them ill prepared to act with any speed."

She gave him a long look before speaking. "Why are you helping me?"

"Because I do not see how this war benefits anyone. Kathleen Bennett was a snake. I realized she had treachery in her heart, but the high priest was blinded by the opportunity she dangled in front of him.

"I want my people to prosper. Perhaps even to one day return to the world from which we came. Not this Earth, but the world that once nourished our muscles and made us strong. It would anger the priests to hear this, but I would be happy if the Masters never returned. Which I will deny having said if you tell them."

She smiled a little. "Your secret is safe with me. I'll gather warriors, and we shall leave tomorrow. Talk with your people and select two others to accompany you back to your planet. We leave in the morning."

8

_____

Brenda stared in awe at the huge city below the lander as it coasted through the dark skies over a dead Earth that she'd never imagined could exist. Even after having been told about it, she hadn't believed it really existed. Not until this very moment.

The bright lights shooting away from the lander illuminated one massive building after another, all dark and frozen. They looked like high-tech versions of structures that might appear in New York or Los Angeles. Only this was supposedly very rural New Zealand. At least it had been on this alternate, impossible Earth.

"And it's like this all over?" she asked. "Seriously?"

"Scout's honor," Harry said. "It looks like a majority of the land masses have grown into something like this, other than what was probably dedicated farmland. We haven't had enough time to even scratch the surface, so to speak, but they probably also farmed the oceans. Just not enough free land to feed what had to be tens of billions of people."

Krueger was looking out the other side of the lander. "Probably more than that. I've been to Tokyo, and this seems like it could pack even more people into that kind of footprint. If it's consistent all over, you're looking at over a hundred billion, easy. Even with ocean farming, that had to be hard to manage."

He turned back toward Harry. "Queen is going to freak. Is this an alternate Earth? Something from our future? Whatever it was, it sure looks like the loss of life was total. That's a vacuum out there, right?"

Harry nodded. "We've found a few contemporary journals. Nothing that talks about what happened, but more what the people went through. It was like the flipping of a light switch. One moment it was a bright summer day, the next it was pitch-black night.

"The sun was gone. Even the moon was gone. Obviously, it was the Earth that had vanished, but most people probably never knew that, or the semantics didn't matter."

Brenda was horrified. "I hope it was quick."

"Not as much as I'd have wanted in their places," Harry said. "It took a few days for the temperature to hit what would otherwise be deep winter. A few more for arctic temperatures. By the end of the week, every place on the planet was indistinguishable from the North Pole.

"People huddled where they could and tried to survive. Perhaps some of them even made it a few weeks in underground bunkers, but when the very air itself froze, they died. Perhaps some deep in the Earth with canned air lasted a while longer. It didn't matter. In the end, they all died."

The lander flared when it came to a large mesa and settled onto a brightly lit landing area beside it. Suited figures told her that the landing area was probably a temporary area manned by people from *Freedom Express*.

Harry hefted his helmet. "Seal up. We're going out."

In addition to Krueger and herself, a representative from New Zealand named Molly Goodwin and Kevin McHugh were seated in the back of the lander, eyes still locked on the dead world just outside their windows.

"I recognize this," Molly Goodwin said, her voice strangled. "This is the mesa with the base in New Zealand. I'd know that slab of rock and the shape of it anywhere."

"It is," Harry confirmed. "I think you're going to find what's here fascinating."

Once he'd personally checked everyone's vacuum suits, he dropped the air pressure and opened the ramp at the back of the lander. The pilot had positioned the rear of the lander so that it pointed at the mesa.

Someone had carefully laid out lights leading up a path toward the top of the large rock beside the mesa. It was buried under frozen atmosphere but looked like it was part of the original landscape.

Designated assistants stepped up beside each of them, helping to make sure no one slipped or fell on the ice. A shattered helmet would be a fatal event, after all.

"This is new," Molly said. "Or rather, it's old and doesn't belong here. Neither does the city all around it, I suppose."

"It's different here," Harry confirmed. "Though to be fair, we weren't sure if that was because it was from the future or not when we found it. This world was a few centuries older than our own even before it arrived here."

"Any idea how long ago that was?" she asked. "Just because the Asharim found it a thousand years ago doesn't mean that was when it arrived."

"Spot on," he confirmed. "We had some of the bodies carbon dated. The people on this world died almost ten thousand years ago, subjectively. The intense cold and vacuum preserved them. Hell, back on our Earth, they found someone who'd died thousands of years ago on a glacier and thought he was a modern accident victim. Bodies on Mount Everest are still intact, even after having been there for over a century."

"That's horrible," she said, surprised that she felt that way. As an FBI agent, she'd seen every manner of horror, but bodies lying where they had fallen for long years—millennia—after they'd died rattled her. Death should be an end. From the Earth they came, and so shall they return.

Only that didn't seem to be the case on this frozen hell.

When they finally reached the top of the large stone slab, she saw other people working at clearing what was obviously a large door in the side of the mesa. One large enough to get a lander into.

"There's a base here," she whispered. "Just like on our Earth."

"There is," Harry said, gesturing toward a smaller door, one obviously made for people. "We can get in here. The larger door isn't functional yet. It's quite literally frozen in its tracks."

The smaller door hadn't been intended as an airlock, but someone had placed one just inside it. It was large enough to pass them all through into a landing bay filled with Asharim ships and people working in cold-weather gear, but without helmets.

Following Harry's lead, she loosened her helmet and pulled it off. Her breath fogged the air, and she guessed it was maybe the low teens. A look around showed her the portable heaters they were using to warm the large chamber.

That also showed her that the overhead lights were on. The base had power.

"It's operational?" she asked.

"Sort of," Harry answered as he led the way to one of the main corridors. "It had power, but it was shut down. We only just got it on yesterday, and the life support was never meant to deal with temperatures like this."

"I can't believe it," Molly said, looking around with wide eyes. "I took a tour of the whole base. There were no ships here. Everything was rotted. What does this mean?"

"We're one level above the gate room, and I want to get Kevin to check something there for me before I answer that. I'm almost certain that I know what the answer is going to be, but I want to hear him confirm it."

Having seen the base in New Zealand, Brenda had to agree with the other woman. This base was in a much better state of preservation. Perhaps it hadn't been breached like the one on her Earth, and thus the elements hadn't had a chance to cause such deterioration.

When they went down the stairs and the group started toward the gate room, Brenda turned the other direction and looked into the engineering space. The machinery there was in excellent shape, and the slots that had contained the massive cubes that had originally provided power were present, glowing cubes a meter along each edge.

Her curiosity satisfied, she hurried to catch up with the others inside the gate room. It was also in excellent repair, with no sign of the make do power supply and control that someone had rigged in the original base.

Harry was waiting for her. "As you noticed, Brenda, this base is in great shape. One problem: the gates won't connect to any of the gates we know the address for. In fact, we haven't been able to make any of them connect at all, with the exception of the other gates in this very room. I'm betting something is very different inside them, and that's what I need Kevin to find."

Without waiting for direct instruction, her young subordinate got out his tools and quickly went to work gaining access to the control nodes on the middle gate. As adept as he was at the work, it only took a few minutes to have data flowing on his slate.

What he saw made him frown. "I can see your attempts in the log. Everything looks valid to me. I'm scrolling back. Wow. The last valid connection was almost twelve thousand years ago, subjectively speaking. It looks like these gates never lost their connection to the main power."

"Any idea why the connections aren't working?" Harry asked.

"Nope. Do you want me to try to connect to the last destination this gate was successful in connecting with? I'll kill it right away if it works."

Harry nodded. "If I'm right, it won't work."

Kevin gave him an odd look and tapped the screen of his slate. "Connection unsuccessful. I suppose I could try others, but why do you think it isn't working?"

"I think this Earth is from another reality. I'll wager there's something that makes the gate network unique, and the gates here are part of another network, if you will. That's why they can't connect with the valid addresses we know but work internally between these three."

Brenda blinked at his guess. "And now that it's in our reality, it can no longer see its original network? How did it get here? The Asharim couldn't have done this. None of the species they had met would have the power or knowhow to do it either. Getting to another universe is science fiction, even for them."

"Yet I think someone did it," Harry said. "Not only that, they did it to an entire planet. One they likely struck at with no warning and did so from space. Other than the large Asharim station in orbit, there are no signs of orbital habitats, even though some of the records we found indicate that this Earth had a thriving presence there, as well as across the rest of the solar system."

"Could they have done it to themselves?" Krueger asked. "Perhaps this was some experiment gone terribly wrong."

Harry shrugged. "I suppose it's possible, but the amount of energy this had to have taken would be immense. We've done a cursory look at the power plants these people were capable of, and while amazing, they would be ridiculously inadequate for the task of bridging realities."

"This must've made the Asharim go crazy," Brenda said. "I'm not sure how they would even know to look out here for this planet once they located our system, but they can't have expected this. It must've frightened them badly."

"How does this world compare with the Asharim technology?" Krueger asked. "Did they have this kind of wormhole technology? Or were these people somewhere between us and the Asharim?"

Harry made a waggling gesture with his hand to indicate a mixed answer.

"They didn't have gates, but they had many things that were almost as good as the Asharim, and even some creations that were more advanced than anything the Asharim could manage.

"Specifically, as Brenda knows, we found a cybernetic cat frozen in one of the buildings. Even after ten thousand years, its power supply was good, and it activated when placed in a shirtsleeve environment. Unless you knew it, you'd think it was a real cat."

"The Asharim couldn't do that?"

"No," Brenda said. "Not only do their power storage units fail after a much shorter time frame, they couldn't make a mechanical cat so realistic. It's damned eerie. Have you found more of them?"

Harry nodded. "Cats, dogs, reptiles, you name it. We took a few up, and they reactivated just the same as the cat. We think with the human population grown so large, the widespread use of living pets was low. It probably happened over a long period when resources became scarce, so there wasn't a die-off. We found a number of real pets in what we think were homes of the very wealthy. They died with their owners."

Before he could continue, a man came in and whispered in his ear. From his sudden frown, Harry didn't like what he was hearing. Once the man finished, Harry sent him on his way. "We're going to have to cut this visit short. It seems Jess is trying to sneak something dangerous past me, and I need to go put a stop to it."

"I'd like to request we send people to help you explore the surface here, or at least to help process what you find," Krueger said. "This sounds like something we could marshal a large group of people to help out on."

"I have no objection to that, though you'd have to clear whatever information you find with all of us," Harry said. "I'm afraid you'd need a minder to make sure you didn't try to get fancy. Also, even the existence of this place is so secret that you'd have to keep it limited to just a few important people. Whoever comes will be here for a while with no communication with home."

Brenda snorted. "As deeply penetrated as the US government probably is, only Queen and the president can know. No one else."

"I can accept that," Krueger said. "Trust is earned, not given. Can I help with whatever Miss Cook is doing?"

Harry opened his mouth—probably to decline—but paused. "Maybe so," he said after a moment. "If you'd like to provide a team like you had on Volunteer World—minus that CIA jerk—I'd be happy to have you along."

"I can have my team back together in an hour at the New Zealand base. The one on our Earth, that is. How should I kit them out?"

"Like you would have if you'd known you were going to be trapped on another planet," Harry said grimly. "Not that I expect that to happen this time, but one never knows."

"I want to come along," Brenda said into the short silence. "I might be able to help."

"You're welcome to do so. Now, let's get back to the lifter so we can get this in place before Jess tries to sneak off without you."

9

Q ueen sat in his armored limousine and fumed as his driver took him to the United Nations building. The paper in his lap was a summary of what Commander Krueger had agreed to with Rogers, and it was far short of disappointing. The US would be tagging along like Cub Scouts on a tour, always under observation, rather than taking the lead as he'd envisioned.

Oh, the man had explanations of how he hadn't been able to convince the alliance of weak nations that guarded the base in New Zealand to accept more —and there might even be some truth to that—but deep down, Queen knew that the military officer had given in without any real argument.

Sadly, Queen could only blame himself. In a moment of weakness, he'd had the not-so-brilliant idea of allowing someone without all the baggage that he and Rogers had to do the negotiating. Obviously a mistake on his part, but one that it was too late to do anything about at this point.

The man had made an agreement that Queen could swallow. That didn't mean that he was going to allow Rogers and the rest to keep him down forever. And actually, the arrangement had one upside that he could use against the enemies of the United States right now.

The United Nations was just about to have the shock of their lives. While their minions now knew about the existence of the base in New Zealand, they hadn't had a chance to return and brief their masters on any of the sensitive details. Even they weren't stupid enough to imagine that they could safely send the images and reports home without every major power intercepting them.

No, that kind of thing had to be hand delivered, and none of them had yet come back in person, though the CIA had informed him that one of them was on a plane to New York even now. He'd be far too late to stop Queen's diplomatic judo, though.

That was likely to be Queen's only source of pleasure today, so he fully intended to enjoy it. The problems with how the US was a junior partner in this endeavor would take more work, but he relished the challenge. It would be all the sweeter when he finally took control of everything.

But first, he needed to give the Chinese bastards a serious diplomatic headache. One that might even be enough to distract them from trying to fight a war with the US. And, as a bonus, one that would put Rogers into the hot seat.

The limo pulled into a guarded garage, and the Secret Service detail that the president had loaned him took up protective positions. After the assassination attempt and the declaration of war by the Chinese, they weren't taking any risks.

Once the men and women protecting him were satisfied that it was safe to proceed, he exited his vehicle and made his way to one of the rooms just off from where the General Assembly met.

Yes, it was even more toothless than the supposed security council these days, but he wanted everyone to hear what he had to say. And they'd all be there waiting, not that they knew he'd be here. No, he'd made arrangements to have an allied country give up their slot so that he could spring his surprise with zero time for the Chinese to prepare.

He arrived just in time to shake the hand of the ambassador from Chile. "I appreciate this, and you can rest assured that we will more than repay this favor, Emanuel."

Ambassador Cepeda smiled and bowed slightly. "I have every confidence in you, my friend. Now, if you will excuse me, I need to return to my seat. I would not wish to miss the show. I promise that I will step in after you take the stage. I wouldn't want to steal your thunder."

"I appreciate it."

Once the man was gone, Queen took a minute to prepare his presentation files and notes. Once he got started, he wanted to make sure that everything went smoothly and without interruption.

The attendant that came for the next speaker only raised an eyebrow at seeing him. "Mister Secretary, I was expecting someone else."

Queen smiled widely. "Ambassador Cepeda has kindly agreed to allow me to use his time."

"I see. Come this way, then. The previous speaker is ending his remarks now, and you will be up shortly. Is there any assistance that I can provide for your presentation?"

"Thank you, no. I'll control it from the podium."

"As you wish. This way, please."

Queen put his papers away and followed the man to the area beside the stage. The ambassador from France was winding down what almost certainly had to be yet one more call for assistance in dealing with the gutting of his nation by the never-ending battle between the forces of order and those they'd allowed to immigrate from the Middle East and Africa.

He had little sympathy for the man or his nation. The US and others had warned them about allowing large numbers of people in that were unwilling to integrate into their society. Did they listen? No.

Now they were fighting against what amounted to a civil insurrection hell bent on setting up a Caliphate right in the heart of Europe. It had reached the point that some sections of the country were already under Sharia law. The fight for Paris made it a burning wreck every night now. It was only a matter of time before the French government became one in exile.

Hell, the Middle Eastern nations represented in this very building were already pushing for the Caliphate in France to be recognized as the legitimate government. They saw it as just one more step towards a total domination of the world.

Queen knew there were a lot of people that saw such a point of view as racism and bigotry, pure and simple. Sadly, nothing he could do could help people like that. People like those in France who only now realized the trap they'd fallen into, far too late to save themselves.

He'd never allow that to happen in the United States. People could loath and revile him as a racist or religious bigot all they wanted. He'd be the villain of that tale and never lose a moment's sleep over it.

His eyes narrowed a little as the wisp of an idea tickled the edges of his mind. Perhaps he could help them and his own country at the same time while still being true to the agreement he had with the alliance.

While Rogers would never frame the situation in France with the same bluntness as he did, he knew the man likely didn't approve of religious extremists warring with the government for control over the land on which his one functional base on Earth sat.

If Queen made an alliance with France to help them, he might be able to get the French government to agree to cede the land to the United States. That might prove advantageous in the fight to come, though he couldn't be too plain in how he framed things.

Yes, that might prove useful if he played his cards right. Definitely something to keep in mind.

Once the current speaker moved away, receiving almost no recognition that he'd even spoken, Queen waited for the man who'd escorted him to announce his arrival to the crowd of delegates at their seats. A low murmur arose as they discussed his unscheduled remarks with those seated near them.

He strode out to the lectern and smiled at the men and women gathered around in their tiered seats, the names of their countries on placards before them. The old movie quote was quite correct. "You will never find a more wretched hive of scum and villainy" suited this building with uncanny precision.

And, to be fair, he was just as bad as the rest. Only he did his dark deviltry in the service of a great nation that deserved to triumph. He'd do everything in his power to make it so. He was his country's Cardinal Richelieu.

Not the buffoon portrayed in the novels or movies, but the staunch servant and advocate of France that did whatever needed doing to see his country survive and flourish. He made a mental note that that would be a good icon to use in speaking with the French later. The French loved icons.

"I'm sure that many of you have heard of the recent unpleasantness," he said, pitching his voice to carry. Most of them wouldn't understand him without the use of interpreters speaking into the headphones they used, but his tone was an important part of his message.

"The Chinese attacked the United States with no provocation, only declaring their intentions after their agents struck us on our own soil. This body is of course deadlocked on doing anything of substance because all of you listening to the sound of my voice are beholden to someone. Many to the Chinese."

That was a lot blunter than his normal style of delivery, but the time for polite, meaningless words was past.

"The same is true of the body that should be acting to secure world peace —the Security Council—and that will not change with China as a permanent member there. Or Russia. Or the United States. One veto removes the possibility of any meaningful action there, and all the General Assembly is good for is mewling. Pathetic."

That certainly stirred up a lot of denial and shouting, which he allowed to play out with only an expression of contempt on his face.

"What you haven't heard is why they felt the need to declare war," he said after a minute, overriding their chatter. "The UN sent a team to New Zealand recently. One of them is on the way back to report, but I think you all richly deserve to hear the truth for yourselves and not the sanitized data that the secretary general might one day tell you about."

He could see looks of confusion on many faces, but a few were enraged or showed consternation. Those he made mental notes of. They already knew the truth.

"The day that many of you were told might never arrive is here," he said, throwing his arms wide. "We've found evidence of an alien civilization that once visited our solar system."

That pronouncement caused a fair amount of laughter, but the Chinese representative merely looked confused. Oh, this was going to be rich. The official government of the country that had attacked him hadn't bothered to brief their envoy on what they'd been after. That was going to prove… awkward for them.

"I can see many of you don't believe me," he said. "That's fine. I brought proof."

With that, he set the presentation in motion by plugging his data chip into the lectern and starting the slideshow. The images started with what Kathleen Bennett had done in her labs, going with pictures of the ship she'd stolen from Clayton Rogers.

It then proceeded to the abandoned base in New Zealand, including the long-decayed bodies of the fighters. Then it went to the flying comet, *Freedom Express*. Finally, it was a parade of views from the inside of the base on Mars, gloriously intact.

The final set of images was taken from Area 51, both before and after the blast that destroyed everything he'd seized from Kathleen Bennett. He'd been explaining in general terms what they'd been seeing as the images had marched across the screen, but he slowed the presentation now and said nothing until the final images were gone.

"The last set of images were of the equipment we were studying at Area 51. The equipment that a Chinese agent destroyed to deny us access to the knowledge they were already pursuing."

That got a reaction from the Chinese representative. He pressed a button that flashed an indicator that he wanted to speak. Too damned bad.

"I'd imagine this is a shock to them," Queen said. "You see, there's an underground movement of genetically modified humans working around the world that have been here for the last thousand years. As one might imagine, that has allowed them to get into many nooks and crannies.

"The Chinese leadership probably doesn't even realize that someone is pulling their strings, and even now a ship they built is on the way to Mars to try and capture that base using alien weapons of incredible power. They've gone to war at the beck and call of spies in their midst that couldn't care less about them. All they want to get their hands on is one of these."

With that, he started a video someone had taken of one of the gates activating in a dark room made of an unknown metal. When the phenomenon stabilized, the camera wielder walked through and out into the bright sunlight of an alien world. One with two suns in the sky.

"This is a video of Harry Rogers, an American citizen who was the first man on Mars and now the first to travel to another solar system an almost unimaginable distance away from here. The man who opened the universe for exploration and exploitation, for good and ill.

"Shadowy figures in the Chinese government don't want you to know about this, but the only way to stop the war threatening to engulf the world is to expose this den of lies and show you what we face if we do not stand together."

The next video was of the heavy-worlders coming through the gate into the French base and attacking the people there with their alien weapons. The bloody attack stopped when he froze the flow of images, leaving the focus of the image on Jessica Cook, who was crouched behind a crate and firing at the enemy fighters.

"That woman is Jessica Cook," he said conversationally. "She is the primary shareholder in the company Clayton Rogers formed before his death. By any stretch of the imagination, she's the wealthiest person on this planet, if one counts the wonders her company controls.

"The base in New Zealand is mostly wrecked, but the one on Mars is fully operational. So is a mobile ship built inside a comet. That is only the beginning.

"An alliance of nations and Humanity Unlimited has been formed to defend the Earth and exploit this new technology. The United States is part of that group, which is made up of New Zealand, Australia, South Korea, Japan, and the island nation of Nauru.

"China wants what they do not and cannot ever be allowed to have. The weapons to subjugate humanity under the rule of alien overlords long thought gone. Ones that are all too real.

"I ask you to demand the report the UN is getting today. Demand answers from China. Demand that they put down their weapons of war and recall their mission to seize the base on Mars. Only by doing those things can they prove their innocence."

He smiled broadly and leaned forward. "And watch their ship in space closely. If it does not turn around, you can be sure that any actions they take on Earth are designed to fool you and continue their program of violent subjugation.

"Do not let them fool you. Do not let the UN cover this up for the large payment that China would gladly pay to sweep this under the rug. Demand the truth and settle for nothing less. With that, I'll leave you to discuss this among yourselves. Good luck."

With that, he unplugged his data chip and headed back behind the stage. Let them bicker and fight. China would deny everything and refuse to cooperate. The other nations would demand proof from the UN. It was even odds whether the idiotic bureaucrats would comply.

The alliance would be angry with him, but that was too bad. Let them stand up in the light of day and show the world what they had. As soon as a few of those damned ships started making public appearances, all doubt would fade, and the war with China would become a lot more one-sided.

The world would not be satisfied with being shut out. Thank God he didn't have to negotiate *that*. Jessica Cook and the rest would hate him for this, but it was now their problem. He'd probably saved the United States, and that would have to be enough.

10

Jess had thought she was going to dodge Harry right up until the moment she arrived in the gate room aboard *Freedom Express*. To her annoyance, he was standing there with a smug expression on his face, waiting for her.

"Fancy meeting you here," he said blandly. "Going somewhere?"

She sighed. "You damn well know where I'm going. I'm taking the heavy-worlder leader and two of his aides back to his planet to try and stop this idiotic war."

As she was speaking, her armed retinue escorted Kerrick Vidar and two of his associates through the gate behind her, the prisoners' arms secured with ridiculously thick manacles. The armed men came from the New Zealand portion of the security contingent.

"Who ratted me out?" Jess asked, annoyed that she'd been caught.

"Does it matter?" Harry asked. "I shouldn't have to say this, but this is a stupid plan. It doesn't matter how many troops you take with you, you're going into enemy territory. These people have already proven how violent they are. Are you looking to get shot again?"

"No, I'm not. But I'm also not going to sit on my butt hoping that this problem solves itself. I believe I can do something to undo the damage your mother caused. And in case it escaped your notice, I am the boss. If I decide that I'm going, I'm going."

Harry simply shrugged. "I know that I can't stop you, but I can at least make certain you're safe. I put in a call to Sandra, and she's going to have a team joining us here in just a couple of minutes. I'll go along with you as well."

She shook her head. "No. It's too dangerous for both of us to go."

"If it's too dangerous for both of us, it's definitely too dangerous for you," he said in what he probably intended to be a reasonable tone. Unfortunately for him, it came across as somewhat condescending.

Of course, he was the military expert and she was an engineer. One who wasn't supposed to be skilled in combat or diplomacy. Unfortunately, everyone was having to take on roles that they were unfamiliar with. She'd make it work, and he'd just have to deal with it.

"I hear what you're saying, but this needs doing, and I'm doing it. You have other very important fish to fry."

She looked over at Brenda Cabot, Molly Goodwin, and Karl Krueger where they were arrayed safely distant from the confrontation. "While we're waiting, what did you think about Earth Two?"

"I'm pretty sure you can't call it that," Kevin McHugh said as he came through the open gate behind the guards. "One of the comic companies has that trademarked, I think. The very last thing you want is to have someone like them coming after you. I can almost hear their lawyers writing cease-and-desist letters as we speak."

Jess put her hands on her hips and stared at the hacker. "Are you serious? That's really a thing?"

"Yep," he said cheerfully. "Maybe you should go with Earth-B or something."

"This is ridiculous," she muttered. "Fine, Earth-B, unless that's taken up by someone else. Which it probably is."

One of the other gates activated, and Sandra Dean walked through at the head of a dozen of Harry's special operations troops. They were all integrating into Humanity Unlimited, but that was going to take a while to get settled, and they had things that had to be done in the meanwhile.

Like making peace with hostile heavy-worlders.

"What's this I hear about a road trip?" Sandra asked, hefting her long rifle. "Can I do some sightseeing?"

Since she was a trained sniper, that simple question had all kinds of hidden meaning.

"Maybe. You'll know when I do."

"I'd better find out first, just to be safe. Gotta line up all the best angles on interesting things ahead of time."

Jess turned her flinty gaze back on Harry. "This makes my life far more complicated than it needed to be, but you win. I'll take the extra people. You, on the other hand, have Mars to deal with."

Commander Krueger perked up at that. "I'd like to see the Mars base, if you don't mind. I've heard bits and pieces that lead me to believe it's big and fully operational. Bigger than the base in France."

"That it is," Harry said. "We're still exploring it, but most of the systems are online, and it has so much stuff scattered around. It was the main base the rebel humans used before the heavy-worlders came.

"I'd be happy to show you, but I really need to start focusing on the Chinese Mars ship. It's full of secret-society heavy-worlder descendants and they'll be in orbit in two months, unless they have a secret to help them get there faster."

Krueger nodded. "And you can be sure they're armed to the teeth. Best to deal with them in space, preferably very far away from Mars."

"It's not that simple," Harry said with a sigh. "We're not officially shooting at one another, so that means the treaty they signed with my father keeps them from openly attacking Nauru and our holdings on Earth. They're powerful enough to take the base in New Zealand, should they decide to do so. Or the island."

Before he could go on, Jess's quantum phone rang. It was one of only four in existence. They'd thought they'd lost the one that Clayton Rogers had had on him at his death, but he'd passed it on to Molly Goodwin before that final mission. Harry had the third, and Brenda Cabot had the last one.

At least having a quantum phone meant that she wasn't getting those stupid robocalls, though it wouldn't shock her if someday some prince of a fallen world across the galaxy was calling to tell her he wanted to give her his fortune but just needed a little money to make it happen first.

"Somehow, I'm betting this isn't a social call, Mister Weller," she said into the phone.

"No," Weller said. "Though it almost falls under the category of someone else's problem if you squint hard enough. Secretary of State Queen just gave a rousing speech at the UN. One where he dropped the bomb about the Asharim, the Chinese heavy-worlders, the base in New Zealand, and a host of other things.

"It's all over the news, and to say I'm being inundated with calls from governments and reporters is perhaps the greatest understatement imaginable. The secret is out, and everyone is now demanding a slice of the pie."

"Perfect," she said, rubbing her eyes. "As if we don't have enough distractions. Get some extra staff hired to take messages and promise nothing. Queen made the statement, so refer them back to him. I'll deal with the most important calls as soon as I make sure that no one is shooting at us. No one is shooting at us, are they?"

"Not to my knowledge, but that could certainly change quickly enough."

She looked back over at Harry. "I'm sending Harry to deal with the public relations aspects of this new problem. Perhaps he can leverage it into getting the Chinese to turn back. He'll call you."

Once she hung up, she raised a hand to forestall his objections. "This just became too important to put off. Let Brenda, Molly, and Karl examine the Mars base, but you need to hustle back to Earth and make sure this doesn't blow up in our faces."

* * *

BRENDA WAS ANGRY. Jealous and angry. The Mars base Harry had taken for Humanity Unlimited was everything the legends of her people claimed and more. It was *huge* and in such good condition. It should've been hers.

But it wasn't, and no amount of envy was going to change that. Her mother had made sure that she understood the consequences of envy quite clearly, so she forced herself to take a deep breath and set the feelings aside, as hard as that was to do.

Good things came to those with the patience to wait for them. There was an entire universe out there, and she had no doubt they'd have their base soon enough. With the Families having power for the portable gate now, it was only a matter of time.

Molly Goodwin and Karl Krueger were much more appreciative of the sightseeing tour.

"This is a lot more than I expected," Krueger said, looking down into the atrium with its lush vegetation. Animal calls floated up to them from below. "Those sound like Earth birds. How could an environment like this still be alive after a thousand years?"

"I'm told it's from Earth," she said. "My ancestors installed gates on the lowest level of the facility, in addition to the ones on the cargo level. One of which was left permanently on and connected to an island on a world somewhere out there. One the Asharim had either forgotten or abandoned.

"They filled it with Earth vegetation suitable to the tropical environment and seeded some species there to help with that ecosphere. I can only imagine what effect it might have had on the other biosphere, but the damage is long done now."

"Can we go see it?" Molly asked.

"I don't see why not, but it's not much to look at. Frankly, it looks like a deserted island. I keep expecting Gilligan and the skipper to pop out from behind a palm tree."

"The professor would be more helpful," Krueger said with a grin. "See? I can do old pop culture references, too."

"I have no idea what either of you is talking about, but I'd like to see another world where I can stand outside without worrying about freezing to death, having my face bulge out because there is no atmospheric pressure, or being shot at by primitive aliens."

"And there you go with an old pop culture reference of your own," Brenda said with a smile. "*Total Recall*. Nice. Come on."

It only took a few minutes to find one of the lifts and take the trip to the bottom of the facility. While they walked, Karl became serious. "Other than being big, what does this base have that the Chinese agents on their ship want? Are there weapons here?"

"Undoubtedly," Brenda said. "I couldn't say what kind, or if they'd be ones usable on more than a personal scale, but my ancestors were staging a rebellion. They'd have plenty of guns lurking about.

"There are small craft here too, including at least one heavy-worlder assault shuttle. It would be a very rude surprise on the modern battlefield, I'd imagine. All that said, weapons aren't what they're after."

"It's the gates," Molly said. "They want to get out into the broader universe, don't they?"

"That's exactly right. They serve the Asharim and want to rejoin their masters. Or perhaps they're expecting the Asharim have fallen and want to take their places. Unless we can get some live prisoners, we'll never know. Hell, even then, the underlings might not know the truth."

"How do we keep them from taking the base in my country?" the other woman asked, a worried expression on her face.

"Easy and already done," Krueger said as the lift opened onto the lowest level. "We have one of the vest pocket nukes there with a team that has orders to arm it if the base is attacked. Then they'll retreat through the gate."

The answer didn't seem to please the woman. "That sounds a lot like taking a sledgehammer to a watermelon. Messy and permanent."

"It is that, but once the Chinese know about it, they'll hopefully keep back. The gates aren't the only ones our side has access to, and they know we'll deny them possession. With the quality of the rest of the base, they have little to gain."

The floor of the atrium was like walking in a jungle. What had probably been a garden in the old days was now completely overgrown to the point that one couldn't see that one was underground at all.

There were three gates along one wall, and one of them was active. Brenda was somewhat surprised that Harry had left it open, but after all this time, it seemed likely no one was going to discover it.

The three of them walked through the gate and into bright daylight. The gate opened up on a small clearing abutting the rock face holding the gate. Over the edge of the trees, Brenda could see the ocean. Interestingly, it had a shade of purple to its greenish blue. What could cause that?

Molly stepped out, looking around in wonder. "Wow. It's gorgeous here!"

Krueger stayed beside Brenda, and she saw him place his hand on the grip of a holstered pistol. Smart. No telling what might be out in the jungle.

"Stay close," she called out to Molly before turning her attention to the military officer.

"So, you're the ally of my ally. And I have my own separate agreement with Queen—in writing—that says he's not going to come after me or my people. What does that make our relationship?"

The man smiled a little. "Complicated. I'm not Queen, though. I'd like to think we can be friends."

"I'd like that. My agreement with Queen is a little on the bare bones side. I'd like to invite you back to my place so we can get something a little more robust and binding."

"You're not going to get me drunk and take advantage of me, are you?"

She laughed. "Only if you want me to."

He grinned and stuck out his hand. "Deal."

11

Harry took one of the troop transports from the French base to the hidden gate in South America, Peru specifically. It was hidden up high in the inaccessible mountains and was only a very short flight to the Pacific Ocean. From there, he could go north, cross Central America, and make his way to the East Coast of the United States over the Atlantic Ocean.

That wasn't as risky as it sounded. The military craft was made to be hard to detect, and the metal of the hull absorbed radar and didn't reflect light in a way that would draw undue attention. It had no engine noise to draw the eye, either. Also, the gate was in an extremely remote area of Peru. It was a risk, but a small one.

The ship was smaller than the heavy-worlder version that he'd seen at the base on Mars but had the same kind of weapons and layout. If he had to guess, someone had taken the heavy-worlder assault ship to use as a model and then built this ship.

His knowledge of how the two compared was hazy, but Black Jack McCarthy had assured him that it was just as fast and nasty as the original. Since the former marine colonel had been a fighter pilot before he'd come over to Humanity Unlimited, he'd take the man's word on it.

Harry could have borrowed Brenda's gate to get to his destination faster and without risking getting shot down, but that wasn't the point. The news was out there, so he needed to make a public statement that couldn't be ignored.

He had the ship packed with his men, armed and armored for a fight. Less because he expected a fight than to make the right impression. He wanted people to ask themselves how many of these ships he had and what he could use them for if they screwed with him.

And speaking of screwing with people, while Black Jack took them out to international waters, Harry pulled out his regular sat phone.

It had taken Kevin McHugh less than five minutes to figure out how to get the assault shuttle to allow the transmission to be handled by the small ship. It would now forward his call out and redirect the incoming signal to his phone, bypassing the hull that would normally block it.

Dawn in Peru meant that it was later on the East Coast, so Queen should be at his office. Harry dialed the number and was connected directly with the man's assistant, Gina Tanner. She passed him right through.

Queen was blunt and to the point as soon as he picked up the line. "What do you want?"

"Good morning, Mister Secretary," Harry said, putting a hint of cheer that he didn't feel into his voice. "I hope your day is starting out well, because I'm about to complicate it in much the same way you did for me yesterday."

"Perfect," the other man muttered. "Though I suppose it shouldn't surprise me. What are you going to do?"

"I'm in a ship, and I'm going to the UN building. I expect to be there in an hour. You might want to be in New York to meet when I land."

Harry heard the other man curse, call for his assistant, and then order a helicopter to get him to a jet. "An hour might be tight," Queen said. "Can you give me a little longer?"

"I'd be inclined to do so if you'd bothered to tell me what you intended rather than blindsiding me at the UN. Now? Not so much.

"I'm going to confirm everything you told them with hard evidence that they can't refute. The ship, my presence here rather than on Mars, and some of the tech I'm going to demonstrate to every reporter I can lay hands on should do the trick. If you want to put some spin on it as well, you'd best get a move on."

With that, Harry disconnected the call and turned the sat phone off. If Queen called back, he'd get voice mail.

"You're kind of an ass," Black Jack called back from the front. "I like that."

"If I let him walk all over me, he'll never give us the respect we're due. He needs to understand his place in the alliance, and I'm going to make it crystal clear to the reporters that the US is the junior partner. Humanity Unlimited calls the shots with the support of the main alliance nations and their little buddy, the US."

McCarthy laughed. "That's great. How will the Chinese react to that?"

"Damned if I know. The Australians have been keeping an eye on them, politically speaking, since Queen made his announcement. Other than denying everything, there's been no sign that they've done anything. Still, I'm sure there's a lot of chaos in their ranks right now.

"They did send an encrypted message to their spaceship on the way to Mars. It didn't respond to multiple transmissions, so I'll wager that counts as confirmation that the heavy-worlders' secret society exists. That has to be a lot worse for them than the revelation that Brenda Cabot and the Families have the US penetrated seven ways to Sunday."

The former marine shook his head. "That means there's a fight for domination happening as we speak. That's gotta be ugly. How will it affect us?"

Harry shrugged. "There are many more regular Chinese people than secret society members, but we have no way of guessing how deep the tendrils go. They've had a thousand years to get influence over that which they want to control.

"If the Chinese come out on top, perhaps we can stop some of the madness. Then again, maybe not. They want the tech, too. If the secret society wins, they become more direct. We already know that they're willing to go to war to get access to the gate system. We have to believe they'll do a lot more to win."

That pretty much killed the conversation, leaving both men deep in thought. Things weren't as dire as they could've been, but they could still get very, very ugly before they got better.

And New York was only his first task. He also needed to get the mission back to the Volunteer World under way. Access to the other human colonies would be invaluable, and the only way to get to them was to have the addresses. As the Volunteers had lost their gate controller when the Asharim had attacked their camp, that meant taking the city away from the devolved Asharim and pulling the addresses from the gates themselves.

Hell, just capturing some of the murderous bastards and bringing them back to Earth would cement the facts of his world's situation for everyone. No way could they fake live aliens.

Wouldn't that be fun?

* * *

CHEN ORDERED his men to remove the dead man from his office. The emissary from the official Chinese government had attempted to bully his way into removing Chen from control of the spaceport and had paid the ultimate price for his temerity.

From what Chen was hearing from his various contacts, both inside the Dragon and in the wider populace, this was far from the only flailing of the suddenly awakened communist government. Too bad for them that they'd awoken with a pillow already on their faces.

The Dragon had had centuries to place their people—heavy-worlder or not—into powerful positions throughout China. Panicked orders were acknowledged and then ignored across the great nation. Those not loyal to the Dragon in important posts were being purged. Those in less important roles would either obey their new masters or die.

Within an hour of that fool Queen's speech before the United Nations General Assembly, Chen had consolidated his control over the Yucatán spaceport. As it had been an important stepping stone to operations in the United States, he'd had more than enough operatives loyal to him personally or to the Dragon to isolate and eliminate any challenge to his control.

The emissary he'd just choked to death had thought a few armed men and his pistol would intimidate the rogue ambassador he'd been sent to quell. That belief had proven a terminal mistake.

The leader of the armed retainers sent by the Dragon to bolster him closed the door once the offal was gone. "What are your next steps, my lord? With knowledge of the Dragon spreading, though no one knows our name, it is only a matter of time before the other nations of the world make common cause against us."

Chen sniffed disdainfully. "Let them. Even before we show them the might of the Dragon, the Chinese military is the most powerful in the world. Better yet, it has long been under our direct control. There was no chaos, as the Dragon had always ruled the warriors."

The man bowed slightly but spoke in a cautious voice. "All true, but a wolf can be brought low by enough dogs willing to die to see his blood."

He started to chastise the man but stopped himself. That was simply the truth, no matter how unpalatable it was. Arrogance killed just as thoroughly as a bullet if allowed to fester. A cautious man would be certain to crush his enemies.

"Your words hold wisdom, and I thank you for them," Chen said, inclining his head. "The larger plan is of course the Dragon's to decide. If I have my way, I will deal with the United States first."

The man nodded but said nothing. Though he owed the warrior no further information, Chen continued. "While we know of the base in New Zealand, the images we've seen show it to be ruined. The gates can be powered remotely, but the US has made certain we know that there is a small nuclear device there to prevent that. It would be little loss to them, as they have access to more gates, so I see no reason to attack them. Yet.

"There is also the inconvenient treaty we have to defend the Republic of Nauru. Clayton Rogers was the primary claimant of the base, and New Zealand has shrewdly chosen to honor that. If we attack that base, it is a direct affront to the treaty, and the rest of the world would see it as proof that we are a mad dog that must be put down."

"Yet we have our ship on the way to Mars on a mission to do exactly the same thing there."

Chen smiled. "Ah, but there is nuance. The base there was not claimed by the president of Nauru. Rather, by his son in the name of a private company. Taking that base is not a direct violation of the defense treaty."

The other man inclined his head. "A fine distinction, indeed. Does the fact Nauru is now allied—no matter how unwillingly—with the United States negate it in some way?"

"Sadly, no. We had no reason to expect a rapprochement between the two when the government made the agreement. We didn't even know that they had already found evidence and relics left behind by the rebels. If we had, I feel certain that the Dragon would have crushed Rogers then."

The phone on his desk rang before the other man had a chance to respond. The warrior bowed and exited the room to give Chen the privacy he needed.

"Chen," he said into the receiver. It was encrypted, of course.

"Ambassador Chen, this is Minister Fa. Are you secure?"

Fa Lao was a full member of the Dragon and had replaced the unfortunate Minister Wu during the coup.

"I am secure, Minister, as is the spaceport," Chen said. "How may I assist you?"

"You need to get on your fastest plane and leave for New York at once."

Chen felt both his eyebrows rise. "I have been declared persona non grata."

"Not relevant. Your UN credentials are still valid, and you are now the Chinese ambassador to the UN. They will allow you to pass, and you must get there as soon as you are able. The son of Clayton Rogers is coming there in a ship made with the technology of the Masters and will be there within half an hour. You must meet with him."

"I will leave at once. I have access to a hypersonic transport and may be able to meet that deadline. Even so, there is no guarantee that Harry Rogers will speak with me. We are sending a ship to take his base on Mars away, after all."

"He will meet with you. In fact, he requested you by name when he called our embassy in Canada just a few minutes ago. He said the two of you had many things to discuss, including the 'secret society of heavy-worlder descendants working behind the scenes in China.'"

That news was shocking and took Chen's breath away for a moment. How could he have known? Did he capture one of the Dragon's warriors in Washington, DC? Well, Chen imagined that was on the table to be discussed as well.

"I'll leave immediately, Minister," Chen said, rising to his feet. "Do you have any specific messages for Rogers from the Dragon?"

"Yes. Tell him that we will make him dearly regret crossing swords with us."

"It will be as you order. To the strong, victory."

Chen disconnected the call and strode from his office, calling for a car to take him to the airfield and for someone to have the hypersonic transport readied for immediate takeoff.

12

J ess watched Kevin McHugh make his modifications to the Asharim troop lander's avionics, not even pretending she understood what he was doing. The hacker didn't leave her in the dark, though. The man couldn't seem to stop chattering on about what he was working on, even if some of the words and phrases made little sense to her.

"There," he said with a tone of smug satisfaction. "That should do it."

"You lost me about five minutes ago, and I'm an engineer," she admitted. "Can you summarize and use less geek speak?"

"Sorry," he said as he put the access panel back in place and sat in one of the handy acceleration couches. "This is comfortable. I may have to steal one for my ship if it doesn't come with one."

"Your ship?" she asked, raising an eyebrow. "I don't think I've heard this story."

The hacker flushed a little. "You were in the healing device, and we had no way to get it off the ship without killing you. It had a slot for a power cube, and I just *happened* to have picked up one to look at earlier.

"The older Mr. Rogers said he didn't mind and that I could have a whole damned ship if we got you out alive. I understand that probably isn't happening, but I do like daydreaming."

She considered the man and nodded. "He gave you his word, and I'll make it good at some point. What would you do with a ship? I assume you mean a small one like this or one of the other landers?"

"That's what I thought he meant. No way I could do anything with a big ship. A small one I could examine and try to learn from. I can't imagine any use in flying it around. That just seems crazy."

"Humanity Unlimited pays its debts in full and on time. We'll find you a ship that's to your liking as soon as we can. That reminds me. Clayton also promised that guy in New Zealand a fast, red car for shooting down the CIA drone. What was his name?"

"Mick Bird," Kevin said.

"That's the guy. We'll fix him up soon, too. Now, what did you do and how will it help us?"

Kevin leaned back in his couch. "I examined the big gate on the side of the station and cobbled together a controller that it will think comes from a bigger ship. These small craft are meant to use only the smaller gates, so the big one would normally ignore it. Not now."

"And we know the gate address that Nathan and Kathleen Bennett used? Is the gate on the other end still there?"

He nodded. "It is. I've had the address for a while. I just couldn't make the gate connect without an authenticated controller. With that fixed, we can go whenever you're ready."

"We'll have to wait for a pilot," she said. "With all the chaos right now, that might be an hour or two. We really need to train more of our people to use ships like this. We've gotten too used to relying on Black Jack McCarthy for the job."

Then a chill ran down her spine. She had other buried skills inside her skull that the healing machine had implanted in her. Was flying one of these ships part of that? She didn't exactly have an index of skills. She had to try each one to see if there were any surprises. Might as well check.

She rose to her feet and stepped into the pilot's cubby, dropping into the right-hand seat, the one Black Jack told her was traditionally the pilot's controls. A swipe of her hand brought the console to life, showing her a series of panels that meant nothing to her.

Only, after a moment, they did. It was as if a switch had clicked in her head and it all made sense. Not only the parts she could see, but she now knew how to get to other screens to accomplish what needed to be done to bring the ship fully online.

That was *super* creepy.

Kevin stuck his head in. "What are you doing?"

"Discovering that I know how to pilot this ship, courtesy of the learning machine or whatever it is," she said grimly. "I get that this kind of thing is useful, but the idea that someone put something in my head makes me crazy mad.

"Not at you," she hurried to add. "I know you were saving my life, and I'm so grateful. I blame the Asharim for making this possible. Maybe if I'd known what was coming and approved ahead of time, I'd feel differently."

"I'd seriously give it a go if it gave me a pile of Asharim know-how," the hacker said. "We're behind the eight ball, and having some people in the know would be a boost. You should look at the machine and see what it tells you about itself."

"I have," she muttered. "The Asharim obviously didn't want their minions to know everything, because there is no extra knowledge on how to work the machine. Its current settings are what they are.

"You're right, though. We need to have more people use it. Harry, for one. You, Brenda, and maybe even Karl Krueger, just to show we're really treating the US as a full partner. Others like Doctors Powell and Young. Maybe Doctor Crockett. Definitely Black Jack."

The young man cleared his throat. "I saw what it did to Kathleen Bennett. That let me see that it did the same for you, though you were younger so maybe not many people have noticed. It's a fountain of youth. That's a bargaining point to recruit people with lots of experience.

"Imagine that as an incentive to a retired space engineer or something. Boom, down from eighty-five to twenty-five. Not even counting the knowledge they get, the healing and extra life would be worth them locking themselves in for a twenty-year or thirty-year contract. Same for curing cancer or other deadly diseases."

"I'd be happy to use the healing without the knowledge implanting," she said. "Not to get people locked in, but to prove some of the benefits of the tech. Keep the anti-aging stuff to yourself."

"Will do," he said quietly. "I'm sure we can figure out how to turn off the knowledge implanting and the age regeneration. It's a matter of exploring the system and learning the interface."

She nodded. "When we get back, I want you to get the full cycle. Hopefully, since you aren't critically wounded or really old, it won't take as long as I did. Then you can figure that machine out. Hell, maybe we'll get lucky and find another one somewhere."

With that, she rose to her feet. "We're not going to find anything if we wait around. I'm going to do a preflight walk-around and then we'll load up. It's time to go see what the heavy-worlder planet looks like and decide if we're making peace or war on one another."

* * *

HARRY WAS ready for trouble as soon as the assault lander hit the helicopter pad near the United Nations, and he wasn't disappointed. A number of New York City police officers closed in on them.

He opened the wide hatch at the back of the lander and stepped down the ramp. He wasn't armed, but his men were, and heavily so. If there was going to be trouble today, he'd deal with it, but he couldn't allow these people to see him as weak.

"What the hell is this, pal?" one of the cops who boasted a lot of stripes on his sleeve asked. "And who the hell are you? This is a restricted pad, and you flew right through restricted airspace to get to it. Are you nuts?"

"My name is Harry Rogers and I'm here to provide some additional testimony about those aliens Secretary of State Queen dropped on you yesterday."

The man frowned. "Rogers? Like the space guy? Aren't you on Mars?"

"I was. Now I'm here, and I arrived in a ship built with alien technology.

So, who do I see about getting in to talk? Or should I just grab all the reporters and have a gabfest on live television?"

A group of men and women in suits came rushing out of one of the doors in the UN building. One of them, a tall, swarthy-skinned man, raced in front of the pack and arrived huffing for breath.

"President Rogers, I'm Friederike Koppenhagen… with the office of the secretary general. She didn't know about your… unexpected arrival until about ten minutes ago and… sent me to greet you."

"Take a breath," Harry advised with a smile. "No need to pass out."

"It seems that I… might need to add more… cardio to my exercise plan." The panting man turned toward the police officer. "It's all right. President Rogers's credentials are in order. He may pass."

"Yeah?" the cop asked, looking less than impressed. "Maybe so, but his troops can't. I'm not letting all these men with illegal weapons off this ship. Hell, I'm inclined to impound it for this damned stunt."

"Good luck with that," Harry said. "They can stay with the ship, but it isn't going anywhere until I'm done. If you screw with it or my people, you'll dearly wish that you hadn't. This ship was designed to fight freaking aliens, and it would be damned embarrassing if you got a bunch of people killed trying to show me that you're a big man."

"Just let it stay and them too," Koppenhagen said quickly. "It's fine. We've had military helicopters land here before, and heads of state often come with armed retainers possessing weapons that would be illegal in New York City. All of this is cleared."

The cop didn't seem convinced but backed up a few steps and gestured for the rest of the police to form a perimeter. Harry watched his men relax just a fraction in response.

"Black Jack," he said loud enough to be heard in the lander. "Keep an eye out for trouble. You and the men are authorized to use force in response to any attack or threat of one. Your call on how lethal."

"Copy that, boss," the ex-marine said. "I want you to tag me every half hour, or I'm coming in after you."

"Understood. Talk to you in thirty." He motioned for two of his men—unarmed for the purpose—to heft the boxes they held and follow him in.

"There is no need for that," the UN official said as they walked at a more sedate pace toward the building. "No one is going to attack you here."

"Someone tried to kill me in Washington, DC, yesterday, in broad daylight, so I'm not convinced that you're correct. People, I might add, with ties to the Asharim."

The other man frowned. "I didn't hear the secretary of state speak, but I reviewed the transcript. He was long on accusation and short on detail. I'm given to understand that he is also on his way here and expects to arrive shortly."

"No need to wait for him," Harry said with a smirk. "He can catch up as best he can if he's late."

"The secretary general would also like to speak with you. Preferably before you speak to anyone else."

"I'll talk with her," he agreed, "but don't fall into the trap of thinking this information won't get out. Now that Queen dropped the bomb, I have no choice but to see that I get as much information as possible to the world. That can be through an address to the General Assembly or to a room packed full of reporters. Either is good for me."

The UN official looked pained. "Secretary General Almen asks that you explain the situation to her first. We cannot compel you to keep any information to yourself, but we need to plan for what's happening. There is already great unrest in many areas around the globe."

Harry didn't know much about Muwaffaq Almen other than her name, so he forced himself not to equate her with Queen. The UN was filled with blowhards, but perhaps a little courtesy might not be wasted.

He nodded. "I'll explain the full situation to her and anyone she wants to have in the room. Then she can decide which group I speak to, the General Assembly or the reporters of the world. I'm not speaking to the Security Council, by the way. That would be a waste of everyone's time."

They stepped into the building, and Harry immediately saw trouble coming. Stalking from one side of a long hall was Secretary of State Josh Queen. From the other direction came Ambassador Chen Jian of China, if Harry remembered his name correctly.

Both looked pissed and not just at one another. Well, this was going to be interesting.

13

Brenda woke late, stretched, and smiled over at her unexpected yet completely welcome companion in her bed. All she could see of Karl was his muscular back, as he was turned away from her, but the urge to run her fingers along the defined creases between muscles was strong.

She resisted the urge, though. Time was short, and if she did that, they wouldn't get out of bed before noon. Instead, she carefully extracted herself from between the sheets and padded into the bathroom on silent feet.

Once she had the door closed, she took an amazing shower. She expected him to still be asleep when she came out, but he was gone. That was a tad irritating.

Her annoyance abated a few minutes later when he knocked on her door, freshly showered and dressed, but also carrying a tray with two cups of hot coffee and a light breakfast of sunny-side-up eggs, lightly crisped bacon, and seasoned potatoes.

"You got all that while I was in the shower?" she asked as she let him in. "I'm impressed."

"I'm a Navy SEAL. We're very task oriented."

"I remember," she said with a somewhat wicked smile. "You weren't asleep, were you?"

He shook his head. "You said we have things to do this morning. I figured it was best to play possum and save round two for later."

"Round two?" she asked, raising one eyebrow. "Round six by my count."

"I count last night as one extended round with multiple engagements," he said, setting the tray on the bed between them before carefully lying down beside it.

"You *are* my hero," she said with a sigh, joining him and loading her plate with food. "And we do have things to do this morning, at least if we can come to terms on what you can pass along to Secretary Queen and when."

He sipped at his steaming coffee, his eyes sharp over the rim. "That depends on what we're talking about. I'm flexible, but I am representing the United States, not just myself."

"You're *very* flexible," she said coyly, lowering her eyelids and smiling a sultry smile at him. "But you're right. I'm representing the Families too, so I have my limits as well. Knowing you as… thoroughly as I now do, I'd wager we can come to some kind of agreement."

His smile widened slightly. "So, I need to know some of the details to know if it's even possible for me to make a deal. What's this about?"

"You know the Volunteers came from the US long after the Asharim-led heavy-worlders crushed my ancestors. We have maps of the general locations of the bases we had a thousand years ago. Nothing in North America, but that's where they came from.

"I've spoken with them and have a very rough idea of where the cave was probably located. Harry and I took them out for a look but didn't find anything worth exploring. It was just the four of us on foot, and we were worried about someone spotting us. I'd like to find it in a more open fashion, and I want you with me, but I don't want Queen to know the details just yet."

"That's asking a lot," he said after taking a long sip of his coffee. "Too much, maybe. That base is inside the US borders, and we want a facility of our own."

"The Families were here first, I'll remind you. Perhaps not physically inside the US, but we've been looking for a base like this for a thousand years. I didn't have to invite you along on this."

He nodded and picked up a slice of bacon. "True enough, but then it would get very awkward between us. Personally, I wouldn't like that."

"Me either, but if we already had the base in our possession, my agreement with Queen would protect it."

"That agreement was for what you already had, not what you might get between then and now. At least I'm sure that would be how the secretary would see it, so that's how I have to play it. How do we find common ground between those two positions?"

"It's called horse trading. If I want something valuable from you, I have to be willing to part with something equally valuable. In this case, I'm talking about knowledge."

"We already have an agreement to share data," he countered, using a slice of toast to sop up his yolk before popping it into his mouth.

"What about the same level of knowledge that Jess Cook has? Or, I suppose Kathleen Bennett might be a more familiar example to you."

"She is now. I missed her change at the time because I hadn't seen her before, but I've seen Miss Cook since she came out of that machine. It didn't just heal her, did it?"

Brenda shook her head. "The sarcophagus healed her, regenerated her body back to about twenty-five years of age, and based on what we've seen from Jess, implanted some advanced knowledge into the woman. Jess can read Asharim, speak the heavy-worlder language, and operate several pieces of equipment that we tested her on. Not all, mind you, but some. She's now also a wicked shot with her flechette pistol, so it gave her some combat skills."

"And she has no idea where the end of it is?" he asked slowly. "That's scary."

"The Asharim used the device on their most trusted minions," Brenda said, nodding in agreement, "but that still doesn't mean we understand the full implications of what it did.

"We *do* know that it never had a whiff of mind control in the legends. It's only knowledge, regeneration, and potentially some other tweaks. We're willing to give you that kind of inside knowledge."

"I'd have to talk that over with Queen. There'd have to be some kind of selection process for someone with that kind of power. Even so, I'm still not sure he'd agree that was a good trade."

"Then we can call it a down payment. Also, when I say you, I mean *you*."

He blinked in surprise. "Me? Are you serious? The risks are incalculable."

"So are the rewards. And you don't need to feel like I'm picking on you. I'll go through it first, you big baby."

He laughed out loud at her verbal poke, showing it hadn't gotten under his skin at all. That was excellent.

"And in exchange for this dubious honor, you want me to keep my damned mouth shut about the base?"

"No," she said, shaking her head. "You can tell them about it. In fact, I'm sure you already have as part of the Volunteer World briefing. All you have to do is keep our search for it quiet. We don't really know who these people were, and I'd like to keep the US from sending people out unescorted into the universe until we have a better idea of what we'll find there. That's bloody dangerous, and I don't trust Queen's judgment."

He seemed to mull that while eating silently and then nodded. "I see your point. We have an agreement, but a gentleman always takes the risks before a lady. Me first."

She stretched her hand over the tray holding their meal and took his with a wicked smile. "We have a deal. We can start after just one more engagement."

* * *

JESS MARVELED at how everything seemed to snap into place as she walked around the Asharim-designed lander and checked the status of every system. She'd have to check with Black Jack but was inclined to believe she was understanding everything.

Well enough to take the chance of taking it for a spin around *Freedom Express*, at least. If that worked out, she'd consider taking it through the gate herself. After coming back for her official guard team and the prisoners, of course.

"You might want to step out while I give this thing a test drive," she said as she strapped herself into the pilot's couch when she was finished.

"Are you kidding?" he asked, settling into the co-pilot's spot. "I wouldn't miss this for the world."

"You say that now. Wait till I crash."

Merely thinking of bringing the ship up and moving toward the gate in the interior landing bay of the dormant comet had her hands on the controls. All at once, the knowledge appeared as she needed it. Like remembering how to drive after being in space for a year or remembering how to drive with a manual clutch.

They'd finally found a concealed gate on the surface of the mobile base, allowing the landers inside it to exit into the same area of space, so all she had to do was tap the code onto the built-in gate controller.

Once the wormhole had stabilized, she took them smoothly through it and out into space, her hands automatically correcting their course as they moved.

The process was captivating. Once she performed a task, she knew how to do it again and what had happened. That suggested that she could move beyond the basic skills with experience and practice.

After circling the comet and then the station a few times, she was satisfied that she had a good grasp on how to fly. She had some experience in regular landers, and that was helping a lot. Getting back through the exterior gate and into *Freedom Express* was straightforward, and she landed without issue.

"Well done," Kevin said. "You looked like you've done it a million times."

"It didn't feel that way," she confided. "I'm more confident now. Let's get our guests and head out."

Summoning her guards and the prisoners, she had them back out in space an hour later. The three prisoners were shackled and secured at the back of the lander under heavy guard, with Sandra watching them. The team Harry had insisted on sat around them.

As soon as she had the lander in front of the large gate on the side of the Asharim station, she gave Kevin a nod. "Open it up."

He responded by activating a handheld controller. "The lander is forwarding the signal, so it should be good."

With a mixture of relief and trepidation, she watched the massive gate come to life and open the universe to her small ship. She nudged them through before she had a chance to change her mind.

The other side of the gate was a mess, and alarms started sounding as soon as she came out. Space around them was filled with debris. She was forced to dodge a large chunk of metal moving energetically past them within seconds, even as the gate closed behind them.

"Hang on," she called out. "We have debris from the nuke, I think."

"It can't have destroyed the station, or the gate wouldn't have opened," Kevin said. "Perhaps it would be safer inside that."

She had to admit that she liked that idea and brought the lander around. A huge station filled the viewscreen, almost completely intact. There was some obvious impact damage, but it seemed the station had weathered the explosion well enough.

It wasn't just a station, she noted. It was a space elevator, and the cable seemed to be intact as well. That matched up with what Kerrick Vidar had told them. The ship that the Bennetts had stolen must've been safely away from the station when it was destroyed.

A few moments later, she found a large set of doors that she suspected led to an interior bay. To her annoyance, the basic command to open them failed. She supposed that wasn't a surprise, but it complicated their choices.

"The hatch won't open," she told Kevin. "I suspect the lander Kathleen Bennett used had a code on it that we don't. Any chance you can get it open for us remotely?"

He shook his head. "I'd have to go out and open it manually. Let me suit up."

Jess considered that and then shook her head. "Hold up. If we go down the cable, everyone below will see us coming. It might be better if we just land in an area near the city and walk."

The hacker's eyebrows rose. "Landing in an atmosphere is a lot harder than puttering around in space. Are you sure you're up to that?"

Her instincts screamed at her that this was inexcusably reckless, but her brain told her she had the skills. "I'm good. Everyone strap in a bit tighter. We're going down."

14

Queen scowled at the smug Chinese man walking casually down the corridor toward him, forgetting Rogers for the moment. Red tinged his vision, and everything else seemed to fade from view.

He imagined it was what it had been like back in the old West when two gunfighters faced off. Too bad he'd had to leave his weapon at the entrance. If anyone deserved to be shot, it was Chen Jian.

Forcing himself to take a deep breath, Queen continued walking until he was standing right in front of the man, with Rogers, two of his men, and some UN flunky just off to his right. "You've got a lot of nerve showing your face in the United States again. How did you slip through customs?"

"Diplomatic immunity," the large man said with a self-satisfied smile. "As the new Chinese ambassador to the United Nations, I have automatic passage. It isn't like in the old days when the US had a say over visas for the UN. Thank your government for that."

The thing that pissed Queen off about that was that he'd supported the change in the damned laws that allowed it. Oh, he'd only been a flunky in the State Department back then, but it still stung.

He considered punching the bastard in his self-righteous face but decided not to. He had things to do that being tossed out on his ear would interfere with. Far better to outmaneuver him and watch him rage.

Queen turned toward Rogers. "What are you going to do?"

"Right now, I'm going to explain the situation to the secretary general. Then, depending on what she says, I'll either speak to the General Assembly or every reporter in New York City. You kicked my feet out from under me with your little speech, so now I'm going to make sure that everyone on Earth knows exactly what we're facing."

"Some of that information probably needs to remain secret," Queen argued. "We need to discuss what you can say and what you can't."

"You're not the boss of me, as they say," Rodgers said. "I'll do what I need to do to protect Earth from the Asharim and their tools."

"When you have an opportunity, we should speak as well," Chen said with a hint of a smile. "There is much we need to discuss."

The look Rogers gave the Chinese diplomat was so cold that it was all Queen could do to avoid stepping back. "You think so? Perhaps you're speaking of the armed mission you're sending to Mars to attack my people? Bring it. Their lives are yours to throw away. Literally, in this case, if I'm right. Are they heavy-worlder descendants like you?"

Chen blinked, likely shocked beyond words.

Queen felt his eyes narrow as the implications sank in. "You're one of them," he said to Chen. "The secret cabal of alien worshipers. How could I have missed it before? I suppose that makes sense, since you're still alive after the coup."

"Don't be ridiculous," Chen said, just a shade too quickly. "There is no such thing."

"DNA doesn't lie," Rogers said. "We have the heavy-worlder gene sequence. One cheek swab will prove it."

"There is no such thing," Chen said again. "My country and yours have an agreement that we will defend Nauru. That has nothing to do with sending our men to Mars so that we can find what luck allows. Are you going to allow these fantasies to nullify our agreement?"

"Since you seem determined to see Humanity Unlimited as a target of opportunity that is something separate from Nauru, I'm not sure why I should look at it any differently. We can talk—and I think we should—but don't mistake me for someone you can fool."

"I feel that I should accompany you to see the secretary general," Queen said, inserting himself into the conversation. "And as a member of the alliance, I think you should refrain from speaking to Chen unless others are present so we can represent our own opinions and needs."

Rogers raised an eyebrow at him. "Where was that thought when you ripped the cover off what we were working on? No. I won't object if the secretary general wants to have you present, but I'll negotiate without someone looking over my shoulder, thank you."

With that, Rogers turned back to the UN man. "Shall we?"

The man inclined his head. "Secretary General Almen has already agreed that Secretary of State Queen may be present. I regret that she has limited the meeting to only them, Ambassador Chen. You may wait to speak to President Rogers, if you so desire."

"I will wait," Chen said after a moment.

"Excellent. I will see that the sitting room nearest the secretary general is readied for you. We here at the UN are always pleased if we can help facilitate discussions among warring parties. If we could moderate a discussion between

China and the United States, we would be more than pleased to see if we can stop any further bloodshed."

"I'm more than willing," Queen found himself saying, somewhat surprising himself by the impulse. He had the threads of a plan but wasn't sure how it would play out. "I have a number of things to say that might make the continuation of hostilities no longer necessary."

Chen was giving him a well-deserved eye, not sure what was happening. Good.

"Again, most excellent," the man said. "If you will come this way, the secretary general is waiting."

Queen placed Rogers's men between himself and Chen as they walked to a bank of elevators. The UN man had to use a keycard to get them to the uppermost floors, but very shortly they were standing in the outer office of the secretary general of the United Nations.

The UN flunky escorted an annoyed-looking Chen away, and the secretary general's personal assistant showed them into her office.

He'd met the woman any number of times and never thought she was very skilled at either diplomacy or leadership. He supposed with a global conflict breaking out between the two strongest nations on Earth, she would either prove her mettle or break.

In person, she was a somewhat stout woman with dark skin. Today she wore a sari of bright colors that swirled as she stood from behind her desk.

"Gentlemen," she said, her voice tinged with her Indian homeland. "I'm pleased that we can meet privately. We have much to discuss."

"I brought a number of items to show the General Assembly, Madam Secretary General," Rogers said. "I believe they will settle any concern that they might have about the authenticity of what Secretary of State Queen said yesterday."

She waved her hand. "I don't need to see trinkets. Your men may wait in the assistant's office with your evidence while we discuss this matter more privately."

That surprised Queen somewhat. He'd expected her to want to see all the alien gadgets. He certainly wanted to.

Once the doors were closed, Almen gestured them toward seats. "We have refreshments, if you like."

"No need for me," Rogers said.

Queen waved his hand in agreement.

"Perfect," she said, sitting primly on her chair. "Now, before you launch into your attempt at convincing me that you have found aliens and their abandoned bases, I'll tell you that that isn't necessary. I've known about them for some time."

She smiled at them brightly. "You've both met my associate, Brenda Cabot. Though it's something of a risk, I'm revealing myself as a member of the Families to you both. That should save us some time and allow us to focus on the most important thing: stopping the Asharim and their henchmen like Ambassador Chen."

Queen sat in stunned silence, words failing him completely for the first time in a long while.

* * *

HARRY BLINKED AT THE WOMAN, her statement knocking him off his stride. "Seriously?"

He looked at Queen. "And you felt comfortable saying so in front of him?"

She smiled at Queen. "The secretary of state knows that without proof, he won't be able to tell anyone else. I've served in the UN for many years, and my reputation is solid. No one is really aware of the Families outside a small circle. Oh, word is spreading that some group might exist because of the witch hunt Mr. Queen started, but he hasn't had any luck finding any moles that belong to us."

"It's annoying that you know that," Queen said, "but accurate. We've found a number of people spying, but they've worked for the normal national intelligence agencies. No one we've spoken with has been part of your group. Other than Cabot's name, can you prove that statement? A spy might know all that."

Harry nodded. "That's very true. We have a lot of players."

"Of course. Your group is exploring a frozen version of Earth out beyond the orbit of Pluto—which is a planet, no matter what those moronic astronomers claim—and you brought back a cat for Brenda to examine."

That proved her claim to Harry, but Queen was frowning. "A cat? Seriously?"

"Indeed. A mechanical construct so lifelike that it's indistinguishable from a real one without the appropriate equipment. It even behaves like one."

"Wait," Queen said. "I'm still not sure what you mean by 'a frozen version of Earth.' Could you explain that, please?"

Harry turned in his seat toward Queen. "We've found a large, frozen world outside the orbit of Pluto with an Asharim station nearby. It really is another Earth, right down to the shape of the continents. Oddly, it's not the same as our Earth."

"Oddly, you say?" Queen said, shaking his head. "Another Earth of any kind is more than odd. How did it get there? How could it exist at all? That's crazy. Not even aliens could do that."

"We agree," Almen said. "The Asharim could not possibly have created something like that or brought it from some other time or reality. Whatever that dead world is, wherever it came from, the Asharim had nothing to do with it."

"From another time? From another reality? What are you saying?"

"That this frozen Earth—which Jess has taken to calling Earth-B—is from hundreds of years in our subjective future. Since the people on it have been dead on the order of ten thousand years, that means time travel on a massive scale or that the world came from another dimension. We're leaning toward another dimension due to data I'm not ready to reveal.

"In any case, the existence of that world is *very* secret. We did show it to Commander Krueger, but he probably hasn't had a chance to brief you yet. Brenda has obviously gotten the word out."

He focused his attention on Almen. "Since I don't have to explain everything to you, what shall we talk about? Chen and his heavy-worlder secret society?"

"Partly," she said. "We also need to discuss what you should and probably should not mention to the General Assembly and the reporters. I do recommend you take the opportunity to speak to both. Since the cat is out of the bag, so to speak, you might as well keep the general populace from dismissing this as a strange hoax.

"You also need to find a way to stop the budding global war. That will kill millions and leave our world in ruins. We have to avoid that kind of senseless violence at all costs."

"I can talk to Chen, but I'm not the one he's at war with, though that'll change soon enough. It's the United States that's in the mud with China—the heavy-worlder descendants, really—and Secretary Queen is going to have to be there."

"We have word that the Chinese state has fallen and that the losers have vanished," Almen said. "I would expect that this group is now running the show there more openly. If the two of you could defuse the conflict enough to avoid mass casualties, that would be extremely helpful."

"I have a few ideas on that," Queen admitted. "Not that I expect to make much of an impact on the damned fight with them directly. No, I think this is going to have to be public relations judo."

Harry felt himself frowning. "What does that mean?"

Queen grinned. "That's going to be a lesson in higher-level diplomatic operations for you, I suspect. You're a man of action. I'm a man of words. Sometimes words can spike things so that a course of action is no longer prudent.

"For example, if I set things up correctly, all the pretext for war goes away and continued fighting makes them a diplomatic pariah. The rest of the global community might be inclined to side with us, and no matter how powerful the Chinese are, they can't fight the whole world.

"If I can make something like that happen, then everything goes covert. They'll still attack you on Mars, no matter what they say publicly, but they'll have constraints on what kind of actions they can execute. That has to be the main goal here."

"It sounds as if the two of you have your plans ready," Secretary General Almen said, rising gracefully from her seat. "I hope you're both adept at making this work. If you're not, China may feel it has nothing left to lose by using their nuclear arsenal. Good luck."

15

———

J ess took the lander down as slowly as she could, but that was still damned fast. Relying on skills she didn't actually know that she had until her hands performed the actions of their own accord was nerve-wracking.

She chose to come down into the atmosphere a long way off from the city where the space elevator was secured. No need to let them hear the sonic boom of her deceleration. She then came in toward it at a much slower pace.

The idea of a space elevator intrigued her. It had to be seriously overengineered for them to be comfortable putting the station above a city. If something broke the cable, the destruction on the surface would be significant.

Once she was close to the city, she asked Vidar where they could land that wasn't too distant from their ultimate destination. She took his advice but landed about an eighth of a turn around the city to make sure he wasn't leading her straight into a trap.

The scent of the foliage was intriguing once they'd all exited the lander. Not at all Earth-like, but still nice. Almost like pine, but with a hint of something sweet that she couldn't identify.

"How are we handling this?" Sandra asked. As the nominal head of Jess's personal security, she actually had the authority to tell Jess how things were going to be, but the woman was willing to accept that there was some risk associated with this mission. Harry's men were following her lead.

"We go into the city and find the heavy-worlder habitation," Jess said. "We're not skulking along, no matter how careful I'm being. We have to speak with these priests, and that means getting up close to them. We just don't want to get shot doing it."

"Copy that," the sniper said. She then started directing the forces at her command—except for the guards watching the three prisoners—to move ahead of them and start scouting the path forward.

The city was amazing. It was obviously in ruins, but the buildings were still standing after a thousand years. That was truly astonishing.

It matched up with what Harry had seen on Volunteer World, with the old Asharim city there. Even the architecture matched the images that they'd brought back, though they'd taken the pictures from quite a distance.

Harry was going to lead the Volunteers and other troops there to gain control of the gates, at least long enough for Kevin to get the addresses to the human colonies, assuming of course that the heavy-worlders didn't capture her people and lock them away.

If so, Harry would be coming here with blood in his eye and an "I told you so" on his lips. So she'd like to avoid that outcome if at all possible.

The area between the buildings looked as if it had always been intended for foot traffic. She supposed the high-tech aliens used antigravity to fly high above the peons who'd be forced to walk below. That sounded like them. Make the lesser races walk where they could look down and see them.

If she ever met an Asharim face to face, she was going to punch his lights out.

"How many people live here now?" she asked Vidar. "The city seems as if it would have once held tens of millions."

"Less than ten thousand, all told," he said, his voice a low rumble. "That's only a rough guess. Not all the inhabitants are friendly to my people. As it matters little, we allow that."

"Do you mean other heavy-worlders?" she asked as she stepped around a hunk of rock that had plummeted from hundreds of feet above them, probably long before she'd been born.

"Some," he admitted. "There are other races that once served the Masters, and they have their own enclaves. Some are friendly, others less so. A couple are outright hostile, but we are nowhere near them. Even this slightly altered path you have chosen should be safe enough to reach my people safely."

The news that other alien species were here both excited and worried her. They'd eventually need to contact them all, and she was certain that there'd be fighting. That saddened her, but they'd do the best they could.

What worried her now was when the first observer spotted them. It would happen before much longer, if it hadn't already happened. With all these tall buildings, it would be very simple for someone to keep an eye out from a great distance.

Would those inevitable watchers rain fire down on the intruders? The heavy-worlders had access to Asharim weapons and some technology. Sandra was an experienced soldier, and as a sniper, she undoubtedly knew the ways of ambushes. That was probably why she had the group so spread out.

When the time came, would that be enough to stop an attack or at least mitigate the risk? Jess hoped so.

Her questions were answered less than five minutes later when a single heavy-worlder woman stepped out from a building ahead of the group, her arms held out to her sides, palms up and empty.

"Stand fast," Sandra said over the com earbuds they all wore. "Jess, I need you up front."

"Coming," she said, but she turned to face Kerrick Vidar. "I'd rather we didn't get into a second battle while I'm trying to undo the first one. Any advice?"

"Take me with you," he said. "I can make certain that you're at least offered safe passage to the temple. After that, your fate is in the hands of the priests."

She considered his plea and shrugged. "Just remember that if we get ambushed, bad things are going to happen to you too. Be convincing."

"If they are talking, they aren't shooting. My guards are in the buildings above us right now and could kill all of you without too much danger to me or my companions. This is a known challenge point, and we have a procedure to give the watchers instructions. Please note that I didn't tell them to kill you all."

"So you say," Jess said back. "I think we understand one another well enough to recognize the consequences of any misunderstandings."

With that said, she gestured for the guards to allow Vidar to accompany her forward. This could turn out very badly for all of them, so she hoped the man was being serious. If not, she might die in the next few minutes.

* * *

BRENDA WAS surprised when Doctor Granger called her back to the makeshift medical center only a few hours after Karl had gone into the sarcophagus. Jess had been inside the machine for three days. This was more like three hours.

"Is something wrong?" she asked as she came through the door, stopping abruptly when she saw Karl sitting in a chair beside the sarcophagus, clad only in a pair of shorts that did nothing to hide his exceptional physique.

Or the missing scars. He'd had a number of healed wounds that she'd taken the time to find in her exploration of his body last night: knife wounds, bullet entry and exit points, and one that he'd had to tell her was a very bad rope burn on his left leg.

All of them appeared to be gone, though she'd have to check more thoroughly later to be sure. The Navy SEAL had been healed of his past injuries.

He'd also lost some of the ruggedness that age had brought him. Rather than a rugged man in his forties, he was now a chiseled one in his mid-twenties. The same biological age that the machine had brought Jessica Cook back to, and from what she'd heard, Kathleen Bennet.

"Well, that was quick," she said, partially covering her gap in the conversation. "How are you feeling?"

"Good," he said. "Really good, actually. I hadn't realized how much low-level pain I was dealing with from some of the injuries I'd suffered over the years. Or from getting older. My knees are particularly happy."

Brenda nodded and pulled up a chair across from him. Todd Granger sat as well, making a triangle of the three.

The doctor picked up the thread. "The process took a lot less time, perhaps because he wasn't as gravely injured as Jess. We have no idea how long Kathleen Bennett was in the box, but it could have been longer because of the age that needed to be regenerated away. We'll have to conduct more experiments as time permits.

"I've spot checked him on a few things. He does know how to speak the heavy-worlder language and has a familiarity with the same test devices Jess was able to work. As far as I can see, it worked the same for both of them."

"Consistency is good," she said. "What do you think of what I was offering now, Karl?"

"The jury is still out, but I'm warming to the exchange. He's got a lot of other things to work on and having more data will help him. No need to get his blood pressure up before we can actually tell him anything."

"What do you remember of the process?" Granger asked.

"Nothing. The lid closed, and I was out like a light with the switch turned off. I woke up as soon as the lid started opening. Needless to say, I feel refreshed. What now? More testing while Brenda takes a turn inside?"

"More testing is certainly on the program," Granger said. "I'm not sure we should be rushing this process, though. We have time. Why do you need to go inside today, Brenda? What do you get out of it that you can't wait for? You're a young woman, so I doubt it's vanity. What makes this something you don't want to put off?"

She started to answer but stopped herself and really thought about it. Was there a driving need to risk this process, which they admittedly knew very little about? Would the gain be worth the risk?

"One of the problems about our understanding of the Asharim is that we don't know what we don't know," she said after almost a minute of contemplation. "We need to understand what we find in this base we're looking for. Hell, we need the same from all the locations we're going to be exploring over the next few months.

"Harry is going to take a force to seize the Asharim city on Volunteer World, so he'll need Jess or someone like her to make sense of what they find. I want the same for us."

He nodded. "But that doesn't have to be you. Why be the first in line?"

"Because she's not going to ask her people to do something that she wouldn't do herself," Karl said. "She'll take the risk to make sure it's safe for the rest of you."

"Forgive me for being blunt, but that's silly," Granger said firmly. "We all know the risks that this might entail. There's no need for our leader to try every dangerous stunt that we might have to execute. I can't stop her if she insists, I just want her to consider why she's pushing this."

Brenda sighed. "I suppose you're right, but this is something that I have to do. Could I wait until we know it's safe? Yes. I'd still be in the same place of understanding if I did. Am I going to wait? No.

"I've taken a lot of risks for the Families over the years. Being an undercover agent in the FBI was a risky undertaking, even with some high-tech help in fooling the lie detector tests. Maybe I'm an adrenaline junkie. In any case, I'm sure that I want to do this."

She rose to her feet. "What do I do? Just climb in?"

"You can do that," Granger said, "but I'd recommend stripping down to your underwear, bottom only, and lie on the blanket I put in there. That'll cause you less discomfort when you wake up."

He turned to Karl. "Why don't you get dressed, and we'll do some more testing while she goes through the process?"

The Navy officer nodded. "After we get something to eat. I'm starving."

Karl turned his attention to her and put his hands on her shoulders. "It'll be fine. I can only barely feel the tentacles that the brain squid is using to control me."

She smacked him on the arm. "That's not funny. Now get out of here so I can get naked."

"I've seen you naked."

"And you won't be doing so again if you don't get your pretty butt dressed and out of here."

He grinned at her, dressed quickly, and left with Granger.

Jokes aside, she was worried. No one did anything so profoundly permanent without some butterflies. Still, she knew it was going to be okay. The legends said so.

Brenda stripped down to her panties, set her neatly folded clothes on a chair, and climbed into the sarcophagus. She waited for a moment, wondering if she needed to do something, but then the door started sliding shut.

She took one deep breath, and her awareness of the world around her vanished.

16

Harry was more confused than enlightened after his meeting with the secretary general. Her membership in Brenda's organization certainly made clear to him how deeply they had their tendrils in governments and organizations around the globe.

Part of him worried about them infiltrating Humanity Unlimited, but as he was already sharing everything he'd learned—for the most part—with them, that was just going to have to be acceptable. He couldn't change what he couldn't change.

That left him with the snake at his elbow—one he also couldn't change. Josh Queen was a tool of the oligarchy that ran the United States—the political class. He and his kind hadn't been of and from the people of they ruled for decades, though they still mostly observed the same forms as they once did. Only those were more for show than actual belief.

Once again, there was nothing he could do to change that. Hell, Harry's father had pulled the wool over all their eyes just to get humanity out from under the thumbs of people like Queen. As much as Harry disliked the man who'd provided half his genetic material, he agreed with the need to leave the chains of the past on Earth.

Which, since they now had to work together to fight the descendants of the heavy-worlder soldiers that had been trapped on Earth for a thousand years, made life interesting.

Their guide led them to a door just down the hall from the secretary general's office. "If you'd like to take a moment to confer before I escort you to see Ambassador Chen, you may use this room."

Queen instantly shook his head. "Not this one. We'll take the elevator down one level and evict a random executive from their office. I don't trust that this room isn't bugged."

Harry was forced to agree that that kind of thing was something the UN was likely to do. A more squabbling group of backstabbing peacocks was hard to imagine. Even the US government looked upstanding in comparison.

The problem with the United Nations was that it was a club of almost two hundred member states that would spare no expense to gain advantage for themselves. Nothing could be trusted to be what it looked like in here. Queen knew these people far better than Harry did, so he'd defer to his judgment, as crazy as that sounded.

The UN guy acquiesced without argument, likely knowing the room in question was monitored by someone. He led them down through the stairs to a level filled with senior UN executives and their staffs. Large offices filled the exterior walls, undoubtedly showcasing offices with wide windows and excellent views.

The interior of the room was a warren of cubicles, one of Harry's personal nightmares. He'd dreaded his father trying to fit him into a place like this and had fled to the military to avoid that fate almost as much as he had his father.

A few people glanced up at them, but most kept their attention on whatever work they had on their computers. Harry wondered with a smile how pissed the unfortunate executive they kicked out was going to be.

Surprisingly, Queen didn't lead them to an office. Instead, he found a room holding office supplies. After taking a good look around, Queen nodded. "This will do. You stand outside and make sure no one tries to listen in on us."

Somewhat nonplussed, the man did as instructed, leaving them alone in the supply closet.

"What is your plan with Chen?" Queen asked after a moment. "Understanding that he'll say or do whatever is necessary to get his people the technology they want."

"If I can keep him from blowing up the planet, I'll be satisfied with that," Harry said. "We've got enough on our plates already."

The other man nodded. "That would help us as well, and I may be able to assist in making him see the downsides of a public war of annihilation. I should meet him with you."

Harry put his hands on his hips and gave the other man a long, hard stare. "You're a big part of why the US is at war. You couldn't leave well enough alone and pushed the Chinese to the point they were prepared to use force to shut you up. Why should I expect anything different?"

"I'm not an idiot. I can see our country is in a bind. I'm not going to make it worse."

"Have you ever had an argument where you knew the other person was wrong, but they just couldn't see it?" Harry asked. "Their version of reality was incompatible with yours. I'm half afraid that's you and me.

"You're so locked into the worldview that you can do no wrong that you'll trample all over everyone else to get the prize you want. To hell with what they want or would be willing to settle for."

He sighed when Queen said nothing. "Fine. What's your plan?"

"They're using the spaceport as a pretext for war," Queen said, as if Harry hadn't just torn a strip off of him. "We'll give him the dammed thing. Then all his maneuvering for a fight has zero basis, and anyone that isn't in their pockets will pressure them to stop the war."

"And how do we know that China doesn't have more of the nations on this planet in their pockets than we can imagine?" Harry asked. "The secretary general of the United Nations is a member of the Families. They've been on Earth almost as long and no one knew to watch out for something that insidious. The heavy-worlders could be everywhere."

"What can we do about it?" Queen demanded, sounding exasperated. "We have to fight them as best we can. If we assume that they're in a position to crush us no matter what we do, we're screwed. Do you have a better idea?"

Harry sighed. "Not really. What's your price?"

"Already paid," the other man said. "We're part of this damned alliance, and we'll eventually get some technology that will give us an edge. If we can keep the Chinese—or anyone else for that matter—from getting out there and beating us to it."

"The universe is a big place, and there are other human civilizations out there," Harry said. "We have to stop thinking that we're the end-all, be-all of the universe. There's no telling how advanced some of these other human cultures are. Or what we'll find on the alien side of things. Someone beat the Asharim, or at least fought them to the point of collapse. We're going to run into them sooner or later."

"My job is to stand up for the United States," Queen growled. "That might not be the place you think it should be, but it's a lot better than some of the other options. Work with me and we'll find a balance."

"If you don't stick a knife in my back," Harry grumbled.

"What's life without challenges?" Queen asked with a grin. "Keep your friends even closer than your enemies. So, let's go make Chen an unhappy bastard."

* * *

CHEN FUMED AS HE WAITED, certain that the man he was waiting for was delaying the meeting to put him on the defensive. In his place, that's what he'd have done, but that didn't make the delay any easier to bear.

After what seemed like an eternity, the door to the room opened and Rogers strode in, Queen at his heels. The latter looked smug, so it was a certainty the two had been plotting how best to thwart him and the Dragon. That could never be allowed.

He rose to his feet and smiled with false congeniality. "Your meeting was shorter than I anticipated," he lied smoothly. "I was under the impression you wished to discuss the matters before us privately. As my people are at war with the United States, I think it… unwise to have Secretary Queen present."

"I'm hoping that as part of our discussion, I can help broker peace between the two of you," Rogers said, dropping into a seat with such casual disregard for propriety that Chen almost winced before he stilled the urge.

"That seems unlikely, but I suppose we must observe the forms," he agreed, injecting a note of polite doubt into his voice.

He resumed his seat as Queen sat beside Rogers. "The rights of my country were taken and provocation worthy of a military response given. How do you intend to just make that go away?"

Queen laughed. "Please. We're all alone here. Let's at least be honest about the events in question. There has been an aggressor all right, but it was you. Not China, I now understand, but this secret organization you represent that has now seized power there. Unless we lay that out on the table, nothing we say means anything."

Chen shook his head sadly. "Once again you've placed a tinfoil hat on your head. I assure you that we have no mind-control lasers in orbit. There is no such thing as the illuminati."

Rogers smiled and leaned back into his chair. "Oh, that's not true and I know it for a fact. You sent men to attack me and Jessica Cook, but you were hoping for a different person. The leader of a group like yourselves, but of wholly human extraction.

"I gave the US the genetic sequence to find heavy-worlders. That won't find all your people, I'm sure, but it will be more than enough to identify the origin of the bodies we left behind. Bodies which I'm sure you already know never arrived at the morgue where you expected to retrieve them."

Continuing his headshake, Chen smiled. "While this is a patently false observation, let us say for the sake of this discussion that everything you imply is true. My country would have even less reason to cooperate with the United States, though something could be arranged with you, Mr. Rogers.

"If we were the descendants of travelers from space, we would undoubtedly wish to return there. All that would need be done is to provide access to a means to do so. The base in New Zealand is wrecked, but the things you call the gates work, if my intelligence is correct. To get peace and security restored, all you would need do is transfer that base to us."

"Perhaps," Rogers admitted. "Perhaps not. The Asharim are still out there, but they've fallen. Their war with some other species didn't work out to their advantage. In any case, I doubt your motives.

"Still, we're not talking about that yet. This is about the war you started with the United States by blowing up the Mars ship they'd bought from the Indian government. And about the Yucatán spaceport that you're squatting on."

"You mean the spaceport that we *legally* own," Chen said, refuting his claim. "We bought it."

"The US is prepared to accept that as legally done," Harry said. "Keep the spaceport. It's yours. They'll even overlook the destruction of their ship and the loss of American lives aboard it. With that done, why would China attack the US any further? Have they attacked you in some other way?"

Chen paused. The way the men had given up on the spaceport and other provocations was problematic. If he admitted that was all he had, then there was no longer a pretext to fight.

Did he need one? His country was the mightiest in the world. They could crush the United States. They could take everything they wanted.

Yet the price would be high. Without the appropriate context, other countries would be disinclined to support China. Though they were powerful, they did not yet have access to the kind of technology they could obtain among the worlds of the Masters.

He had to be honest. He himself didn't care one bit if the Masters had fallen. He didn't see them as almost deities, as did others inside the Dragon. That wasn't a point of view he could publicly admit, but it did bear on his negotiations.

"The situation has become more complex than that," he ventured. "With the United States engaged as a member of this so-called alliance in New Zealand, I can see through this sham. They are searching for the military power to overwhelm us. That cannot be allowed."

"There's a lesson in politics for you, Rogers," Queen said. "Accuse your opponents of what you're doing to throw the public off the scent."

"There's the small matter of your spaceship," Rogers said, ignoring the aside. "It's loaded with heavy-world soldiers and likely has Asharim weapons of some kind. I'm not going to let that thing keep coming toward Mars when I know you intend to attack my ship there.

"That, however, is not part of the discussion about the US and the situation here on Earth. Let me lay it out for you, Ambassador. In ten minutes, I'll be in front of the General Assembly telling them everything we've found and what you and your people are doing. Most support for this conflict will vanish, leaving you hanging in the wind.

"Keep this conflict on the down low, break off the posturing here on Earth, and I won't tell them about your people and what they're doing from the shadows today. That doesn't mean that people like Secretary Queen won't know about you. A number already do, but they have no reason to tell the man on the street. I do. Test me and find out. The choice is yours."

Chen sighed. His options really were that limited. "Very well."

17

———————

Jess joined Sandra at the front of her party, Vidar and his guards right behind her. The sniper looked at the prisoner and then raised an eyebrow at Jess.

"Kind of taking a chance, aren't you?" the woman asked, knowing that the prisoner didn't speak their language.

"They already know we're here. We might as well see where this takes us. His assistance could be invaluable, and we could hardly be in more danger."

"Optimist," the other woman said darkly.

The heavy-worlder woman that had confronted them stood about fifty meters away, her arms crossed over her chest as she waited patiently to see what the intruders to her territory were going to do.

She was tall and muscular. Not exactly unexpected when confronting a heavy-worlder. They were designed to live on a planet with three gravities after all.

What *was* surprising was how feminine her form was. Jess had expected females built for heavy gravity would be short, blocky, and not at all curvy.

She was wrong. The woman ahead of them was definitely a woman, even if she was built like a bodybuilder. She was far less blocky than the males of her society.

Without waiting for Sandra to say anything more, Jess strode forward until she was about five meters away from the female warrior. There she stopped, holding her hands out at her sides to show that she was not a threat.

She started to say they came in peace but realized that wasn't true. They'd come in response to an act of war, and she couldn't just pretend that it hadn't happened. No. Sometimes you had to show your strength.

"Your attack force has been defeated," Jess said in an even tone, using the heavy-worlder language, still shocked at how easily it came to her. "As you can see, we have your military leader in our custody. We have come to speak to your priests and determine whether we continue to fight or allow you to start over."

The woman nodded slowly, her eyes never leaving her leader's face. "What say you, Leader Vidar?" Her voice was deep and serious, pitched at a melodious tenor that was deeper than most women on Earth.

"She speaks the truth," the prisoner rumbled. "Our attack failed, and all the priests that accompanied us perished. These people have treated us well and have come to speak to the priests under the rules of parley."

"My squad leader dispatched a runner to notify the temple of your arrival. Do these people understand the rules of parley? Do you order us to allow them through?"

"It would be best if you explained the rules to them, just to be certain there is no misunderstanding. I and my men have given our parole and it is best that we not be seen as dictating the events that happen today, so the decision is yours."

The woman nodded and turned her full attention to Jess. "Those who come to parley are forbidden violence, though they are allowed to keep their weapons. In return, the People will keep their peace and allow you to depart when the parley is complete. Should you violate the terms of parley, you will be exterminated. Do you understand?"

"The same will happen if you attack us," Jess said. "Our failure to return will draw a heavily armed response. Let's be polite so that we don't have to kill one another for nothing.

"When we depart, we take our prisoners with us unless we come to an agreement to release them. Under no circumstances will you attempt to separate us from them. We took them in battle, and they are ours until we release them of our own free will."

The woman hesitated but nodded. "It is agreed. Do you have any other conditions you wish to lay upon this parley?"

"Not a condition, but I would like to know if the priests will abide by our agreement. I have heard that they were the ones that decided to attack my world. What guarantee do I have that they will not continue to scheme against us?"

The woman laughed. "Of course they will continue to scheme against you. They are priests. What they will not do is violate the terms of this parley. If they were to do so, the warriors would not allow them to survive the betrayal. Of that, you have my word."

Jess smiled slightly. "It seems that you don't have a particular fondness for your priests. If you don't like them, why keep them?"

The woman shrugged. "It's the way of the People. Since we were created, we have followed the dictates of the Masters and the priests that they have appointed. So it has been, and so shall it be. Whether I like it or not is irrelevant."

The woman turned slightly and looked Jess's party over. "If we proceed immediately, we can arrive at the temple about an hour before dark. While it is safe enough to travel after dark, it is perhaps unwise to risk any misunderstandings when we don't know one another."

"How are we going to do this?" Jess asked.

"You have given your word to abide by the rules of parley, so I alone will accompany you to the temple. My squad will continue their watch here."

Jess turned to Sandra. "Form up in whatever order you think best, and I'll keep her with me. If we need to change course, I'll give you a signal over the radio."

"Are we going to keep going forward?" the sniper asked.

The woman nodded once Jess had translated the question. "The temple is not directly ahead but is in that general direction. As we come closer, I will announce any changes in course long before we are ready to make them."

As Sandra organized her people and prepared to set out again, Jess extended a hand to the heavy-worlder woman. "My name is Jess Cook. What shall I call you?"

"My name is Vera Vidar. Your prisoner is my father."

Well, that certainly had the potential to complicate matters.

"I'm surprised that you're being so restrained," Jess admitted. "Aren't you worried about him?"

The woman laughed. "My father is a warrior, as am I. Either one of us— or both of us together—could die in battle at any time. Such is the life of the People.

"I can see that he is in good health and not under duress, and that is enough for me. You can remove his shackles, if you like. He has given his word. He will not attempt to escape your control."

At her gesture, the guards removed the shackles from the three prisoners, though Jess could see their uncertainty about whether that was a good idea.

Kerrick Vidar rubbed his wrists and smiled at his daughter. "It is good to see you again, Vera. What has transpired in my absence?"

She shrugged. "Very little. With the majority of the priesthood gone, we have carried on with our lives while awaiting word of your return. I confess that I did not expect you to return defeated, though. Are these Earth people great warriors?"

The large man laughed. "They defeated us, so I would say yes. I commend their bravery under fire. The words of Kathleen Bennett have proven false. This world called Earth was not nearly so ready for picking as she led us to believe before her death."

Vidar looked at Jess for a long moment before nodding as if to confirm something he had been thinking. "In fact, I think our failure to form a bridgehead on their world may have been a great stroke of luck for us. The story of what happened to the Masters seems more complicated than we would have believed possible, and it is time for us to determine what our place in the universe truly is."

Now if only Jess could convince their priesthood of that fact. These people would make great allies but getting them on board would take a lot of work.

She didn't imagine convincing a dogmatic religious leadership to abandon their reverence of a long-fallen alien race would be easy.

If she could do it, Earth would benefit. If she failed, the war was only beginning.

* * *

QUEEN SAT in the chair normally reserved for the US ambassador and listened to Harry Rogers layout everything he'd found in the solar system, except for the frozen version of Earth out beyond Pluto and the secret society of heavy-worlder descendants. Or, he noted wryly, the descendants of the regular humans that Brenda Cabot led.

The man was a surprisingly good public speaker. His cadence and delivery seem practiced and easy, and he never missed an opportunity to engage with his audience using a glance here and a nod there.

The crowd seemed even more uncertain than they had during Queen's speech the day before. They'd had time to think about what they'd been told, and it was obvious to him that many had decided that they were being sold a bill of goods.

That was until Rogers brought out his bag of tricks. One of the items inside it was a small sphere that looked almost like a glob of liquid mercury the size of his fist. It was shiny and drew the eye. It certainly did so when Rogers released it and it stayed hovering there in midair with no obvious support.

"I'm sure that many of you view this as a magic trick," Roger said with a hint of humor in his voice. "It's not. This is a toy that uses antigravity to remain unsupported in the air. I won't pretend that I understand how that works in a technical sense, but I can make use of it. I'm sure each of you can see the implications as well.

"Perhaps some of you have heard about how I arrived this morning in an alien ship that made no sound. It uses a propulsion system like this built on a large scale. It's capable of going from Earth to Mars far more quickly than I was able to in the ship my father cobbled together.

"I'd be happy to give each and every one of you a tour of a ship just like that. Not personally, because I've got a lot of things that I need to be doing to protect us from the Asharim and heavy-worlders that serve them, but I'd be more than happy to make a ship available to ferry you around the planet and back to your home countries.

"Hell, they can even take you around the moon before returning you here or there. That should prove beyond a shadow of a doubt that this technology is real."

He fell silent for a short time, looking over them one final time before he continued. "Make no mistake, we are not alone in the universe. We never have been. We've allowed ourselves to fall into the trap of believing that we humans are the center of the universe. That we are the only intelligent life in all of space.

"I suppose that's understandable. We've listened for the inevitable sound of other life from the first moment we were able to do so. Unfortunately, due to the distances involved and the technologies being used, we've failed to hear what's been going on all around us.

"A thousand years ago, we were visited by an alien species that took people from our world and changed them in ways that we cannot begin to understand. The Asharim saw us as primitive tools that they could use to enhance their society. We all know what the word to describe that is: slavery.

"Unless you'd like to see all of humanity enslaved by the next group of aliens that comes along with that kind of urge, we've got to get ready. We have to be able to defend ourselves."

Queen found himself nodding. This was what he'd been saying since he'd discovered what was going on, but no one had listened to him. Well, they'd listened and then proceeded to do whatever *they* thought was best.

Perhaps now he could convince the alliance that it was time to allow the United States to play a more important—a leading—role in the conflict. They just didn't have the resources or experience for a fight like this. His country did.

Or they would as soon as Queen spoke with the president and started the process of getting the money that he needed to start rebuilding the military and bulking up the science groups that they could call on.

Oh, he realized that wasn't going to be a quick process, but if he didn't get it started now, they'd never finish in time to do any good. Sadly, Rogers was right when he said that the US military was in a shambles. They had far more people than Rogers did, but they probably weren't of the caliber needed to fight an enemy like the Asharim or the heavy-worlders.

Though Queen would never admit it, Rogers and people like Commander Krueger were the right people to lead this fight. They had the skills and tenacity to win against the superior technology they'd be facing. For at least the time being, Queen wouldn't contest Rogers being in command of the military contingent.

In fact, Rogers might be able to collect a crew of highly skilled warriors that the United States military had let go over the last decade. They wouldn't trust the government because of how they'd been treated, but they'd trust someone like Rogers. He had the kind of reputation that was needed to create what amounted to the largest mercenary force in existence.

What had he called his organization? A private military company? With the blessing of the United States government, he could grow that small group while adding elements from both inside and outside the US military and even other countries.

Queen would have to keep a very close eye on Rogers, because that was the kind of power that allowed someone to conquer the world, but the man already had access to the kind of technology that could do that, even with his small number of troops.

Just one look at the ship he'd arrived in would convince anyone of that. It was far faster than anything the US possessed, and it was stealthed to the point that their radar hadn't even picked it up right over New York City. It was basically invisible, other than being in plain sight. A fleet of ships like that could destroy any resistance.

Yet he was certain that wasn't what Rogers had in mind. He wasn't the kind of person that wanted to rule the world. Rather, he was the kind of man that humanity needed to lead it into battle against alien hordes.

Of course, Queen would continue to do whatever he could to get an edge for his country. The United States would not play second fiddle to anyone for one moment longer than it had to. With this kind of technology, they would once again be the leading power on Earth.

Now, perhaps even the universe. He'd certainly do everything he could to make that into reality.

And that meant figuring out how to take down Chen and his genetically enhanced supermen. Rogers was an idiot to think that he could intimidate those people into dropping their war against the US or trying to take him out.

The Chinese might publicly stop their posturing, but they'd keep striking from the shadows, just as they had when they'd destroyed Area 51. Queen couldn't allow that to pass, but he had to keep his actions below the threshold that would start up the overt fighting again.

He grinned to himself. He knew just how to make them squirm while making sure they couldn't actually prove he was responsible. Time for some payback.

18

B renda woke as the lid to the sarcophagus slid away, and she blinked up into the florescent lights mounted in the ceiling. It took her a moment to remember how she'd gotten inside it, but her confusion passed quickly, and she sat up to take stock of her body.

She'd kept herself in good shape over the years, but it was still easy to note how her skin had tightened and her flesh had firmed after the treatment. The body of a fit woman in her early forties was certainly different than one in her mid-twenties, which was what she seemed to be blessed with now.

She stretched her back and was pleased to note that the low-level pain along her spine and lower back was gone. That was one hell of a perk, because being an FBI agent meant stressing your body in ways that were detrimental to your long-term health and comfort.

Knowing that it probably wouldn't be long before the boys came back, she climbed out and redressed herself. Based on how her bra fit, she'd need to buy some new ones. She suspected Karl would approve of the changes. She certainly did.

One perk of being in good shape before the event was that her outer clothes still fit, so she wouldn't need to completely update her wardrobe. Though, if she wanted to blend in with the people around her, she'd do so anyway. A woman in her twenties that dressed as if she were almost two decades older stood out, and not in a good way.

Once she'd dressed, she walked over to the table and picked up several printouts in the Asharim language that they'd been using to test Karl's new skills with. She'd been able to read the language before, but it had been a struggle. She'd had to work hard to comprehend the meaning of many words because the language was complex and sometimes maddeningly obtuse.

Now she found she could read the papers with ease. The meanings of the words and phrases were so much clearer than they had been before. That meant that whatever education this machine had been designed to perform on her had worked.

From what Brenda had understood, Jess had been able to utilize some of the equipment that the Asharim had designed. In fact, she'd flown one of their ships. Brenda hoped that she could do the same, because that would be *really* fun.

She checked her watch and found that only two and a half hours had passed. That was a little bit less than it had taken Karl, so the machine must've had to do some extra work inside him because of damage from wounds he'd suffered in combat.

Speaking of that, she checked where she'd been winged during a hostage rescue situation a few years ago and found that the wound was completely gone. It hadn't really pained her that much because it had only been a graze, but the scarred skin was now smooth and unblemished. That was amazing.

There was a knock at the door, and it slid open a crack to reveal Todd Granger's face. Once he saw her, the door opened wider. "Ah, I see you're awake. How are you feeling? Do you mind if we both come in, or would you rather just have me for the first part?"

"You can both come in."

Todd pushed the door open and came inside with Karl at his heels.

"How are you feeling?" Karl asked. "Like a new woman?"

"Like a younger woman," she corrected. "One who hasn't been banged up nearly as much by life. Though, I suspect, you had a lot more repairs than I did."

She smiled at him and switched to the heavy-worlder language. "Let's see if this works. Holy crap, I'm really speaking an alien language."

His eyes widened slightly. "And I'm understanding it. That's just freaky. I knew after reading the papers that I could, but that's not quite the same thing as having a conversation in a language you've never dealt with before. It's kind of scary how they can implant that sort of thing directly into your brain."

"It's still a mystery to us as well," she said. "Have you had a chance to go test out some of your other skills?"

"I went down to the secret range you guys have rigged up in the basement, and I gave one of the flechette pistols a try. Using one is a lot like using a regular pistol, but there are some individual quirks, and it was as if the required information was implanted straight into my muscle memory.

"It didn't interfere with the skills I already had, and that seems impossible. How can they implant muscle memory that doesn't conflict with what you already have?"

She shrugged. "I haven't got the slightest idea. Their grasp of technology was amazing. How they translated that into the human brain is a mystery that I doubt any of us will ever really understand."

"So what do you think of my offer now? Is this worth keeping the knowledge that we're searching for the base to yourself for the time being?"

He nodded without hesitation. "I think so. Secretary of State Queen put me into an awkward position when he gave me the orders to be his face in this matter. As anyone in the military can tell you, the United States government is not exactly the most trustworthy of groups. It hasn't been so in a long time.

"Whatever we find in that base might be too dangerous to allow the United States to possess. The agreement that we signed with the alliance says that we can't have alien tech with military implications. Until we're certain what's down there, I think I should abide by the spirit of the agreement and keep the details to myself. I'll make a report when I know more."

Brenda felt herself smiling widely. "That's just what I was hoping to hear. What say we go ahead and ditch all this testing, gather up a group of people, and go for a hike in Virginia?"

"I'll need to get some boots and suitable pants, because I'm sure it's going to be rough, but that sounds great. I've got a lot of energy that I want to burn off."

Her grin turned a bit wicked. "We don't exactly have to leave this building for that."

Todd's eyes rolled upward. "Oh please! Can we keep the bedroom talk to a minimum? This is a professional setting."

"You don't have to watch," she said transferring her "we could" look to the doctor. "Unless that's your thing."

"That's it," Granger said repressively, pointing at the door. "Get out of my office. Go do something that isn't going to scandalize everyone around you."

She could tell from her friend's poorly hidden smile that he wasn't scandalized in the least. Still, she rose to her feet and held out her hand toward the Navy officer.

"Let's go find out what's hidden in the hills of Virginia and who might still be working in the area. We know it's not any of us and we're certain that it's not the heavy-worlders, so that means we have a third group in play.

"Or at least we did a few hundred years ago. It's time to find out what they left behind for us."

* * *

HARRY HAD BARELY FINISHED his speech when his cell phone rang. He saw that it was Molly Goodwin when he fished it from his pocket and glanced at the screen.

"Hey, Molly. It has to be late there. What's up?"

"We've got a problem," she said, her voice grim. "A big one. I need you down here as soon as possible."

"What's wrong?" he asked as he headed for the assault lander at a jog.

"We've been sending people back to Volunteer World to make sure everything stays the same, and they're telling me they can hear someone digging into the hill. It sounds like shovels and picks, but that means they're not too far off from getting control of the gate in the cave."

That wasn't good. That gate was their only bridgehead on to Volunteer World. If they lost control of it, they wouldn't be able to access the gates located in the old Asharim city. Without them, they wouldn't be able to get to the other human colonies that the Volunteers had contact with.

"I can be there in a few hours, though I might be able to make it in less than thirty minutes if I can get Brenda to allow me to use her gate. One way or the other, I'll be there shortly. Start gathering what troops you can and be ready to repel an incursion."

As soon as he'd disconnected, he broke into a fast jog and arrived at the assault lander minutes later. The diplomats would have to wait for a second vehicle to arrive to take their joy rides.

His troops swarmed in behind him, seeing his urgency. Everyone was strapped down, and the lander was lifting off less than sixty seconds later.

Harry dialed the number to Brenda's quantum phone. She answered a few moments later.

"This is Harry," he said somewhat needlessly. It wasn't as if everyone on the planet had her number. "Can I use your gate to get to New Zealand? Molly said they can hear someone digging into the tunnels with picks and shovels. Odds are good that's the Asharim slaves. I'm going to need to find Commander Krueger and get his people on standby so we can go defend the gate."

"Hang on a second," she said.

Moments later, Krueger's voice came out of his handset. "I caught a little bit of that. I'll put the call in to my folks and have them standing by in New Zealand. I figure we can have the full team ready in maybe forty-five minutes."

"What are you doing with Brenda, Karl? That's just about the last place I expected to find you."

There was a long hesitation and suddenly Harry knew *exactly* why Karl was with Brenda. He almost laughed out loud, but he stopped himself. The man's love life was none of his concern. Neither was Brenda's.

What they were doing might be a somewhat dangerous game to play if Queen found out, but Harry wasn't going to raise any kind of stink.

"Never mind," he said. "Get your folks together, and I'll meet you at Brenda's place. We'll go to New Zealand together."

"Thanks for giving me a little space," the Navy officer said. "I promise this isn't going to complicate what we're doing."

Harry did laugh that time. "Of course it's going to complicate things, but that's okay with me. I suggest you don't tell Queen, though. I don't think he'd take it very well."

"Probably not. Let me hand you back to Brenda."

"How are you going to get here?" she asked a moment later. "I was watching the news and saw you land at the United Nations. You can't bring that thing to my place without telling everybody where I am."

That was certainly true. While Queen had agreed to leave Brenda and the Families alone, that didn't mean he wouldn't necessarily take action against them if he knew where they were located. Best not to tempt him.

"I'm going to have them drop me a few miles away from where you're located. I'll find my own way there without giving them anything to follow."

"You can't take any cabs," she said. "They keep records, and so do the ridesharing companies. All of them cooperate with the government, too. Tell me where you're setting down and I'll send one of my people to pick you up. You can circle overhead and make the dive down at the last minute so that they can't track you. Make sure you're at least twenty miles away from my place."

"That works. It'll give me time to ditch the helicopters and jets I've got following me now. If I take off at maximum speed, I'll lose everyone. Once they don't have eyes on me, I can circle back around and have Black Jack drop me off with no one the wiser."

"Excellent idea," she said. "And Rogers? Don't give me any crap about my love life. I'm the one that gets to make the decisions about what I do, and Karl gets to make the decisions about what he does. I'm not going to take any judgment from the likes of you."

Even though it had been said in a stern tone, Harry picked out the humor buried in her tone and smiled. She was both being serious and letting him know not to make an issue of it.

"You got it," he agreed. "I look forward to hearing what you two have been up to—outside of the bedroom—when we next meet. I suspect you both have other things to tell me about."

"Other things?" she asked slyly. "I'm not sure what you mean."

"You can't pull the wool over my eyes," he said with his own version of mock sternness. "You invited Karl down there to look for the Virginia base, didn't you? Did you find it?"

"We haven't looked for it all," she said with a slight sniff. "In fact, we haven't left this building."

"But we were going out to look for it in just a few minutes," Karl said from a short distance away, obviously overhearing what they were discussing. "Let's not hide this from him. He needs to know that we intend to find that base. Once we've dealt with this intrusion on Volunteer World, we're still going to do it."

"Screw that," Brenda said. "You two go deal with the troublesome aliens, and I'll go find this hidden base. I promise I won't do anything disastrous until you get back, and I'll take lots of pictures."

Harry shrugged. They were going to do what they were going to do, no matter what he said, so he might as well get on board with the program.

"That sounds fine to me. Be careful. Now let me look at the map and find out which park looks good for a rendezvous. See you shortly."

19

———

Jess walked through the ruins of the Asharim city with Vera Vidar by her side. The place was an ancient ruin, but the buildings still stood. It was amazing. She could only imagine how badly Michael Crockett and his family, as well as the restorationists, Doctors Rachel Powel and Paulette Young, would love to get into these buildings to see what they could find.

That would have to wait. Rather than daydreaming, she needed to find out what kind of situation she was walking into. The outcome of this meeting spelled either war or peace. There was no room for error.

"Without putting yourself in the middle, could you tell me a little bit about the priests that were left after the battle?" she asked the warrior woman.

Vera raised an eyebrow but didn't stop walking. "I shall betray no confidences. Unless I am told differently, you are an enemy of the People. My father led a war band to attack you. Unless the priests say differently, that still holds."

"I'm just looking to get what kind of personality I'm going to deal with. Are they going to be difficult, or will they at least listen to what I have to say before they lose their minds?"

That made the woman smile. "They are priests. Of course they will be difficult. I will tell you that all of the senior priests went on the incursion into your world. Those left behind are junior priests. They may perhaps be less difficult than you would otherwise have had to deal with, but all things are relative. I shall say no more."

They traveled in silence until they finally arrived at a small settlement constructed in the valley between the monstrously tall buildings. These structures were not of the same caliber as the Asharim edifices and showed every indication of being much more recently built.

They'd begun encountering individuals and small groups as they approached the settlement, but word had obviously spread before them, as no one approached, though they did give them a thorough looking over. Warriors assessing warriors, looking to see the kind of people that had captured their war leader, she wagered.

The temple was different than the general structures. Where the other buildings were at most two stories, it was four. It was also covered with what she recognized as bas-relief religious carvings of the tall and willowy Asharim set into pale stone.

Standing on the steps leading into the building were three heavy-worlder males. Each wore long robes that seemed as if they'd hamper any attempts to move at more than a slow pace. The one in the center wore a tall hat that was obviously ceremonial and somewhat similar to what the Pope wore. She'd seen men dressed like that before and killed them.

If she had to make a guess, none of the men in front of her was more than perhaps twenty-five years old. Of course, if they had access to a sarcophagus, their appearances could be deceptive.

Vera approached the priests and bowed. Just based on the relative depth of the bow and its speed, Jess didn't think that it showed a lot of respect. From the central priest's expression, he agreed with her assessment, though he showed less anger and more resignation than she'd expected.

"What have you brought us, daughter?" the man asked.

The woman's lips twitched upward into the ghost of a smile. "Daughter? Gavin, I'm two years older than you." The latter was said in a low tone that Jess only barely picked up.

The man sighed and whispered back. "You know as well as I that the way you refer to me and the way I refer to you is based on tradition. Work with me, Vera."

He focused his attention on Jess and raised his voice. "Who is this that you have brought to us? Is this a woman like Kathleen Bennett?"

"First, she can understand what you're saying," Vera said. "Second, I don't believe so. She leads this war band though. None of the rest appears to understand our language."

The man's eyes rolled slightly. "Perhaps you should have mentioned that to me first. We should not be familiar in front of outsiders."

Not waiting for her response, the man stepped forward and looked down his nose at Jess. "You have come to this place under parley and with our war leader your prisoner. What are your demands? Where are the priests of my order? What have you done with our warriors?"

If she hadn't heard the man speaking softly with Vera, she'd have formed the initial opinion that he was going to be a real hard case. Her hearing was excellent, so he probably wasn't aware that she'd caught those low words that he'd exchanged with someone that Jess suspected was probably a childhood friend or perhaps even a lover.

That actually put her at ease. She'd have been much more defensive if she hadn't known that there was a real human being somewhere inside this officious-looking fellow.

"My name is Jessica Cook," she said levelly. "I prefer Jess with my friends. I'm one of the leaders of the people your war band attacked. Many of your warriors were wounded or captured. Unfortunately, a number of them died in the fighting, as did a number of my own warriors. As for your priests, none of them survived the encounter."

Rather than looking angry, she thought she saw just a flash of interest in his eyes before his expression became sterner. "These are grave words you bring me. What do you seek?"

"Peace. We didn't attack you, and we believe that you were tricked into attacking us. I want us to have a second chance to discuss the matters at hand before we are drawn into a war that need not happen.

"You seek word of the Masters. I know something of their fate. I'm willing to discuss them and other matters with you, so long as we are working towards coming to an understanding that will leave us a more peaceful path forward."

The young man slowly nodded. "Your words have weight, and we shall speak. You may have two of your warriors escort you into the temple. Rest assured that the rules of parley will be observed. You are safe here until our talks have completed, and then you will be allowed to depart without harassment or harm."

Jess made a gesture toward Sandra. The other woman selected one of her men, and they bracketed Jess as she followed the priests into the temple. Vera and two additional heavy-worlder guards followed them inside, along with Kerrick Vidar.

This was it. Either she would be able to negotiate peace between their peoples, or there was a larger war on the horizon. There was a lot at stake, and everyone at home was counting on her. She was an engineer, but now it was time for her to be a diplomat. God save them all.

* * *

BRENDA MET Harry when the van that had picked them up arrived at the loading dock at the back of the building. They didn't have a lot of time to exchange information, but she confirmed what he knew about the incursion on Volunteer World. She also told him that she would be taking a group out as soon as they left to look for the hidden base in Virginia.

All of that took place in the three minutes before he and Karl made their way to New Zealand through the portable gate in her base. She really needed to see about finding him something to use for his own needs, because it was awkward having people show up just to use her gate. She'd prefer her secret base to remain... well, secret.

Once the boys were safely through the gate, she called Victor Holyfield and Todd Granger in to see her. She didn't offer them seats because they weren't going to be there that long.

"Get dressed for a hike," she said, gesturing at her hiking boots and jeans. "We're making a trip to Virginia to look for that hidden base that the Volunteers used."

Todd frowned slightly. "I thought you were taking Karl to go look for it. What happened?"

"Trouble on Volunteer World. Karl went with Harry, and they're going to take care of it. That leaves this to us. While we're no longer officially on the police watch lists, I'd prefer that the government doesn't figure out what we're doing. We need this base."

Victor nodded, smiling a little. "I see you've come to an agreement with Commander Krueger. That's good news. Are you sure he's not going to tell anyone?"

"No, but I'm relatively certain that he's going to hold his tongue until we have our hands on the base. Possession is nine tenths of the law, as they say.

"We'll take a few other people along with us, but I want you two to herd them in different directions. Working together, I think we can find the cave entrance based on the description of the rocks that General Norris gave us. We'll be looking for an outcropping that resembles the rising sun."

Norbert Norris, the commanding general of the Volunteer militia, bore a striking resemblance to one of his ancestors: George Washington. It was spooky how much the man looked like their first president.

They'd be leaving him here this time rather than trying to shepherd him along on the search. While he had more experience in rough terrain than they did, he stood out when traveling through the streets of a modern-day city.

Even dressed in regular clothing, something was off about him. The way he moved, the way he spoke, and the way he gawked at everything. He just stood out, and they didn't have time to deal with that right now.

Twenty minutes later, she was in the passenger seat of a van full of her people headed toward rural Virginia. Specifically, federally owned land that had been set aside as wilderness.

Once they arrived in the area, they parked the van on a small side road and left a note under the windshield that they were hiking and not to tow the vehicle. Better safe than sorry.

She and Harry had searched a fairly significant area the last time they were there and come up empty. In the intervening time, she'd researched more carefully using modern maps as well as some historical maps of the area to try to see if she could locate a more productive area.

While she had no idea whether or not the new locations would prove more fruitful than the last, at least they were still looking. If they didn't find anything here, it very well might mean having to bring in equipment to scan through the ground. That would draw undue attention, so she'd prefer to avoid it.

Hefting her pack as soon as they were ready, she set off into the wilderness. Five hot, grueling hours later, Victor called for her on the short-ranged radio, and she saw him waving at her from a rocky hill off to her left. She used her bandanna to wipe the sweat from her face and headed over to meet him.

"Did you find something?" she asked when she'd finally climbed up to meet him.

He pointed off toward the south. "Does that kind of look like a rising sun to you?"

She shielded her eyes and squinted. There was a large rock protruding from the side of a rocky crag that, if one used enough poetic license, might possibly resemble a rising sun.

"It beats what I've been looking at all day," she said with a shrug. "Let's go check it out."

Using the radio, she gathered up the rest of the searchers. They wouldn't be leaving anyone behind while they wandered off to look at something cool and shiny.

Getting down to the area below where they were searching and making their way to the new target took them another hour and a half. If they didn't find something relatively quickly, they were going to have to break off and retreat to the van, or they might get lost in the approaching darkness.

She made a mental note that if they came out again, she needed to bring along more camping gear. They had enough food and water to last them a couple of days, but other than a fairly thin sleeping mat, she had nothing to rest on if they stayed overnight. It would get pretty cold out here, she suspected.

When they arrived on the ground underneath the suspicious outcropping, it only took a few moments to find something interesting. The rock face had a rather large crack that was big enough for two people to enter side by side. That might very well be the cave that the Volunteers had spoken of in their legends.

"Nothing ventured, nothing gained," she said as she turned her flashlight on and climbed up about five feet so that she could get into the crack. Luckily there were plenty of handholds, and it wasn't a difficult climb.

She knew the moment that she shone the light inside that they'd hit pay dirt. The rock inside quickly grew into a tube moving deeper into the hillside in a smooth, perfectly circular tube.

Brenda turned and looked down at her people with a grin on her face. "Somebody get me the geolocation on this and pass it back to our people. Have them bring another van out with camping supplies. I think we're going to be here a while."

20

Once Harry had everyone gathered in the New Zealand base, he dialed the address for Volunteer World on the sole functional gate. Kevin's people were disassembling the other two gates, as they might be useful elsewhere.

The other side of the wormhole was just as dark and gloomy as he'd remembered. Not surprising, considering that it was inside a cave that had been sealed off by a deliberate collapse of the only exterior entrance.

Being underground, it was cool, but not as much as the lowest level of the New Zealand base. The latter had much more rock piled above it to keep the heat away and maintain a constant temperature.

The air was still heavy with the scent of detonated explosives, sharp and unlike anything found in nature. The floor of the passage was covered with small debris jarred loose in the blasts that had closed the cave system off from the world outside. The small stones and bits of rock crunched under his boots as he made his way forward, his weapon up and at the ready. Just in case.

Commander Krueger and his Navy SEALs were right behind him, and a strike force of New Zealand special operations men and women backed them up. There was an even larger force in the base behind them, prepared to hold the gate room if he was forced to retreat.

He hoped that didn't happen, because it would make getting back onto this planet extremely difficult. Not impossible, but they'd have to lead with an explosive large enough to clear an entrenched hostile force, and that would likely bring the roof down onto the gate. Not the best possible outcome.

To his relief, it appeared that the diggers had not yet reached the cave system itself. Though from the sound of it, they weren't all that far off.

One of the New Zealanders gestured toward the pile of rocks covering the entrance. "This still looks about the same as it was before, but I can see some signs of shifting. Whoever's doing the digging is close enough to be pushing the rock forward. It won't be long."

Harry nodded. "That gives us a chance. We weren't ready to fight them while you were retreating, Commander Krueger. This time we can set up a defensive line in here to force them back once they clear the entrance enough for us to do so.

"We've basically got an unlimited supply of ammunition and as many support troops as we need to form a perimeter. All we have to do is push them off the hill."

Krueger grimaced. "That's going to be some ugly fighting. No matter how we play this, we run the risk of having an unstable ceiling come down on us as we try to push them out. We've got to have some experts right behind us to finish bracing the tunnel.

"Once we get out there, you're right about us having enough firepower to keep them back. It certainly seems as if their weapons systems are primitive, and that's a big help. Unfortunately, there are a lot of them. When they overran the Volunteer camp, it was a never-ending stream of those aliens."

"Do we have any idea what the alien slaves are like?" Harry asked.

Krueger shook his head. "It was dark, and they never got close enough for us to get a decent look. Bipedal, about our size in general, two arms and two legs. That's all we were able to get during the firefight.

"We had a drone up, and it got some IR images. Those back up what I remembered, but they didn't give us any real information, other than the fact that the aliens had a slightly lower average body temperature than humans."

"What about weapons? Were they using black powder like the Volunteers?"

The Navy officer nodded. "The weapons seemed different, but the rate of fire was similar, and the sound of them firing was very much a black powder sort of affair. That doesn't mean that the Asharim leading them don't have access to high-technology weapons, though. We've got to assume that they do, otherwise we're putting ourselves at great risk."

"True enough, though I doubt we'll see the Asharim leading a charge into this cave. They're going to send their minions in first. That's going to give us a chance to shove them back with our superior firepower. Once we get outside, then the Asharim and their potential weapons come into play. Do you have anything that can scout from the air?"

"We've got several drones, but they're not armed," Krueger said. "We're going to need more space to assemble and launch the larger, armed drones. The top of the hill would be perfect for that, but that means we've got to capture it first. Unfortunately, I suspect we're going to have to do this all the hard way."

The pile of rock shifted, and some loose stone slid to the floor. Whoever was on the other side was probably just about through the blockage.

"Everybody back behind some of the outcroppings," Harry said. "We'll wait for them to clear the opening enough that they feel safe coming in. They're undoubtedly bracing as they go, otherwise the ceiling would've collapsed on them. That means we only have a small section to brace on our end.

"When I give the signal, I want everyone to attack with small arms. No explosives, grenades, or rockets. Short, controlled bursts. Keep their heads down and force them back.

"Commander, when I give the command, take your team forward and clear the tunnel. Get out of the cave and form a bridgehead. Hold it until we get the heavy weapons in place behind you."

"Copy that," Krueger said, turning to give his men orders.

Harry turned his attention to the New Zealand commander. "Be ready to take your forces out and secure that bridgehead once they've cleared it. Place the heavy weapons in whatever locations make the best sense at the time. We can always move them once we're more secure. Be sure to get as much cover as you can for your men, because we can't count on the enemy having only primitive firearms."

The man nodded and turned his attention to his people. That left Harry contemplating the rockslide, which was continuing to flow slowly down toward the floor of the cave. It wouldn't take long before they broke through and had a useful opening. Then the real fun started.

* * *

QUEEN SAT IN HIS OFFICE, surrounded by his principal deputies, and smiled coldly. "It's time to make those Chinese bastards pay for what they've done to us, but we've got to be careful. We can't let this publicly blow back on us."

"It's about damn time," Darryl Dickman said, his tone pleased. "We can't just let them get away with making monkeys out of us. We've got to make them hurt before they have a chance to recover their confidence."

"Have you lost your mind?" Lana Bohannon said, her expression aghast. "We've got them on the defensive. There's no way they can credibly come up with a reason to attack us openly, and you're going to give them one? We should be thinking about the long game."

The third person at the table, Philip Judge, shook his head. "I can see reasons why it might be in our best interest to kick them in the balls when they're not looking. If the end results can't be traced directly back to us, they'll still be limited in what they can do.

"And if you think that they aren't going to be acting against us covertly, you don't know the Chinese like I do. They'll smile to your face while they get ready to stick a knife in your back. You can't trust them."

"I agree," Queen said. "We don't have to go overboard, but we need to take at least some of the pieces off the board while we have an opportunity to do so. Specifically, the Yucatán spaceport."

Darryl grunted in agreement. "That's a good one. It's not something they directly need right now, but them having a presence on our continent is unacceptable. If they moved nuclear weapons to the spaceport, they could have a straight shot right up our skirt."

Queen rubbed his eyes, trying to get the mental image of Darryl in a skirt out of his head. "First of all, Darryl, that's incredibly sexist. I don't care if people have been saying it forever, it's not going to be said in my office. Second, I agree with you. We can't let them have weapons of mass destruction just south of our border.

"I mean, who knows what they have. Nukes are just the beginning. Maybe they've got alien weapons that are even more destructive. Do we want to give them a base to launch attacks on our country that almost certainly would kill millions of people?"

Darryl frowned at him. "And kicking someone in the balls isn't sexist? Whatever, you're the boss. How do we go about making sure they can't trace this back to us?"

Lana rolled her eyes. "Of course they're going to trace it back to us. There's no way that anything that happens there is ruled an accident. I don't care if a meteor fell from the sky right now and made a big crater where the spaceport used to be, we'd be blamed.

"The key is making certain that there's enough reasonable doubt that our allies will still support us. If we can argue that it was something the Chinese did, or some other party, our allies will stand by us. If they do, the Chinese won't be able to act overtly."

"They'll be able to act covertly," Judge said. "But, as you say, they're going to anyway. We might as well do what we can to secure our borders and make certain that they don't pull another trick like blowing up Area 51. Speaking of which, this would be a tit-for-tat payback. I like that."

"Speaking of Area 51," Lana said, "where are we on getting some additional alien technology to study? I'm given to understand that you made an agreement to get some of the nonmilitary tech. Where is it, and where are we keeping it for study?"

Queen grimaced slightly. "We haven't gotten any new alien technology. At this point, Rogers and the alliance are claiming that they have too many fires to put out to hand over the technology they owe us.

"I'm willing to let that go for a little bit, but not too much longer. They're going to need our help getting weapons capable of defending Mars against the Chinese when they show up. If they want those weapons and troops, they're going to have to pony up some juicy tech for us to start studying.

"As for where we'll keep it, I think Area 51 is still a good location for us. It's isolated, and we can control who goes in and out without any question. We just need to vet whoever is there a lot more thoroughly."

Darryl scowled. "Have we gotten anywhere on catching the bastards that did this to us? I'd like to see somebody executed for treason. That'll send the kind of message we need to be heard around the world."

"Focus, Darryl," Lana said. "We need to figure out exactly what we're going to do at the Yucatán spaceport before we start getting ourselves involved with tech and traitors. You said you had a plan, Josh. What is it?"

He grinned at his subordinates. "Something we can thank Clayton Rogers for. He built self-destruct charges into every critical component on that base.

I'm quite sure the Chinese have been diligently disarming them, but from what I'm given to understand, they aren't easily removable.

"If we can get a team to go around rearming the charges, we can blow the spaceport up and blame their own incompetence for the loss. Something like what they've done with their public reaction to the attack they made on Area 51."

"Getting into the buildings is going to be challenging," Judge said. "The launch gantries and other exterior facilities are probably easier to access, but there'll be guards everywhere. In any case, whatever we do to them, they're going to be able to rebuild. It's just going to be a matter of time."

"What's that old saying?" Queen asked. "'Ask me for anything but time.' Well, that's how damaging the loss of time would be to the Chinese. They need those facilities operational and useful now, not a year or two in the future. If we can take it out of play, then they're going to be scrambling, and that's exactly what I want.

"Now, let's figure out who we can send that has a reasonable chance of getting in and out without being caught, and who has the technical skills to be able to rearm these charges and blow the spaceport up."

21

Jess looked around the temple's foyer and was impressed. The entrance was filled with small works of art set in nooks, paintings, and either precious or semiprecious stones set into the walls and ceiling. It should've been gaudy, but it meshed together in such a way that it worked.

The dominant theme, of course, were the Asharim. The aliens were represented everywhere. They were inside the paintings, doing things that looked like either helping humans or dominating them. It was hard to tell which. They were the little statues. Even the semiprecious stones showed hints of the Asharim form inside them. That was kind of spooky.

The priest called Gavin led the way to a small sitting room deeper inside the temple. He gestured for the other two priests to go get something called Veristar juice and cakes. Once they were alone, he motioned for Jess to sit in one seat and Vera in the other. He took the third and didn't seem concerned that the guards were forced to lean against the walls.

"My name is Gavin Stone Fist," the priest said once he had leaned back in his chair. "It seems that I am now the high priest of the People. With the deaths of the priests that went on this ill-conceived outing, there are no others senior to me in rank."

He shook his head. "Let me be honest. Other than the two under priests that you have already met, I am the only priest left. We were never a numerous lot. There was no need. Considering how much the previous high priest had doubted my suitability to serve the order, there is some irony in me taking his place."

Jess nodded. "I'm not unfamiliar with that kind of situation. I never expected to be in charge of an organization like the one I control. I certainly never expected to be searching the universe for answers to questions I didn't even know to ask. The Asharim came to our world a thousand years ago and left behind many mysteries. Ones we're only just beginning to decipher."

"I heard Kathleen Bennett speak of this," the man said in an unreadable tone. "I recall thinking at the time that she sounded as if she were shading the truth. I have always been fairly adept at knowing when someone is lying to me, and the woman just seemed to ooze something nasty from every pore of her being.

"You don't seem like the same kind of person to me, Jessica Cook. It makes me wonder what falsehoods Kathleen Bennett told us. She was quite convincing. She persuaded the high priest not only to lead an incursion onto your world but to bring the majority of his priests to assist in its subjugation and reeducation. Why don't we start with you telling me what the situation on your world is actually like?"

Jess smiled slightly. "I have absolutely no idea what that woman told you, but Earth is not the same kind of world as this one. The Asharim never showed their faces to us openly. They took isolated people from our world and used them as servants or slaves—the exact details of the relationship are still somewhat confusing.

"There was some kind of secret rebellion against the Asharim by the humans under their control, and some of them managed to return to Earth with high technology. They then proceeded to build hidden bases and fight some of your ancestors sent to subdue them. Interestingly enough, their descendants still live on Earth."

She allowed her gaze to grow harder. "And here is where your people once again invade my world, with no provocation and the intent to subdue us for the Asharim. I don't care whether or not you revere them as gods, but humanity is not their plaything. We will not submit to them or to you.

"I've come to seek peace, but if I can't find it, then I'll deliver a warning instead: come to Earth looking for a fight and you'll find it. We'll defend our home, and if need be, return the fight to you.

"Personally, I'd rather find some kind of accommodation. I don't see any reason for us to fight over a race that collapsed into a primitive state a thousand years ago. Don't let the past dictate our future. Let's forge something that actually works for both of us."

The young man smiled but didn't say anything as one of the under priests returned with a tray holding a pitcher filled with liquid cold enough to bead condensation on the exterior. The tray also contained three small cups and a platter with small cakes piled high.

The priest poured for himself and the two women. "I am going to assume that you have never had Veristar juice before, so allow me to warn you that it is perhaps different than anything you have experienced before. It begins with a sweet flavor, but that is overtaken by a rush of sourness. The cakes are quite good at cleaning the palate and preparing you for more. I think that you will enjoy it."

Nothing ventured, nothing gained. Jess took a sip. The initial flavor was very much like apple juice, but it quickly became something far more like lemonade. Tart and sour.

She took a bite of the small cake and found that the sourness faded. The cake was also quite good. On the whole, the combination was excellent. She suspected trade in the Veristar juice might be quite lucrative if things worked out. People were always looking for new taste sensations.

She nodded her appreciation. "It's good. Thank you."

After a few seconds of looking at him intently, she continued. "You've heard where I stand, high priest. I'd like to know what you think. Shall we have peace, or shall we have war?"

He took another bite of his cake and shrugged slightly. "It is far too soon to say what is appropriate. Deep in my heart, I would need to believe that war was necessary before I would order such. Yet the state we find ourselves in is already one of conflict.

"No one on this planet knows the code to get to your world, even if the ancient gates could be made to function again. Is there a point in having a state of war where one can never actually strike at one's enemy? I think not."

He stared at her with a serious expression. "I shall have to speak with Kerrick Vidar and hear his side of what occurred. Based on the large explosion in orbit—one we were able to see here on the surface—it certainly appears that the ship that Kathleen Bennett arrived in was destroyed.

"That once again leaves us in a state of being trapped upon this world. You have said that the Masters have fallen from their position of dominance. We know that they were engaged in a war with another species. That provides certain... opportunities for the People.

"Yet for us to take advantage of those opportunities, we would have to trust that you are telling us the truth. We would have to have a basis upon which to build a negotiation that benefits us both. Trust is earned, not given. How do you suggest we both earn credit in that column?"

"Small steps," Jess said promptly. "We're willing to release the men we've captured. Also, if you would like to have an opportunity to see the Asharim in their current state, one of my associates is currently engaged in a conflict with them to control gates on one of their worlds. I believe that could prove my words without too much difficulty. If, of course, you don't feel the need to rush in and save them."

The large man leaned back in his chair and smiled sadly. "My opinion of the Masters is perhaps somewhat different than the priests who fought you. I am not going to form an opinion of what the Masters are now, but I have always had my doubts about how much veneration they truly deserved.

"I am certain that some would see such a view as heresy, but my position is not new to anyone that knows me. It is one of the reasons that the previous high priest did not believe that I was suitable for the priesthood. Unfortunately for him, I managed to pass all the tests, so he could not reject me out of hand.

"I believe what you are telling me, Jessica Cook. I ask that you take our military leader, and what number of his men you feel comfortable allowing, to this new world to see what the situation with the Masters is. He will return to me and report once you have done so. Then we can speak again."

Jess bowed her head. "That's acceptable. If we can come to an agreement between your people and mine, it may be possible to restore your gates to operation. I have people that are skilled in that sort of thing.

"I look forward to trying to forge a friendship between our peoples. There's no reason we need to fight one another. There are plenty of dangers in the universe, and we'd be far better off standing shoulder to shoulder. You may not see yourselves this way, but you came from Earth. You're as human as me. We are one people."

The priest rubbed his chin and smiled. "You have a strange way of looking at the world, Jessica Cook. Let us take the small steps together and see what happens."

*   *   *

BY THE TIME Brenda saw the approaching lights of the additional people she'd requested to come out to the site, it was dark, and the temperature had dropped significantly. It made her glad that she'd brought along a windbreaker. By dawn, it was probably going to be down into the low fifties.

She'd considered going into the base before the rest had arrived but had worried something would happen where the extra people would be extremely helpful. This wasn't the time to rush, so she'd waited.

With the reinforcements, she now had three dozen people and plenty of camping gear. If push came to shove, she could survive for weeks off what they had.

That wasn't going to be necessary here in the wilds of Virginia, where help was a phone call away, but if something happened inside the base and left them trapped, they might need all of the food, water, and other survival implements to make it until someone came looking for them.

By the time they were fully ready, it was after one in the morning. She carefully climbed back up into the entrance, using her bright flashlight as she started inside and looked over everything as she walked.

The tube wasn't actually completely circular like she'd thought earlier. The area where she was walking was flattened and made it easy to keep her footing. It was also somewhat rough and provided a surface that her boots could grip. Still stone, but better than something smooth.

She'd expected to find lighting in the ceiling, but there was nothing. Perhaps the people that constructed the space hadn't wanted anyone outside to see a light that they couldn't explain.

The tunnel began sloping downward within five meters of the entrance, but the slope wasn't very steep. It also curved slightly. That meant that she was quickly at a place in the tunnel where no one on the outside could have seen her.

That was when the overhead lighting units appeared. They were dark but obviously of Asharim manufacture. She expected them to turn on as she and her people proceeded, but they remained unresponsive.

Even with their lights, the tunnel felt like it was closing in around her. Some water from the outside must've gotten into the tunnel, because she could smell organic rot and possibly mold. It was possible something—or many somethings over the years—had used the tube as a den. They might find bones and scat ahead.

As she continued forward, the floor changed from stone into a black material that the Asharim favored for their exterior walking needs. It was nonslip and extremely durable.

After twenty minutes, Brenda estimated they were now thirty or forty meters below the surface, not even counting the hill. She thought they'd made at least one complete circle, but that was also impossible to determine without a compass reading, which she hadn't thought to take at the start of this walk.

Ahead, she saw that the tunnel was sealed by a heavy metal door. She was not familiar with this specific style, but it was similar to ones she'd seen in the bases that Harry Rogers had discovered. Still, it wasn't precisely the same.

A minute later, she was standing directly in front of the door and looking for a way to open it. Victor Holyfield and Todd Granger stood beside her and watched.

The door had an access pad rather than one of the simple Asharim keys that normally opened such doors. The lettering on the pad was in the Asharim language and represented the twelve digits of their base numeric system.

"Looks like you need a code," Granger said. "That's going to make things awkward. We might need to get Kevin back so he can crack it."

Victor leaned forward and used his flashlight to look at the numeric pad more closely. "Maybe not. If you look closely, you can see that some of these numbers have wear and the rest don't. Four numbers, it looks like to me.

"It's possible some of those repeat, but we can certainly attempt to open this via trial and error for a little bit before we call Kevin. He is on another planet, after all."

Brenda shrugged. "It's not as if we have anything more pressing on our schedule. Let's see, the simplest answer would be to press them in ascending order."

She firmly pressed the four worn keys, and a low buzzer hummed for half a second. "Wrong guess, but at least the door is powered. That's a plus."

With four keys, that gave them two dozen potential combinations, if there were no repeating numbers. They made it through seven attempts before the door began sliding into the wall.

"Hot damn," she said, rubbing her hands together. "I can't believe it was that easy."

"I can't believe you're *saying that*, because now things are going to go really bad," Granger grumbled. "That's a basic rule that you need to adhere to, Brenda. Never say things are going easy."

She laughed, hefted her light, and stepped inside the base. The area just past the main door widened out significantly. It became something of a grand foyer.

The air smelled decent, as far as Brenda was concerned. The life-support system and lighting on the inside were obviously still operational. As to who had been here to escort the Volunteers and where they'd gone after they'd done so, she certainly hoped that they'd be able to figure that out, but there was a possibility that they'd never know the answer.

The lack of an answer was irking, but they'd found a base. That made it all worthwhile.

"Let's go a little bit deeper into the facility and see what we find," she said. "Is this just a very basic operation or something much larger? Personally, I can't see why anyone would bury a small base, so I'm hopeful we have something of consequence."

"That would be good," Victor said. "While I don't mind living in the city, it would be nice to have a place to call our own. Especially since Harry and Jess found all those other bases. We need resources of our own."

The three of them, with the other people following along behind them, made their way through the foyer and into one of five tunnels radiating out from the entrance. That was another clue that this was a significant base, because something smaller wouldn't need so many different paths moving forward.

She chose the central tunnel and was not disappointed. There were side corridors and even stairwells and lifts going down. She double-checked to make sure that the stairways only went down, just to be sure.

The stairwells were also another sign of the size of the base. Her light was insufficient to see the bottom of the stairwell clearly, but she could see at least eight levels below them. Victor flourished the metal cup that came with his canteen and dropped it down the open area in the center of the stairwell. He counted without speaking as it dropped until they all heard a metallic clatter from far, far below.

She glowered at him. "Didn't you see the *Lord of the Rings* movies? This place could be filled with nasty creatures, and we might start hearing drums from the deeps as they start coming for us."

"This is an old base, not the mines of Moria," the large man said with a grin. "No orcs or goblins here."

"Still, I'd prefer you didn't do that."

He held up his hands in surrender. "Sorry. Judging by the relative height of the levels that we can see from here, there are at least two dozen levels below us. That's significantly larger than even the Mars base that Harry had found. Whoever put this here, whatever they were doing, they weren't screwing around."

"But what *were* they doing?" she asked, staring down into the darkness. "None of our people were living in the United States when this base was built. Did they know we were out there? Did they have some other purpose in mind? What was their end goal?"

"I suppose we'll have to finish exploring the base to find out," Granger said. "If it's like the base on Mars, there's going to be some kind of central atrium. That seems to be a common Asharim design feature. We should see what it looks like."

They proceeded on and found the atrium right where she'd expected it about ten minutes later. Based on what she could see, this base did indeed dwarf the one on Mars. The atrium was three times as wide and so deep that the bottom was lost in gloom, even with their bright lights. It probably went all the way to the bottom level.

While that thrilled her, she was growing even more concerned about who was responsible for putting the base here. What had they hoped to accomplish? Were they still around somewhere? If she found them, would they be her enemies?

All good questions. She could only hope she liked the answers.

22

————

C hen sat in his office at the Yucatán spaceport and drummed his fingers on the desk he'd appropriated. Something was wrong. Queen had been too quiet. Backing down from a fight wasn't the man's style. If confronted by a superior force, the buffoon was more likely to meet it with everything he had rather than back away. He had no subtlety.

Really, the man wasn't a very good secretary of state. He believed in the dominance of his country under all circumstances and didn't favor compromise. Not that China was any different in this matter. Not now.

Queen was smart enough to understand that though they'd declared a truce, that was only for public consumption. The battle would continue to quietly rage. Much as his people had attacked and destroyed the facility holding the artifacts at Area 51, the Americans would continue to act behind the scenes. Which meant that the United States would be looking for weak points to strike at. As would Harry Rogers, he was certain.

Though with Rogers, the target of that strike had been stated explicitly. He would attempt to stop their Mars ship. He would use whatever force he thought was necessary to protect the base he'd found on the Red Planet.

That might turn out very differently than Rogers expected. Chen's people had sent along a few tricks with their ship. The man might have access to more Asharim technology than the Dragon did, but the Dragon was descended from warriors. Warriors who had not left all of their weapons behind on the battlefield.

That fight, when it came, was going to be brutal and exceptionally one-sided. The base that Rogers had commandeered was built by rebels who didn't have access to the most advanced weaponry the Masters could provide. Oh, Rogers's forces would undoubtedly fight valiantly, but they would still lose.

Yet that fight was still weeks away unless Rogers came to meet his people.

Something he hadn't shown any indication he was ready to do. Well, all good things came with time.

Once the Dragon controlled Earth and had regained contact with the Masters, it would fall to people like Chen to subjugate the masses and make certain that any further resistance was met with blood and death.

A soft rap at his door broke him out of his reverie. "Enter."

One of his guards leaned into the room. "There has been an incident. The locals seem to be gathering outside the main gate."

Chen rose to his feet and buttoned his jacket. "Have they attempted to cross into the spaceport?"

The man shook his head. "No, but I'm growing concerned. Their numbers are increasing, and it feels as if they're headed towards a more direct confrontation with our guards."

"Do we have any idea why they're feeling the need to be so demonstrative? What precisely are they protesting?"

The large man shrugged, his bulky shoulders raising his well-tailored suit shoulders only slightly. "They believe that the lease their country originally signed with Clayton Rogers and Rainforest does not allow us to 'steal their land' and that we are violating the agreement.

"There doesn't seem to be any sign of official sanction for this event, but the lack of Mexican officials in the vicinity is quite meaningful in its own way. Perhaps they don't wish to be seen as supporting a rebellion against us, but they apparently don't wish to be seen as endorsing our takeover either."

"Double the guard around the perimeter," he ordered. "Have everyone be wary of intrusions by people we have not yet located."

The guard frowned slightly. "That will reduce patrols inside the spaceport significantly. What if there are already intruders inside our perimeter?"

Chen raised an eyebrow. "Do you believe that we would have missed rioting civilians wandering around? One would think that sort of thing would stand out."

"Perhaps the rioters are a distraction for an organized force," the guard countered. "There is some sense to having a distraction while a more covert unit moves into place. Since the Mexican government doesn't seem to be overtly supporting the rioters, it may be that they have trained individuals inside the spaceport to take control while their people have our eyes pinned outside the gates."

Chen considered that and slowly nodded. "I want every worker we have gathered together and paired with some of our troops. That will give us more coverage inside, even if we have less actual firepower. I want every area checked for potential sabotage. Keep the majority of our trained fighters facing toward the outside, because if a larger attack comes, it will be from that direction."

The guard didn't seem to be overly enthused with Chen's plan, so he suspected there were gaps in what he'd just ordered. Since they were short of manpower, that was just going to have to do. There was no way that anyone could do more with troops they didn't yet have.

If the Mexicans felt that they had a chance of evicting the Dragon from their spaceport, they were sorely mistaken. Chen would grind whatever force they sent to seize this area under his heel.

"What if it is the Americans?" the guard asked hesitantly.

The thought made Chen chuckle. He'd just been thinking of how Queen would react and how he would strike. Unfortunately for the Americans, their lack of true military skills made such a rapid operation impossible. It had only been hours since he had thrown the gauntlet down to Queen at the UN.

No. It wouldn't be the Americans. He'd bet his reputation on that.

* * *

It took a bit more than half an hour for the Asharim slaves to finish digging their way through the rock fall. Harry had ordered Krueger to leave a small drone perched on a rock down the tunnel, all but invisible in the darkness, and it showed them the scene in infrared.

Harry, Krueger, and the New Zealand commander stood in the side chamber where his father had hidden himself during the first excursion and watched on the small screen as the aliens buttressed the tunnel and began spreading out into the cave.

"Time to roll," Krueger said over his com. "Engage, Gunny."

Two snipers, positioned behind handy obstructions, opened fire on the leading aliens. Even suppressed, their gunshots were loud in the enclosed area. Everyone was wearing hearing protection. Hopefully that would be enough.

The drone's feed showed that the slaves might have been strong, but they weren't invulnerable to being shot. They also weren't unarmed. The loud and unmistakable boom of black powder weapons came in response to the snipers' fire.

Still, having both sides armed didn't make them equal. The snipers were trained shooters with modern weapons, capable of pinpoint accuracy in the dark due to their night-vision goggles. The aliens, bipedal, tall, and wide, with details that he couldn't quite make out in the IR view, went down hard and fast.

"Team two, go," Krueger said.

That set off a controlled rush as the rest of his people raced forward, covering one another as they stopped behind preplanned obstructions in order to fire, taking down the remaining aliens inside the tunnel. They then proceeded forward into the tunnel themselves in order to secure it for the rest of the troops.

Without waiting for the all clear, Harry stood and followed the last of them into the tunnel with Krueger on his heels. The other man probably disapproved of the commanding officer being so forward in the combat theater, but that was tough. He was going to have to accept that Harry did things his own way.

Stepping over the dead and around what looked like a primitive mining machine, Harry stepped out onto the surface of Volunteer World and took up pretty much the position he'd occupied when he'd last visited.

This time, there wasn't a huge army fighting to get up the hill and kill him. It was actually more of a small army, based on the campfires out in the early gloom. Sunset must've taken place less than an hour ago.

The aliens didn't seem to have anticipated having someone on the other side of the rock fall ready to push them back out. If they had, there would've been more troops on the hillside. As it was, the survivors were racing down the hillside, putting their own lives at risk as many of them tumbled and fell to their deaths.

Using only night-vision goggles, it was impossible to tell if any of the figures were Asharim. They'd have to wait until daylight to look over the corpses and wounded to see if they'd laid their hands on one of the mystical alien overlords.

Right now, he had a hill to secure. "How does the tunnel look?" he asked over the com.

One of the New Zealanders responded at once. "Pretty solid. It looks like it could do with a bit more support in a couple of places, but I'll be able to get my guys on that as soon as the main forces are out on the surface. Shouldn't take me more than twenty minutes to be completely confident of the work. These aliens knew what they were doing."

Already, the rest of the New Zealanders were pouring out behind Krueger's team. They spread out, going up the hill and off to the sides. Their orders were to make certain that the hilltop was secure and to push back any intruders. By dawn, Harry wanted to be in complete control of this hill.

Going from memory and drone records, he and Krueger had worked out where to place heavy weapons and anti-aircraft guns to command all approaches to the hillside. By dawn, if they held on, the aliens would have a difficult time retaking the hill without the use of high-tech weaponry.

Of course, if anyone had access to high-tech weaponry, it would be the Asharim. Personally, Harry doubted they had a lot in reserve. Otherwise they'd have used it to attack the Volunteers. That was the threat that kept coming back to haunt them year after year, so if they had the ability to do so, they would've stopped them long ago.

Not that he was counting on that. He actually planned for them to have a cache of alien weapons that could set him back on his heels. That way, if that ever happened, he'd be ready. If it didn't, they were in even better shape than he'd hoped.

If things actually went according to plan, they'd have the hilltop secured within the hour and have settled the heavy weapons emplacements in less than an hour. Then they'd dig in and prepare to repel any counterattacks.

The dark was the perfect time to launch those attacks, based on the behavior Harry had seen and been told about by the aliens. Unfortunately for the Asharim, Krueger and his people would quickly be bringing through large drones, assembling them on the hilltop, and launching them. Unlike their smaller brethren, these could stay in the air for a long time and were visually undetectable at any real range.

As they were armed, any grouping of aliens that looked like officers could be taken out before the primitives realized they were in danger. That would really screw with their command and control. They'd also see any large-scale attacks coming a long time in advance. Those could be harassed by the airborne drones, which would then return to the hill to be refueled and rearmed.

Honestly, Harry hoped it didn't come to that. If he had to, he'd kill as many aliens as he needed to in order to secure both this hillside and the gates in the city itself, but negotiation was a much better option.

He hoped that after his troops had occupied this hillside, the Asharim would send a delegation to talk. If they started talking, some kind of compromise could probably be worked out.

Of course, from what they'd discovered on the crown of the hill the last time, Krueger was convinced that the Asharim performed human sacrifice there. If there was some type of religious component to this, finding a reasonable solution was going to be much more difficult.

He hoped it didn't come to "kill them all and let their gods sort them out," but that was still the most likely outcome to this war.

Well, no matter how things eventually worked out, right now he needed to focus on securing the hill so that the remainder of the troops and their equipment could be brought in and set up. Only once that was done could he start seriously worrying about what came next.

23

Jess discovered that taking off from a planet was significantly easier than landing. Even though her mind seemed to have all the required skills, that was very reassuring.

Once she'd come to an agreement with the high priest, they'd returned to their lander with one addition and a few subtractions. Vidar had asked to leave his two associates behind to continue telling the priests the story of how things had gone so wrong but had offered to bring his daughter along to see the world that they had tried to conquer.

Of course, they wouldn't be seeing it for a while. They'd be going directly to the New Zealand base and then straight through to Volunteer World.

She'd called ahead to make absolutely certain that Harry was ready for her and her guests. He'd said to bring them along and that they had the hill secure, at least for the moment. Her partner seemed to think that allowing the heavy-worlders to see his troops in action would be educational and give them additional reasons why they shouldn't come looking for a fight.

Jess didn't think he understood the heavy-worlders as well as he thought. These folks were not afraid to fight when they thought the situation warranted it. They weren't the kind of people that intimidated easily.

The trip up to the station went without a hitch. This time she decided not to stop there but did give it a close pass to make sure that her guests saw what was above their world.

"I did not get such a good look at this the last time," Vidar said in a low voice. "We traveled up the space elevator and then took a small craft out to the ship that Kathleen Bennett controlled. From there, we used a gate to travel to Earth. The view was far too short for me to truly comprehend what I was seeing."

Jess nodded. "Is this something that the Masters built, or was it built by the people of this world? Who were they, by the way? This is obviously not a heavy-worlder planet."

The large man shrugged slightly. "I am not certain. This world once held many species. The Masters decreed which of them were present and in what number. I am uncertain that anyone truly remembers what species had come first.

"It is possible that the Masters developed this world for use as an administrative center where no species had been present before. They were very capable terraformers and could shape marginal worlds into paradises. Of course, they reserved their greatest efforts for low-gravity planets that mirrored their own home world."

"Does anyone know where their home world is or how to get there?" Jess asked. "We captured a lot of information, but I don't recall having seen anything that identified what world they came from."

Vidar smiled. "Whether I knew that information or not, I suspect my answer would be the same. I cannot tell you. The Masters are the Masters. Until the high priest determines that we are no longer bound by their dictates, we could not betray them to you.

"However, I will point out that we have been trapped here for almost a millennium. Such knowledge, particularly when gate access has been cut off, would be lost fairly quickly. As a warrior, I would never have needed such information in the first place.

"Perhaps the high priest could find it, but he would not tell you any more than I would. Not unless he determines that it is in the best interests of the People."

Jess nodded, understanding where he was coming from. She set the shuttle into a gentle arc coming around the station toward the massive gate in the side of the station hosting the space elevator, having to dodge a small piece of debris.

That reminded her that she wanted a much better idea of what the area around the station looked like after the small nuke had taken out the warship Kathleen Bennett had commandeered. The desire to take that looked prompted her hands to dance over the controls, and some kind of scanner activated.

The data that filled the screen over her head was alien—literally—to her, but she smiled as the meaning of the various bits started making sense. Interestingly, the debris was gathered a short distance away from the station in a small area enclosed in some kind of energy field. That explained why the station was intact but not why the space there was restricted.

It took a few moments to locate what was creating the energy field. There were dozens of spheres globing the area, and they had contained the shrapnel from the blast. Jess wasn't sure how, and as an engineer she really wanted to take the time to explore that angle but didn't have time.

The scanners didn't have much range beyond the general area, but she could also see a number of what she guessed were real ships at the edge of her detection range, orbiting almost around the curve of the planet. One of them was significantly larger than the others. She longed to go see what she'd discovered, but she had more pressing matters on her plate.

Being certain to shield her hand from Vidar's gaze, she tapped in the address to take them back to the Asharim space station orbiting Earth-B. The gate on the outside of the space elevator station activated, and the small craft edged through.

After a few minutes of maneuvering, she went through the gate on the surface of the dormant comet, and they were inside the landing bay. She killed the gate behind them and started shutting down the lander.

"Welcome to *Freedom Express*," she said. "This is one of our bases. From here, we'll make a transition to another abandoned facility and then on to the world where we found the Asharim."

That plan lasted approximately two minutes. As soon as they were on the way to the gate room on the dormant comet, she found herself buttonholed by Susanna Adorno and General Norbert Norris. The two of them looked very intent.

"Miss Cook," Adorno said as she came to a stop in front of Jess. "It is my understanding that your forces have once again opened contact with my world. Is that correct?"

Jess didn't bother denying it. "That's right. Harry Rogers just let me know that they were out on the surface of the hill and had pushed the Asharim slaves back down to the plain below. It's dark there, so they're planning on maintaining that position until dawn. Then they'll see what they can do from there."

"It is urgent that my forces join the attack," Norris said. "It is our world and our responsibility to be there for our people. We must have a hand in pushing the enemy back and securing the gates inside the city. That was our agreement. Will you honor it?"

As much as she wanted to decline their assistance, she really couldn't come up with a good justification. The man was right. They'd made a deal. Now that they were actually fighting, she really should allow them to be part of it. Otherwise, the trust they'd built would suffer.

"May I suggest that you lead off with a smaller force?" she suggested. "The situation is still uncertain, and I wouldn't want you to commit your entire force to an operation where we might be withdrawing come daylight if the fighting goes against us."

The two glanced at one another and nodded simultaneously.

"That sounds wise," Norris added. "I've taken the liberty of having several of my best squads prepare for battle. I understand that our weapons are not as effective as your own, but it is what we have.

"Now, with your assurances, we will accompany you back to our world and assist in the operation to capture the city. I should warn you that even with your advanced technology, capturing the city will be no easy task. Particularly if you intend to hold it for any length of time. The fighting will be quite intense, growing more so as the enemy brings more of their forces to bear."

While they'd been talking, Kerrick Vidar and his daughter had been watching quietly from the side. Their expression showed only interest at the strange clothing worn by the Volunteers.

Adorno wore what could only be described as a pirate outfit: tight leather pants, a white shirt with ruffles and long sleeves, and a jacket that hung down to her knees that would be suitable for service aboard a ship. She wore a cutlass on her hip and looked prepared to do battle.

General Norris, on the other hand, was dressed much like one would expect from a fighter in America's Revolutionary War. His jacket was just as long as hers but seemed more for style and warmth than protection from the elements.

Seeing the opportunity, Jess introduced the two groups to one another. Once names were exchanged and handshakes given, she explained who the heavy-worlders were.

"Kerrick Vidar and his daughter Vera are descendants of the Asharim warriors. We found them on a world where the aliens abandoned them almost a thousand years ago. We're still negotiating to see if we can form an alliance, but they are coming along so that they can observe the current condition of the Asharim civilization."

Adorno's eyes narrowed. "I have heard something of your people. Great fighters, very strong, and loyal to the end and beyond. Many of the other human colonies speak of your kind in the legends. It is said that you were once human like me. Is that true?"

Jess translated her words.

Kerrick Vidar shrugged slightly. "Considering how alike our two peoples are, I am inclined to accept that we were once raised from the same stock. Others have told us that we are modified humans, but the source was suspect. Now? I personally believe it to be so, though I have no proof.

"As for my people, we are very loyal. When the Masters command us to fight, we fight. At least that is how it used to be, before the Masters left us separated from the home that we came from. Now the People live on a world of light gravity and have lost the way back to our home with true gravity.

"It is my intent as the leader of the warrior faction of our people to see what the condition of the Masters is. If it is true that they have fallen, it is uncertain that the priests will feel the obligation to follow any orders given by them. I warn you, though I have given my parole and my daughter is acting under the terms of truce agreed to by Miss Cook, if the priests determine that we should go to war, we may yet be enemies."

"I'm not certain we should jump to the conclusion that that is the inevitable outcome," Jess said quickly. "Let's look on the bright side. We could come into this as enemies and leave as friends. That would be the preferable outcome."

She passed Vidar's words to Adorno and then looked at General Norris. "General, how long will it take you to prepare your people?"

The man smiled, his resemblance to George Washington very spooky to her once again. "They stand prepared in the gate room. As soon as we arrive, they will be ready to depart."

"Then let's go," Jess said as she walked forward and found a lift to take them to the gate room. Just a few minutes later, she was dialing their destination on a handheld pad.

"The base on the other end of this gate is protected by armed guards that are unaware of our impending arrival," she warned. "I'll go through first and make certain that there are no misunderstandings."

The guards on the other end recognized her once she'd opened the gate and stepped through and lowered their weapons. She informed them that there was a large number of troops coming through and going to Volunteer World.

They didn't put up any argument.

When they'd first found the base in New Zealand, only one of the three gates at the bottom level had had power. That was still true, but in reality, there was only one gate there now. Kevin McHugh's people had mostly disassembled the other two gates and were removing them.

Once Humanity Unlimited set up a base somewhere in the United States, they'd put those gates in so that they could have access to the greater universe. Without power, they weren't doing any good here.

Frankly, the New Zealand base was pretty much a write-off. The shell was good in most places, but it was going to take a lot of work to make it operational again. They just didn't have time for that right now.

They also didn't have time to try to set up a base in the United States. They had to go about it nice and slow, or the US government would figure out where they were. Even though they were supposed to be allies, she had no doubt that Secretary of State Queen would take those gates in a heartbeat.

If that happened, a bunch of arrogant fools would find themselves in far over their heads with the universe at large and humanity would be in terrible danger. Neither she nor Harry was prepared to allow that to happen.

Pulling her mind away from problems that she couldn't solve at the moment, she used the tethered controller to activate the gate going to Volunteer World. From this side of the gate in New Zealand, it was impossible to open any other gate because of what the engineers had done to make it work back when the base had fallen.

Once the gate was stable, Jess began moving the Volunteer troops through. Harry was going to be surprised. Hopefully, he wouldn't be mad. In any case, there was nothing either of them could do about it. They'd made a deal. She just had to hope that it worked out for the best.

24

B renda and her people searched for the base computer to isolate it before they tried bringing main power back online. That proved unnecessary. They found where the computer should have been, but it was gone. Not erased but physically removed.

In fact, someone had gone to the trouble of taking every bit of data storage in the facility, so far as she could tell from spot checking. The various offices were neatly cleaned and empty. No paper, no data chips, nothing.

The power center, on the other hand, was completely intact. All of the power cubes were in place, and only the massive breakers were turned off. It took several people each to get the breakers turned back on, but as soon as they did, the overhead lights came on and the life-support system came back to… well, life.

The gate room was a real surprise, mainly because it wasn't a single room at all. The Asharim basic floorplan called for a large area serviced by three gates. This facility had three exceptionally large gate rooms, each serviced by three gates, connected by a cavernous chamber servicing all of the gate rooms.

Brenda stood in the center of the massive space and swiveled her head around. From where she was standing, she could look into the three adjacent gate rooms and see all nine of the gates.

It was damned impressive. She couldn't imagine why the original builders had needed so much capacity. From everything she'd been told, these people had been active here on Earth until just a few hundred years ago. Hell, they could've been here last week for all she knew. Probably not, just based on the general conditions inside the base, but it hadn't been all that long.

Realistically, they'd probably been gone no more than fifty years. That meant these people had been present during the Industrial Revolution, all the way through the moon landing and beyond. They'd seen Earth as a technologically advanced civilization. Why had they stayed so long, only to depart abruptly? What had their true goals been?

"We should check the gates to see if we can pull any addresses off them," Victor said from beside her.

She turned to face the large man. "Do you think they'd have left the buffers in place? If it was me, I'd have erased all the destinations that this base had record of. They took the computers, for God's sake."

"Never hurts to check. You're probably right, but if we don't look, we don't know."

She nodded. "Give each of them a check and then open a wormhole to the gate in our building. If we need any other people or supplies, bring them through. They need to know how to dial us here."

The large man nodded and trotted off toward the first gate room. Granger stepped up beside her and watched him leave.

"This is kind of spooky," the doctor said. "I've been trying to figure out exactly why someone would be behaving like this, and I can't exactly come up with a decent answer. These people pulled up stakes pretty recently. Why did they do that and where did they go?"

"I was just wondering that myself. Do you think there's any way we can determine how long ago they left, just to verify?"

He nodded. "Somewhere in this base is going to be a hydroponics room. We should be able to look at the plants there and do some double checking. It's not an exact science, but I'd be very surprised if we couldn't at least determine within a decade how long everything had been dead.

"Hell, I can't imagine they got every single tablet out of this place. We may be able to find enough information to figure out when they were here. This is a huge place. It's going to take us a while to search it from top to bottom, so let's not get ahead of ourselves."

"They had to have stripped the computers because they were afraid that the regular humans here would find this facility," Brenda said. "By the time they'd departed, they had to have known that destroying the base would draw far more attention than just leaving it abandoned.

"The area around it was declared federal land at some point in the past. I'd be willing to bet that whoever built this place pulled some strings to make that happen. Until they departed, they were probably plugged into the United States government, much like the Families are today."

Granger rubbed his chin. "Do you think they still are? Could they still have spies in place to tell them what's going on? If so, word that we've started discovering old Asharim-based facilities scattered around the system might draw them back."

"There's no way to predict what they might do, since we have no idea who they are and what their original goals were. Since they cut off the power, I can't imagine that they intend to return here via the gates."

Granger shook his head. "Someone threw those breakers. Someone had to leave via lander or on foot. The people that built this place still have some contact here on this planet."

"Perfect," she said with a scowl. "Just what we need. Another player."

Victor came trotting back a few minutes later. "No dice on the buffers. Someone wiped them clean. That means that someone was here after the rest left."

She nodded. "We were guessing that. Did you find any gate controllers?"

The large man shook his head. "And there aren't any ships or cargo movers that have gate controllers either. If we hadn't brought our own, I'm not certain that we could've gotten into the gates at all."

Well, they weren't going to figure out what happened today. Karl was going to be pissed that she was just taking this base over, but she'd make it up to him.

There was no way that she was going to turn this thing over to the US government. Not a chance. This base belonged to the Families, and they were damned well going to keep it, no matter what Queen said. Let the bastard pound sand.

* * *

QUEEN SAT in a secure bunker below the Pentagon and watched via remote as the Special Forces teams worked their way deeper into the Yucatán spaceport. While there were guards searching the port for intruders, they'd started too late. His people had infiltrated the area hours before the demonstration had started. The Chinese were behind the curve, but they didn't realize it yet.

Part of the information that the CIA had dug up on Clayton Rogers included complete schematics and plans for the spaceport. Those pilfered files included the locations of the self-destruct devices as well as how they operated.

He'd made certain that the teams had specialists with them that were more than capable of rearming and reconnecting the systems as was required for them to operate. It might seem counterintuitive to reconnect the self-destruct devices to the general systems and controls, but plausible deniability demanded it. They had to make this look as if it was a rogue signal that set them off. If the systems were still isolated, the finger would point squarely at saboteurs.

"What's the status of our people?" he asked the general who was seated at his side. He'd already forgotten the man's name and didn't feel like looking at his name tag. That would make it seem as if he didn't care—which he didn't —but he didn't feel like getting into that particular pissing contest.

"All six teams are on schedule, Mister Secretary. We should have everything lined up and reconnected within the next twenty minutes. Once everything is in order, we'll exfiltrate our people. They'll kick off the self-destruct via remote timer planted in the system before they leave the spaceport."

"Highlight the locations that we are rearming," he ordered. "I want to see exactly what we're working on here."

Six areas lit up on the screen. Three of them were in the midst of the refueling tanks, two of them were on the launch gantries, and the final one was inside the control center.

"I can see how we're going to get people to the five exterior positions, but what's the plan for getting the team into the control center itself? It's going to be heavily guarded, since that's where Chen has his office. I can't imagine they're going to leave any side doors unlocked."

The general nodded. "You put your finger on the most difficult portion of this exercise, Mister Secretary. That's going to be the sticking point if there is one. That team will go in last so that the other teams have an opportunity to finish their work. At that point, all the other Special Forces operators will be in position to assist in the extraction of the final team if things go bad.

"As for entry, there are some underground tunnels servicing the building. Those are out of general view of the guards, and not all of them are very well marked. In fact, one of them seems to have been erased from the maps. We suspect that it was supposed to be used by Clayton Rogers in case he needed to evacuate the building in a hurry."

Queen nodded. That made sense. The old bastard wouldn't have trapped himself someplace that he couldn't run away from. Not on purpose.

"What's the status of that last team?"

"They're in the tunnel and have scouted far enough ahead to disarm all of the sensors that might allow anyone to know that they're there. Once the exterior teams have completed their work and are in position, they'll move forward.

"From the basement, they go up two levels and into one of the backup computer centers. They can rearm the entire security system from that location and plant a Trojan horse that will set off the explosives and then erase itself. By the time everything goes boom, all our people should be away from the spaceport entirely."

The two of them watched the operation play out through little dots on the screen. The exterior teams completed their work and moved to the secondary locations where they could support the lead team. Then the lead team infiltrated the building.

Things couldn't go smoothly. That was just the way it was. The interior team ran into a pair of guards inside the building and had to take them down. At least their suppressed weapons made it less likely that any of the other guards would become aware of their presence before the sabotage was complete.

Queen wasn't concerned at all that his people had had to kill the guards. Chen hadn't exactly cried over the people he'd murdered when he'd blown up the lab at Area 51. Compared to that operation, this one was going to be relatively bloodless.

After what seemed like an eternity, his people were done and moving out. They'd relocated the dead guards to the area inside the control center where the self-destruct device would go off. It was in the middle of the computer center and would vaporize all the controls and files in addition to the bodies.

It was conceivable that the Chinese wouldn't be able to prove what had killed those guards. That would be the best outcome.

Of course, it was also likely that others in the control area above the computer center would be killed in the explosion. His experts had given 50-50 odds that the floor would collapse and dump a number of people into the computer center after the explosion.

If that happened, there would be no video record of who was in the control room, and so the guards might have been assumed to have been there as well. Honestly, he didn't care how it worked out, so long as the Chinese didn't catch his people red-handed. The United States had plausible deniability, and that was good enough for him.

Chen was going to go through the ceiling when this happened, so Queen needed to be ready to deal with the fallout. Hot accusations would be coming his way, and he needed to make certain that he looked the part of a wrongly accused man.

The goal of this was to sting the Chinese without actually goading them back into overt conflict. Queen thought that he'd be able to pull that off, but one never really knew until push came to shove.

"The primary team is moving, Mister Secretary," the general said. "All the teams are on their way to the extraction point. The timer is set to blow all six self-destruct charges in exactly nineteen minutes and twenty-four seconds."

A handy timer at the corner of the display showed that countdown. When it had spooled down to less than a minute, the general spoke again.

"Our teams have extracted from the spaceport grounds. They're all in vehicles moving in different directions and will rendezvous with the helicopters some distance away. At this point, there's no reason that any of them should be bothered. All we have to do now is wait for the explosives to go off."

"Put up the real-time satellite image," Queen ordered.

It was still dark in the target area, but he was going to be able to see the explosions due to the high-tech visibility the satellite conferred upon him. It was able to see into the infrared and ultraviolet. Nothing would be lost.

Right on the tick of zero, a number of massive blasts appeared on the monitor. A quick count showed five. The one he didn't see was inside the building, but that was most likely because the building itself had shielded the exterior from the explosion.

"Zoom in on the control building," he said tersely. "Did the explosion there go off?"

The general nodded even as the image zoomed in. "There is significantly more IR going on inside the building than there should be. That's the sign of a massive fire. The explosive went off, and the building is most likely going to burn down. We should be able to see the fire in short order."

In less than three minutes, he could see the flames licking the outside of the building. The entire control center was on fire. Excellent. With the loss of the fueling tanks, which he double-checked and made certain that they were all gone, the main gantries, and the control center, the spaceport was now just an expensive office park. The amount of time and money that it would take to rebuild it into a working spaceport would be significant.

With that piece off the board, Queen stood and headed for the door. "Excellent work, General. Discreetly pass my congratulations on to your troops. I think I'll head home now. I'm expecting an angry phone call shortly and want to make the gentleman wait while I supposedly get dressed, drive in to work, and deny everything."

Queen walked toward the interior parking area with a smile on his face and a bounce in his step. Today was going to be a good day.

25

Harry made sure he was standing by when Jess led her group through the gate onto Volunteer World. "What's going on?" he asked quietly as he pulled her aside.

"A lot," she said with a smile. "The Volunteers are insistent that they take part in your attack. I'm not sure how we can protect them while that happens, but we did make them a promise. If I could've snuck past them, I would have, but they caught me, so here we are.

"The initial negotiations with the heavy-worlder high priest seem to be going well, but he was insistent that his people see what condition the Asharim are currently in. I think seeing them in this fallen state will help forge an alliance between the heavy-worlders and us.

"I'm sure you recognize Kerrick Vidar. The woman next to him is his daughter, Vera. They're both warriors. He's given his parole, and she is under what they call a truce bond. Neither of them should cause us any trouble. What about you? What's the situation here?"

He considered her for a few moments and then inclined his head, accepting what she'd said. "We've formed a firebase at the top of the hill. It took a couple of hours to fully push the Asharim slaves off the high ground, but we're in control now. I figure it's about four hours until dawn, so that's about how long we have before the counterattack begins. They'll want to see what's going on before they make the push.

"How many Volunteers are we going to have to fit into our lines? I need to work with Krueger to get them situated so that we're still strong all the way around and can protect our allies as well as we can when the counterattack comes."

"Not that many," Jess assured him. "At this point, they only brought along a couple of their best squads, so it's more making a point than anything else.

Once we expand away from the hill, they plan to bring the rest of their armed forces back through and participate in capturing the city."

He considered that and slowly nodded. "They have a much better knowledge of the layout inside the city and know where the gates are. If they can do the primary pushing to get there while my forces provide overwatch and heavy firepower, we may be able to secure the city faster. There's really no way to know until we start trying."

He gestured toward the tunnel leading out to the surface. "Let's go up to the top of the hill so you can take a look around. The enemy is on the plain below us, and there's still some shooting, but it's a pretty random affair. The range is pretty long for black powder weapons."

It took five minutes to get everybody out of the cave and up to the crown of the hill. As they were moving, Harry made a decision to speak to the heavy-worlders. That presented a challenge, since he didn't speak their language. Jess was going to have to translate.

After laying out to his partner what he intended to do, he escorted the two heavy-worlders up to the platform looking out over the remains of the Asharim city.

"My name is Harry Rogers," he said, allowing time for Jess to translate. "I understand that you're Kerrick Vidar and this is your daughter Vera. Is this correct?"

The large man nodded. "Your understanding of the situation is correct. I assume that your associate has passed along that I am under parole and my daughter is operating under truce bond?"

"She has," Harry said with a nod. "We call this place Volunteer World. The origin of that name is probably going to be somewhat obtuse to you, so if you'll forgive me, I'll leave it unexplained for the moment. The city that you see there was once occupied by the Asharim and their slaves. In fact, it still is.

"As best we can tell, the Asharim and their slaves continue to assert dominance over that city because of the gates that are inside of it. The humans on this world occasionally seize the gates and communicate with other human colonies out there in the greater universe. I'm not certain how long either group maintains control, but they take it back from one another on a fairly regular basis."

He gestured down toward the altar that they discovered on their first trip. "Over there is an altar that either the Asharim or their slaves had been sacrificing humans on for some time. It seems to have some type of religious significance. Is that something the Asharim commonly did when your people had contact with them?"

Vidar shook his head. "The Masters were never religious. If anything, they promoted themselves as gods over those who served them. None of the legends speak of any kind of sacrifice. I am also unaware of any of the servant races having that particular trait. I find it somewhat… unsettling."

Harry could certainly understand that. The idea of murdering sentient beings in some type of ceremony made his stomach turn.

"It will be dawn in about four hours," Harry continued. "At that point, we'll see what type of forces have been drawn up below us, and we'll plan our attack accordingly. We're going to make a beachhead down on the plain and move more forces through the gate onto this world.

"The Volunteers had relocated to our world, and they will be providing the majority of the troops and the knowledge on securing the city. What are you hoping to see during this operation?"

The large man grunted. "I hope to see the condition of a live Asharim. If they have fallen from the heights of their knowledge, that is important for the People to know.

"I can understand why you might want to keep me and my daughter away from the fighting. You have no reason to trust us. I find that acceptable. If you can capture an Asharim and bring him to me for questioning, I believe that I can provide information to the high priest that will settle any question of what we should do."

Harry thought that was a pretty tall order. The Asharim no doubt kept themselves as safe as they could during the fighting. Somehow, his people would have to locate one of the aliens and perform a raid to get a living prisoner.

Wasn't that going to be fun?

* * *

BRENDA CALLED in every available person she had in Washington, DC, and set them to searching the abandoned base in Virginia. By the time they'd finished, it was almost dawn, and none of their mysteries had been solved. To her annoyance, they'd found no overlooked material whatsoever.

No data chips, no tablets, and no paper of any kind. Nothing. Whoever had abandoned the space had done an exceptionally thorough job of cleaning it. Anything that was portable was gone, with the exception of the power cubes.

For whatever reason, they'd decided to leave those in place. Perhaps in case they ever needed to return, though that didn't quite make sense either.

What her people did have was more infrastructure than they'd ever had in the United States. Hell, in the entire world. Not since the heavy-worlders had crushed the resistance on Earth.

One thing she knew for sure was that they'd need to seal off the entrance as soon as possible. If it had been anyone else that had chanced upon the tunnel leading down to this base, the United States government would be all over it at this very moment. She needed to prevent that from happening without leaving any telltale signs that her people had done so.

She pulled Victor and Granger back from the search of the base and laid out her concerns. "If we want to keep this facility, we're going to have to make absolutely certain that it's not found again. Victor, I want you to get a team busy gathering whatever you need to seal this entrance so that anyone who chances across it thinks that it's a natural wall of rock.

"If we can put a doorway in that we can use, that's fine, but I want to be sure that no one ever stumbles into this place. Even if we do have a door, we'll have to use it *very* sparingly."

Granger shook his head slightly. "That's going to be complicated. You promised Harry Rogers that if he didn't compete with us for this base, you'd give him the portable gate we've been using. That leaves us a little bit short of places to go, if you know what I mean."

The rangy doctor was right, but that didn't change anything. "He allowed Kevin to disassemble two of the gates in the New Zealand base. We're keeping one of those and will put it in the Vault. Cyrus will make sure it stays secure."

The Vault was an abandoned subway station under DC that the Families had converted into an intelligence center. It was run by Cyrus Patterson, an ex-CIA officer, and had plenty of room for something as important as a gate. The professionals there would never let word of it slip out, and if the US government ever located the Vault, it could be destroyed along with the rest of the facility. That would be a blow but not nearly as painful as losing the portable gate would've been before they'd had other options.

Granger was nodding at what she'd said. "Okay, we can do that. And if we seal off the only exterior entrance to this place, the odds of us being located go way down. They'd have to bring some pretty impressive scanning equipment into the area to detect this base from the outside. It's shielded pretty well.

"My next question is what are we going to do with all of this space? I thought the Mars base was large, but this dwarfs it. Even if we brought every member of the Families into this facility, we'd still be underutilizing it by a huge margin."

She laughed. "I'm perfectly happy with room to grow. I'm thinking of offering to share with Harry and Jess in exchange for some other concessions in the solar system. We could certainly use some of those ships that they've got their hands on, at a minimum."

And the Humanity Unlimited team certainly had a number of ships they could part with. More than enough that they wouldn't be concerned about sharing. Just based off of what she'd seen in *Freedom Express* and in the French base, they had to have dozens of Asharim-designed landers, and that was probably only the tip of the iceberg.

"On a completely unrelated note, I had a chance to look at the plants down in hydroponics," Granger said. "I'm going to have to perform a few tests, but it certainly looks as if they were abandoned less than a hundred years ago. My gut tells me that it's been more than fifty years, but I'll have to take some samples back to my lab to be absolutely certain."

One of the other security men came into the room and hurried over with a piece of paper in his hand. "I found this fallen behind some machinery," he told Brenda as he handed it across to her.

Even before she looked closely, she recognized that it was part of a newspaper. It was yellowed with age but not brittle. One glance at the front told her all she needed to know.

She held it out so that the others could see the headline and picture on the front. It was an issue of the *New York Times*.

"I believe we know what triggered our friends' departure," she said.

The edition was dated July 21, 1969, and the headline was "Men Walk On Moon." It amused her that it had only cost 10¢. How times had changed.

"So, right in the middle of my guess. Let's see, 2036 minus 1969 is... sixty-seven years. Almost sixty-eight. They haven't been gone all that long."

Brenda shook her head. "My guess is that they aren't truly gone at all. I think they're probably from somewhere in Asharim space, and they have other ways to get back here. Or we're making a false assumption that they were human at all. There were plenty of races that could have been interested in humanity."

Victor scowled. "That's an unhappy thought. If somebody went out and got a newspaper, they were able to blend in. There had to be humans involved somewhere."

"Probably, but we're going to have to do a lot more digging to find out where they vanished to before we'll ever know for sure. For right now, let's start securing the base. Get all the help you need to seal up the entrance and start installing a permanent gate at the Vault. The clock is ticking."

26

Jess huddled behind a handy rock and tugged her borrowed coat closer. She hadn't been dressed for the nighttime wilderness and even though Volunteer World was a fairly temperate place, it was chilly.

Dawn was just breaking. The valley below was still bathed in shadows and would be for at least another fifteen or twenty minutes, but she thought she could see movement in the gloom.

The Asharim slaves were maneuvering to position themselves for an assault, she was certain. Unfortunately for them, Harry and Commander Karl Krueger had had all night to prepare for this and they were ready.

"Are they going to attack as soon as they can see us?" she asked Harry as he knelt beside her.

"I don't think so," he said with a shake of his head. "I think they'll take at least some time to assess our forces before they make their move."

"That's going to work in our favor. We've got drones in the air that will be looking them over. By the time they're ready to attack, we'll know where to strike first to cause the most damage to their forces. Better yet, we'll know if there are any Asharim down there for us to try and capture."

She wasn't sure how she felt about capturing one of the aliens. They were like boogie men. "If you do see any of them, how do you intend to isolate them without killing them? They're going to be heavily guarded."

Her friend nodded. "Getting down to the plain is going to be a slow process. We're up on the top of a fairly steep hill and can't just relocate at a moment's notice. If we had helicopters, or even one of the assault landers, we could sweep right down and land on top of them. As it is, we're going to have to work with the forces we have at hand."

"So what you're telling me is that we're not going to be able to capture any

TERRY MIXON

of the Asharim until we break out from our positions here. That means we have to stop the enemy attack and chase them as they retreat, right?"

"That's about it."

He panned his binoculars over the area around the hill, and she let him do so without interruption. She knew that his gear allowed him to see in the infrared and ultraviolet, so he'd be able to see what they were facing better than she would.

If the enemy only had black powder flintlocks, the more advanced weapons her people brought with them would decimate the Asharim and their slaves. Part of her quailed at the mass slaughter that was about to happen, but she was smart enough to realize that it was either the aliens or the Volunteers. Not the ones on the hill with her but the ones in their settlements.

If the Asharim and their slaves gained the upper hand, it was virtually certain that they'd subjugate the humans on this world. Most would be converted to slaves, and the rest would be sacrificed to whatever sick gods the aliens now worshiped.

"They're moving," Harry said after a few minutes. "It looks like they're gathering off to the west in the shadow of the hill we're on. I'm not sure what that gains them, but we can definitely work with their move. They've left forces all around us, but nothing that we shouldn't be able to break through."

Harry lowered his binoculars and focused his attention on her in the growing light. "If we can penetrate their lines, we can swing our forces around behind their strongest units and pin them in a crossfire. It's really hard to defend against two separate attacks at the same time.

"If we break them, they'll run, and a retreating enemy isn't very effective. The panic that they'll spread to the rest of their forces will let us take the area around us with minimal losses."

Not being a warrior, all she could do was nod and trust his experience.

"I got something," Krueger said over the radio bug in her ear. He was talking to both Harry and her, as well as his senior people and the New Zealander officers, over the command channel.

"With the upgraded lighting conditions, we've started cataloging what the enemy forces look like. One of my drones has zeroed in on what seems to be a command pavilion off to the north. It's behind some trees, so it's not visible from our current location.

"The bottom line is that a lot of the aliens we've been fighting are gathered around there, but they're not alone. I'm seeing at least six beings that are not of the same species. Based on your descriptions, they look like Asharim."

Harry smiled coldly. "If so, that gives us a chance to get a team to their location. We have to work that into the breakout options we've already discussed. This complicates the process, but it gives us a chance to finally get our hands on one of them.

"These aliens might not be responsible for what happened on Earth, but they certainly know what's going on in the ruined city. If we can break some of their leaders, that should give us a number of benefits.

"First, it would allow the heavy-worlders to take a good look at their former Masters. Second, it would finally allow us to communicate with the enemy forces on this planet. Since Jess can speak their language, we can start putting the screws to the bastards."

"Actually, I can speak heavy-worlder and read what we think is Asharim. I won't know if that's true until I meet one, but I'm not certain they shared their language with their slaves. If the written language isn't Asharim either, that's going to open up some interesting new questions."

She had to admit that she badly wanted to talk to one of the aliens. Just getting a grasp on how they thought might help Humanity Unlimited figure out a number of things that had been puzzling them.

Sure, the mysteries were a thousand years old and the aliens here would almost certainly not be aware of the details, but if she didn't start getting some of the answers, they'd never dig down to why there was a frozen version of Earth in their outer system. That was a mystery that only the Asharim could shed any light on.

It was possible that some details would come out as they continued evaluating the research data that the Asharim from the past had gathered on that world and on the station that they'd placed above it, but that was slow going. They just didn't have the people to make that happen, not even having formed an alliance with the Families, Brenda Cabot, and a host of other nations.

Another angle that Harry probably hadn't thought of was that a live alien would be something that he could use to prove to any skeptic back on Earth that everything they'd said was true. A surprising number of people had thought this was all some kind of scam, even with the high-tech ships that Harry had demonstrated for them.

To make this happen, she'd have to rely on Harry's battle skills to pull off what amounted to a miracle. She hoped he was up to the task.

* * *

CHEN STOOD outside the burning control building and raged. Not just verbally, either. Anyone that was stupid enough to stray inside his reach earned a fist to the face at his full strength. His minions quickly learned to leave him be.

This had to be Queen. There was no other conceivable option. That son of a bitch had blown up the spaceport, including the control building. While Chen had been inside it.

The damage reports were still streaming in, but it was obvious that the launch towers and refueling facilities were gone. With the addition of the control center and its computer hardware, the spaceport was wrecked.

It didn't matter that they hadn't intended to use it anyway. It was the principle of the matter.

The American had not only managed to strike back at him but had gotten away clean. His security forces had searched the spaceport from one end to the other and found no indication of intruders. The only non-Chinese people nearby were the locals outside the gates cheering the fires.

Oh, how he wanted to order his men to shoot them down. Those scum, laughing at his misfortune. He hungered to see their blood.

But that would be a mistake. He'd lost the spaceport, but if he attacked the Mexican nationals outside the gate, that would turn public opinion around the world against China. That would be bad for the Dragon.

As much as he wanted revenge—and he knew that those bastards outside had been part of this plan—he couldn't take it. At least not here in Mexico.

Forcing himself to calm down, Chen searched the area around him and located his chief security officer. The man stood nearby with a handkerchief over his broken nose, otherwise impassive. He gestured for the man to approach.

"What are the Chinese Navy's disposition around New Zealand?" he asked coldly.

"I will have to check, Ambassador," the man said, his voice sounding odd because of the injury. "In general, it is my understanding that we have a number of small ships in the area, with some larger ones near the island of Nauru."

"What about submarines?"

The man shrugged slightly. "The movement of such vessels is more secretive than the surface units. I will have to check with someone in Beijing to know for certain, but it would be surprising if there were not at least one subsurface unit in the area around New Zealand."

"Do so. Now."

While the man departed to discover the information that he required, Chen thought about his new plan. It entailed serious risks. In some ways, it was akin to reopening the blatant warfare with United States, only adding in the rest of the world.

He was going to have to argue cunningly to take this action, but he intended to see the New Zealand base removed from the control of their enemies. It was likely they had other gates, but this action against the Yucatán spaceport could not go unanswered.

Ten minutes later, his guard returned and bowed slightly. "My sources in Beijing indicate that there are two submarines in the area. One is armed with nuclear weapons and the other with a mixture of those and old-fashioned cruise missiles. I'm given to understand that the conventional weapons are quite powerful."

Weapons of mass destruction were a step too far in this case. All he needed to do was use conventional weapons to deny them the use of that base. The tit-for-tat war with the United States and Humanity Unlimited would notch forward, and they would pay for their insolence.

"Gather our people at the airstrip," he ordered. "We depart as soon as I finish making this call."

As soon as the man was gone, Chen removed his satellite phone from his pocket and dialed a number from memory. The recipient answered on the second ring with a curt grunt.

"This is Chen," he said softly. "I must speak with the master."

There was silence from the other end of the line for a few moments and then another grunt.

Chen allowed his people to drive him to the airstrip as he waited patiently to be passed along. It would not happen quickly, he suspected. This was a power play to show him that he was not in control of his own destiny. Such games were common inside the Dragon, and in China generally.

His guess was proven correct when he was kept on hold for over half an hour. He was already aboard the hypersonic transport by the time someone spoke again from the other end. A different man.

"I have been reviewing the news reports, Jian. It seems that you were unprepared for the American counterstrike."

As gallingly true as that might have been, Chen could never admit such a lapse. "It is my belief that the enemy was already present on the facility, my Lord. It certainly seems as if they had spent some time reconnecting and reactivating the self-destruct equipment."

"That sounds suspiciously like an excuse, old friend. While we had no intention of utilizing the spaceport as such, its loss damages our prestige. How do you propose regaining face under the circumstances?"

Chen smiled. That was the perfect opening to offer his new plan.

"That's quite simple, my lord. They took the spaceport from us, so we should take the New Zealand base from them. We have a number of ships in the area, including a submarine with conventional cruise missiles. I propose that we counterstrike and remove our enemy's access to the universe at large in response to their temerity."

"This Humanity Unlimited seems likely to have access to other gates," the man said with a note of disapproval. "This will not deny them access to that which they already have."

"True, my lord. However, the United States is a lesser partner in this alliance. They only have access through the gates in New Zealand because they have not been informed of other locations on the planet.

"Not only will this hamper the United States, it will make it more likely that further activity will eventually highlight the location of other bases on Earth that we can capture for ourselves."

The line was silent for several long seconds. "Your plan comes with numerous risks. It is completely possible that the situation will spin out of control and China will find itself at war with the rest of the world. While that is a battle we could likely win, I do not believe that the Masters would thank us for handing this planet to them in such poor condition."

"If we do nothing, we will never hand it over to them at all," Chen said, risking disagreement. "The decision is yours, my lord, but I urge you to be bold."

The other man sighed. "So be it, but on your head the results lie. If this plan is successful, you will have somewhat redeemed yourself. If it fails, you will not have another chance to make things right. Choose wisely and execute well."

The call ended without another word, and Chen put his phone away. This plan was very risky, but without bold moves, he would be eliminated from the great game, and that was unacceptable. Let the world burn, so long as he lived.

27

Harry studied the aerial map they'd put together and turned his head to gauge the degree of sunlight in the valley below the hill. It wouldn't be long before the aliens decided to test his defenses. If he wanted to avoid a protracted siege, he needed to set them on their heels fairly quickly.

There was one side of the hill that would be easier for them to climb en masse. It had a path, but there were also several fairly gentle slopes that were amenable to climbing. That was the area in which the Asharim slaves were gathering below.

If Harry had been limited to operating with regular troops, that might be the only area he could utilize to get them down too, leading to a head-to-head fight that would be bloody and protracted. It would be much better to descend where the enemy weren't holding themselves in strength.

To that effect, Krueger had had his specialists run rappelling lines down the steepest part of the hill while it was still dark. They'd cleared out some of the worst obstacles, but there was still plenty for a person to get hung up on, so they couldn't just move down in the darkness. They had to wait for the light.

Now that they could see where they were going, all they needed was a decent distraction to get the aliens looking elsewhere while he moved a force into position to flank them.

The distraction was easy. They had drones in the air that were capable of firing missiles of relatively impressive power. The aliens didn't seem worried about attacks at this time, based on the way they were clustered together. The missiles would be deadly.

"Is everyone ready, Commander?" he asked Krueger over the dedicated command channel.

"We're ready."

"Have the drones launch their payloads into the largest concentrations of the enemy. Try to keep the shots from an altitude where the drones aren't visible from the ground. I'd like to be able to do this again if an opportunity presents itself.

"As soon as you fire, I want all of our long-range shooters to engage any of the enemy still on this side of the hill. Take down anyone that looks like an officer or senior noncom. As soon as we've that done, send the lead teams down the ropes. They'll secure the base of the hill while the rest of us come down."

"Copy that."

They wouldn't be taking all their forces down, and they certainly wouldn't be moving the Volunteers via rappelling. That would be a real mess. They also had to defend the hill, and once they started shooting up the enemy formations, Harry expected the aliens to start boiling around like disturbed ants.

The explosions on the other side of the hill were distant enough that they were just loud booms, but Harry felt the ground shake and could faintly hear screams and shouts wafting up on the breeze.

The dedicated snipers began firing at targets below, their suppressors keeping all but the supersonic crack of the bullets themselves to a bearable level. Clearing out the visible officers and noncoms took less than a minute, so the lead teams were headed down the ropes in short order.

As much as he wanted to be out front for this, Harry knew that he couldn't be. That was Karl Krueger's job, with Rex's competent assistance. He'd secure the beachhead below and start directing the initial deployment based on the plans they'd made a few hours ago.

The aliens hadn't expected to be shot from this distance. That and their shock at the rapid descent of his troops via the ropes kept them from counterattacking in a cohesive manner, putting the aliens at a disadvantage. Krueger's forces reached the bottom of the hill and dispersed to cover the entire area around where the rest of their forces would be congregating, opening fire on any of the alien slaves they could as they moved from cover to cover. Rex took one side while Krueger took the other.

When it came time for him to head down, Harry hooked his D ring around the rope and made certain that his harness was secure. Using heavy gloves to help control his descent and slow him where needed, he made his way down, dodging small shrubs and jutting rocks.

Once he reached the base of the hill, he unhooked from the line and moved forward so that no one behind him would have to worry about running into him.

The fighting was getting heavier as the Asharim slaves advanced and tried to stop his people from expanding into their area of operations. This was where their modern Earth firearms proved decisively that Harry's troops had very little to fear on a case-by-case basis. The black powder rifles couldn't reload with any speed at all.

That still didn't mean that there were no casualties among his people. The man immediately to Harry's right took a hit from a heavy slug fired by one of the black powder rifles and went down hard.

Harry moved to check on the man's condition and perform first aid but saw immediately that the wound was far too serious for him to make a difference. While the man wasn't dead yet, even with body armor, his chest had been caved in. There was no way that Harry could do anything about that.

"Medic!" he shouted, looking over his shoulder at where they should be setting up a makeshift triage area under what cover they could find. Two of them immediately darted toward Harry and the downed man.

Harry started to turn back toward the fighting when he saw Jess unclipping herself from the rappelling line. Someone had given her body armor, but he'd just seen how useless that could be.

With a curse, he started toward her. That was when a large group of aliens came around the base of the hill and engaged his troops guarding that quadrant of the perimeter. They seemingly came out of nowhere, so they engaged quickly and overwhelmed the troops defending the area.

Harry immediately called for reinforcements and raced toward Jess. She was directly in their path, and they'd mow her down if he couldn't get her clear right now.

* * *

Brenda Cabot walked through the massive control center situated on one of the lowest levels of the base. Her base. It rivaled the size of the control room she'd seen at the NASA Johnson Space Center that had guided the space shuttle into orbit back in its day. Actually, it was probably a bit larger.

What had it been like back when it had been fully manned? What had all the people done? What had they monitored? What had been their goal in being here at all?

She wished she could've brought it back online but lacked the requisite computer system. Harry was unlikely to give up any of the ones he had access to. Why would he disable one of his bases just to give her a leg up, after all? She'd just have to make do.

Her phone rang, surprising her. It shouldn't be able to receive a signal this far down without something in the base providing a relay of some kind. However, when she pulled it out of her pocket, it was still dark. Another ring came from her pocket.

Ah, it was the quantum phone they'd given her. She supposed being underground wouldn't be an inhibiting factor for something that was supposed to be able to call someone on the other side of the universe.

"Cabot."

"Miss Cabot, this is Molly Goodwin. Mister Rogers left me his phone, and we have something of a situation and require your assistance."

"What kind of situation and what can I do to help?"

"I don't have a lot of time to explain all the details, but I've just received word that someone has fired a number of missiles at the base I'm standing in," Molly said. "They've also done something to the communications in the area. The only way I can call for assistance is via this phone.

"We need to evacuate the New Zealand base immediately, but the only operational gate in this facility is hardwired so that it can only call Volunteer World, and that's currently a war zone. To get anywhere else, someone will have to call us. We desperately need you to do so."

Brenda headed out of the room at a run. It wasn't far from where she was to the gate rooms.

"What kind of time frame are you looking at? I can have a gate open to your location in a couple of minutes."

"The last word we received before all communication ceased indicated that we had approximately eight minutes. I called you at once. I'd deeply appreciate it if you could hurry."

"Text me the gate address, and I'll get it open as quickly as I can."

She disconnected from the call and dug her radio out of her pocket. "Victor, tell me they you're somewhere near the gate room."

"Not exactly, but I can get there pretty quickly," he answered a few seconds later. "Why?"

Brenda ducked into one of the stairwells and started down toward the gate rooms. "I need you to open a gate right now, because we've got impending visitors that need to get here in a hurry."

"On my way. I'll call you as soon as I get there."

The quantum phone updated with the gate address. Brenda resisted the urge to call Victor back, because it wouldn't do any good if he couldn't enter the code immediately. With twenty Asharim characters, that wasn't the kind of thing that one just remembered.

When she was about thirty seconds away from the gate rooms, Victor called her back. "I'm ready."

She stopped running, took two deep breaths, and slowly read him the gate address. This wasn't the time to make a mistake because she was in a hurry.

"Gate activating," he said as soon as she'd finished. "We have a good connection. There's a bunch of people coming through. A lot of them are in uniform and armed. What do we do if they try to take over?"

"These are allies of our allies," she said. "They asked for our help and we're giving it to them. They're not going to stick a knife in our backs."

She fervently hoped that was true.

By the time she arrived in the gate rooms, over fifty people had made their way from the New Zealand base. Most of them were soldiers of one kind or another, but Brenda saw a sprinkling of civilians in the mix. She also saw Molly Goodwin heading her way with a determined stride.

"Are you going to be able to get your people through in time?" Brenda asked.

The other woman nodded. "We should be able to shut the gate down at least a minute before the missiles arrive on target. It has to be the Chinese, though I'm uncertain why they suddenly felt the need to start a war with New Zealand and the alliance."

As Brenda watched the gate, she saw a new flood of civilians coming through. A number of them were pushing large crates on hand carts or carrying other artifacts. They were probably trying to salvage what they'd found in the base.

"I understand that you're not formally a member of the alliance," Molly said, "and I appreciate your assistance. Trust me when I say that if you want a more formalized relationship with us, I'd wager that you could get it."

The woman looked around. "Good Lord, I thought Harry had said that you only had a temporary base and gate. This looks more like the Mars base."

"Our circumstances have changed," Brenda said smoothly. "We can talk about all of that once we get your people in here and know what's going on. If China—and by China, I mean the Dragon—has decided to go to war, we need to know why and figure out what we can do to counter them fast."

The trio of people in military uniforms came through the gate and waved their arms toward Molly.

"That's it," she said, glancing at her watch. "We're still ninety seconds away from the projected impact, but perhaps we should close the gate down now. If they say we've gotten everyone out, then we've gotten everyone."

"Victor," Brenda called out. "Shut the gate down."

Moments later, the gate closed, leaving the abandoned base in New Zealand to its fate.

Brenda turned toward Molly and gestured for her to walk with her. "The first thing we need to do is get your people situated. We have access to a relatively large base, but the primary services other than life-support are offline. It doesn't have a computer."

The other woman smiled. "Then we just might be able to help you out. A number of those crates over there hold the computer that was left in the New Zealand base. It was sealed in a room and protected from the elements. It may be functional enough to serve your needs.

"I'm certain that the alliance is going to be peeved at me, but I'm willing to gift it to you in exchange for the service you've just performed for us. I feel quite confident that we can find another one someplace out in the universe with your help. If this is useful now, we should use it now."

Brenda smiled. "Molly, I think we're going to get along just fine. We can have some coffee while we wait for news from New Zealand and talk over a more formal alliance."

28

Jess had expected there to be consequences for coming down from the hill while the fighting was still taking place, but she hadn't expected a bunch of alien warriors to break through the lines right where she was coming down the ropes.

Her initial inclination was to haul ass in the other direction, but there were still people coming down from the top of the hill, and they were vulnerable. She wasn't going to see the enemy warriors just tear them apart.

She wasn't stupid enough to come to a battle unarmed, but she wasn't sure exactly how much use her little flechette pistol was going to be. Well, it was better than nothing.

Just the inclination to draw her weapon was enough to send her hand darting down to the holster at her waist. Muscle memory that she hadn't earned quickly drew it and had it lined up on the lead alien.

This was the first good look she'd gotten at an alien species firsthand. The bugger was tall—probably a bit more than two meters—and wide. He wasn't as stout as a heavy-worlder, but he'd be strong. She had no doubt of that.

His skin was the color of pewter and looked rough to the touch. Almost scaly but not quite. He wore what looked to be some kind of leather pants and a rough-spun shirt. He wore a harness holding a number of things that she couldn't identify across his wide chest.

His face had very little in common with humans. While he had two eyes, they were set wider apart than a human's would be, and he had no nose.

Instead, he had a wide mouth with a lot of *very* sharp-looking teeth. She could see them quite clearly because he was screaming at her as he raised what looked like a flintlock rifle that he intended to use as a club.

She took that all in as she was raising her pistol. As soon as it was lined up, she fired a burst into his chest. Neither his harness or his skin proved to be an impediment to the lethal projectiles, and blood flew everywhere as the alien went down.

To say that enraged his companions would've been something of an understatement. Whereas before they seemed to have been looking for any target to take down, now they all focused on her. That was so unfair.

She planted her feet into a wide stance and continued firing short bursts at each of the aliens in turn. They'd get to her before she could possibly take them all out, but it wasn't exactly like she had a choice at this point.

Just as they were about to overwhelm her, someone off to her right fired an automatic weapon made on Earth and cut a number of the aliens down. She didn't have time to see who it was, but she mentally thanked them as she swapped her nearly empty magazine for a fresh one and resumed firing.

Together with the other shooter and a few additional people who joined in, they quickly took out the aliens that had penetrated their lines. Even counting the fight in the sewers just a few days ago, this was easily the grisliest scene she'd ever witnessed. There was blood so dark it was almost black, guts, and other horrible-looking things scattered all around the bodies. And the smell almost made her throw up.

A few of the dying aliens still twitched and groaned. She wondered what she was supposed to do about their suffering. Could her people even perform any kind of surgery on an alien?

"What the *hell* are you doing?" Harry demanded from beside her. "You shouldn't be here."

With her hands trembling slightly, she replaced her partially spent magazine with a fresh one and holstered her weapon. Only then did she turn to face her enraged partner. It must've been him that had been shooting into the aliens, so he'd saved her life. Again.

"I had to be here," she said quietly. "I couldn't just stay up there and watch the fighting."

"Well, coming down here was the wrong thing to do," he growled. "If we didn't have people coming down the ropes, I'd send your ass right back up there. Since you're here, I'm going to put you under guard. Where the hell is Sandra?"

"I left her watching the heavy-worlders. She probably thinks I'm still up there."

Harry cursed under his breath, not quite loud enough for her to make out the words over the fighting around them. "You make me crazy, Jess. What did you think you could do down here?"

While they'd been speaking, several other soldiers had been checking the aliens, including Krueger. He stood up from where he'd been kneeling beside one of the fallen and walked over to them.

"Almost all of them are dead or dying," he said in a matter-of-fact tone. "We don't know anything about their physiology, so wounds of this caliber are beyond our medics. One of them looks like he might make it, though. He took some hits in the legs and his right arm, but we were able to stop the bleeding.

It looks like one of the shots grazed his head, too. Probably knocked him out. He's coming around, so I had my people bind him."

"I need to talk to him," Jess said, forgetting her argument with Harry. "I might be able to get some information from him."

The Navy officer looked skeptical. "In the middle of the battle?"

"It's not exactly in the middle of the battle anymore," she hedged. "The battle is out at your front lines. We're back here and should be safe now, right?"

"As this intrusion has already proven, we can never count on being completely safe," Harry said in a repressive tone. "Still, I suppose it won't hurt to try and see if you can at least understand what he's saying. We're not going to do any in-depth questioning until I move him—and you—back up to the top of the hill though."

She ignored the implied accusation in his tone and walked over to where the alien lay. He looked in pretty bad shape, but he did look as if he was going to live. His eyes were a flat green color that looked completely unnatural but seemed to go well with his skin color. His shoulder-length hair was a deep black and only covered his head. Either his people didn't grow beards or mustaches, or he'd shaved recently.

Making certain to stay clear of his reach—even though several soldiers were holding him down and his hands and legs were bound—Jess waved her hand to catch the alien's distracted attention. He might have the equivalent of a concussion, because he didn't seem like he was completely focused.

"Look at me," she said firmly in the heavy-worlder language. "Do you understand what I'm saying to you?"

The alien blinked in what looked like surprise and then shook his head. "Yes. How can you speak the tongue the Masters use to command us?"

The dichotomy between the headshake and his acknowledgment that he understood her momentarily confused her, but then she realized that she couldn't count on gestures meaning what she expected in an alien society. For him, shaking of the head seemed to be agreement.

"That isn't important," she said. "I have some questions to ask you, but I want to start by telling you that we will do what we can to save your life."

Her words only seemed to confuse him more. "Why would you do that? The wounded are expendable to the Masters." Those last words held a hint of what certainly sounded like bitterness.

Maybe there was an opportunity here after all. "That's not how my people and I work. We fight when we need to fight, but we don't kill those that we can save. I'm sorry that none of your companions are going to survive, but you will."

The alien man grunted. "So that you can torture the secrets of the Masters from me? You shouldn't make it sound as if you're offering me a gift."

She smiled but made certain not to show her teeth. That might have negative implications for his culture. "That's not how we work. What's your name?"

"Lastark," he said after a few seconds.

"Cheer up, Lastark. This might just be your lucky day. If you help us, we might be able to help you get out from under the heels of the Masters."

The alien made a noise that sounded like a chuckle. "No one escapes the Masters. The Masters will continue to rule, and one day they will decide to eliminate your kind. I have no idea why they haven't done so already."

"It's complicated," she said. "We call our species human. What do you call your species?"

"My people are the Peret," he said. "It is our lot to fight for the Masters."

Remembering the head gesture that the alien had used, she shook her head. "They once had other races that fought for them. Humans, similar to myself, but redesigned to be stronger. Have you ever heard of them?"

The alien raised his elbows slightly away from his body. "I have not. Our people have many legends and myths about the Masters and the time before the great collapse, but I do not believe that I have heard of humans ever fighting for the Masters. It seems to me that you've always been fighting against them."

"Do you think you can sit up?" she asked.

He seemed to hesitate for a moment and then shook his head. "I believe so."

"Help him to sit up," she said in English.

"Are you sure that's such a good idea?" Harry asked. "What has he said?"

She felt like slapping her forehead. Of course they hadn't understood anything that she'd said or the alien's answers. Though, interestingly, Krueger didn't share her partner's blank look. Something to explore later.

"I think this will be fine," she said, gesturing for the soldiers to help the alien sit up. She then explained everything she'd learned.

"I think I might be able to get him to cooperate more fully with us," she concluded. "Maybe it would be best if we moved away from the dead bodies."

While she'd spoken with the alien, the remainder of his companions had perished from their wounds. That was ghastly and horrible, but it didn't seem to overly concern the wounded man. That was sad and sick and said something terrible about the Asharim.

"I think that would just emphasize that we just killed all of his friends," Krueger said with a brief headshake. "If he's talking now, I suggest you keep talking. Don't change any of the variables unless there's a purpose to it."

Harry nodded and took a step away from the group. "Commander, I'm leaving Jess in your hands. I've got to get back to the fighting. We've repulsed a number of attacks, and I think it's time for us to go capture a few of the Asharim for ourselves."

With that, her partner walked off. She was pretty sure Harry was still angry with her and that this discussion wasn't over by a long shot, but she was glad to see that he wasn't going to dwell on it at this particular moment.

She needed to consider carefully what she was going to do next. She had her hands on someone familiar with the disposition of forces inside the Asharim city. If she nurtured a relationship with Lastark, it was possible that she could save hundreds of lives over the course of this battle.

Hell, she might be able to end the war without more fighting. If she knew how to open a dialog with the Asharim, it was conceivable that she could negotiate a cease-fire that led to something more permanent. There was no need for the fighting to continue.

Of course, stopping something that had been going on for longer than anyone on this planet had been alive would be difficult. People held grudges. Aliens probably held grudges too. None of that would be easy to work through. But if she didn't at least try, then it certainly wouldn't end without one side absolutely crushing the other.

It was her duty to try and find a less violent conclusion to this problem. If that worked, great. If not, she'd done what she could. She might still come out of this with a number of people willing to talk to her. That had to be worth something.

She refocused her attention on the wounded alien sitting on the bloody ground in front of her. "We've got a lot to talk about and very little time to do so. Let's begin."

29

Q ueen sat with his elbows on his desk and his head in his hands. How had his move gone so wrong? He'd been certain that the Chinese wouldn't dare strike back. For Christ's sake, they hadn't even been using the Yucatán spaceport. It had just been scoring points.

Only that hadn't proven true. The Chinese had retaliated by firing cruise missiles at the ruined alien base in New Zealand. It had been completely destroyed. He had no idea how many people had been inside the thing, but that hadn't slowed those bastards down one little bit.

It wasn't as if the militaries in the area could stand up to them, after all. China—all posturing aside—was the strongest military on the planet. If they wanted to conquer Japan, New Zealand, Australia, South Korea, and the Republic of Nauru, there was nothing anyone could do to stop them, as long as they were willing to pay the price in blood and global condemnation.

And it seemed that they were, at least to the point of making a counterstrike against what he'd ordered done in Mexico.

Of course, now everyone's hair was on fire. Accusations and counteraccusations were flying across the globe, and nations were aligning themselves on one side or the other. The world was closer to war than it had ever been during his lifetime. He'd made a terrible mistake in judging how they would respond.

How could he fix it? What could he do that would change anything?

A rap at his door drew his gaze and ended his introspection. It was Gina Tanner, his personal assistant. Her expression was both sad and grave.

"You have a visitor," she said quietly.

"Not now," he said. "I have to think about what we need to do next."

"I think you can make time for me," George Blankenship, the president of the United States, said as he stepped past Gina. "That will be all, Miss Turner. Make certain that we're not disturbed."

Gina nodded, stepped back out of the office, and closed the door quietly behind herself.

George shook his head. "Dammit, Josh. What the hell did you do? And I mean that in a rhetorical sense, since I know exactly what you did. Why did you do it? What did you think would happen?"

Queen sighed. It was worse than he'd thought. If the president felt the need to come over to see him, then the situation was dire.

"I was just trying to put them back on their heels," he said, rubbing his eyes. "If we let them keep walking all over us, they're not ever going to stop. This game is for keeps, George."

Blankenship sat in one of the chairs in front of the desk. "This isn't a game, Josh. While you might think it is, the consequences are far too significant for playing around.

"The United States has been underestimating and misunderstanding the goals and intentions of China for as long as we've had relations with them. There's something to the fact that we just don't think alike. It's happened time and time again, where one side or the other thinks they've understood what the other will do and then found out that they were completely and utterly wrong. This situation is an excellent case in point."

The two of them sat in silence for a few seconds before Queen spoke. "What should I have done? What can I do?"

"You're not going to like hearing the answers to those questions," the president said heavily. "The first thing you *shouldn't* have done is attacked them. For God's sake, you'd just arranged a public cease-fire. Sure, they'd have been maneuvering behind the scenes, but the blatant military action would've been off the table.

"When you attacked the spaceport, what did you really gain us? Nothing. It was just posturing because your opponent had pulled something off that you hated. You couldn't stand the thought of them getting ahead in this game that you're playing."

Blankenship rubbed his forehead with the back of his hand. "You got into a pissing contest with Chen, but the man wasn't willing to take what you did lying down. Worse, he convinced his government to back him with solid retribution.

"You, on the other hand, didn't bother to get me to back you at all. You do realize that military action requires my input, right? I gave you permission to use some of the forces but not for combat with China. I authorized off-world action against aliens.

"Now we find ourselves in a very difficult situation. One that I can get us out of, but the price is going to be significant."

Queen set up abruptly at that last sentence. There was a way out. Even if it was painful, that was better than being trapped in a shooting war.

"What is it? What do we have to do?"

Blankenship stared deep into his eyes for a few seconds. "We don't have to do anything. *I* have to do something you won't like and that I wish I didn't have to do. Josh, I'm going to need your letter of resignation on my desk within the hour."

Queen blinked. "What?"

The president stood. "We've known each other a long time, so I came to tell you in person that the price to put this genie back in the bottle is your job. The Chinese see you as personally responsible for what happened at the Yucatán spaceport. For once, they actually got it right. It was you.

"They've demanded that I fire you and, for the sake of our country, I'm going to do so. I don't really have a choice. You abused my trust and I'd probably have fired you anyway, but with this being the only chance we have to stop this from growing into something uncontrollable, I'm afraid that you're going to have to go."

Queen knew he should've said something, but his mind was blank. He just sat there with his mouth halfway open and watched as the president walked out of his office and closed the door behind him with a final-sounding click.

Fired? He was the damned secretary of state. He had too much work to do for the United States to be sidelined like this. Was that what the Chinese really wanted? They knew how dangerous he was and had to get him out of the picture?

That had to be it. There was no other answer.

He couldn't let them get away with this. He had to do something to stop them.

Then he slumped back into his seat. He'd been fired. There wasn't anything that he *could* do.

But maybe—just maybe—there was something still within his power that would make a difference. It was far from optimal, but it was something that he'd been working out the logistics of for a while.

The president would have his resignation on his desk in an hour as ordered. That gave him at most half an hour to set his final gambit into motion. He retrieved a phone number from his desk, picked up his phone, and started dialing.

The president was going to be seriously pissed, but what was he going to do? Fire him twice? Screw the bastard. This was the last chance he had to make one final move in the game, and he was going to take it.

* * *

HARRY TRIED his very best not to stomp as he walked away from Jess. How could she be so irresponsible? She could've been killed! And in spite of his good intentions, he found himself stomping.

He sighed as he resumed his oversight of what was going on through the drone feeds. Nothing he did would change how Jess behaved. Nothing at all. He might as well just get used to it.

What he needed to focus his attention on right now was stopping the enemy, who was trying to regroup. His surprise attack had sown chaos among the forces arrayed against them, and their quick descent had formed a bridgehead that broke the will of a good number of the aliens on this side of the hill.

Now he needed to capitalize on that and send them packing. If he continued to hit the forces on this side as hard as he could, they'd run. Well, any humans in their place would run. He probably shouldn't make that assumption about aliens doing the same.

"Snipers," he said over the general net. "Increase rate of fire. I want you to break the forces trying to take back the bottom of the hill near our forces. Get them off our necks so that we can turn our attention to the main group.

"Firebase Alpha, start dropping mortar rounds into the middle of the forces on the other side of the hill. Soften them up or send them packing, I don't care which."

As the two groups acknowledged his commands and started carrying out the attacks he'd ordered, Harry gestured for Rex and Gunnery Sergeant Danvers to join him. Once they were huddled down beside him, he gestured off toward the forest.

"The drones still show our Asharim friends sitting out there. If we can get the group of aliens around us to move, I want two teams ready to go. Jess says that one of the Asharim would be useful to question, and I'd like to oblige her, even if she has pissed me off."

Rex laughed. "I saw this coming a mile off, Boss. You should've too. She's going to do what she thinks is best, and the only way to keep her on the sidelines is to chain her up. I'm not even sure how well that would work, now that I think about it."

Harry sighed and shook his head. "You're probably right, but I'm still going to keep trying. Be ready to move out as soon as we have the opportunity. Rex, I want your group to scout ahead and make sure that the rest of us come through clean. We don't need to run into an ambush."

"You got it. It seems like the herd is thinning out a bit, so I should be able to get moving in about five minutes at this rate."

"Do you think we'll be able to capture one of the head honchos?" Danvers asked. "Judging from what we can see via the drones, they're pretty well protected. It's going to take most of the people we bring along to deal with the escort those aliens have protecting them. We might want to bring a little extra."

Harry shook his head. "We're going to have to move fast. They have people in the woods watching the hill, so they're going to see us coming. The only way we're going to corral them is to strike fast. We can always call for backup once we have them cut off from the city.

"I don't want to take too many people away from this fight, because it might still end up being a really ugly affair, but if we ever want to settle this, we're going to have to get our hands on one of the Asharim."

He waited almost five minutes and then decided that the path across the plain was as clear as it was going to get. With hand signals, he got both teams into motion and made certain that they had people on both flanks to catch any stray aliens as they raced across the grassland.

The aliens they'd been fighting seemed disinclined to attack a force as organized as his. That suited him fine. It took ten minutes to cross the field and get to the tree line.

Just as they were entering the trees, the woman overseeing drone operations called him over his radio. "The alien leadership is on the move. It looks like they're headed off to your right under heavy guard, while the remainder of their protective forces is moving into the forest to engage you. Should we intervene?"

"If you can drop some mortar rounds into the forest ahead of us, that would be good. We'll hold position for sixty seconds and then cut off to our right. We're going to need you to vector us in."

"Copy that. Stand by."

Harry stopped both teams and informed them that mortar rounds were on the way. Less than twenty seconds later, he heard the unmistakable whistling sound of incoming munitions, followed by some pretty intense explosions ahead of them.

The mortar teams at Firebase Alpha would have the benefit of using the drones as forward observers. They'd continue to chew up the area where the enemy was while Harry took his forces around and tried to intercept the Asharim before they broke contact.

"Take us around to the right," he ordered Rex and Danvers.

With the enemy unable to see their changing course, they might be able to skirt even the outliers of the reaction force coming after them. That would be the best option. It wasn't likely, but he'd take it if he got it.

There was some small-arms fire off to their left as some of his troops engaged a few of the aliens. None of his people seemed to have been hit by the few black powder shots that came their way, and within three minutes, his people had broken away from the enemy.

"I've detached a squad to interdict our pursuit," Danvers said as they ran through the woods, jumping over fallen debris and dodging around bushes and trees very similar in form to what they'd find on Earth, even if the exact plants were different.

Before Harry could respond, he got another call from the drone operator. "We've got incoming to your position," she said. "New forces coming out of the city. Looks like three airborne units. Something open topped. Must be some kind of antigravity, because I don't see any engines."

"Are they headed for our position or to pick up the Asharim fleeing the area?" he asked.

"I can't tell. Could be either."

There was only one way to find out. "Everyone advance at full speed and be ready to fight airborne units with high-tech weapons," Harry ordered. "It looks like we've got company."

30

Brenda sat in one of the base's conference rooms and listened as people on the ground in New Zealand reported the destruction of the base there. They weren't speaking to her, but Molly Goodwin was kind enough to allow her to listen in.

The weapons had been nonnuclear, but that hardly mattered. The cruise missiles had smashed into the mesa one after another, each one digging deeper than the last before it exploded. They wouldn't know if the lowest levels survived the attack for quite some time, but Brenda privately bet they hadn't.

The only way to find out faster would be to try the gate there. She hadn't suggested that yet but would bring it up when the time seemed right. She expected it was destroyed, but there was only one way to be sure.

The pictures of the destruction didn't leave much room for anything to still be intact. No, far better to count the base lost. Frankly, in as bad a shape as it had been in, that might actually save the alliance a lot of work. They'd been trying to decipher what amounted to wreckage. Now they could focus their attention on other locations that might prove a lot more productive.

Joining the alliance had proven a lot simpler than Brenda had anticipated. It turned out that she and her people had a lot to bring to the table. Yes, they'd been helping Humanity Unlimited with their know-how, but her people still had far more intimate knowledge of the Asharim technology and their history than Harry or Jess at this point.

Speaking of them, while Harry hadn't answered his phone, Jess had. It turned out that Molly was correct in her assumption that they were in the middle of pitched battle on Volunteer World. Going through the tunnel from the New Zealand base would have been the wrong call. They might not have gotten everyone out alive. With the assurance that Jess would call her back once things were settled, Brenda had let the other woman be about her business.

And now that the report on the devastation in New Zealand was complete, things were shaping up to get pretty ugly as both the New Zealand and Australian navies were confronting their Chinese counterparts and ordering them out of the area with the other option being their destruction.

That was a lot more restraint than Brenda would've had. She'd have just started shooting. It was probably a good thing that she wasn't in charge.

Part of her was angry enough at how those heavy-worlders were manipulating the Chinese people to be in favor of shooting. Unfortunately, the people on those ships wouldn't be heavy-worlders. They were witless dupes, thinking they were following the orders of their duly appointed superiors, when almost certainly the heavy-worlders had overthrown the rightful Chinese government.

Now that her people were members of the alliance, she needed to guide this burgeoning confrontation into something a bit more constructive. Somehow.

Molly rested her head in her hands once the call was over. "I can't believe the bloody bastards actually started shooting. I get it. They were mad at the Americans for blowing up their shiny new spaceport, but the Americans were never a large partner in the alliance. They're going to be ejected now, which is going to cause all kinds of unanticipated complications. Idiots."

"You sound like this is your personal problem," Brenda said as she reached out and squeezed the other woman's shoulder. "This is what those governments of yours actually have to negotiate and figure out how to respond to. You're just the representative on the ground."

"Now that the base is destroyed, I'm not exactly sure what I'm supposed to be representing."

Brenda laughed. "That's easy. You're the diplomatic envoy to the Families. We'll do what we can to help you understand the Asharim and their technology, and you're our point of contact. Almost an ambassador, really. You should push for that title."

"God forbid," the other woman said fervently. "I absolutely do *not* want to be responsible for negotiating anything. I think I might just retire to a small sheep station in the middle of nowhere."

They sat in silence for the next several minutes. Brenda was about to invite the other woman to take a tour of her new base when her phone rang. They'd set up a repeater so that they could make and receive regular cellular calls, though with some encryption and other tricks to hide exactly where they were. A quick check showed it was her least favorite person in the world: Secretary of State Josh Queen.

She considered not answering but sighed. She'd end up dealing with the bastard one way or the other.

"Are you happy now?" she asked in a tone that she hoped conveyed exactly how displeased she was.

"We don't have time for this," he almost snarled. "I made a mistake and

I'm going to pay for it. Hell, I'm already paying for it. The president wants my resignation on his desk shortly."

"Good!" Brenda said. "That's the first piece of positive news I've heard recently."

"Ha ha," the man said in a flat tone. "Like I said, I don't have time for this verbal sparring. If I'm going to make the deadline that the president set, I'm going to have to type up that resignation letter and leave here in twenty-five minutes or so. The question is, do you want me to do something for you before I go?"

Brenda frowned. What the hell did that mean? "Go on," she said cautiously.

"I've been queuing up a number of things since this whole alien affair started to offer in exchange for technology. Things like personnel with specialized know-how, money to put together real research teams, and equipment that might be useful in some way. All approved by the president ahead of time, mind you, if I decided to proceed.

"We're talking thousands of people from universities, high-tech firms that can be paid to subcontract and assist, and other organizations that have the scientific and educational know-how to help decipher that frozen planet and so many of the other things you found. All of that can be yours in exchange for one thing."

Dreading the answer, she nonetheless asked the question he was waiting for. "And what exactly do you want in exchange for that assistance?"

"Why, the same thing that every government employee wants when he leaves Washington: a cushy job. If you bring me into your organization with a contract that's good for five years at top-tier pay, then all of this can be yours. But only if you decide you want it right here and right now."

Well hell.

"The administration will never stand for that," she said. "They'll see it for exactly what it is and cancel everything. It's illegal."

"You underestimate their hunger for this new tech. I'm exchanging all of these things for the purpose of getting the United States all the current nonmilitary data you've gathered. It isn't as if we've received anything from Humanity Unlimited at this point, and we'll get kicked out of that damned alliance for sure. This is their only way to get what they want. They'll let it stand."

Inviting him into her organization was the absolute last thing she wanted to do, but he was right that they could use those resources. Was it really worth it?

Then she smiled. "I hope you can type fast, because I have a few conditions of my own. Everything that my organization has in its possession at this time remains in our possession—full ownership, mind you—no matter where it's located or what it is. You either agree to that, or no deal. Also, I get to decide which information and tech is suitable to share and when we share it."

"That's no skin off my nose," he said with a sniff. "Deal. Give me a fax number, and I'll have the contract to you in five minutes. Read fast, sign it, and get it back to me so I can get it certified and filed. And remember, you're on the clock."

As soon as she gave him the number to the fax machine in her old base in Washington, Queen hung up.

Brenda really didn't want to have to deal with that man, but getting title to the base they'd just found would be worth almost any level of inconvenience.

Oh, the US government would scream when they finally found out, but she'd have an actual agreement in hand from their secretary of state. If they tried to undo it at some later date, there'd be hell to pay with other countries that worried their deals would be unilaterally canceled as well.

And it wasn't as if she had to admit that she had possession of the base up front. She could append a general list of facilities and equipment that they had in their possession. It didn't even have to list everything out and could be very general. "Asharim-style base with all equipment in US wilderness, concealed facility underneath American city, and the appropriate number of residential buildings with facilities."

That was going to make somebody start demanding to know where exactly their facilities were located, but she could say that wasn't required information. This was proof that they had possession of these facilities when the deal was signed. She'd make certain to have Queen sign off on the addendum so that there would be no questions later about whether or not she had revealed the existence of this base when the deal was signed.

She'd send them select images so that the bases and facilities could be positively identified later, just as an insurance policy. She'd also list the sarcophagus while not mentioning all its capabilities. Taken all together, that would get Karl off the hook for concealing things, too.

In fact, she'd appoint him as the verifier of their possessions with a clause that he couldn't reveal the details beyond confirming that the Families had them.

Since this was a deal with the United States government, they were granting her ownership and possession of the base in their own federal lands. She imagined Congress might scream if they had a clue, but those idiots hadn't had any real power in decades. All they did was beat their chests about their ideology and get embroiled in whatever corruption was handy.

Yes, this was going to be worth it, even if she had to accept that Queen would be in her face for five years. She could find some way to shunt him off into doing something that wasn't going to be dangerous or give him information that he shouldn't have. She'd just have to deal with the ass whenever he complained. Compared against having title to this base, it was completely worth it.

All of those thoughts had gone through her head in just a few seconds. Molly Goodwin was still staring at her with narrowed eyes.

"Was that who I thought it was?" the other woman asked. "Was it that idiot Queen?"

Brenda nodded even as she rose to her feet. "It was. It looks like he's being fired, but true to form, he's going to stick a knife in the president's back and give us a lot of resources in exchange for the nonmilitary information and technology we possess.

"The bad news is that I have to give him a job for five years. The good news is that whatever we have in our possession as of right this moment we get to keep, including this base. That makes it worthwhile."

"What a nightmare," Molly commiserated. "I can barely stand speaking to his subordinates. You have to deal with him for *five years*? I'd hang myself."

"We all have our crosses to bear," Brenda said as she headed for the door. "If you'd do me the favor of coming with me to witness me signing this, then the alliance will be in on the details of what we've agreed to and can stand witness to the fact that I had this base before I signed the agreement."

Molly stood and stepped out into the corridor behind her. "Of course. After all you've done for us, it's the least I can do. I find it rather particular that since Queen did something that's going to get the United States thrown out of the alliance, their only access to Asharim technology is going to be through you and Harry's people.

"The United States used to be so powerful, and now they've gotten themselves into a position where they have no influence on events that are currently taking place, unless they work with a group that's been infiltrating them since before their government was formed and what amounts to a rebel company."

"If there's one thing I've learned in life, it's never to underestimate how ironic things can get," Brenda said. "They can always get stranger. In fact, it might be best if I show you one of our secret bits of technology that I'm going to list on the addendum but not explain in any detail to the US government.

"You remember how Jess was critically injured in the fighting at the base in France? When we recovered her, she was in a healing unit shaped like a sarcophagus. We found out after the fact that it does so much more."

The two of them continued toward the gate room as she explained. If the woman was amenable, Brenda would offer her a session inside the sarcophagus. It would be good if someone else in the alliance really understood what the Families had to offer.

If Queen ever found out exactly how she'd used the deal to her advantage, he was going to be super pissed. Maybe she should tell him herself. Or just let him figure it out on his own. Either way, that aspect of the situation was going to be delicious.

31

Jess had to restrain herself from questioning the captured alien while the medics moved him to the area near the ropes. Exactly how they were going to get him up the hill was beyond her, and she didn't want to interfere and cause an accident.

At least Harry's forces had pushed the aliens back so that no one was shooting at them.

She felt relatively confident that he was going to tear a strip off of her as soon as this was all done. Still, it had been worth it. They had someone that she could question. Perhaps the prisoner wasn't as good as an Asharim would be, but she still wasn't ruling out getting her hands on one of the aliens. It could still happen.

The medics worked as quickly as they could and got Lastark on a tethered stretcher and up to the top of the hill in about fifteen minutes. While they were pulling him up, several other men and women were helping her follow along behind.

Her plans of following the wounded alien to wherever they were taking him were shattered when an extremely angry Sandra confronted her.

"You snuck off!" the other woman almost shouted, waving her finger in Jess's face. "You intentionally distracted me and then snuck off so you could go down and join in the fighting. If you weren't my friend, I would punch you in the face right now."

Jess had no doubt that Sandra could do exactly what she was threatening. The woman was a warrior and Jess was not, even counting the weird alien training in her brain. None of that seemed to contain any hand-to-hand muscle memory.

"I'm sorry," Jess said raising her hands defensively. "I shouldn't have done it. I won't do it again. I promise."

Sandra's eyes narrowed even further. "I don't believe you. I think you're going to string me along until the next time it suits you to do whatever you want.

"Dammit, Jess. You're the leader of the entire company. If you die, everything we're doing could go up in flames. You need to figure out that you're important to the rest of us as well. Seriously, how could you do these things? What were you thinking?"

Jess shrugged slightly. "I'm not really sure. I didn't set out to ditch you. I just saw all the fighting going on down there, and I felt like I had to be there too."

Sandra poked Jess in the chest. Hard. "And that's the reason I can't take my eyes off you. You're going to see something shiny, and then you'll be off to do whatever idiocy you think is more important than protecting your own life.

"For Christ's sake, you almost died in France. If Nathan Bennett hadn't stuck you into that sarcophagus, you'd have bled out."

Jess rubbed the spot on her chest where Sandra had poked her. "What exactly do you want me to do, Sandra? What can I do that will make you happy?"

"Happy? You could make me happy by trotting your cute little ass right back through the gate and going to *Freedom Express*. I don't expect that to happen, mind you, but anything less isn't going to make me happy. I don't suppose I can guilt trip you into doing it, can I?"

"Probably not, but I promise that I'll stay up here until Harry says I can go down. I'm not going to run off. You can stand right here and watch me."

"Don't think I won't," the sniper said grumpily. "You've obviously lost your freaking mind. There's no way I am taking my eyes off you until we're clear of this planet. Thankfully, it looks like the fighting is winding down.

"Once we secure the area around this hill, we can start focusing our attention on the Asharim city. And don't think for one second that I'm going to let you go along with the expedition to take the city and those gates. Not going to happen."

She started to open her mouth to argue, but Harry's voice came over the bud in her ear. "All units, attention. Our spotters indicate that we have hostile aircraft inbound. They look like atmosphere-only antigravity cars.

"I want everyone to take cover immediately. Do we have any troops with antiaircraft capability? Respond on this channel."

Before anyone could answer, Sandra had Jess by her elbow and was steering her toward the cave. "We're done here. Back inside you go."

Jess yanked her arm back. "I'll get under cover, but I'm not leaving this hill until the fighting is over. We've got troops that can take out those ships. Hell, we're probably not the targets anyway. It's going to be the troops on the ground."

Sandra looked as if she just wanted to throw her over her shoulder and take her off to the cave anyway but stood there grinding her teeth for a moment before shoving Jess toward a large outcropping.

"You make me crazy. Get behind this rock where I've set up my sniper's nest. If I think you're going to run, I'll taze you. Is that clear?"

As much as she wanted a better view of what was going on down below, Jess knew that was folly. The enemy was going to be shooting at them with either flechettes or something else high tech. Being in the sights of someone like that was not a recipe for long-term survival.

As she crouched behind the rock, Jess started scanning the sky toward the city. She saw something that might be birds or perhaps aircraft at a great distance. She wasn't sure.

"How can they have advanced technology?" she asked. "If they had access to something like that, they should've destroyed the Volunteers already. This makes no sense."

"When someone is shooting at you, you'd be much better off ducking and fighting back than trying to figure out what you got wrong. There'll always be time for that later."

As she was speaking, Sandra had gotten her sniper rifle up onto the rocks and was using the stone as a support while she swiveled the weapon and looked through the sight.

"There they are," she said slowly. "Three vehicles, open topped and flying along just like they were airplanes. No wings, and I don't see any pylons with heavy weapons. It's a bit too far to see what the occupants are carrying. Settle down while they get closer. It's time to see exactly what the Asharim are bringing to the party."

* * *

CHEN WAS STILL in the air when he got word of the successful strike on the New Zealand base. Rather, his senior guard got it from his own contacts in Beijing. Satellite images indicated a very high probability that the base had been completely destroyed.

Excellent. That denied the enemy access to at least one gate that was far too close to the shores of his home country. There was nothing he could do about the ones off planet. At least not until such time as he had access to a gate himself.

While the ship China had sent to Mars would still take weeks to get there, the outcome of that mission was certain. If the American was stupid enough to send one of his little armed ships against it, he'd find out what kind of weapons the Dragon still had at its disposal.

For the moment, Chen would continue to focus his attention on events here on Earth. There would be more fallout from the attack on New Zealand. He didn't believe the alliance would actually go to war with China over the incursion, but he'd been wrong before.

If they did, the fighting would be brief. All of the nations involved might have a decent level of technology, but they didn't have very many ships. China could swamp them with numbers.

And it wasn't like the old days. China was a true superpower now, with all of the sophisticated weapons that anyone else had at their disposal. Of course, they'd stolen most of the technology from the United States, but they still had it.

America was in decline now. The corrupt oligarchy that they called Congress had defunded the military and neutered it to the point where it wasn't capable of fending off a war with even the false face of China. If they added in the weapons that the Dragon had access to, the fighting would be over even more quickly.

His phone rang with a number that he didn't recognize.

"Chen."

"This is Hyde," a familiar voice said. "Congratulations on your strike. It seems to have borne fruit."

Arthur Hyde was the American-born member of the Dragon that he'd met just a few days ago. The one that was overseeing operations inside the United States.

"Mr. Hyde," Chen said, easing back to relax in his seat. "I hadn't expected to hear from you so quickly. What news do you have for me?"

"My spies inside the White House indicate that President Blankenship has asked for and received Secretary of State Queen's resignation."

Chen allowed himself a dark chuckle. The irritating man that had decided to stand up to him was now thrust out of his seat of power in disgrace. Perfect.

"Excellent news. Do we have word who will replace him?"

He was certain that it would be one of the assistant secretaries of state, but it could be any one of the three. Some would be easier to deal with than others.

Darryl Dickman would be the worst possible outcome. He was just as arrogant and stubborn as Queen, only less polished and more impulsive. Lana Bohannon would be his preference. She was cautious and tentative. He could bully her.

That made the most likely possibility Phillip Judge. He wouldn't be a pushover and could negotiate in a give-and-take situation.

"There's no word for certain at this point, but my money is on Phillip Judge," Hyde said. "He's got the best set of qualities for the job. But that's not really the reason that I called you."

Chen raised an eyebrow even though the other man couldn't see him. "Oh? What else is happening?"

"In between the time that Blankenship asked for Queen's resignation and the time he delivered it, Queen initiated a number of actions. I don't believe that the US is aware of them yet, but something is going on."

"Do you have any idea what? Even if you don't know the full scope of the action, can you give me an example?"

"A good bit of money has been paid to at least three major universities in the form of significant grants. Those call for hundreds of reputable scientists being reassigned to some secret project. Probably ten times that many graduate students are accompanying them. Nondisclosure agreements have already been signed, and the people are disappearing even as we speak.

"We're trying to keep track of them, but it's not certain that we'll be able to do so. Someone is taking a lot of care to make certain that no one follows them to their ultimate destination. I don't know precisely what that means, but it's probably not good for us."

"And you say that there are a number of other suspicious activities?" Chen asked, his brow furrowed as he considered what the man was telling him.

"I believe that there are, but I have no information to be sure. There is other money being relocated from the Department of State and some special accounts that Queen had access to. Encrypted orders have gone out to a number of military units as well. As of yet, with everything being done so quietly, I'm uncertain exactly what is taking place."

"Find out as much as you can as quickly as you can," Chen ordered. "It sounds as if that pathetic man is making one last play. I need to know where those scientists are going. Most likely, he's loaning them to Rogers. If so, I'm not that concerned.

"What I *am* concerned about are surprises that come from unexpected quarters. We still believe that there is at least one player we haven't identified in this grand game. That former FBI agent that was on their most wanted list. Cabot. The one we believe that stole some Asharim technology.

"We still need to know who she is and who she represents. The Americans no longer are searching for her, which means that they've made some kind of deal. If they'd captured her, we'd have heard, so there's still something happening there. If these orders revolve around her and those who she works for, I need to know immediately."

"I'll keep you informed," Hyde said. With that, the man disconnected.

Chen put his phone away, frowning at the unexpected news. Just when he'd thought that he had the upper hand, something new was taking shape. He didn't like it. He had to get to the bottom of it as quickly as possible so he could stop it now.

32

H arry moved his troops through the dark forest and to the tree line on the other side. He knew approximately where the edge of the forest would be simply because he'd watched hours of drone footage overnight.

Once they were in place, everyone spread out and began looking for the incoming aircraft, if aircraft was even the right word. For all he knew, these could be anything from military strike craft to civilian ships appropriated for use in battle. They knew far too little of the Asharim and their current circumstances to even guess.

"Should I try to interdict the Asharim battle commanders before they get away?" Rex asked over the command circuit.

"Negative. I don't want you caught out in the open. Let them go."

"It's possible those ships are coming in to pick them up."

Harry considered that and slowly nodded to himself. "Probably. If so, we won't have to deal with strafing runs. I'd much rather have the Asharim get away than use some type of super weapon on us."

The drones were still keeping an eye on the incoming aircraft and, as they got closer, he was able to determine more about them. As indicated, they were open topped, but once they became clearer in the drone's view, he was able to see that there were no dedicated hardware mounting points.

They wouldn't be dropping bombs then. Not unless somebody inside the damned things flew over them and dropped something over the side. Which, he admitted to himself, was still possible.

One of the aircraft began dipping lower in an obvious bid to meet up with the fleeing Asharim. Rex had been right. This was a rescue mission.

The other two aircraft were coming toward where Harry was hiding. Well, not specifically toward him. As they split apart, it became obvious they were bracketing the explosions in the woods. They didn't know specifically where he or his people were.

The video feed showed that the craft were occupied by a mixture of Asharim and the slave race that had been fighting just below the hill. It looked as if two of the Asharim were piloting the craft and the rest of the occupants were warriors carrying what certainly appeared to be Asharim-designed flechette weapons.

So much for just having to face black powder rifles.

"It looks like we're going to be dealing with some flechette weapons," he said over the channel dedicated to the two teams. "We've got one of the aircraft heading toward us, and the other one is circling around where the mortars struck inside the forest."

With that, he changed channels on his radio to talk to the snipers. "Sandra, what's your status?"

"I've got them in my sights," she said. "The range is ridiculously long, but I might be able to get a hit if I empty my magazine."

"How about the aircraft on your left? It's the one going on the far side of the mortar impact zone from us. It's possible it will overfly the forest and try to come up behind us when we engage the other one."

She was quiet for a moment. "If they do that, they'll be in a better position for me to give them a couple of rounds. Are you sure you can take the other aircraft? We don't know what makes these things tick."

"We're about to find out. Fire when you're ready, but try to let them get as close as you can. There are two Asharim piloting the damn thing. If you take them out, I'll bet it crashes."

"Copy that, Boss."

With his orders given, he settled in. The aliens must've spotted something, because they opened fire. The range was still long for his weapons, but it didn't look like they were firing at his people anyway. It was possible that they'd seen some of their comrades and mistaken them for his troops.

It was obvious that the alien slaves wielding the flechette weapons didn't have any skill with them. They opened fire at too great a distance and seemed unfamiliar with the process of reloading them.

In fact, they seem so unfamiliar with what to expect that more than one of them dropped the weapons as soon as they squeezed their triggers, shocked expressions on their faces.

This was obviously a scratch force brought together because of the advanced—comparatively speaking—weapons that his people had brought to the party. In any case, both his own troops and US military Special Forces were far better trained, and he began to feel a little bit more hopeful that they'd come out of this fight on top.

He watched the approach of the air car—that's what he'd decided to call them—through the short-ranged scope of his weapon. Second by second, the vehicle grew closer to their position and began reducing altitude in small dips and jerks.

Personally, he'd have preferred a smooth descent, but it was obvious the pilots were also somewhat unfamiliar with their craft. Oh, they knew enough to fly them, but they didn't have true skill with the controls or flying in general.

When he was confident that they were within range of his weapons, he gave the signal over the channel to his teams. "Target the pilots and fire for effect."

As soon as he finished saying those words, the woods echoed with the sound of suppressed shots ringing out. He added his bullets to the hail rising to meet their enemy and saw the short windscreen that protected the pilots from the air in front of them crack and divot as a few lucky shots struck them.

The material was tough and protected the pilots from the incoming fire but not their own reactions to it. One of the pilots must've done something epically bad, because the air car flipped over, dumping all of the troops in the back out. They fell screaming to their deaths.

"Well, sucks to be them," Gunnery Sergeant Danvers said with a grunt.

"Sure as hell does," he agreed.

The pilots were strapped in and didn't fall, but their recovery from the unexpected roll once more highlighted their inexperience. When they finally leveled their craft, it was dangerously close to the trees. And to Harry's people.

One of his men, who was equipped with a grenade launcher, fired a round into the bottom of the craft as it passed overhead. The explosion and resulting shower of debris were too far away to be dangerous to them, but the air car lost all lift immediately and crashed into the trees somewhere behind them.

Harry was about to ask what the status of the other air car was when it came barreling overhead from behind them, completely out of control, and crashed into the open field in front of them. It wasn't a pretty sight as bodies flew from the wreckage while it skidded sideways and began flipping over, instantly disintegrating.

"Good work, Sandra," he said over the radio. "What's the status of the other vehicle? If we hurry, can we ambush the alien leadership before they get away?"

"Afraid not," his sniper said. "They've already taken off and headed back toward the city. I tried to take them out, but none of my shots hit. We're going to have to do this the hard way."

It looked like they were going to have to invade the city after all. So much for taking the easy way out.

* * *

BRENDA COMPLETED her addendum to the agreement she'd made with Queen and sent it back to him. Twenty minutes from the time he'd called her, she had a signed agreement with the United States of America in her hot little hands. One that guaranteed her possession of the base she'd found.

Of course, he also had an agreement in his greasy hands that meant she had to start handing over some of the tech and know-how to them. Not any of the gates or weapons tech, but it still soured her stomach a little.

Well, it was no different than the agreement the US had with Humanity

Unlimited, but the Families actually had enough data to get them started doing something.

She also had several phone numbers and an assurance that various people would be contacting her in the next few days to fulfil the agreement from Queen's end. He also assured her that he'd file his copy with his people formalizing the event.

To make certain that none of the little details got lost, she sent a copy of the agreement back to the base in France. From there, it would be couriered to New Zealand to make absolutely certain everyone had copies of what these documents said.

Since the alliance had not yet formally expelled the United States, the US government would get a copy of the agreement from that end as well. That meant that whoever replaced Queen wouldn't be able to back out.

Hell, just to be thorough, she should probably make certain that Harry sent a copy to the United Nations. That would make getting out of this deal really, really difficult.

Then she'd convince Molly to try the sarcophagus out. Brenda had explained what would happen, but she wasn't sure the other woman had believed her. She'd find out when she woke up in a few hours.

This would really bind the Families to the alliance. She'd also share everything she passed to the US with them, adding in other tech and historical details that the US couldn't be trusted with.

With all that done, she returned to the Virginia base. She cleared one of the gate rooms and had Victor dial the base in New Zealand.

The gate activated, which showed that the receiving end was intact and functional, but there was only a pocket of space on the other end. It looked like the ceiling to the gate room there had collapsed.

The New Zealand base was a total loss, though with a little bit of work, they might be able to extract the last gate and set it up somewhere else. Honestly, that was almost all that they'd found in the base that was worth recovering, unless the computer system proved functional. She hoped it did, because that would give her a fully operational base that would turn Harry green with envy.

Brenda waved Victor to close the gate and then had him dial Volunteer World. She knew there was a battle taking place, but she should be safe enough inside the caves. She needed to interface with Jess and find out how her people could assist in the fighting there.

Once the gate cleared, she made her way through and found out that Jess wasn't in the caves. On the crown of the hill, she spotted Jess standing next to Sandra Dean, both women beside a rock outcropping.

"How's it going?" she asked the blonde scientist as she walked up.

"It looks like we've won the battle, but the war still up in the air," Jess said as she turned toward her.

"Perhaps a little bit better than that," Sandra said grudgingly as she put her rifle away. "We've routed the forces around the hill, and they're retreating. We took out a couple of aircraft that the Asharim sent out, but a third one picked up their leadership and took them back into the city.

"At this point, the best we can do is bring the Volunteers in, along with whatever other troops we can find, and push forward. If we're going to take the gates inside that city away from the Asharim, it's going to take blood, sweat, and tears."

Brenda looked at the rotting city in the distance. "Fighting is never pretty. Is Commander Krueger okay?"

Jess frowned a little at that but nodded. "He's busy, but he came through fine."

She relaxed a little at that and changed the subject before the other woman could follow up. "I've got a little good news on my end, though some bad, too."

She filled the two women in on the deal she'd made with Queen.

"It sure seems like you got the crappy end of the deal," Sandra said with a genuine laugh. "You might get a good bit out of it, but you've got to work with Queen for *five years*? Sucks to be you."

"Nothing worthwhile ever comes without some pain," Brenda agreed. "It also sucks that the New Zealand base is gone, though it's certainly probable that we can recover the gate if we dig down and disassemble it."

She looked around. "Weren't you hosting a couple of heavy-worlders? Where are they at?"

Jess frowned and began looking around. "I'm not sure. Sandra was watching them before she came over to tear a strip off of me. I don't believe that they ran off, though. Both of them gave their word. They'll be around here somewhere."

Interested in finding out the answer to that mystery, Brenda followed Jess and Sandra as they searched the hilltop, finally locating the two heavy-worlders locked in a conversation with an alien unlike anything she'd ever seen before.

The wounded male had kind of a dark-grayish skin with a rough texture and vaguely humanoid facial features. He lay on a cot inside a large tent with the two heavy-worlders sitting on either side of him. They were conversing in the heavy-worlder language.

"I can't decide if this is good news or bad news," Jess said. "Let's go find out."

33

Queen smugly walked through the security checkpoints and into the White House. The Secret Service agents outside the oval office must've been informed about his change in status, because they were watching him more closely than usual. Fine by him.

The secretary to the president gestured for him to proceed in, and he did so. The handover between the Secret Service agents outside the Oval Office and those inside went smoothly. At no time did they leave Queen without one of their number ready to deal with him should he decide to cause trouble.

He wasn't inclined to. Nothing he could do or say would change the outcome of this meeting, so he might as well embrace his future. Everyone had been fired at some point. That was just part of life. Often, such things were stepping stones to more prestigious posts, ones that were more satisfying, or ones that led to more power.

Queen had to admit that while being the secretary of state had been a prestigious position, it certainly hadn't been an easy task. It was a thankless job, if one was honest. And thankfully, in just a very few minutes, it would be someone else's problem.

George Blankenship rose from his desk and gestured toward the comfortable seats, surprising Queen a little. He'd expected the man to take his resignation and send him packing with no fanfare.

"I understand this isn't the high point in our relationship, Josh," the president said as he settled into his seat. "I take no pleasure in having to do this. Honestly, I can't see how anyone could have done a better job in your position, right up until the end.

"I wish you hadn't put me into a position that made me choose between you and the safety of the United States. I know the Chinese pissed you off—

hell, they pissed me off too—but you should've just let the spaceport matter drop. In the end, that's what got you."

"So you said," Queen said as he took a seat. "I'll admit that my response was probably too forceful in hindsight, but I'm not going to apologize for doing what I thought was right for the United States of America."

He smiled at the president. "I'd imagine that whoever you pick as my successor is going to have quite the hot potato on his or her hands. My actions are certainly not going to make their jobs any easier."

"Probably not," Blankenship admitted. "We came into this as friends, and I want us to leave the same way. I understand that you're angry with me and I regret that. That doesn't mean that we can't work together again at some point. I'm sure that you'll land on your feet."

Queen chuckled. "I will. In fact, I've already accepted a position that I'll move into as soon as I hand over my resignation and you accept it. It's something of a step down, but the prospects for personal growth are truly impressive. I suspect that I'll look back on this moment with a degree of fondness, once a certain amount of time has passed."

He reached into his jacket, pulled out the envelope with his resignation in it, and handed it to the president. "You'll find everything in order. Just your standard everyday mutually agreed-upon resignation so that I can pursue other goals in life."

Blankenship opened the envelope and scanned the resignation letter, nodding when he finished the brief missive. "Everything is in order. As of right now, you are no longer the secretary of state of the United States. I thank you for your service. If you don't mind my asking, what exactly are you going to be doing now?"

"I think I'll just keep that to myself for the moment," Queen said with something of a smirk. "Let's just say that it's going to be rewarding on a number of fronts.

"By the way, speaking of rewarding, I think you should know that one of the last things I completed in my official position was an agreement with Brenda Cabot and her associates.

"It's something that I'd been working on for quite some time, nailing down the specifics of exactly how they could assist us in understanding the Asharim technology while at the same time benefiting from association with the United States. I left a copy of it in my files for my replacement."

The president frowned. "Why would you do that? We already have an agreement with that Humanity Unlimited company and their alliance for substantially the same thing."

"Our agreement with Humanity Unlimited does have a number of the same sorts of clauses and requirements, but they don't have the same level of knowledge that Brenda Cabot and her associates have. They've been working with this tech and the knowledge of the Asharim for a thousand years.

"Tell me, would you rather trust a startup company to solve the problems in space or the people that have been here as long as the ones ruling China right now?"

Blankenship stood and scowled down at Queen. "What exactly did you promise them? What precisely are we getting from them?"

Queen stood slowly and smiled at the president. "All I can say is that I only bartered things that you'd previously approved—and I have that in writing, mind you. I can't say that it's been a pleasure working for you, Mr. President, but it has certainly been educational."

"Get the hell out of my office, you little piece of crap. Whatever you did, I'll undo it."

"Good luck with that. Everything I had was looked over by the department lawyers and is ironclad. I've made certain that a copy of the agreement was shared with the members of the alliance, too. Here's a pro tip for you: if you're going to fire someone, don't leave them time and access to cause you mischief.

"Oh, and by the way, you asked about where I was going to be working? Brenda Cabot is my new boss. Irony there, right? With any luck, when you start negotiating with them in earnest to try to do anything else, I'll get to be their front man. Wouldn't that be fun?"

With a laugh, Queen headed for the exit, leaving the president cursing behind him. Time to go see what the future held.

* * *

JESS CLEARED HER THROAT. "Did I miss anything good?" she asked in the heavy-worlder language, though she was now sure that the name wasn't accurate. The Peret spoke exactly the same tongue, so it might be the language the Asharim used to converse with their slaves so they didn't have to sully their own language. The same was likely true for what they'd thought was the Asharim written language. She'd have to ask to be sure.

Kerrick Vidar turned toward her and shook his head. "Discussing issues like these is rarely a good thing for anyone involved."

His daughter shook her head. "You miss her inflection, Father. She was speaking about interesting rather than good or bad."

The man smiled slightly. "Ah. My mistake. In that case, you could say that Lastark, my daughter, and I have had quite an interesting discussion. As one might imagine, the subject of the Masters came up."

The wounded alien nodded slowly. "I confess that I did not believe you when you said that humans had fought for the Masters, but they know far too many things about the Masters for this to be anything but the absolute truth.

"Their legends match with many of ours, but they are not always congruent. Their tales of the cruelty that the Masters have displayed toward their slaves is one thing that has not changed. He tells me that you are negotiating with his people. What exactly do you hope to gain by some reunification with humans that are former slaves of the Masters?"

"I don't think you quite understand where I'm coming from," Jess said, finding a chair nearby, placing it at the foot of the cot, and sitting. "I'm not negotiating with them because they're human. I'm negotiating with them because I believe that we can be allies and both benefit from sticking a finger in the eyes of the Masters.

"Frankly, the same is true of your people and mine. We don't have to be blood enemies. What would you do if you didn't have to fight and die for the Masters? What kind of lives would you have? Isn't that something worth fighting for?"

The alien shook his head. "I cannot envision a future such as you describe. My people have been slaves for centuries beyond measure. This freedom that Kerrick speaks of is a foreign concept to us. Something almost incomprehensible."

"It doesn't have to be a mystery forever," Vera said softly. "Our people were once as downtrodden as yours. Once the Masters abandoned us, it took us lifetimes to learn how to be as free as we are.

"The children are the ones that teach you. The ones that are born after the hold of the Masters is broken. They see life in a different way than you. Or they will. All you have to do is imagine a future without the Masters and help us bring it into being."

Jess smiled slightly. It looked as if the heavy-worlders had made up their minds about the Masters. Excellent. She still didn't know what that would mean in the long term, but it was better than fighting them to the death.

As if reading her mind, the woman turned to face Jess. "And before you believe that means that we have decided to take your side against the Masters, I caution you against thinking that. We still need to see and speak to one of the Masters, and then we will take what we learn back to the high priest. He will make that decision, as is his right."

Jess held a hand up signaling her acceptance. "I don't want to rush things, but I'm allowed to feel somewhat hopeful. My partner is fighting the Asharim down below, trying to capture one of them so that we can all speak and learn of them, but I'm uncertain how that will turn out.

"Now, I have a side question. Until we spoke with the heavy-worlders, we assumed that the language we were finding and speaking was the Asharim tongue. You both speak it but say it isn't the language they use. Does that mean it's a specific language for dealing with their slave races?"

"It is," Kerrick said. "And the scrap of written language that I've seen is also used for the same purpose. The Masters were never ones to sully themselves with the lower beings. Even knowing how to converse with slaves was a black splotch on them. They reserved that for their own lower social classes. No slaves are ever allowed to learn their own language."

That was when a group of men made their way into the tent carrying someone on a stretcher. Jess turn to watch them, trying to see who'd been injured, and saw Harry walking beside the group.

He spotted her and changed direction toward her. "Good news. One of the pilots survived the crash of their air car because it got hung up in a tree. He's hurt, but unless some type of internal injury kills him, he'll probably make it."

Her mouth partly open in surprise, Jess stood and walked over to where the soldiers were securing the new patient/prisoner. Based on the images she'd seen, this was definitely an Asharim: tall, slender, and, even injured, arrogantly sneering at everyone around him.

Seen this way, he didn't seem that much of a threat, but she wasn't fooled. These people had mastered technology far beyond anything that humanity had dreamed of just a few years ago. Even having fallen from their pinnacle of achievement, they still had access to things she could barely imagine, even with the download in her brain. It wouldn't do to underestimate them.

As she was staring down at the alien, Kerrick Vidar stepped up beside her. "He looks smaller than I expected."

In spite of the gravity of the situation, Jess laughed before she could slap a hand over her mouth to smother it. The corner of his mouth curled upward, showing that he'd known what his words would cause her to do.

His daughter smacked him on the arm before turning to Jess. "If he survives, we will question him. You can of course be present and ask your own questions. He is after all your prisoner, as is my father. As I am under truce bond, I will not press my case too strongly.

"I will say that you have met many of the expectations we have set for you, and that will weigh in your favor when we speak to the high priest. If what I expect to hear comes to pass, I believe my old friend will decide that we do not follow the Masters any longer."

"Fool," the wounded Asharim said, his voice weak and cracking. "As if we care whether you decide to follow us or not. All are our slaves and will serve us."

Jess shook her head slightly. This was going to be a very informative question-and-answer session. She doubted the Asharim would give them any useful information, but his words would probably convince their other prisoner to help them. All she had to do was get this guy on a roll.

34

Harry quickly became bored trying to follow Jess's questioning the alien. He didn't even speak the language. Since Jess was focused on the Asharim prisoner, he stepped back without saying anything and went off in search of Krueger.

He found the man at the bottom of the hill directing the troops in securing the area against further incursions. There were a lot of dead aliens scattered across the landscape, and based upon a few sheet-covered bodies at the base of the hill, his forces hadn't gotten off completely unscathed.

"What's the damage?" Harry asked softly once he was next to the other man.

Krueger dipped his head slightly. "Surprisingly light, but not painless. Seven killed, twenty-three injured in one form or another. We're evacuating the wounded through the gate to *Freedom Express* right now. They'll perform triage there and get the very worst of the injured taken to better facilities as quickly as possible."

Considering the number of people that they'd been fighting and the number of bodies he was looking at on the field, that was a remarkably low casualty count. Still, Krueger was right.

Every single one was painful in its own way. Somebody's mother, father, sister, brother, wife, or husband would get the worst news of their entire lives shortly, and they'd be broken.

Harry had done those kinds of notifications before. When any member of his company had died, he made the notification in person if he could. If not, he followed up in person as soon as he could possibly do so. His people deserved that.

It never got any easier. As soon as they saw him, they knew. He could see it in their eyes. The fear and horror followed by the despair. It tore at his heart every single time.

"I want a listing of each and every one of them, and for those that aren't in my company, I'll need to know more about them. As soon as we get clear from here, I'll make the notifications."

Krueger cocked his head slightly. "Most of them aren't troops from your unit. They already have superiors and processes in place to perform notifications to the next of kin."

"I know that," Harry said with a nod. "But that doesn't change my duty. These people died under my command, and their families deserve to hear what happened from my lips. One day I might command enough troops so that's not practical, and I'll address that then, but today is not that day."

"I'll get the information to you as soon as I can. It's going to have to wait until after phase two of the fighting, I'm afraid. The surviving aliens pulled back toward the city, and I expect they're forming a defensive zone to receive us.

"Based on the air cars that they sent after you, we have to assume that they have other weapons in reserve for emergencies. Why they didn't feel they could use them in fighting against the Volunteers, I don't know, but we're going to have to make the assumption that we'll face more advanced technology and perhaps larger numbers than we expected."

Harry stared off at the distant city, its tall spires decayed, leaning, and occasionally fallen onto their neighbors. It was hard to imagine anyone there retaining any kind of technological sophistication, but the air cars hadn't been mirages. They'd been real. And if used correctly, they could've been quite deadly.

"I just saw Brenda Cabot up top with the prisoners and Jess," Harry said. "I didn't speak with her, but I'd expect that we can count on some technical assistance from her in the planning stages and perhaps even something of a surprise during the execution. We need to bring the Volunteers over once we've secured the area. We made a promise to them, and we need to keep it."

Krueger looked unconvinced. "Is that really the best idea? No offense to Miss Adorno and General Norris, but they're more in line with the technological level of the targets. They don't exactly have sophisticated techniques for going door to door in what's going to be the ugliest fight of our lives. They'll be slaughtered."

"This is their land," Harry said firmly. "Who are we to tell them that they can't defend it? We can do everything possible to shield them from the worst of the blowback, but we have to let them fight their own enemies. That's what free people do.

"That doesn't mean we can't be there with our advanced weapons and blow the living snot out of any resistance they run into. We can protect our friends, but we can't coddle them."

"You're the boss." The other man looked up at the sun and did some obvious mental calculation. "We've got another six or seven hours of daylight. That's enough time to get all the troops we want to bring through the gate, get them into place, and set up in a real defensive perimeter. We can use our night-vision gear and some scouts to make absolutely sure no one sneaks up on us, but we're going to bivouac here tonight.

"We'll need to speak with our allies and our military commanders for as long as needed tonight to find out what we're facing, how we're going to break through the enemy lines, and take possession of those gates. Which brings up a couple of questions for you.

"I thought this Asharim civilization was filled with people using these gates. All I've heard about are a couple of gates in the center of the city that we're going to be pushing for. Shouldn't those buildings be filled with gates?"

Harry shrugged. "Perhaps they are, but there's no power supply for them. The Volunteers said they had to secure a certain specific set of gates. On the heavy-worlder planet, the Asharim locked the gates down so that no one could use them. Perhaps they did something similar here. Until we can actually get Kevin to look at them, we won't know the answers to those questions.

"One thing that will be a huge bonus, if we win, is salvaging as many of the nonfunctional gates as possible. If we can lock them down to specific addresses, which Brenda says is possible, then we can give them to our allies on Earth."

"Sounds dangerous. They could undo whatever you did and gain access to the galaxy at large."

There was something to Krueger's objection, but Earth needed something like this. The idea of having a bank of gates open in a major airport, allowing people from all over the world to just step from New Zealand to Los Angeles in a single heartbeat, would change the world instantly.

"We won't do it if we can't secure it," he said at last. "In any case, that'll have to wait until we've secured the city."

Harry put his hands on his hips and stared off into the distance when Krueger only nodded. That brought his thoughts full circle. Those aliens would be defending their homes. This was not going to be an easy fight.

But the Volunteers were also defending their homes. In many ways, they were the patriots of this story, much as their ancestors had been the patriots of the Revolutionary War. They were fighting for hearth and home.

He looked forward to having time to talk to the Volunteers and learn more about their society. He suspected that they still had many of the honorable traits his forefathers had once had. The ones that had made them great leaders and had made the United States the shining jewel of the world.

Perhaps that knowledge and spirit could salvage the nation he'd grown up in. He certainly hoped so.

"I'll leave you here to continue getting everything in order," Harry said after a few minutes. "I'll start sending down the Volunteers as quickly as they arrive. We'll use the path, since the fighting is over. Set them up wherever makes the best sense, but make sure that they're covered against surprise attacks. After the last time, I'd rather not have them hit in the dark again.

"We'll meet in the command post on top of the hill when everything is done. I'll make sure we have food and that everything is set up for us to make our final plans as quickly as possible. Tomorrow, we attack."

* * *

BRENDA STARED at the Asharim city through a borrowed pair of binoculars. "Holy cow, can you imagine the amount of high-tech gear just sitting there? Even though most of it has to be junk, we know that the gates survive that kind of time, so there has to be other stuff that still works. This is almost like exploring that frozen Earth."

"Except that Earth-B doesn't have people trying to kill you hiding in every building," Jess said. "Not that having an atmosphere and survivable temperatures wouldn't be a nice change of pace."

Taking one last look at the city, Brenda set the binoculars down on the rock she was leaning against and turned to face Jess. "You realize that you're not even going to scratch the surface of that mystery during your lifetime, right? Just like I'm never going to learn everything I possibly can from the Asharim. This is going to be a multigenerational task."

"That's where bringing in all those scientists that Queen promised you—and me for that matter—comes in," Jess said. "It's like a long-term research project where people will gain a lot of experience and bring in fresh viewpoints with new classes of graduate students. Then they'll see things that their teachers never imagined possible. In a lot of ways, this is like the Manhattan Project, only bigger."

Brenda immediately realized that the other woman was right, but she was also wrong. "It's like the Manhattan Project, sure, but this is like World War II hasn't ended. We're making the breakthroughs, but we can't count on the information we learn stopping the Asharim or some other alien race from being a threat.

"We literally have no idea what's out there waiting for us. Humans never really had a good grasp on galactic civilization. We know the Asharim had enemies that fought against them, though we had no real grasp of who or what they were. Those enemies provided humans with some tech and some assistance when we needed it, but that was always behind the scenes. No one really knows what their true goals were.

"We don't even know if they were the race that the Asharim got into a knock-down, drag-out fight with. Someone ended the Asharim's supremacy, but it might not have been those shadowy aliens that helped humanity. They might have been thrashed as well. Until we get out there into the wider universe, we'll never know."

Jess sighed and rubbed her face tiredly. "I know, but we've got to take care of the problems closer to home before we can even start exploring. Just look at this place. This is really a side fight. I wish we could've spent our time elsewhere. We'd get a lot more mileage out of working on turning the heavy-worlders into allies than fighting these degenerate Asharim and their slaves."

"You're wrong," Brenda said with a shake of her head. "Fighting here and showing the heavy-worlders what the Asharim have become is the best way to make them feel that they can safely become your allies.

"Just think about it. They've had the Asharim hanging over their heads like the Sword of Damocles. If they strayed too far, the aliens would crush them if they returned. Now that they know that fate isn't waiting for them, they're finally free to grow and become the kind of people they want to be. Whatever that is."

"That sounds pretty touchy feely," Jess said. "We can't count on anything like that. We have no idea what they'll do."

"I'm serious here," Brenda pressed. "Once the fighting is finished inside the Asharim city, I'll bet everything I have that they return home and argue ferociously with their priest that it's time to break away from that religion. What they do next, I don't know, but there's a very good chance that they'll be allies to humanity."

"They want to find their home world," Jess said. "Not Earth, but the heavy-gravity planet that they were transplanted to. That's where their population is the strongest. And convincing these heavy-worlders that they should be our allies isn't going to do anything to convince the others."

"You might be surprised. I think that wherever the larger portion of their race is, they'll pay attention to these members of their subspecies. We might as well admit that's what they are: a subspecies of humanity. I'm not sure what the scientists would call them, but even though the genetic change is artificial, they're not exactly *Homo Sapiens* anymore."

Jess opened her mouth to respond, but a shout from back at the cave caught both of their attention. When they turned, they saw Susanna Adorno leading a long string of Volunteer fighters onto the planet. The men behind her cheered when they saw that they were home.

"She and General Norris must've returned to bring the rest of their people here and get them ready to fight," Jess said, her tone somewhat worried. "I really do hope that this isn't a mistake. They're so vulnerable."

Brenda put her hand on Jess's shoulder. "They been fighting the Asharim for hundreds of years. They aren't helpless. Whatever happens, we'll be standing beside them and doing our level best to make certain that we come out on top.

"But even if they suffer losses, this is their world. It's their place to fight for their homes. Isn't that what their ancestors did?"

Jess slowly nodded. "This war is a just one for them. Like Jefferson once said, the tree of liberty must be refreshed from time to time with the blood of patriots and tyrants. The Volunteers are patriots and the Asharim are tyrants. We just have to do our very best to make sure that the tyrants shed more blood than the patriots."

Brenda tugged Jess toward the arriving soldiers. "Let's go see that they get settled in. Once everyone is together, you can give them one of those motivational speeches that leaders always give to urge their followers on to greater heights."

Her friend blanched. "I'm an engineer. I hate talking in front of people at all, much less trying to raise their enthusiasm to new heights so that they can go conquer their enemies. That's Harry's job."

"I think you're selling yourself short. Pretend they're your engineering team and conquering that city is just finishing a project on schedule. Trust me when I say that you'll motivate them then."

They'd almost made it to Susanna when Kerrick Vidar and his daughter came racing out of the tent where the prisoners were being housed. They immediately spotted Jess and Brenda and ran toward them.

This couldn't be good.

"Lastark has decided to cooperate with you," the elder Vidar said. "He has grave news. You must come at once."

Jess immediately turned away from the arriving Volunteers and ran toward the tent. Brenda shared a glance with Susanna and ran after her. A minute later, all of them were clustered around the alien warrior in his cot.

Lastark looked up at them with an expression that Brenda couldn't decipher. "I have considered what you said and decided that I will help you. Perhaps that will help my people as well, but it will certainly help bring an end to this continual war between the Asharim and the humans on this planet.

"I have never known anything other than living under the heels of the Masters, and I find the idea of making decisions for myself, though strange and frightening, is one that appeals to me. With that in mind, I will tell you something that the Asharim would execute me for speaking of if they knew."

He cast a glance over at where the Asharim they'd captured lay. He was rolled over in the cot and so busy ignoring the presence of everyone else in the tent that it didn't seem that he was listening. There was a bit of irony in him missing the big reveal.

Lastark seemed to take a deep breath and then continued. "The forces that you are fighting here are not the largest group of my people. In fact, the Masters have called two other colonies of their own kind and summoned warriors to end the human presence on this world once and for all.

"Even as we speak, a force much larger than the one you defeated travels to where the humans live on this planet. They intend to exterminate them. As they departed two days ago and will be travelling fast, it may already be too late for you to stop them."

Jess translated what the alien had said to Susanna Adorno, and the other woman paled. "Gods above! Our people cannot stand off a force that large. We must race to their defense, or tens of thousands of my people will be exterminated."

"I'm going to go talk to Harry," Jess said resolutely. "We'll save your people or die trying."

35

Jess raced out of the tent and called Harry on the radio. "I need you up here right now. I'm near the medical tents."

"Can it wait fifteen minutes?" he asked.

"No. Bring Commander Krueger if he's anywhere near you. We've got a serious problem."

"Copy that. We're on our way."

She paced back and forth in front of the tent as she waited, her mind racing. Various plans to intercept the attacking force came up and were discarded. None of her ideas seemed realistic. They were days late in responding and didn't have the kind of equipment that could get them to the settlements in a hurry. What were they going to do?

Harry and Krueger came running from where the ropes went down the side of the hill a few minutes later, both skidding to a halt beside her.

"What's going on?" Harry asked.

"Lastark decided to help us," she said grimly. "He said that an army about five times the size of the one we fought here left toward the Volunteer settlements two days ago. They're going to exterminate them."

Harry cursed. "We don't have aircraft. How are we going to get ahead of them?"

"Can we even get ahead of them?" Krueger asked. "A two-day lead on foot is almost insurmountable."

"Maybe we can bring something through the gate," Jess said. "I realize that the tunnel is too small for aircraft, but surely something can be disassembled and brought through that will give us a speed edge. We've got three days to get ahead of them and form some kind of defense of those settlements."

Harry began pacing, massaging his temples with his fingers. "If we can bring through some ultralights, we could get some air cover. They have two-seat versions where one person is piloting and the other can act as a gunner or spotter for mortar rounds.

"I realize that's not much when it comes to air superiority, but we're pretty much fighting people with black powder weapons. I understand that they might have a few flechette rifles, so it's not a settled deal, but it beats having nothing at all."

"We're not going to be able to get any vehicle of size through the tunnel," Krueger said. "About the biggest we can manage are motorcycles. With this rough terrain, I'm thinking dirt bikes. If we can bring through a bunch of dirt bikes, we can give the troops that don't have any knowledge about using them a couple of hours of training that will be sufficient to get them where they need to go.

"If we have some of the bikes carry nothing but fuel, we should be able to catch up with the enemy before they reach the settlements. We'd have to keep sending even more bikes with fuel to keep that going, but it should erode the lead that they've got. The question will be if we can shave off enough time to stop them before the attack begins."

Harry turned his head and looked at the sun. "By the time we get things in motion back on Earth, it's going to be dark, so here's what we're going to do. The bikes can be gathered and brought here overnight. That should get us a sufficient number by the time dawn arrives.

"That's going to be an expensive undertaking, and it's going to draw attention. I mean really, who comes in and buys out a complete showroom of dirt bikes?"

"I might be able to help with that," Brenda said as she stepped out of the hospital tent. "Things have been a little hectic here, so I haven't had an opportunity to tell you that we found the base in Virginia. It's a big one, and the gates are operational. There's nothing else inside of it. Whoever ran it back then cleaned it out, but it's not very far away from DC.

"With the Chinese blowing up the base in New Zealand, it makes more sense to use the portable gate I have and the other gates in the base to get here. They should be able to handle the load."

Harry blinked. "The Chinese destroyed the New Zealand base? Why haven't I heard about this?"

"You were a little busy fighting a war," Jess said before she turned to face Brenda. "Do it. I've heard a little bit about some of the new resources you've got, so get us what we need to defend the Volunteers. Ultralights, too. Whatever you can get."

Brenda raced toward the cave without responding.

Jess faced her partner. "Let's say that we get all the dirt bikes you need, and all the fuel needed to get you to the settlements. Let's even say that we get a dozen ultralights. How are you going to stop an army five times the size of the one you fought here with a mobile force? We had surprise last time. They'll probably know we're coming this time."

Harry smiled grimly. "We do what we have to do. If we can interdict the

Asharim forces, that gives time for the Volunteers to catch up. If we can delay the fight long enough, they'll smash them in the rear."

"And what do you do if you can't hold them?"

Her friend chuckled grimly. "Then I'm not going to be in a position to care what happens next, because I'll be dead. This is one of those missions where the outcome is more important than our lives. We'll find the Asharim and we'll stop them, no matter the cost. There'll be no atrocity here. I swear it."

* * *

HARRY WORRIED that he wasn't going to be able to keep that brave promise he'd made to Jess. There were so many things that could go wrong. He had no idea what kind of weapons the Asharim would've taken to exterminate the settlements. Even here, they'd used three air cars to try to change the odds of battle.

What would they take with them to finally break the Volunteers? If he were in their place, he'd take significantly more airpower than he'd left behind. That made it all too likely that they were going to be facing mobile elements in the air with high-tech weapons, even if they were mostly untrained in their use.

What was he putting up to fight them? Ultralights. Unarmed, small engines, and limited to low-speed maneuvers. Such a fight would be brutal, one-sided, and ultimately fatal for his forces.

The fight on the ground had the potential to be more favorable, but he could only count on the motorcycles to get them where they needed to go. They weren't going to provide any great advantage during battle.

"Penny for your thoughts," Krueger said as he walked up.

"I think we're in a lot of trouble," Harry admitted. "The Asharim are going to control the air, and they can use those weapons of theirs on us from up there. Our ultralights are no match for their air cars. We have to accept the fact that the forces here probably notified them of what we did to their air cars by ambush. They're going to be ready for that.

"And once we deal with the forces that are trying to keep us from attacking the Asharim, we have to figure out how to take the relatively small number of troops we can move and hold back what amounts to a massive army. Their weapons are not going to be comparable to ours, for the most part, but as they say, ten men with clubs can take down a man with a gun."

Krueger shook his head slightly. "You did a lot of special operations in your day, but you never fought this kind of fight before. There are some techniques that might substantially alter the outcome you have in your head."

Harry stopped pacing and stared at the special operations officer. "What are you talking about? What kind of techniques?"

"Have you ever heard of General George Armstrong Custer?"

Harry felt his eyes narrowing. "Sure. If that's meant to be some kind of incentive to cheer me up, I don't think we're going to stand a lot better chance than he did."

"That was hubris," Krueger said. "General Custer thought he was invincible. Even when warned that he was biting off more than he could chew, he raced in, utterly confident that he could achieve victory. That's not you. That's also not the comparison that I'm making.

"What I'm saying is that he was an exceptionally skilled cavalry officer. He knew how to maneuver troops mounted on horses to achieve the very best outcome from their very different mode of transport. Dirt bikes are not horses, but they can provide a lot of the same benefits as horses when we're fighting people on foot."

Harry stopped to ponder that unexpected advice, scratching his head as he tried to figure out how he could use the dirt bikes more effectively. Probably some method of using them to circle around the Asharim forces and strike from many different areas and keep them off balance.

That was easy to say, but it didn't come naturally to him. Other than watching a bunch of westerns where the Native Americans utilized similar tactics against less mobile foes, he really had no idea how something like that would work.

"I hear what you're saying, but I'm not certain it's going to make a lot of difference for me," Harry said. "We're little short on time, and I'm a lot short on the background that I'd need to use something like that effectively."

Krueger clapped him on the shoulder with his right hand. "Then you're in luck. The U.S. Army still has cavalry, though not in the same way as it did in the past. Now they utilize vehicles for their mobility, though stuff bigger than dirt bikes. That doesn't stop them from studying the past and learning from it.

"By morning, I'd wager I could have a team of experienced cavalry officers and noncoms here to take charge of the actual combat. You'd still be in overall command, of course, but they'd be able to advise you about specific actions that'll make those dirt bikes one hell of a lot more effective."

Harry wasn't certain about that, but it wasn't as if he had a lot of choice. "Make some calls. We'll have Black Jack pick them up and take steps to make sure they can't identify any of the bases Brenda is using to get them here. We'll need to have them here before dawn to examine the equipment and the riders. As much as it annoys me, we're going to have to take the time in the morning to do a basic orientation for dirt bike riding in the wild. People need to know how to operate the equipment."

Krueger nodded. "Are we going to have the dirt bikes here by then?"

"I sure as hell hope so. That's going to be on Brenda and her ability to get enough bikes for us and get them to a place where we can utilize them. And she's going to have to do it all without tipping her hand to the US government. They'd stop whatever she was doing and try to seize the gate if they get wind of it."

"I wish I could say that you're wrong, but you're probably not," Krueger admitted. "This operation is going to revolve around those vehicles, so we'd best pray she comes through. If she lets the US stop her, tens of thousands of people are going to die, and there's not really anything we can do to stop it from happening."

Harry stared off at the stars beginning to appear in the sky as darkness took over the landscape. This was a beautiful world. One that would make a great second home for humanity. To make that happen, he needed to do everything in his power to make certain that the people here survived.

If he failed, he'd have a terrible atrocity on his conscience, or he'd be dead. Neither one of those options sounded all that good to him, so he was rooting for Brenda Cabot. She had to come through. She just had to.

36

Brenda wasted no time summoning every member of the Families in Washington, DC, to the base in Virginia. She had the folks at the Vault tied in by secure, encrypted com.

Hopefully, that would make it too difficult for any spies to trace them, though the United States government was *supposed* to be honoring their occupation of that facility. Time would tell whether they could be trusted that far.

When she had everybody listening, she got right down to business. "We need dirt bikes. I know that seems like a very strange request, but we need them in as great a quantity as we can get them. It's late afternoon here in DC, and we have to hit any place that sells them and buy up *everything* they have in stock. Once we have that, we have to get them back here and take them to Volunteer World."

Victor raised a meaty hand, his expression somewhat befuddled. "I thought they were fighting a war there. Why do they need dirt bikes?"

"The bottom line is that they have to catch up with an army that has a two-day lead on them. There's no way to get larger vehicles through the cave the gate is in. That means they're going to have to use motorcycles, and since it's rough terrain, that means dirt bikes. The easiest places to hit first are the ones that sell these things for a living. We're going to clean them out."

Cyrus Patterson shook his head over the video link. "If you try that, they're going to think this is some kind of scam. Credit cards are going to make them suspicious for that kind of purchase. Cash, they'll wonder if it's fake or stolen. What you're proposing is going to make them turn us down."

"So what are you suggesting?" she asked. "Gold Krugerrands? That certainly wouldn't be suspicious."

Cyrus chuckled slightly. "No, that wouldn't work any better. What you need is for someone they already have a relationship with to make the deal. Someone that will tell them that this isn't a scam. Somebody here has to know someone that's into dirt bike racing. Anyone?"

A couple of hands went up in the big hall, and Cyrus indicated he had a couple as well. "That's good," Cyrus said. "These folks know people inside the industry. They have a relationship. What they need to do is contact their friends and find someone that knows some of these dealerships. That way they can vouch for our people and the cash we're offering.

"And they're going to want to see cold hard cash in their hands. Not gold, not digital, just regular money that they can check to make sure it's not fake."

Todd Granger shook his head. "Do you know how much dirt bikes cost? They're not cheap. Do we have that kind of cash on hand? If we don't, can you imagine going to a bank and asking to withdrawal hundreds of thousands of dollars? Or a million? That's going to bring all kinds of attention that we don't need."

"The Families have money stashed away for various purposes, and I'm going to raid that fund," she said. "Humanity Unlimited will reimburse us. The purchases are still going to raise some eyebrows and have people checking into us. I guess this is the point where we find out whether the treaty we have with the US government is worth the paper it's written on."

She gathered those with connections to the racing industry and started them contacting their friends. By the time she had enough cash on hand and had paid their friends a handsome fee for assisting them, it was going to be just a couple of hours before these showrooms closed.

Once that was started, she tasked others with going through the papers and finding dirt bikes for sale by individuals. That was something that could be handled more easily and wouldn't raise any eyebrows.

The number of bikes they could get that way would probably be fairly low, but in a city the size of DC, there would still be dozens of bikes for sale. Everyone would help. She had no idea how many troops Harry needed to move, but they probably wouldn't be able to get enough bikes for everyone.

"Todd," she said, gesturing for the doctor to come over. "We need ultralight aircraft as well. None of us is going to know anybody with an in on that angle, so I want you to find out if there's a dealership and head over there right away. We'll get you enough cash to buy as many as they have on hand. If that sparks them to call the police, then we'll deal with it, but I need to get Harry every piece of equipment that we can."

He nodded and headed for the gate.

She racked her brain, trying to figure out if there was anything else she could do to improve their odds of winning this fight. She really wished that she had access to high-tech weapons other than the flechette rifles that they'd recovered in various places.

Still, she supposed that those would be helpful as well. She'd gather up everything she had on hand and get it sent through the gate with the dirt bikes when they arrived. Then it would be all up to Harry and Karl.

The idea that her lover was going to be in such dire circumstances made her stomach roll, but she knew that she wouldn't be able to stop him from doing what he thought was right. That was one of the things she liked about the man.

One way or the other, this was a throw of the dice. If they came up good, they might be able to break the Asharim on Volunteer World once and for all.

This was a pivotal moment in their expansion into the universe. If they blew it, a lot of people would die, and they'd be back where they started. She didn't want to see anyone else die, so she was going to do everything in her power to make this work.

* * *

JESS MANAGED the arrival of the dirt bikes as Brenda Cabot delivered them. They started as single units, and then, after about an hour and a half, the first large shipment arrived. By the time dawn was close, they had several hundred dirt bikes ready for use. She was amazed at how well the other woman had done.

Transporting the fuel was significantly more complicated, as everything had to be brought through in containers. Not only what they needed to fuel them up, but more containers to transport fuel with them as they tried to chase down the Asharim forces. They also needed things like helmets, gloves, and jackets to protect the riders. All of those things were coming in a flood.

There were also additional troops arriving every hour. Forces from New Zealand, Australia, and even the United States. All transported in a way that didn't reveal the locations of the gates. She wasn't sure how that last was going to play out when the alliance got around to throwing the US out of the group. That wasn't going to be fun, and she was glad she didn't have to be involved.

Somehow, Harry managed to keep track of all the frantic activity and force order onto the chaos. He and Commander Krueger were able to keep everything moving and organize the incoming troops into appropriate units and get them armed.

Brenda had sent along some of the Asharim weapons they had in storage. They'd been useless with no one able to charge them but were now available. There were a bunch of them on *Freedom Express* as well that her people were sending over. Maybe even enough to arm the mobile forces entirely. She hoped that those advanced weapons made a difference.

She'd expected everyone to go tearing off into the wilderness as soon as dawn broke, but Harry surprised her and held organized training for those who were unfamiliar with the use of motorcycles. There were surprisingly many that didn't know how the little devices were operated.

She'd have expected more military people to be familiar with motorcycles. They seemed daring and dangerous, so she'd expected there to be some type of correlation. Apparently not.

He was also training the troops in the use of the flechette rifles and pistols. There was a lot of hooting that she could hear from the shooters. It sounded as if they were pleased.

Also coming through the gate were ultralight aircraft that could be used for scouting. They could probably also be used for firing down from great height, but that seemed like a sure way to invite the counterattack. The little things had no way of protecting the riders from being hit by birds, much less bullets.

Being someone that had gone into space before, she'd always found herself attracted to aircraft. Her training in flying them was limited to the lifters, but she'd enjoyed quite a bit of time flying around in ultralights. One of the engineers that she'd worked with had been a fan of that sort of thing.

She'd suspected that he'd hoped taking her up for a couple of rides would lead to some kind of romantic entanglement, but she hadn't been looking for that sort of thing at the time.

He'd been a good sport about it, and she'd made sure to introduce him to one of her friends that she thought might find him interesting. Since they were now married with three kids, it seemed she'd guessed well.

That passive knowledge about the small craft, added to what she knew about flying from the implanted Asharim skills, gave her the impression that she might actually be able to fly one of these things. Perhaps not as well as a trained pilot, but they didn't have enough of those in any case. Brenda had brought far more ultralights than they had pilots.

Jess paid close attention to the familiarization spiel that one of the trained pilots was giving the rest of them with any experience. Everything made sense, and she was confident that she could remember what the controls were and how to use them if she needed to.

Harry would be severely pissed if he knew that she was going along. Hell, Sandra would be furious. That last might be able to be rectified.

Once the familiarization class was over, Jess went to find her bodyguard. She didn't have to look far. The woman was watching her from about fifteen meters away.

"You were going to do it, were you?" Sandra demanded.

"Not without talking to you first. We're going. Both of us."

Sandra's eyes narrowed. "We have plenty of ultralights. Why would I allow you to go charging in like that?"

"We might have enough aircraft, but we're really short on pilots. Harry isn't going to wait much longer. As soon as he has those people down there able to go without falling over, he's going to head out. I'd give him no more than an hour.

"I suggest you arm up with your sniper rifle and some of the Asharim weapons, and we'll follow along. We can communicate with the scout teams from the air, and if Harry runs into trouble, you can use that sniper rifle to help make sure he gets clear.

"I don't have to tell you how important he is to Humanity Unlimited and me personally. I don't want him dying in this fight. It's up to us to make sure that he doesn't find himself in a place where he's going to plant his feet and roar his defiance at the enemy, knowing that he's going to die."

The other woman stared at her without speaking for twenty seconds and then slowly nodded. "It's a crazy idea, and he's going to be super pissed, so I suggest we just don't tell him. If everything goes according to plan, he never needs to find out.

"But here's the deal. I'm not going to put you in danger either. If it looks like the enemy has a means of dealing with these ultralights, then we're pulling out. I'm not going to take any chances with your safety, Jess. Is that clear?"

"Perfectly," Jess said as she headed toward the stacks of Asharim weapons. This time she wasn't taking just her little pistol. She wanted a rifle and plenty of ammo. They were about to fight the fight of their lives, and she'd be damned if she'd be underarmed.

37

Harry wasn't completely satisfied with the performance of his makeshift cavalry troops, but they were out of time. If they didn't leave now, they'd never stop the Asharim and their slaves short of the Volunteer settlements. He gave the order to mount up.

The Volunteer forces had started marching hours ago, but his troops would quickly skirt their planned marching path and get in front. The locals were determined to save their people, but they'd arrive days after the battle was over, one way or the other. Their people's fate was in his hands now.

The dirt bikes were capable of holding a driver and a passenger as long as they were willing to get comfortable with each other, so he'd be able to move a significant force into the area of conflict quickly.

A second group of dirt bikes was outfitted with makeshift harnesses capable of holding gasoline to refuel the bikes when they ran low. The little things didn't use that much fuel, but they had a long way to go, and they didn't want to run dry just short of their destination.

Everything about this mission was on a shoestring. He'd just have to pray that nothing serious went wrong.

He slid onto a bike behind the driver assigned to him and looked up into the air as a swarm of ultralights circled overhead. They were going to be the scouts that made certain nothing went wrong as they raced forward.

The bikes carried fuel for those as well, which cut into the number of combat troops he could bring along, but he'd rather have sufficient air cover to know what the enemy was doing. Drones would help, but they weren't the same thing as having people in the sky watching what was going on.

Since the air cover seemed ready as well, Harry made a motion and sent the force forward. The enemy had a three-day lead now, and he didn't want to be late to the party.

They didn't dare drive after dark. There was just too great a chance for someone to find a deep rut and kill themselves. It was much better to be a little bit cautious and make certain that they all got where they needed to go as quickly as possible.

He quickly determined that this was a beautiful world but difficult to drive through. The underbrush beneath the trees made passage slow and troublesome, but the helmets helped, as they didn't have to worry about limbs smashing them in the face as they drove.

If the Asharim were having to deal with the same problems, that was going to slow them down as well. This was going to end up being one of the weirdest battles in history.

"Lead elements, this is Liberty Six," he said over the radio. "Keep an eye out for any lookouts that the Asharim might have left behind waiting for them. We don't want to walk into an ambush. Report *anything* that seems out of place.

"We'll take breaks every hour and let everyone stretch their legs. If you have any kind of mechanical issue, report it quickly. Let's not screw this up. A lot of people are counting on us."

With that, he settled back in his seat and did what he could to enjoy the ride. At this point, he was a passenger and just had to accept that this was a waiting game. When they reached an area suitable to bivouac, they'd land the ultralights and let the drones keep watch as they slept.

When they caught up with the Asharim forces, he'd do his very best to exterminate them. He wasn't going to stand by and watch the aliens kill unarmed men, women, and children. He'd die first.

* * *

BRENDA STEPPED out of the cave just as the motorcycles and ultralights were heading out. She looked around for Jess but couldn't find her anywhere. Eventually, someone told her that they thought the woman had gone off on one of the ultralights with her bodyguard.

Harry was going to be really pissed about that.

She worried about the fight ahead. They didn't know what kind of forces the Asharim were taking to attack the settlements. If they brought along some kind of superweapon, that could spell the end of Harry, Karl, and Jess. She really wished that she had something to add to the mix that would help them out, but until they got control of a gate that wasn't obscured inside a hill, that wasn't possible.

That didn't mean that she felt useless. There were plenty of things that she could bring to the party here that might be useful if Harry and the rest ran into trouble. It would be a lot better to have them retreat here and find a lot of extra equipment waiting to help them defend the place.

Some of the assistance that she'd negotiated with the United States via Josh Queen was beginning to come into play. She wasn't a military commander, but she now had one to assist her with the new troops that the United States had grudgingly loaned her.

They weren't special operations soldiers by any measure, but to hold this hill against counterattack didn't require those kinds of specialized skills. The light infantry brigade that Queen had managed to sequester for her would certainly make a difference in securing this place.

If they had to take the city, it would free up a lot of people to be in on the attack. That was outside her control, but she could go ahead and make certain that the people here on the hill were as safe as they could be.

She ordered Lieutenant Colonel Albert Montalvo to deploy his companies in defense of the hill. She left all of the details of that up to him and had him interface with the people that Harry had left behind. The new troops poured through the gate and began setting up machine-gun emplacements and extra mortar batteries. The Asharim weren't going to take this place easily.

Considering how the enemy had used air cars in the past, she made certain that her troops had brought along anti-aircraft weapons. If the Asharim tried that kind of nonsense again, the forces here could deal with them firmly.

Humanity was going to claim this world. The Asharim could go screw themselves.

* * *

JESS HAD FORGOTTEN how liberating flying like this was. She could feel the wind on her face and smell the trees and forest below. It was nothing like traveling in a lander or an airplane. The experience was visceral. Personal.

"This is awesome," she said over the short-range radio to Sandra. "It's like I have wings."

Sandra shook her head. "You don't even know how to fly this thing. Not really. You're kind of making this up as you go. That's like the opposite of awesome."

Jess laughed. "I've flown landers before, and a bunch of the Asharim knowledge included how to fly their ships, including inside an atmosphere. I've also flown as a passenger in ultralights before. It just didn't make much sense until I had all this other experience. It doesn't matter that the experience was implanted. Seriously, I'm good to go."

"What could possibly go wrong?" Sandra asked grumpily.

"According to the briefing, we're at three days behind them," Jess said. "It's possible that we'll catch up to them before dark tomorrow, but that seems unlikely. We'll probably run up into their business sometime day after tomorrow. Hopefully, still short of the settlements."

The sniper looked around without speaking for a while. "I have to say that this forest is going to make my job harder. Yours too. We can't see anything under the canopy. There could be an entire army down there, and unless they were using fires that created smoke, we'd never know.

"You'll find places like this on Earth, though not with this many big trees.

Maybe the Amazon rainforest, but that got cut way back a couple of decades ago, so it's not even the same there."

Jess understood immediately what her friend was talking about. She'd seen the Earth from space and knew how much smaller the green space had been getting over the years. Demand was outstripping the protections that people had placed on their natural habitat. That was another thing that getting off the planet would help with, because eventually that kind of nonsense would kill off the majority of humans on Earth.

Of course, that brought in a whole new set of problems. How did they keep from exporting all of the terrible things that they had done on Earth to these new worlds? Volunteer World was pristine in so many ways.

Perhaps it hadn't been back when the Asharim were more advanced, but she wasn't willing to bet on that. With advanced technology came easy ways to protect the environment without disrupting what you were trying to build.

She swung the ultralight far off to the left of the formation and looked back toward where the motorbikes were running. There was a little bit of dust and smoke in the air. If someone was looking back from the Asharim forces, they might see that if they were observant.

Hopefully all those trees that were blocking the view forward would do exactly the same sort of thing looking backward. It wasn't as if the Asharim had reason to expect that they were chasing them, at least not at this speed.

Or, with the communication systems that were probably on board the air cars, that might not be true at all. The aliens might know exactly how quickly they could go. It was possible they'd run into an ambush. Harry had said that he was prepared for that, but they still didn't really know the capabilities of the enemy.

She'd just have to trust that her friend knew what he was doing. If anyone could protect them from ambush or counterattack, it was him.

"I think I see something," Sandra said, peering forward with binoculars raised to her eyes. "It looks like smoke up ahead."

Jess did as she'd been instructed and passed word back to the head of scouts. The man in charge of the ultralights immediately ordered her to move closer to determine what the source of the smoke was. He indicated that he'd be dispatching a couple more ultralights to back her up in case she needed it.

He didn't know who she was. She'd concealed her identity from him easily enough because he'd been one of the new folks coming in from the United States. He hadn't understood exactly who was supposed to be on Volunteer World and had expected that she was a civilian brought in to help with the scouting. He'd been happy to have her skills, and that had been the end of the matter.

Rather than approaching the smoke directly, Jess decided to come in on a big arc so that she could approach from the side of the travel path that the dirt bikes were using and get a longer look at what she was scouting without showing herself as a target.

It quickly became clear that the smoke was coming from what was left of a fairly large rural building. No, two buildings set somewhat close together. It was hard to tell what they'd been because both had burned to the ground.

The original fire was out, and all that was left was lazy smoke rising from the ruins. Based on the tilled fields off to one side and a number of what were probably some kind of domesticated animals native to Volunteer World wandering in the fields, this had been some kind of farm or ranch. She wasn't sure if there was a name for something that incorporated both.

Whatever had happened here, it had happened at least a day ago. Maybe more.

"Look at the crops," Sandra said. "A lot of people moved through here. They trampled everything. I think we found the direct path that our friends from the city took to get here.

"That was probably a human homestead. I don't envy what Harry will find inside and around the buildings. These bastards seemed the kind that'll execute men, women, and children without pause or self-recrimination."

For once, Jess was glad that she wouldn't have to do the exploration herself. It was hard enough forgetting some things. Seeing a dead child? She wasn't sure she could ever get that out of her head.

She made a report of what they'd found and then, after circling the burn buildings several times, rose higher into the air and began moving forward along the path that the aliens had taken.

This probably wasn't going to be the last set of burned buildings they found. If they wanted to keep the number to an absolute minimum, they needed to catch up to the Asharim and put an end to them once and for all.

38

Harry stopped long enough to allow his people to conduct a quick search of the burned farmstead. He didn't send anyone inside the buildings, but he didn't have to. They found three bodies between the buildings in the trees. Human bodies, two women and a man. They'd been shot multiple times with large caliber bullets.

That was all the proof he needed that the Asharim had passed through here. And it was all the motivation he needed to spur them on to catch the bastards. There was no way in hell he was going to allow this to occur to anyone else if he could help it.

"Mount up," he said over the general channel. "We keep riding. I want the scouts to be extra careful about running into pickets. If they've left someone behind to keep an eye out for us, I want to make absolutely certain no one gets away to tell them about us. If we run into any Asharim or their slaves, I want that area swamped with riders to take down any outliers as fast as possible."

"How far behind them do you think we are?" Krueger asked from where he stood next to Harry.

Harry shrugged. "Hard to say. If I was going to guess by the condition of the bodies, I'd say this took place a day ago. It's getting dark now, so it's questionable whether or not we're going to catch them tomorrow."

The Navy officer nodded. "What are we going to do when we do catch them? Hit them from the rear? Circle around and block them from their targets?"

"That's really going to depend on how many troops they have and how they've arrayed themselves. With the mobility that the dirt bikes give us, I'd like to hit them from all sides and keep them from being able to effectively counterstrike.

"At least that's what the cavalry officers in direct command of the units advised me to do. With the slow reload rate of those black powder rifles, we should be able to hurt them badly if we can keep them from shooting any of us.

"The wildcard is going to be the Asharim and their high-tech weapons. We've got a number of people that have flechette rifles to counterattack that kind of thing, but we need to identify them quickly and take them out as hard and fast as we can."

Krueger nodded again and eyed the sun. "We've got maybe a couple of hours of ride time before we have to set up camp. The scouts are going to need to keep an eye out for a place that we can easily fortify before the sun sets and still have enough time for the ultralights to perform an overhead sweep to make sure that they don't see signs of the enemy in our vicinity."

Harry put his helmet back on. "Make that happen. I'd like for everybody to get as much sleep and food as they can. We might be fighting tomorrow."

* * *

SHORTLY BEFORE DARK, Jess brought her ultralight in for a landing. Troops with flags provided a visual cue for the best ground. In a pinch, they could do the same in the dark with glow sticks, though she didn't relish the thought.

She'd done this several times over the course of the day to refuel and stretch her legs, but it still made her nervous because she couldn't really be sure what was under the grass. A hole or big tree branch could tip the aircraft and send them tumbling.

Once she had the ultralight shut down and secured on the ground, she tossed her helmet into the seat and stretched her back. "I don't mind flying rather than driving, but it sure does mean having to sit in the same spot for too long. My legs feel like jelly."

"Pansy," Sandra said as she did some squats. "In sniper school, we had to stay in one place and not move for a day or more. It didn't matter whether ants were biting your leg or a snake slithered along over your back. If you twitched, they'd fail you."

"I'm glad I'm an engineer not a sniper," she said with a shudder. "I smell food. Those ration bars may have kept us from starving, but why can't someone design one that tastes good? It was like chewing glue and sawdust."

Sandra laughed. "That's been a complaint since the beginning of time. Army rations made for the field will keep you alive but not satisfy you in any way whatsoever. It looks like the chow line is over to the right, so let's get something inside our bellies and find a place to crash for the night."

"I'd prefer a different word, if you please. I don't even want to think about crashing."

There was still just enough light to get into line and get their food. Jess had pulled a hat out of her pocket and pulled it down over her hair to keep from being so recognizable that people would know her at a distance.

Harry was eventually going to find out she was here, but she'd prefer to put that off until tomorrow when they were too far out to just send her back.

Dinner consisted of some kind of stew that they were reheating. It was delicious. Thankfully, they were encouraging folks to come back for second helpings, which she did.

Once they'd cleaned their plates and put them away, Sandra led her to a tent that she'd set up. It was small, so they were going to be cozy tonight. That might be just fine considering how chilly it was already getting.

"The smaller drones are going to keep an eye on everything while we sleep," Sandra said. "They have infrared modes, so we should get some warning if we have visitors."

Jess raise an eyebrow. "Do you think they're going to attack at night? Wouldn't they have to know we were here first?"

"The Asharim have advanced technology. Just look at the air cars. Who's to say that they don't have some kind of communications devices with them? They may already know that we took out their forces back at the hill and are behind them. That would make it perfect for them to come roaring back and attack us at night. Makes a lot of sense for them, if they can manage it."

"But the drones will spot them, right?"

The sniper nodded. "Commander Krueger said that they could see the aliens just fine in infrared when they assaulted the Volunteer camp. They didn't quite look like humans, but they weren't invisible. Infrared will work through the trees, though I'd bet these big growths are going to give them a little trouble. We should have plenty of warning if we have infiltrators."

Jess was certain that was meant to sound reassuring, but she still lay awake worrying about an attack for almost an hour before she finally nodded off. Whatever was going to happen was going to happen. She might as well be rested if trouble came knocking.

* * *

BRENDA WOKE ABRUPTLY but realized after a moment that it was only Colonel Montalvo touching her on the shoulder. She sat up on the cot and blinked at him, trying to clear her mind.

"What's wrong?" she asked.

"We're about to have visitors," he said grimly. "The drones we've got watching the alien city have picked up a pair of slow-moving air cars headed our way. I wanted to get your input on how you wanted to respond to their intrusion if they come too close.

"Under other circumstances, they'd already be in range of our anti-aircraft weapons, but we weren't able to bring in the bigger stuff. They'll be in range of the smaller weapons before much longer, and the drones can engage them if they keep moving this slowly."

Brenda scrubbed her hands across her face before standing up. She'd laid down on the cot fully clothed, only removing her shoes. It only took a few seconds to get those on, and she was headed out of the crowded tent and into the night air.

"Only two air cars? That seems like a scouting mission to me. Do we know if they have any troops on the ground?"

The man shook his head. "Not that the drones are picking up. You're probably right that these two are just scouting us, but considering the fact that the aliens have access to high-tech weaponry, the possibility exists that they have something capable of clearing this hill on board one or both of those air cars. Can you shed any light on that possibility?"

"My knowledge of the Asharim is a thousand years old and passed down from generation to generation," she said as they walked toward where the drone operators were set up in the large tent. "A lot of the specifics have been lost over the years. I'm not going to rule anything out."

The inside of the tent was well lit. She hadn't noticed anything from the outside, so the canvas walls must've been well sealed to keep even a hint of light from leaking out.

Colonel Montalvo stepped over to one specific table, and she followed him, staring over the shoulders of the operators at the images they were seeing. In infrared, the air cars were cool. Whatever kept them aloft didn't generate sufficient heat to mark them strongly at all. Frankly, the aliens inside the air cars were brighter on those frequencies.

From what she'd heard before, the air cars used a pilot and copilot, and these were no different. Rather than being filled with troops, each air car had only another pair of beings in the open-topped rear of the vehicle. Based on their heat signatures, all four beings were probably Asharim. Their slaves gave off a slightly different appearance in infrared.

"Can we get any greater detail of what they're messing with in the back of the vehicles?" she asked.

One of the operators, a young woman with bright red hair in a military uniform, turned to look at her. "No ma'am. Whatever they've got back there isn't putting off heat. We're moving some drones into place that have ultraviolet capability.

"Honestly, I'm shocked that the drones they brought in didn't have both already. I'm guessing they were old or just whatever the New Zealanders had on hand."

Colonel Montalvo cleared his throat. "I believe those were drones from the Navy destroyer the New Zealanders captured. It's probably not a good idea to assume that we always have the best technology at hand, Corporal."

The woman's face reddened, and she nodded. "Sorry about that, sir. In any case, we have a drone with ultraviolet capability that should be in position in a minute. If we decide that these vehicles are threats, we can use the onboard weaponry to take them out."

"Is there any way that we can capture one of these vehicles?" Brenda asked. "We've got no air transport, and one of these would be damned helpful."

The colonel turned to face her, raising an eyebrow. "Do you know how to fly one?"

Even though Brenda wasn't completely certain of the answer, she nodded.

"I do. Or at least I should be able to figure out enough to get it onto the ground. If they've got a weapon on board that's capable of clearing this entire hill, I'd like to take a look at it as well."

"We were lucky to spot them on the way in. What if next time they just send a couple of people on the ground to open fire on us?"

"I can't argue the logic of that," he admitted, "but even if we can take out the people on one of these air cars, it's probably just going to crash. That's what vehicles without people at the controls do."

She smiled. "I think I have an idea about that if they hang around."

Just as she was about to tell them about her idea, one of the drone operators turned his head and looked at them. "We have a change in status. It looks like they're pulling back toward the city."

Brenda watched the display as the two air cars turned away and move back toward the city. She was somewhat disappointed that she wasn't going to get a chance to carry out her crazy plan, but maybe that was for the best.

"What do you think that was all about?" Colonel Montalvo asked. "Was it a scouting mission? It certainly didn't look like they were ready to attack."

Brenda shrugged. "It's as good an excuse for them to be doing what they did as anything, I suppose. We'll just have to keep a close eye on what happens next. If they come back, we'll deal with them."

"What was your plan?" he asked as they walked away from the drone tent.

"I think I'll keep that to myself," she said with a grin. "If I told you ahead of time, you might just forbid me from doing it."

The Army officer sighed. "The sad thing is that I don't know whether you're kidding me or not. We'll just have to hope that they don't come back looking for trouble."

"They'll be back," she said with a dark chuckle. "I think we can take that to the bank."

39

J ess woke far too early the next morning, stiff from sleeping on the cot. To her annoyance, Sandra was already up and looked as fresh as a daisy.

"How do you manage to sleep on that cot without being twisted up like a pretzel?" Jess asked, trying not to sound petulant and failing.

"Practice," Sandra said with a grin. "If you do this long enough, you'll get used to sleeping on anything."

Breakfast consisted of scrambled eggs and coffee, with something that was supposed to pass for bacon but failed miserably. Jess just shrugged, forced it down, and went out to preflight her ultralight.

By the time she got into the air, it was just after dawn. She and Sandra flew throughout the day, trying to catch up with the Asharim forces. To her irritation, they failed.

They found more burned homesteads but no sign of the actual enemy. Those aliens could travel a lot faster than humans could under the same conditions, it seemed.

That changed as they went into the third day. The signs of the enemy started growing stronger, and they could see what looked like active fires up in the distance.

Based on the maps that they'd been given, they weren't so far away from the largest of the Volunteer settlements. If they had a few more hours to spend traveling, she was pretty sure that they'd make it.

"Liberty Air Seventeen," a voice said over the radio in her ear. "I want you to press ahead and see if you can get any visuals of the enemy."

"Copy that," she responded.

She opened the throttle on the ultralight, and it shot forward. Well, shot forward as well as any ultralight could possibly manage. These craft weren't exactly designed for speed but for fuel efficiency and fun.

It took her about half an hour to raise her altitude and go far enough to start seeing things that were actually interesting enough to report. There were definitely signs of the alien force down below, because the destruction was much more recent. She could see buildings actually on fire, which indicated that whoever had set the fires had done so recently.

She also started seeing groupings of the Peret moving about below. The enemy army was definitely down there.

"I see something in the distance," Sandra said. "Can you take us up a little higher?"

"You got it," Jess said as she pulled back on the stick.

With a little bit more altitude, it was obvious that Sandra was right. She could see something that looked like a city on the horizon. That was almost certainly the Volunteer settlement they'd been heading for.

It looked like it was under siege. There appeared to be a vast army spread out on the plain around it. The aliens didn't seem to be attacking but appeared more focused on digging in. They were setting up fortifications of their own.

"Why don't they just attack?" Jess asked. "They've got so many soldiers. They could just swamp the walls and take them out."

"I'm not sure," the sniper answered, sweeping her binoculars over the scene that was unfolding in front of them. "It may be that there are a lot more troops behind those walls than we expected.

"Or they may have trained the civilians to protect the city. If that's the case, the aliens would run into a wall of lead as they approached. It makes sense to at least take a look at the lay of the land before they rush in."

"We can't count on them holding off," Jess said grimly. "As soon as they know we're here, they might attack. If they get inside the walls, they could kill everyone in there. How many people do you think that city could hold?"

"It's big. Tens of thousands, I think."

Jess increased their altitude and turned back toward Harry's forces. She activated the radio and called back to the person in charge of the scouts. "This is Liberty Air Seventeen. We have visual on the Asharim forces. They look like they're setting up for a siege on the Volunteer settlement. What are your orders?"

"Circle around the city at a distance," the commander said. "Try to get a decent count of the attacking forces. I'm sending other scouts forward to assist in documenting what you're seeing. I'd imagine that we should be in position to strike them from behind in a couple of hours.

"Make certain that you stay high enough not to be a target. They can see you now, I'm sure, but don't let them shoot you."

"Copy that." Jess said, tweaking her flight path to take her just a little bit further away from where the enemy was settling in. She could already see some of the troops below pointing toward the ultralight. Now that they knew she was there, it wouldn't be long before they decided to do something about it.

With black powder weapons, she wasn't precisely sure what they could do about her, but she really didn't want to find out the hard way.

"We're supposed to get a good count of the enemy forces and how they're laid out," Jess said to Sandra. "I assume you've got better skills than I do in that arena."

"No doubt," Sandra said with a chuckle. "Go ahead and circle while I make some notes. Just based on what I can see from here, it looks like they've got a lot more troops than Harry has. We'll know more once we've made a complete circle.

"What I can say for sure is that this is going to be an ugly fight. Even with superior weapons, a lot of people are going to die."

Jess took a good look at where the sun was. "By the time we're in position, it's going to be close to dark. Do you think Harry will attack at night?"

"Almost certainly, though he might wait until a few hours before dawn. We have night vision and they don't."

"Actually, we don't know that. They're aliens. Their normal visual processes might allow for them to see a little bit into the infrared or ultraviolet. We don't really know."

"Well crap," Sandra said with a sigh. "I hadn't considered that. Whatever's going to happen is going to happen. We'll just have to do the best that we can."

With that, Jess continued her circle around the Volunteer settlement. There were a lot of men and women on the walls facing off with the aliens. If the Asharim forces attempted to attack these people, they were going to pay a heavy price.

Perhaps not a heavy enough one to stop them, but they'd certainly bleed. She hoped Harry could work together with the Volunteers to pinch the aliens between their forces and the walls and that that would be enough to turn the tide, but the only way to find out what was going to happen was to wait for events to unfold.

* * *

WITH THE USE of the ultralights and scouts moving through the forest, Harry was eventually able to get into position to take a look at the city for himself. It wasn't that his own eyes were better at seeing the layout of the aliens than the drones traveling overhead or the reports of the ultralight pilots, but he needed to see things for himself.

The army that the Asharim had dispatched to destroy the Volunteer settlements was significant. By their best estimate, there were probably six times as many troops as he'd brought with him. Their advanced weapons would more than even the odds in individual fights, but there were a lot of enemies out there willing to shoot them up if they had a chance. It was his job to make certain that they didn't get that chance.

Taking a good look at the settlement through his binoculars, he guessed that there were probably twenty thousand people living inside what had to be a walled city very similar to what one would see in medieval times.

True, it was built in the style of cities from the Revolutionary War period, with some modifications that he wasn't sure he understood, but even with the precautions that they were taking, he didn't think the walls could hold for very long against this force.

It was an hour before dark, and he couldn't position his forces in time to make a difference before the sunset. That might actually be a point in his favor. He had night vision and could utilize the dark as a shield against their return fire.

Of course, that assumed that the enemy couldn't see in the dark either. Something that wasn't known at this time.

"What do you think, Rex?" he asked his scout commander.

The man lay beside him and was looking through his binoculars toward the city. "It's going to be a bear. Even with our superior weapons, they can still swamp us if they want to.

"It would be something like the Zulu wars that the British had to fight. We might have better weapons, but they've got numeric superiority and, based on the last battle, they're not afraid to charge into the face of overpowering firepower. We're going to have to be very careful in how we choose to fight."

That pretty much matched up with what Harry had been thinking. "So, do we attack at night, or do we wait until morning and force our way in towards the city and push them back?"

"Why can't we have both? We can attack early in the morning and shoot them up really good using our night vision, and then we can attack at dawn with more force. With the way that they've surrounded the city, we're not going to be able to take them off guard. They already know about our ultralights, so they have to know we're here. One good thing is that we haven't seen any Asharim. That may mean that we're not dealing with advanced weaponry. That would be nice."

Harry considered that for a long moment. A two-staged attack like that would carry some risks. If things went badly during the first part of the attack, the enemy could be in position to counterstrike with devastating effectiveness as soon as it was light out.

But the benefits of doing both couldn't be ignored. If they could knock the enemy off balance during the hours just before dawn, it was entirely possible that they could push them away from the city walls when they attacked in force.

He couldn't discount the possibility that they'd have their scouts out during the dark hours looking for exactly what he was planning on doing. If they discovered him while he was positioning troops, they could hurt his people badly.

"We'll do it," he decided at last. "Pull most of the ultralights back to get the pilots rested. We're going to want to have a clear spot to launch them from safely behind us when we're ready to attack. We need to have human eyes watching what's going on as well as the drones. If anything goes wrong, it's going to go really wrong."

He hoped that he was being overly cautious, but he knew just how dangerous this fight was going to be. They'd have one chance to smash this army before it fractured if things went well. If they went poorly, it would be his people retreating under heavy fire and hot pursuit. That was a possibility that he prayed never came to pass, but only the gods of battle knew for sure.

40

Brenda again woke in darkness, but this time she knew it was Colonel Montalvo waking her before she reacted. She sat up, rubbed the sleep out of her eyes, and looked up at him. "What's happening?"

"Our friends are back. The same two air cars, or at least they look the same through the drone feeds. They're at about the same place they were last time, but it looks like they're moving forward with a little bit more purpose this time. I think they may actually intend to do more than scouting tonight."

She nodded and started putting on her shoes. A minute later, they were standing in the tent with the drone operators again. Colonel Montalvo stepped up behind the woman that she'd spoken to last time. "Why don't you show Miss Cabot what we've got, Bridget."

The redhaired woman nodded and focused her attention on Brenda. "Two air cars are inbound from the city with the same number of people. This time we have ultraviolet-capable drones in the area and can see that there is definitely some kind of weapon in the back.

"They're proceeding past the point they stopped last time but are still moving slowly. Based on their projected trajectories, I wouldn't be surprised if they split up and came at us from different directions."

Brenda had been examining the screens while the woman spoke and nodded. She could see a dotted line that showed the projected paths and a solid line that showed where they'd picked up the air cars. This definitely didn't look like a scouting mission to her.

"I'm going to need someone to get the ultralight ready," Brenda said. "I need to get up there before they do something to us."

Colonel Montalvo put his hands on his hips and narrowed his eyes. "You never really did explain your plan. I think it's time you trotted it out, Miss Cabot. If it's too dangerous, I'm going to nix it right here."

Brenda laughed. "There's dangerous and then there's *dangerous*. We don't know what the range is on their weapon, so everyone on this hill is in grave danger as long as they're out there.

"What I've got in mind may put me in a little bit more danger than you, but it gives us the opportunity to capture one of these air cars. Those people think they're safe out there in the dark. We need to prove them wrong—dead wrong."

The Colonel watched her without saying anything for a few seconds and then slowly nodded. "There's something to what you say. Based on the clues you've given me, I think I understand what you have in mind. If you've guessed wrong, you'll be a sitting duck.

"Worse, if you're not nimble enough, you're going to fall straight down to the ground. Let me assure you that falling to your death is no fun. I've never personally tried it myself, but the outcome is pretty inevitable and gory."

Brenda knew that if something went wrong during her attempt to capture one of the air cars, it might flip over and send her falling hundreds of feet to her death or simply crash. She had some ideas on how she could mitigate that risk. If she blew it, this might be the end, but if she got it right, this would give them mobility that they desperately needed at this point.

"I'm willing to take the risk," she said. "We're going to get one chance at this, and we need to make sure that we do everything possible to make this mission a success. I assume you've already got your snipers watching the pilots?"

The colonel nodded. "We've got them covered. We only have four accredited snipers left in this force, but we have several other folks that are exceptional shots under normal circumstances. If things go right, we should be able to take them all out in a single volley of fire.

"I've got the trained snipers focused on the people operating the weapon. If we take them out, the pilots won't be firing at us."

Brenda shook her head. "You need to reverse your priorities. I want to take out the pilots in the first salvo. If one of those pilots moves at the last moment, I'm going to go all the way down. If one of your folks miss one of the people manning the weapons, you can deal with that with follow-up volleys. If you miss a pilot, a moving target is much more difficult to take out."

That made the officer scowl. "This isn't some kind of game, Miss Cabot. If you guess wrong, hundreds of people could die in an instant. This is no time to act as if this were a chess game and that we're just moving pieces on the board. We've got to get this absolutely right the first time."

"You're damned right we do," she said firmly. "We need those air cars. The odds of us getting one with me dropping on it are pretty good. The odds of both of them crashing if we do this the wrong way are damned high. If you've got any suggested alterations to my plan, now is the time to let me know what they are, because I'm leaving shortly."

Montalvo sighed but nodded. "First, I want you to lay out explicitly what your plan is so that we can make this happen in the safest manner."

"I plan to fly up in one of the ultralights and have the pilot drop me into one of the air cars as soon as your snipers take out the Asharim. I'll have the ultralight come in as slow as possible, and I'll use a rope to get into position.

"The key is going to be timing so that the ultralight doesn't overshoot the target. I'll let go when I'm directly over it and fall into the back. From there, I'll go to the controls and bring it down safely on the hilltop."

He shook his head. "That's too risky. If you botch the timing at all, you'll go over the side. If you're too early and you hit the side, you'll drop. You need to be secured to the rope until you're ready to let go.

"We have specialized harnesses with quick releases. You can go over the side on the approach and the ultralight will make its pass, just above stall speed, and the pilot will tell you when to release your harness. You do that right, and you've got your best chance of landing inside the air car. Otherwise there's just a little bit too much motion for my comfort."

"Fine," she said. "Let's do it."

Someone had already taken the liberty of getting the ultralight prepared, and it was running softly at the bottom of the hill on the far side from the city and the air cars. Climbing down the path in darkness took more time than Brenda was comfortable with, but it wasn't exactly like she had a choice.

The radio earbud told her that the air cars were splitting apart and coming in on both sides of the hill just as they'd guessed they would. No one knew the exact range at which they could open fire, but if it looked like they were setting up for a shot, the snipers would immediately take them out. That meant she needed to get into position as quickly as she possibly could, or this plan would collapse.

One of the men got her into the harness and attached a rope to her. The ultralight operator quickly took the other end of the rope and secured it to the frame.

"This should be secure enough, Miss Cabot," the man said. "We'll circle around and come in from the rear of air car two. If they take an interest in us, I'm going to try to dodge as well as I can, but no promises."

If the enemy saw them and started shooting, they'd probably die in the air before they hit the ground. Yet one more thing that she hoped didn't happen.

The little craft was surprisingly quiet as it taxied out into the grass between two men holding glow sticks. The pilot sped the ultralight up and quickly pulled into the air. Being off the bumpy ground was something of a relief, as Brenda wasn't sure that they wouldn't hit a pothole and flip over.

Once they were in the air, the pilot began circling around the hill and pulling out over the forest. As he did so, he handed her a set of night-vision goggles similar to the ones he already wore.

"Put these on. There's a button on the side to activate them. That should give you a better view of what we're coming up on."

She did as instructed, and the darkness gave way to a greenish-colored view of the landscape below them. It was kind of weird, but she could clearly make out the trees in the forest and the hill they were leaving.

A few minutes later, she saw the air car that was their target. It was floating slowly toward the hill, four beings either controlling the craft or manning some kind of equipment that certainly looked like a weapon with a wide barrel pointing toward the hill.

"I sure hope they don't get into range to open fire before we get there," she muttered.

"You and me both," the pilot said. "Get ready to go over the side. You'll be hanging directly below the seats here. The disengage for the harness is right there in the center of your chest.

"Grab the ring when I say, twist it 180 degrees counterclockwise, and then pull. The harness will pop open and you'll drop, so keep your arms pointed up until you land. Don't touch the ring until you're ready to drop."

"You can bet I won't," she said fervently. "How long will it take us to get there, and how am I going to know that you're ready for me to drop?"

"It shouldn't be more than two or three minutes. You're going to feel the aircraft slow down greatly as we get near the air car, and I'll shout loud enough for you to hear when it's time. I'll say, 'go go go!'"

Brenda nodded. That wasn't something she could get easily confused over. It also sounded vaguely familiar. She thought she'd heard something on a television show about people parachuting and using that same kind of command.

Her plan started going awry just as they were beginning to approach the air car. It spun toward them and began moving in their direction.

"Crap," she muttered.

Moments later, the pilots she was watching slammed sideways in their seats. A few seconds later, distant cracks announced the shots that had killed them. A quick look showed no one standing in the back of the air car. The snipers had gotten the weapon controllers too.

The air car began to spin in place and drift sideways as she watched. One of the pilots must have struck the controls. She instantly knew this air car was a loss. It was already falling toward the ground and moving in a way that made it impossible for her to board.

"Change course," she ordered. "Take us to the other air car."

The pilot obeyed and lifted them over the hill even as Colonel Mulvaney was calling on the radio.

"I think we've disabled everyone," he said crisply. "The second air car is still upright, so it might be salvageable. Or somebody inside might be playing possum. Be very careful."

The approach to the second air car went a bit more quickly than she'd anticipated. She climbed out on command and lowered herself under the ultralight, her heart pounding as she swung and twirled in the wind. The ultralight flew up above the air car and pulled back, almost into a stall, before she heard the pilot shouting for her to go.

Brenda released the harness and fell. She had to admit, her actions terrified her more than she'd imagined they would. At first, she thought she was going to miss the air car entirely, but she landed just inside the back on the far side of the interior compartment.

She slammed against the side of the vehicle and bounced back into the interior, her ribs complaining at the abuse. Once she was on her unsteady feet, she drew her flechette pistol and put some precautionary shots into both of the bodies sprawled in the back of the air car next to the weapon. She couldn't be sure that they were dead and wasn't going to take any chances.

Neither of them twitched, so the snipers had done their work.

She did the same to the pilots, being careful that none of the trajectories led toward the controls. The very last thing she wanted to do was damage the air car after she'd captured it.

Now that she was certain the Asharim were really dead, she unstrapped one of the pilots and dragged his body into the back with the two weaponeers. The seat that opened up was a gory mess, but she forced herself to sit anyway and fumbled with the unfamiliar straps as she secured herself. If something went wrong, she didn't want to be thrown from the air car.

The controls were unfamiliar to her, but just the action of trying to figure out what they meant gave her the memory prompts that she'd been hoping for. The knowledge of how to control the air car slipped into her mind, and she reached out confidently to manipulate the controls, starting the air car toward the hill.

"I'm in control," she said. "Don't shoot."

"Copy that," the Colonel said. "We're standing down, and you're cleared to land. We have a spot opened up for you and some men out with glow sticks."

It took a couple of minutes and a few false starts to get the air car settled down safely on the ground, but she managed it and was finally able to unstrap, stand up, and get out of the air car. Triumphant hoots from the soldiers who'd gathered around the air car greeted her.

"Get those bodies out of this thing," she said brushing her hands across her filthy clothes. She desperately needed a shower, but she'd settle for just changing her clothes and getting the blood off her skin.

Then she could go over the vehicle and the weapon. Harry and Jess might need something like this desperately by morning, and if they called, she wanted to be ready.

41

Harry felt like he'd only just gotten to sleep when Rex shook him awake. He sat up abruptly and rubbed his eyes before standing.

"They're on the move," Rex said. "Looks like they're attacking the city. I guess that means they can see in the dark well enough to manage."

"What time is it? How long until our scheduled attack?"

"It's only a little bit after midnight. Our attack isn't scheduled to kick off for another three hours."

Harry walked out of his tent and headed toward the larger command tent nearby. Inside, he found his senior people already hard at work trying to interpret what the drones were sending in.

Since it was late night, they didn't have any ultralights in the sky. They'd probably have to change that if they wanted to have decent real-time operational data that had actual human beings with a wide-angled view of the entire battlefield.

"Tell me what they're doing," Harry told the lead drone operator. "Are they attacking all around the city perimeter, or are they focusing their attention on a single location?"

The man turned in his seat, though he kept one eye on his screen. "It seems like they're running a general attack all the way around the settlement, probably to keep the defenders guessing which way the primary attack is going to come from. The drones have already picked out a major force that's going to be moving on a specific section of the settlement wall. Based on the equipment I'm seeing, they intend to scale it."

"How are we positioned to respond? Can we get to their major force before this kicks off?"

The operator shrugged. "I'm not certain how long it'll take us to get into position. Their location is about ninety degrees around from where we'd planned to strike, so we could flank them easily enough, if time permits."

"I have our people gathering," Rex said. "We should be ready to attack in about half an hour. Commander Krueger has the main forces standing up for battle. Even with a good chunk of their forces spread around the settlement, this one force is probably twice our size. If they catch a smaller group of us coming out, they'll thrash us."

Harry ground his teeth in frustration. Why hadn't the bastards given them just a few more hours to get into position?

"Twenty-five minutes," he said. "Have everybody hustle. We can't afford to let them take the wall before we attack. We've got to sidetrack them so that they don't get into the settlement."

"Copy that," Rex said as he sprinted out of the tent.

Twenty minutes later, Rex was back. "We'll be ready to go in five. You should be able to guide the attack from here without any trouble. We've got a couple of ultralights up already, and as soon as the fighting kicks off, we'll send some more up with snipers to try to take out enemy leadership."

"Good," Harry said. "As soon as you're ready, kick off the attack. I'll make sure that the main force is ready in case you run into trouble. Turn their attention to us so that we can kill them."

The other man nodded and grinned ferociously. "You got it, Boss. Let's go kick some ass."

* * *

THEY'D WOKEN Jess hours before her scheduled flight time and ordered her off to scout the enemy surrounding the Volunteer settlement. The way the camp was moving around like a disturbed anthill, something was wrong. The enemy must be moving sooner than they'd expected.

The scout commander was giving her and several others a hurried briefing before he sent them into the air. "As you've probably surmised, the enemy is attacking the city. It looks like they intend to scale the wall. Mister Rogers is going to flank them shortly.

"Your job is to give him the intelligence he needs, the kind of thing he can't get from the drones. Pilots, stay high and get a good idea of what's going on on the ground. Snipers, once the attack begins, I want you to take down anyone directing enemy forces. You'll operate at your own discretion and shoot as need be. Any questions?"

There were none, so she and Sandra went to their ultralight, started it up, and were quickly airborne.

Once Jess was flying over the dark forest, she felt like everything was becoming a bit too real. She felt like she was in a war movie. The terror of getting into a fight was finally settling over her. Panic from the firefight where she'd almost died flooded her.

"Breathe," Sandra said. "We'll be in the air and they aren't going to be shooting back at us effectively. The real danger is going to be on the ground. Just focus on the task at hand, and everything is going to be fine."

"I don't see how you can be so sure," Jess said, hearing the quiver in her voice. "If they take Harry and the ground forces out, we're not going to be landing anywhere because they'll have overrun our camp. We've got enough fuel to fly around for a little bit, but landing in the dark with just night-vision goggles is not something I ever want to try."

Sandra patted her on the shoulder as she inspected her sniper rifle. "Focus on the positive. Harry's a smart commander, and he'll use our forces effectively. They'll never know what hit them.

"In any case, he's not going to be leading from the front. He'll send Rex to lead the troops on the ground and guide everything from the command tent. He won't get into the thick of the fighting unless things go seriously wrong."

Jess thought about that for a while and slowly nodded as the Volunteer settlement came into view. There were a couple of fires down below and many torches inside the walls, so she had a decent idea of where people were positioned.

The night-vision goggles didn't like the bright points of light, but they were modern units and more than capable of toning down the brightness while still showing her what was going on.

She could see a huge gathering of enemy troops that must've been just across a small rise from the settlement. They seemed to be in a large, wide line, and many of them in the front were holding pieces of equipment that looked like they might be useful in scaling the walls.

They were ready to attack. That wasn't good.

Even as she watched, the enemy forces let up a howl and charged toward the settlement. There were scattered shots from the walls, but it looked like the defenders were evenly spaced around the circumference of the settlement, and not enough of them were going to be in position to deter the charge.

From the trees below her, she saw a lot of their own troops began coming out in wide lines, laying down fire as they moved forward. The range was long, but a miss was almost impossible with that many targets.

To her shock, the heavy fire didn't deter the aliens from charging the city, and they kept going until they were there. They then began scaling the walls. The fight for the settlement was on.

"This is going to be bad," Jess said even as Sandra opened fire, her suppressed weapon stepping down the cracks to a bearable level as she started shooting at whatever targets she saw below.

Jess had to do something. If this went the way she expected, Harry was going to get involved and that might leave him dead on the field below.

Making certain that they were in a good flight pattern and far above the range of the black powder weapons, Jess pulled her quantum phone from her jacket pocket and called Brenda Cabot. She needed to make the other woman aware that if things went bad, they'd be on their way back in a real hurry.

* * *

BRENDA HAD JUST FINISHED washing and changing when Jess called. She answered the phone, worried that something had gone wrong.

"Cabot."

"The aliens have kicked off their attack, and it looks like they're trying to overrun the walls on the settlement. We're attacking them, and I'm worried that things are not going to go smoothly.

"Harry's a great military leader, but we're so outnumbered. If things do go badly, I'm going to try to get him into the ultralight with me and get as far away as fuel allows. You guys are going to have to be prepared for things if they turn on us."

Brenda looked at the air car and the strange weapon that was still mounted in its rear. "We'll be ready, but would some extra air support be helpful? We just captured one of the air cars with some kind of weapon mounted in the back. I'm not sure how fast this thing goes, but we might be able to get there in time to make a difference."

"Do that," Jess said, relief in her tone. "Even if you've only got a squad with heavy weapons in the back of that thing, that might be enough to break the Peret. Thank you."

Brenda put her phone away as soon as Jess had hung up and gestured for Colonel Montalvo to come over. "We need to get the blood cleaned off of this thing as quickly as possible, and then we need to get a team of folks with an appropriate heavy-weapon mix to relieve Harry and his people. I'm not sure what you can get into the back of this thing, but grenade launchers would be a great start."

The man nodded and called for one of his aides to come over before giving him a sharp series of orders. He then turned back to Brenda. "We'll be ready to go in about fifteen minutes. Are you sure that we can get there in time to make a difference?"

She shrugged. "I'll do my very best. If we don't make it in time, a lot of our friends might die, and I'm not going to stand still if I can change that. We fight tonight."

42

Even before Rex and his forces had hit the Asharim at the wall, Harry knew they weren't going to be enough. The Peret weren't being forced back nearly as much by the incoming fire as he'd hoped, and their morale seemed to be unbroken as they counterattacked. Even through the green of the drones' night vision, he could see the enemy's resolve. This was going to be an all-or-nothing event.

"Send in the reserves," Harry snapped. Even as he said the words, he was running out of the tent and headed toward those same reserves. He slapped his night-vision goggles down as he ran.

The forces he'd set aside for an event like this came to about a third of his forces and were heavily armed. Their purpose was to turn the tables when that type of martial judo would make a difference. In this case, he needed to relieve Rex so his scout commander could pull back enough to regroup and fight on.

"We got a serious problem," Rex said over the command frequency. "It looks like they're not just scaling the wall. They're planting charges, and they're going to blow a big hole in the sucker. Once they do, they'll go right through. It's going to be a massacre."

"Continue to engage the enemy," Harry ordered coldly. "I'm bringing the reserve force. Be prepared to get in between them and the wall."

"That's the very last place we want to be," Rex warned. "The Volunteers don't know who we are. They could shoot us in the backs while the aliens are shooting us in the front. That's a suicide move."

"It's a desperation move," Harry corrected. "We've got to keep the Peret out of the city at all costs. At. All. Costs."

There were a few seconds of silence before Rex responded. "Copy that. We'll be ready for you."

The reserves were prepared, and as soon as he reached their position, he gathered their senior squad leaders and Commander Krueger.

"Rex is going to try to push the Peret away from the walls, but the possibility exists that he's going to fail. He said that the enemy have explosives rigged up and that if we can't stop them from setting those off, there's going to be a large breach that we'd have to protect.

"His forces are going to help us with that, but we'll have to spread out enough to cover the area around any breach and keep the Peret from breaking through."

"We've got a lot of ammunition, but I suspect it's not going to be enough," Krueger said. "My people have as much as we can carry, but if we can get more brought out to us before the fighting gets really bad, that'll help us to set up a defensive perimeter to keep these bastards off of us."

Harry considered that and nodded. With the use of the dirt bikes, they could move a fairly decent amount of ammunition out to the fighting lines and get the riders back to safety in fairly short order. There was always going to be the risk that someone was going to get shot, because the couriers were going to be prime targets, so it would have to be a volunteer-only effort. He'd give the orders and hope for the best. Needs must when the devil drives.

The relief force couldn't just jog out like Rex's forces, because the scout hadn't been trying to get there fast. He'd been trying to conceal his approach for as long as possible. Harry needed to get there as quickly as possible, and that meant they were sacrificing stealth for speed.

He mounted one of the bikes and was just securing his helmet when a loud explosion sounded in the distance. That couldn't be good.

"They've breached the walls," Rex said over the command channel. "We're holding as best we can, but if you could speed up a little, we'd appreciate it."

"Let's get a move on," Harry said as he gunned his bike and shot forward.

As a group, the entire force raced out from the forest and onto the plain surrounding the Volunteer settlement. It might have been cleared of trees and underbrush, but the ground was certainly not what anyone would consider flat. There were ruts and holes, probably created by some kind of burrowing animal, and that slowed them down.

As soon as he had a clear view of what the situation was like at the wall, Harry knew they were in trouble. The Peret were grouping behind a large line of their fellows, and it was obvious that they were preparing to crush Rex and his people against the walls at their backs.

Rex and the main force were arrayed, protecting the city. There wasn't time to dig in and make foxholes, so they were standing fast and taking the heavy fire coming at them.

Thankfully, it seemed that the defenders were disinclined to attack fellow humans, because they were firing their black powder weapons at the Peret rather than Rex's people.

The hole in the wall was rather significant, perhaps twenty-five meters wide. Of course, the wall was made of wood, and the debris was smoldering or on fire.

"We'll hit them from the left flank," Harry ordered. "Use cavalry tactics. Zip right in, shoot them up, and ride out. Always keep in motion and never give them an easy shot at you. Try to force them to turn, and face us because that will open up their flank for Rex to take advantage of."

Having said that, Harry had absolutely no intention of harrying the enemy flanks while Rex was in deadly danger. Even as they raced closer to the enemy, he was already looking for a good way to get around the Peret so that he could join the defenders. If he was going to fight, he was going to plant his feet between innocent civilians and the ravening hordes. They would take the settlement over his dead body.

The aliens were shooting at every motorcyclist. Harry heard a couple of bullets whistle past him and thought he was going to be safe enough, and then one of the shots struck his front wheel, and his bike flipped over, throwing him into the air.

This was not the first time that Harry had been unceremoniously tossed through the air, so he tucked himself into a ball and regained control of his potential impact position, landing on his feet but rolling to absorb as much of the damage as he possibly could. The unexpected flight had taken him over a couple of the enemy, and he saw a clear path leading through the last few enemies between him and Rex's forces. He leapt to his feet and staggered forward, becoming steadier with ever step. He wasn't hurt. He was going to make this.

He drew his pistol and shot the Peret that were between him and Rex. Several of them turned and leveled their black powder rifles at him, but there weren't enough of them to form a strong defense. The one that actually pulled the trigger missed Harry in all the confusion. A few seconds later, Harry was on the other side of the Peret and sprinting toward Rex.

"A little help here, buddy," he said over the command channel.

The forces against the wall seemingly turned their attention to the quarter that Harry was coming from and opened fire. Bullets flew past him in every direction at the enemy as Rex's forces engaged the Peret. Harry had no idea how many people were shooting at or around him, but it was more than he'd like.

Seconds later, he spotted Rex and raced to the man's side.

"Glad you could make it," his scout commander said as he continued firing at the enemy. "I wish you hadn't come, though. It looks like they're going to rush us."

"We've got reinforcements out there harrying their flanks, and we have folks with more ammunition headed this way. Can you hold out?"

"Isn't that the kind of question you ask *before* you stick yourself into a blender like this?" Rex asked with a snort. "I don't know. It really depends on how determined they are. If they really want to take this settlement, they're going to roll us."

Almost as if on cue, a huge shout went up from behind the alien lines, and every one of them seemed to charge forward.

"Well, my timing *does* suck," Harry agreed with a dark grin. "Everyone stand fast. None of those bastards gets through."

An answering shout came from his people as they increased their fire at the charging enemy.

There were a *lot* of aliens out there, Harry decided as he emptied his pistol and grabbed a rifle from one of his fallen comrades. In truth, he didn't know if they were going to win this fight. He just knew that he didn't have a choice about whether to defend this place.

The Peret were seemingly unimpressed with their stand and charged in ever-growing numbers. Even against the Asharim flechette rifles his people had, they were turning the tide. They seemed willing to climb over piles of their own dead to kill his people and get into the city.

All around him, his troops were dropping, wounded or dead. This defense was rapidly becoming a last stand.

"Krueger, we need immediate support," Harry said over the radio as he continued firing. "And by immediate, I mean ten minutes ago."

"We're trying to break through," the Navy officer said. "They've closed their lines, and we're not making much progress. Hang on."

Before he could answer, Rex toppled backward, his head almost exploding from the impact of a large-caliber bullet. Harry wanted to scream in denial, but he couldn't spare his dead friend even a single moment. If he did, they'd all be dead.

"Cluster together," he shouted. "Stand fast. Stand fast!"

As soon as he finished giving the order, something struck him in the left shoulder like a sledgehammer. He staggered back and fell. The world seemed to be spinning around him.

He glanced at his arm groggily and saw that the enemy had shot him in the left shoulder with one of those big-bore black powder rifles. He had to be in shock, because the amount of blood he was seeing and the bone sticking out of the injury indicated he was in bad shape.

"Krueger," he gasped over the radio. "Take command. stop them from getting into the city."

The world faded to a pinpoint and went dark before the other man could respond.

* * *

JESS CIRCLED the ultralight over the battle with her heart in her throat. Word had just come in that Rex was dead and that Harry was down and seriously injured. The news tore at her heart, and she desperately started looking for a way to get down there.

It didn't look like she was going to have the chance, though. The fighting was too intense, and the forces were too jammed together. The Peret were killing her people.

The only place she could land was far outside the fighting, and she had to do that in the dark on terrain that she was completely unfamiliar with. Terrain that had never been inspected for things that could destroy the ultralight and probably kill Sandra and herself.

"We got to do something," she said, almost growling in frustration.

Sandra was busy firing down into the enemy, taking out whatever people she could and trying to make a difference. Still, she managed to respond, never slowing her shooting.

"We're doing what we can," she answered, her voice filled with despair. "If Krueger can just hold out, we might still be able to push the Peret back and find a way to land. Harry can hang on. He's tough."

Jessica knew from experience that being tough wasn't enough sometimes. Rex had been tough, and now he was gone. She had to come up with some way to get Harry out of there before the Peret killed them all.

A buzz from her pocket startled her. Someone was calling on the quantum phone. It had to be Brenda.

"Give me some good news," she said grimly as she continued to look for a survivable landing spot.

"We're on our way," Brenda said. "In fact, we're almost there. What's the situation?"

As quickly as she could, Jess explained what was going on and told her that Rex was dead, Harry was down, and their forces were being exterminated. "You've got to hurry. I don't know if we can clear an opening to get him out, but we've got to try."

The other woman chuckled. "I think we might be able to help open a spot for you. We figured out the weapon in the back of the air car. I think it'll probably help turn the tide.

"I'm going to have to go so I can fly this thing, but you better call the people on the ground and tell them to be ready to duck when the time comes. They'll know when that is."

With that, the connection went dead, and Jess put the phone away. She explained what she'd been told to Krueger.

Sandra, who'd been listening, chuckled darkly. "I bet that's going to be an unpleasant surprise for someone."

Jess began scanning around, trying to spot the air car. In the darkness, that wasn't going to be an easy task, even with night vision.

A few minutes later, she spotted it coming over the city itself. It was a little higher up than she was and almost obscured by the wings of her ultralight.

Her phone rang again, and she answered it.

"Jess, you need to get the ultralight forces out of the way," Brenda said. "There's one in particular that's directly in my firing path."

"Yeah, that's probably me. I'm changing course now, and I'll give a signal to clear out over the radio. Please hurry."

Jess did a hard bank and pulled the ultralight away from the enemy forces and signaled on the radio that all scout forces needed to withdraw from the area over the battlefield. Rather than argue, the scout commander gave the order for everyone to pull back.

She had just enough time to turn her ultralight back around when she saw a bright-green spark leap from the back of the air car and strike into the center of the attacking Peret. That transformed into a writhing, energetic globe the color of moss perhaps ten or fifteen meters across, which then transformed into an explosion and blew a huge hole in both the enemy lines and the ground.

"Holy shit," Sandra said. "Is that Cabot?"

"You're damn right it is," Jess said with a grin. "We might just be able to hold them off yet."

The rate of fire of the alien weapon seemed to be about one shot every five seconds. It took less than a minute to break the will of the attacking Peret, and they started racing away from the settlement and back toward the forest. Brenda's people didn't hesitate to continue firing into their ranks as they fled.

As soon as the pressure was off, Jess turned her ultralight toward the site where Harry had been holding the line against the Peret.

"Hang on," she said grimly. "This might get a little rough."

She brought the ultralight down as low as possible and reduced its speed to just above a stall as she came in to land near the forces there. She spotted Krueger just before she was about to set down and goosed the throttle enough to bump them further along and brought her aircraft down about ten meters away from her partner.

The landing was just as rough as she'd expected. The ultralight had barely touched down before one of the wheels dropped into a hole and the entire thing flipped over. Thankfully, even though it was a rough landing, it was one that both she and Sandra managed to walk away from.

Throwing her helmet back at the wrecked ultralight, Jess raced over to Krueger.

"Where is he?" she demanded.

Without speaking, he gestured toward a group of men huddled around something. Someone.

A couple of steps and she dropped next to Harry. He was breathing, so that was good. His arm was a mess though. It looked like he'd been shot in the shoulder, and there was blood everywhere. The massive wound had lots of bone splinters in it, too.

She scanned the faces of the people working on him and saw one of them was a medic. "How's he doing? Is he going to live?"

The man shrugged as he tried to do something with the wound. "We're doing our best, but I'm not sure. It's bad. We need to get him some better care immediately. Even if we do, he's going to lose this arm."

She was about to speak when a gasp went up around her. The air car was coming down with Brenda waving at them. Someone must've spread the word that these were friendlies. Thank God for that, because she hadn't thought about it at all.

As soon as the air car was on the ground, Brenda jumped out, and a number of soldiers followed her. She marched right up to Jess.

"We need to get him and his medical team into the back of the air car. If I push it to max, we can be back at the gate in half an hour. Move."

Jess didn't even hesitate, ordering the men around her to find a stretcher to carry Harry and get him into the air car. The clock was ticking, and she had to get him back to the sarcophagus before he died. She only prayed that they'd make it in time.

43

B renda watched as a group of medics loaded Harry Rogers into the back of the air car and secure him as well as they possibly could. He looked bad. Really bad. She was concerned that he wasn't going to survive the trip back to the hill.

Once they'd finished loading him, Jess, Sandra, and a host of soldiers and medics climbed into the back of the air car. Jess took the co-pilot's seat while the rest of them settled in.

Without further ado, Brenda brought the air car back to life and took it up into the air. She set the course toward the decaying Asharim city and the hill where the gate was located. She increased the speed as high as she dared.

Even with her obvious concern for her partner, she watched Jess stare at the controls. The other woman shook her head slowly. "I can't believe that these implanted memories tell me how to operate this thing. That's crazy. How can they do that?"

Brenda shrugged. "It doesn't really matter, does it? What matters is that we can fly things like this air car and control their spaceships. It gives us a bit of leverage to try to stop them from sending their minions to eliminate us.

"Not that they're that dangerous in their degenerate state. Honestly, I think even regular army troops without the special weapons might have been able to take out these forces if we'd had more time and gotten a little bit more help from the US government."

"Do you think Queen will ever give us any meaningful assistance?" Jess asked. "The man is a snake. All he wants to do is get one over on us so that he can smugly claim to his boss that he's gotten alien tech all by his little lonesome."

"You must not have heard," Brenda said with a rueful smile. "The president forced Queen to turn in his resignation. He's no longer the secretary of state. Now he's just a working schmo. Sadly, a working schmo that I'm responsible for over the next five years, but it got him to release a lot of the stuff that he'd promised.

"I'll get you all the information I can once everything settles down, but he did loan us an infantry battalion to stick on the hill and provide overwatch. As soon as we can turn our attention back to the city, I suspect that we'll have the force to take it."

As they'd been speaking, Jess had shot glances back at the medical team working on Harry. Based on their activity, it certainly didn't seem like he was out of the woods. In fact, it seemed to Brenda as if the medics were doing what they could to keep him alive and perhaps not succeeding completely.

She focused her attention forward. She needed to be concerned about getting to the hill as quickly as possible, and that meant not going off course. A couple of minutes might mean the difference between life and death for Harry Rogers.

"We have company," Sandra said.

She looked back and found the woman standing behind her with her night-vision goggles on. She held a second set that she slipped onto Brenda's head and activated. The darkness became green, and she could suddenly see much further away.

There was something ahead of them.

"It's an air car," Sandra said. "I can't see what kind, but considering that only the Asharim have stuff that flies, this isn't going to be good. How capable is this thing of evasive maneuvers without dumping everyone out the back?"

"I'm betting it sucks," Brenda said grimly. "This isn't a combat aircraft. It's more like a transport. There are spots back in the back where cargo can be secured, but it's not really made for passengers unless some kind of seats are installed. Seats that this unit didn't have when I captured it."

Sandra grunted. "Then we'll just have to do the best we can. Let me get my rifle."

It only took a few moments for the other woman to grab her rifle and step up between the control chairs, settling the barrel on the short windscreen that protected the drivers of the air car.

She knelt and stared through the scope at the oncoming air car. "I'm seeing two pilots and potentially a couple of people in the back. It's a little difficult to tell from this angle.

"Hold it. The people in the back are standing up. They look like Peret. They've got flechette rifles. Based on the way they're looking toward us, they can tell we're here."

Brenda watched as the other vehicle grew larger with unsettling haste. With the combined rate of closure, they'd be in firing range way before she could dodge out of the path of the other vehicle. They were going to have to do something about it.

"You need to take it out," Jess said grimly. Obviously the blonde had been thinking the same thoughts that Brenda had.

"It's going to be chancy," Sandra said. "I can only get a couple of shots before we're all tangled up with each other. We better get everyone else shooting, too. We're going to need all the firepower we can get if they get to point-blank range."

Without waiting for any further instruction, Sandra steadied her rifle one more time and fired. The noise was both startlingly loud and yet less than it should have been. That must've been because of the suppressor on the end of the weapon.

Brenda stared forward as Sandra continued to fire and saw that she could now discern individual people on the approaching craft. Since the pilots were behind glass like she was, she wasn't certain how effective the shots would be.

Jess was shouting for the rest of the soldiers to get their weapons up and open fire as soon as the other craft was in range. At this pace, that would be in about ten seconds, and it was probably going to be brutal.

Brenda considered the 3D aspect of the encounter and the Asharim's relative lack of experience in operating the craft. She might be able to use their degeneration from the master race of the galaxy down to people that didn't really understand their own technology against them.

"Everybody hang on," she shouted. "I'm going to raise our altitude and tilt us to the left. That should give you a shot down into the other craft as it passes. Don't miss, because I think I'll only get to try this once."

And with that, the other air car was in range, and Brenda sent their air car shooting upward even as she started tilting it slightly to the left. She paid close attention to the angles, because she needed to tilt enough to give them shots but not so far that anyone fell out. Especially Harry.

Both groups exchanged fire. The Asharim and their slaves used flechette weapons. Jess had an equivalent weapon, but most of the soldiers in the rear did not.

In the end, that didn't matter. The angle of attack made their fire devastating and the other air car spun before flipping over and smashing into the dark forest below.

Brenda quickly brought the air car level and resumed her course toward the hill. "I hope we don't run into any more of those things. I really don't want to have to fight in the air with this thing again."

"You did just fine," Sandra said with a cold grin as she clapped her hand on Brenda's shoulder. "This might even count as an air kill. Get four more and we'll call you Ace."

Brenda laughed in spite of herself. That thought was ridiculous. "I'll just be happy to get us on the ground safely." With that, she turned her attention back to the task at hand, and the air car settled back into its course.

Twenty-five minutes later, the hill was in sight and they hadn't spotted another air car. Brenda breathed a sigh of relief and brought the air car down onto the hilltop, where soldiers were waiting to get Harry through the gate and back to her base in Virginia.

Once they were there, they could get him into the sarcophagus and see if he was going to pull through. She sent her prayers for him, because there was nothing more she could do. His fate was in other hands now.

* * *

JESS SAT by the sarcophagus and waited. She'd been there for two days now and expected that Harry would be waking soon. She'd been afraid they wouldn't get him inside it in time, but he'd still been alive when they'd put him in, so she expected him to fully recover.

She'd spent most of her time sitting here, but she'd still managed to stay busy. People had been coming in waves to see her about issues over the last forty-eight hours, and she'd been guiding the situation on Volunteer World via remote control.

She'd released the Vidars from their oaths and returned them home, though she'd hated taking the time away from Harry to do so. They would talk to their high priest, and she nursed hope that they'd become her allies.

Susanna Adorno and General Norris had come to visit yesterday, praising Harry and his troops as patriots for shedding their blood in defense of the Volunteers. The people of the settlement were helping to gather the dead and care for the less seriously injured.

The woman had said that they wouldn't forget who their friends had been when their need was great. Based on everything that Jess had heard about these people, they held their honor in extremely high regard. Debts were paid promptly and in full.

Since the battle, she'd had a lot of time to grieve and cry for Rex and the others that she'd lost. That the Asharim had taken from her. Even now, Sandra was seeing her old friend and occasional lover back to his home town to see him buried and spend a while with his parents.

Part of Jess was glad that she could hide here, as she didn't want to face anyone. How could anyone survive telling parents or spouses that their loved one was dead? It would wreck her.

She forced her mind back to the situation on Volunteer World. The Army troops were preparing for the assault on the Asharim city, since there was no way her people could lead that attack. Not now.

Brenda had taken the air car up and observed the Peret that had fled the Volunteer settlement via infrared. It looked as if their spirit had been broken and that even though they were returning to the Asharim city, they were not currently a force worthy of considering a threat until the Asharim regrouped them.

That was why the attack was going to take place tomorrow morning. The Army colonel that Brenda had brought in would lead the assault on the alien city with his infantry battalion, stiffened by people with Asharim weapons, and drive the enemy from it before the majority of the Asharim forces could return.

Then, when the Peret arrived back at the city, Lastark would try to get them to surrender. If more bloodshed could be avoided, Jess wanted to make that happen.

If their Peret prisoner wasn't persuasive, she'd kill every last damn one of the hostile bastards. They were a loose cannon and couldn't be allowed to threaten the Volunteers again.

Her thoughts were interrupted by a low hum from the sarcophagus. She turned her attention to it and saw that the lid was sliding open. She sprang to her feet and rushed over, looking inside.

Harry lay in the cavity, seemingly still asleep. They'd put him inside in his underwear, so she could see that the awful wound in his shoulder was gone, his skin smooth and unblemished. She imagined he had a lot of other scars that were gone, both on the outside and inside of his body. A lifetime's worth.

He also looked so young. Not that he'd been all that much older than her, but now he looked like he was in his mid-twenties. Just like she did after the sarcophagus regenerated her and reset her age. Somehow, his rugged handsomeness was still there, though blunted by his new youth.

Even as she thought that, his eyelids flickered and then opened. Before he could say anything, she put her hand on his newly rebuilt shoulder. "You're okay, Harry. The battle is over, and you're safe."

"My people," he rasped, trying to sit up. "How are my people?"

"Brenda Cabot arrived like a Valkyrie right after you were hit," she said, keeping her voice as soothing as she could. "She blew the snot out of the Peret, and they broke. I won't lie. We lost more than half our people, including Rex."

He closed his eyes in obvious anguish. "Did we keep them out of the settlement? Please tell me that all those deaths meant something."

"You kept them safe. Susanna Adorno is probably going to pin a medal on you. She called you a patriot, and that seems to mean a lot to her.

"The attack on the city happens tomorrow, and since I know that I can't keep you from going, I want you to wait here for Doctor Granger to examine you."

He tried to speak, but she put a finger over his lips. "No argument. You'll be back in the race in a little bit. Relax, just for a few minutes."

She stepped over to a panel on the wall and called for Todd Granger. He'd get Harry back on his feet, and then they'd deal with the Asharim. This phase of the fight was almost over, and she was eager to get out into the universe and see what they could find.

* * *

WANT to get updates from Terry about new books and other general nonsense going on in his life? He promises there will be cats. Go to TerryMixon.com/Mailing-List and sign up.

. . .

DID YOU ENJOY THIS BOOK? Please leave a review on Amazon. It only takes a minute to dash off a few words and that kind of thing helps Terry make a living as a writer and gets you new books faster.

WANT MORE BOOKS BY TERRY? Flip to the next page and grab one.

VISIT TERRY's Patreon page to find out how to get cool rewards and an early look at what he's working on at Patreon.com/TerryMixon.

ALSO BY TERRY MIXON

You can always find the most up to date listing of Terry's titles on his Amazon Author Page.

Note: the links below (ebook only, obviously) redirect you to my website where you can click a button to go to Amazon. This allows me to participate in Amazon's associates program and earn a little more. Sorry for any inconvenience.

The Last Hunter

The Last Hunter

Bonds of Blood

Alpha Strike

The Enemy Revealed

Command Authority

The Grand Conspiracy

Shield of Humanity

Fog of War

Ships of the Line

Operation Liberty

The Empire of Bones Saga

Empire of Bones

Veil of Shadows

Command Decisions

Ghosts of Empire

Paying the Price

Recon in Force

Behind Enemy Lines

The Terra Gambit

Hidden Enemies

Race to Terra

Ruined Terra

Victory on Terra

When Luck Runs Out

Gunboat Diplomacy

The Imperial Marines Saga

Spoils of War

Imperial Recruit

Enemy Action

The Humanity Unlimited Saga

Liberty Station

Freedom Express

Tree of Liberty

Blood of Patriots

Single Novels

Scorched Earth

Storm Divers

The Vigilante Series with Glynn Stewart

Heart of Vengeance

Oath of Vengeance

Bound By Law

Bound By Honor

Bound By Blood

Box Sets

The Empire of Bones Saga Volume 1

The Empire of Bones Saga Volume 2

The Empire of Bones Saga Volume 3

The Empire of Bones Saga Volume 4

Humanity Unlimited Publisher's Pack 1

Humanity Unlimited Publisher's Pack 2

ABOUT TERRY

#1 Bestselling Military Science Fiction author Terry Mixon served as a non-commissioned officer in the United States Army 101st Airborne Division. He later worked alongside the flight controllers in the Mission Control Center at the NASA Johnson Space Center supporting the Space Shuttle, the International Space Station, and other human spaceflight projects.

He now writes full time while living in Texas with his lovely wife and a pounce of cats.

TerryMixon.com

[a] amazon.com/author/terrymixon
[f] facebook.com/TerryLMixon
[p] patreon.com/TerryMixon
[BB] bookbub.com/authors/terry-mixon
[g] goodreads.com/TerryMixon